THE CHOSEN ONE

ALSO BY JAMES RILEY

The Revenge of Magic series

The Revenge of Magic

The Last Dragon

The Future King

The Timeless One

The Half Upon a Time series

Half Upon a Time

Twice Upon a Time

Once Upon the End

The Story Thieves series

Story Thieves

The Stolen Chapters

Secret Origins

Pick the Plot

Worlds Apart

THE REVENGE OF MAGIC

THE CHOSEN ONE

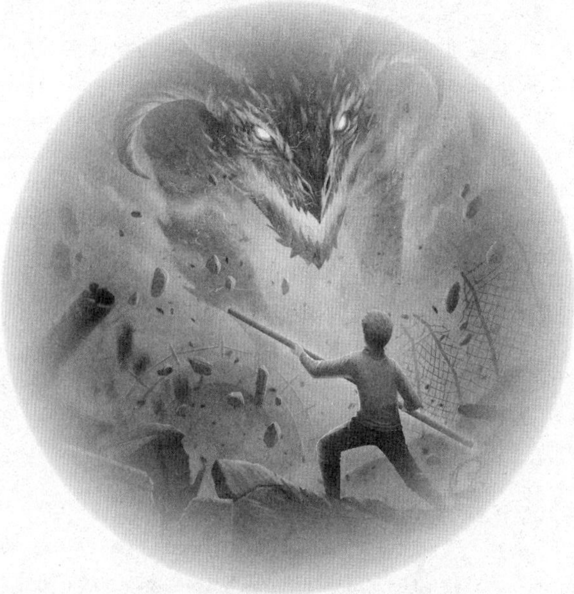

JAMES RILEY

ALADDIN

NEW YORK LONDON TORONTO SYDNEY NEW DELHI

ALADDIN
An imprint of Simon & Schuster Children's Publishing Division
1230 Avenue of the Americas, New York, New York 10020
First Aladdin hardcover edition March 2021

Jacket designed by Laura Lyn DiSiena
Interior designed by Mike Rosamilia
The text of this book was set in Adobe Garamond Pro.
Manufactured in the United States of America 0121 FFG
2 4 6 8 10 9 7 5 3 1
Library of Congress Cataloging-in-Publication Data
Names: Riley, James, 1977- author.
Title: The chosen one / by James Riley.
Description: First Aladdin hardcover edition. | New York : Aladdin, 2021. |
Series: The revenge of magic ; 5 | Audience: Ages 8-12. |
Summary: Fort and his friends face more perilous ancient magic as they prepare for the final battle to prevent the Old Ones from returning and destroying humanity.
Identifiers: LCCN 2020035717 (print) | LCCN 2020035718 (ebook) |
ISBN 9781534425842 (hardcover) | ISBN 9781534425866 (ebook)
Subjects: CYAC: Magic—Fiction. | Healers—Fiction. | Friendship—Fiction.
Classification: LCC PZ7.1.R55 Cho 2021 (print) | LCC PZ7.1.R55 (ebook) | DDC [Fic]—dc23
LC record available at https://lccn.loc.gov/2020035717

For Mara Anastas, my publisher
through my first three series.

Thank you for taking a chance on me!

THE CHOSEN ONE

- ONE -

"GOOD MORNING, STUDENTS," COLONEL Charles said from a podium in the cafeteria of the Oppenheimer School. "I apologize for taking you away from your studies, but it's important that you all be made aware of some events that have happened in the last week."

Sebastian Thomas rolled his eyes as a low murmur passed through the assembled students and even some of the soldiers guarding the doors, of which there were at least twice the usual number. This was going to be good.

"As many of you know, and some of you were involved in, we had a break-in at the school two days ago," the colonel continued. "Unfortunately, the thieves were able to escape with their objective: a sword of great historic value. But hunting down these thieves will unfortunately have to wait, as there's a larger threat that needs to be dealt with first."

That was unexpectedly honest. Sebastian had half expected the colonel to lie and say they still had the sword. But too many of the students had been there, watching as Rachel, Jia, and Fort—aka the Annoying Kid—had taken it.

Even worse, they hadn't bothered to include Sebastian! Oh, they needed his help to fight the Old Ones back at the old Oppenheimer School, using Healing magic on that former student Damian to push out the Old One mind controlling him. And there was no one better at Healing. Even Dr. Ambrose admitted this, since Jia clearly didn't count, having secretly been at the school for at least a year longer than Sebastian had been.

Jia and the others were lucky Sebastian hadn't turned them in to his mother, the head of the congressional committee that decided how much money the TDA would get. Because she was *not* happy about the theft of Excalibur and had already decided to replace Colonel Charles within the next week or two, as soon as she found a new headmaster she trusted. And if this briefing was any indication, the colonel knew it was coming and was trying to distract everyone with some new threat.

"This theft, while obviously concerning, is *not* our primary worry at this time," Colonel Charles continued, glaring at the assembled kids in front of him. "All of you are by now aware of a group of creatures that call themselves the Old Ones and of their intention to return to our world. We've been given credible intelligence by one of our Clairvoyance students, Cyrus, that these Old Ones mean to strike in the next few months."

Okay, *that* was new. Last Sebastian had heard, the Old Ones were stuck in some other dimension. But that was before everything in London and whatever had gone down with the sword.

But now Rachel had been expelled, Jia was locked in her room, under guard, and the Annoying Kid . . . well, who cared where he was.

Whatever they were up to, it would have gone down much better with Sebastian in charge. That he knew.

"But *because* of that intelligence," Colonel Charles said, "we've taken steps to ensure this attack will not happen. We will stop the Old Ones, ladies and gentlemen, before they can even start their attack."

Sebastian had to cover his laugh with a cough. *Really*, though? The colonel expected any of them to believe that? The TDA couldn't even control the Oppenheimer School students, let alone whatever the Old Ones were.

The colonel narrowed his eyes. "Did you not hear what I

said? The world is safe only due to the actions of the TDA. We will avert a major incursion by horrific monsters, and I expect some *recognition* for our brave men and women of the TDA!"

Two or three people started clapping softly, only to stop as no one else followed suit, making Sebastian cough even harder.

Colonel Charles sneered. "Perhaps it's time you students realized how much we've done for you. TDA soldiers have kept some of the most powerful magical items out of the hands of terrorists, animals who mean you and your families harm. We have researched and developed cutting-edge magical weapons to keep the Old Ones out of our world and will preempt any future attacks by their Dracsi. I think a little appreciation is in order!"

Again there was silence . . . until one voice rose toward the back of the room.

"You're lying," said a girl with black hair dressed in an Oppenheimer School uniform. "The Old Ones are coming, and there's nothing *you* can do to stop it."

Sebastian turned around and couldn't help but grin. *Finally* they were getting somewhere!

The colonel looked up in shock at this newcomer, his hands gripping the podium so tightly the wood creaked. *"Jia,"* he said quietly, before turning to the soldiers at the back of the cafeteria. "How did she get out of her room? Remove her, *now*!"

The guards nearest Jia moved to grab her, only to fly back against the walls, stuck there as if they were on a spinning carnival ride. "No, I think I'm done with all of that," Jia said, slowly walking toward the podium.

Awesome. This, Sebastian wanted to applaud for.

"Stop her!" Colonel Charles shouted, gesturing at the other guards. "Take her down! She was in league with the thieves!"

These new guards moved more cautiously, but the result was the same, and a moment later, they were hanging on the walls as well. A few students stood up to confront her, some glowing with red or blue magic, but a look from Sebastian sent them back to their seats.

"Nice of you to finally step up," he said to Jia, who rudely ignored him. As usual.

"Colonel Charles is lying to you," she told the assembled students. "We did take Excalibur, yes, but it was used to *beat* an Old One. And the other Old Ones won't be stopped. In fact, they're on their way now, and Cyrus?" She paused, like she didn't even want to say the words. "He was on *their* side."

Whoa, what? Cyrus was a traitor? That couldn't be true,

could it? Immediately all the students began talking at once, most disbelieving but more than a few sounding scared. This was irritating, since it stopped Jia from explaining, so Sebastian waved a hand, and the assembled mouths froze in place. "She's not done," he said, crossing his arms.

"Enough!" Colonel Charles shouted. "I will *not* let you—"

And then his mouth closed by itself as well, glowing with blue Healing magic. Sebastian lowered his hands, the glow of his Healing magic disappearing. They'd heard enough from the colonel at this point.

"Thanks, Sebastian," Jia said. "But you can let them go. We need to all trust each other, or we're never going to make it through this."

He winced at that. "We might be in trouble, then."

"How can we trust you?" Moira asked as Sebastian freed the students—but kept Colonel Charles quiet. "You, Rachel, and . . . that other kid—I forget his name—you all attacked us and took that sword. Why should we believe anything *you* say?"

Jia nodded. "I get it. I don't know that I'd believe me either, especially after I just said you've been lied to all along. But does *anyone* really believe Colonel Charles is telling you the truth anymore?"

No one spoke up, and the colonel growled through his closed mouth. This time, Sebastian didn't hide his loud laugh.

"Exactly," Jia said. "Anyway, don't take my word for it."

With that, she stopped and gestured toward the stage.

A circle of green light opened next to Colonel Charles, who leaped away from it in surprise, then pulled what looked like some kind of wand out of his holster, glowing with red light.

The wand immediately exploded, and he clutched his hand in pain as he stared at the two children passing through the green teleportation circle. One was Rachel, whom Sebastian was happy to see. After all, she was his counterpart in the Destruction school, the best of the best.

But the other kid . . . ugh.

"What's up, Opps School?" Rachel said with a wide grin, her hands raised in the air, still glowing red from destroying Colonel Charles's magical wand. "Nice to be back. Now, we're going to need all of your help. Jia's right: We took Excalibur to use against the Old One of Time magic. And guess what? *We trashed him*. And we can do the same to the others."

"But we can't do it alone," said the Annoying Kid, Forsythe, and he gestured for something to come through the teleportation circle behind him. The head of a large black dragon passed through it, and Sebastian's eyes widened. *That* was new.

He readied a spell as half the rest of the students leaped to their feet, only for Jia to freeze the others in place. "But it's not the Old Ones who we need to face right now."

The dragon nodded and snorted fire in annoyance. "No, you ridiculous humans," Ember said in English. "It's Damian, a fellow dragon, who apparently has lost his mind and is bringing the Old Ones *here*. As much as I despise setting a precedent of humans attacking dragons, we need to hunt him down and eat him—"

"We need to *stop* him," Fort immediately interrupted, shaking his head at the black dragon. "No eating!"

The dragon rolled her eyes but went silent. The rest of the room followed suit, as did Sebastian, considering everything the new kids had just said, none of which sounded good. And what was worse, he knew—*he* knew—that there was no way Rachel, Jia, and Fort would include him in all of this, in spite of the fact that he was the number one Healing student and could probably take all three of them down if he needed to.

Just as Sebastian decided it was time for *him* to take charge of things, Annoying Kid stepped on his moment by turning to the colonel. "So, Colonel, it's time we filled you in on what's really been going on. Mind if we use your office?"

Sebastian couldn't help but roll his eyes again. Of course they'd tell the *colonel*—who'd failed time after time—everything but leave *Sebastian* out of things yet again.

And what could they *possibly* have been up to that was so important they could only share it in private?

- TWO -
YESTERDAY

FORT, RACHEL, AND JIA HAD SOMEHOW done the impossible: They'd defeated the Timeless One, the Old One of Time magic.

Only now everything was falling apart, starting with the fact that the Timeless One had turned out to be Fort's best friend, Cyrus.

Maybe Fort could have dealt with that, by itself. He'd known ahead of time, after all, having figured out Cyrus's true identity from hints he'd gotten from his friends and Merlin—who was also Cyrus's older self, another huge shock.

All of that was bad enough. But combined with Jia's deal with the faerie queen, the deal she had hidden from them—that if they beat the Timeless One, Jia would hand him over to the queen—it was just too much for Fort to take. Especially when Jia had used her Corporeal magic to freeze Fort and

Rachel as a shimmer appeared over Cyrus, just after their battle with the Timeless One.

"Fort!" Cyrus screamed. *"Please—"*

But a humanoid shape within the shimmer grabbed him, and together they disappeared, taking Fort's complicated feelings about Cyrus to a whole new level of awful.

Jia quickly released them from her spell, and Fort immediately sprinted to the spot where Cyrus had lain and bent down, making sure this wasn't some illusion, some sort of glamour.

Then he looked up at Jia, who was covering her mouth like she might throw up.

"Was it worth it?" he asked quietly. "Tell me it was worth it. Tell me that the queen didn't just trick us all."

She looked down at him and shook her head, then began to quietly cry as Rachel hugged her close.

Fort sighed, rubbing his forehead. Maybe Xenea could find out what happened to Cyrus, try to keep him safe, but he doubted it. The faerie queen had been holding a grudge against Merlin/Cyrus/the Timeless One for centuries, and now that she had her old enemy in her hands, Fort didn't think she'd ever be willing to release him.

Not that Cyrus didn't deserve a few hundred years in a

dungeon for what he'd done to them. But he'd also sent Damian and Sierra off somewhere in time to find the last two books of magic, and when they returned, Damian would be ready to summon the Old Ones, Cyrus's plan all along to bring his family back to their home.

And without Cyrus, they had no way of knowing when or where Damian would come back.

"We *might* be in trouble," Fort said, standing back up.

"Nothing new about that," Rachel said as she let go of Jia and turned to him. "Got any ideas?"

Fort swallowed hard, hating what he was about to say. "Just terrible ones. We're going to need help. And there's only one place left to find it."

Rachel groaned, shaking her head. "They'll never take us back."

Fort nodded. "I know. But we still need the TDA and the other students at the Oppenheimer School." He looked up at Jia and Rachel. "Hiding magic away for over a thousand years didn't keep the Old Ones from coming back. If we can't stop Damian before he summons them, then this time, we'll have to *destroy* magic altogether."

"Wait, *what*?" Rachel said, her eyes widening, as Jia just

stared at him in shock. "Did Cyrus hit you in the head at some point? Because you're not making any sense, Fort."

He started to respond but stopped as he noticed Ember, his dragon, a few yards away, cleaning the dirt off her scales like a cat would, her attention thankfully absorbed by her bath. The last thing he wanted was for her to overhear this, since ending magic would probably be fatal to a creature like Ember, who had been created from it. Not to mention he'd just spent the last few days realizing he didn't want her to go to Avalon and be raised by the elder dragons who'd escaped there.

But wouldn't that be better than for the Old Ones to return and transform her into one of the Dracsi, like they'd done to the other dragons? Better for her to live on Avalon than to become some mindless monster.

Better to destroy magic for good than let humanity be taken over by the Old Ones.

The future they'd just come from was *worse* than apocalyptic: The Old Ones were in control, and humanity served them. Even the idea that his friends, his aunt, his father would be under the Old One's Spirit magic, like the dwarfs in the Dracsi dimension, enraged Fort.

It wouldn't happen. Whatever needed to be done to avoid that future, Fort would do.

"It might be the only way," he said finally, nodding at Ember so Rachel and Jia would hopefully get the hint to cover what they were talking about. "Whatever made it go away the first time, we'd just make it permanent."

And just like the last time, that'd still leave Avalon and other dimensions with magic, so Ember and the faeries would be okay. Or so Fort had to hope.

"Doing that would leave us with *nothing*," Rachel said, giving him a long look. "We'd never be able to fight back again. Stopping Damian before he summons the Old Ones is our only option."

"Ray, he might have a point," Jia said. Rachel looked at her in surprise, but Jia just shrugged sadly. "If we can't stop Damian, if we lose . . . It's better than the future Cyrus just showed us, where humanity is serving the Old Ones underground."

"If only we still *had* Cyrus, we might have a better shot at stopping Damian," Fort growled, glaring at Jia. She blushed, looking incredibly guilty, which didn't help Fort's mood, weirdly. "As it is, we have no idea when or if he's even coming back. For all we know, he'll find the other two books and just summon the Old Ones from whatever year he's in."

"Cyrus would never have talked," Rachel said, stepping between Jia and Fort. "You think he'd have set this all up just to help us stop it? No way. We're better off without him."

"Maybe Jia can just hand Damian over to the faerie queen too, then," Fort said, hating that he was so angry about this, but not able to help himself. He knew Jia had made the bargain to stop a war, not to mention that Cyrus was an Old One and didn't deserve his pity, but he couldn't help it: The silver-haired boy still felt like his friend, even after everything Fort had learned.

"Whoa!" Rachel shouted. "You know why she did it, Fort. And at the time, Jia thought she was giving up an Old One, not . . . well, Cyrus *is* an Old One, but you know what I mean. And do I have to remind you that *you* made a deal with the faerie queen too?"

"Shall I eat them for you, Father?" asked Ember in the language of magic as she walked over, her bath apparently now finished. *"I know you said I should protect the other humans, but you seem to have changed your mind about them. I can give them a head start if you like?"*

"No, we're not hurting anyone," Fort told her quickly, not

liking the excited look in the dragon's eye. He'd promised he'd take her hunting a few too many times now and didn't want her chasing down his friends, even the ones he wasn't too thrilled with at the moment.

"Watch what you say in that language," Rachel said, still looking furious with him. "If you 'accidentally' throw a spell Jia's way, I *will* take you down, New Kid."

"No, Rachel, he's right to be mad," Jia said, moving out from behind her to face them both. She turned to Fort, her face contorted with sadness. "I'm so sorry, Fort. I wish I never had to do it. But even if I'd known it was Cyrus, I still would have made the bargain. I'd do anything to save the world from going through a world war like what we saw, and if I have to hate myself to do it, then that's a price I'll pay."

Rachel pulled her in for a hug, though she glared at Fort over Jia's shoulder. "Which you shouldn't, because now that it's all out in the open, we *all* completely understand—don't we, Fort?"

He turned away, not feeling like this was very fair, considering Rachel had been pretty upset with Jia herself once she'd found out about the bargain—though not what it was for. "I *do* understand, Jia," he said, and oddly, realized he meant it.

Whatever Jia had done wasn't the real reason he was so upset. That was all on Cyrus. "I . . . I might have even made the same decision. Besides, maybe your deal with the queen is why she fixed my father, took away whatever magic he could do, which is what would have actually caused the war. So I probably have you to thank for getting him back."

Jia looked at him like he'd just thrown her a life preserver when she was lost at sea. "That could be true. I *hope* it's true. But I'd still get it if you hate me."

"Can we turn our attention to the *real* bad guy here?" Rachel said. "Cyrus has been lying to us for . . . well, *ever*! He's been manipulating all of us to get his family back, and whatever the queen does to him, he fully deserves. Not to mention that we have to stop the Old Ones from returning as it is. Like Fort said before he brought up the awful Plan That Shall Not Be Named, we're going to need the TDA's help, and probably a bunch of the Oppenheimer School students'."

"Or *all* of them," Jia pointed out, looking a bit relieved that they'd moved on. "You know how powerful Damian was, back when we fought him in the UK. If he's learned Time and Spirit magic, he's going to be almost impossible to beat."

Rachel and Jia continued on, but Fort stopped listening, lost in his own thoughts as Ember trotted over to him and pushed her dragon head against his hand, like she still wanted to be petted, even when not in her cat form.

Hopefully Rachel was right. If they could get the TDA and the other students on their side, maybe there was a chance . . . but Fort doubted it. Damian was already too powerful when they'd fought him last, just like Jia had said. And with two more books of magic . . .

Even with a dragon, Fort couldn't see how they'd win. Ember might be able to put up a fight, but she was too young to do much against the older Damian, even as fast as she was growing.

And if they lost—*when* they lost—that was it for humanity.

The future that Cyrus had shown them just couldn't be allowed to happen. And if there was no way to beat Damian, then destroying magic really was the only way, no matter what Rachel thought.

"Hey, you still there?" Rachel said, waving a hand in front of Fort's face. "I asked if you were with us. We all are going to have to work together on this if we have any shot of beating Damian."

Fort cringed. "I don't think we *have* a shot, Rachel. Plan, ah, *B* is our best shot here. It's the only way to be sure the Old Ones can't come back."

"Oh, that's a *great* point, except for three reasons," Rachel said, ticking them off on her fingers. "One, we have no idea how to do that. Two, there'd be no coming back from it, so if we needed our spells again, they'd be gone. And three, we have *no idea* how to do that!"

"You said that twice," Jia pointed out.

"That's because it's doubly important," Rachel said. "I get what you're thinking, Fort. I really do. But if it comes down to that, we've already lost. Now, if you're with us, and we can stop Damian, then we don't even need to worry about your plan B."

He nodded, realizing arguing about it any further was useless. Rachel wasn't going to listen to him, and while Jia seemed a lot more open to it, she'd insist on trying to stop Damian first. And if they could keep him from summoning the Old Ones, then Rachel was right, that was the *far* better plan.

But if not . . .

"I'm in," Fort told them. "But before we go back to the Oppenheimer School, there's one more thing we need to do. Or at least, *I* need to do."

"What's that?" Jia asked.

"Shower?" Rachel said, wrinkling her nose.

"Well, that," Fort said. "But I need to see my dad, to . . . talk to him." He swallowed hard. "Because we don't know what might . . . you know."

Jia and Rachel both went silent and nodded.

Fort had no idea what they were in for with Damian, or worse, the Old Ones. But if things went badly, like he feared they would, then he had to tell his father everything, *now*.

Just in case it was his last chance to do it.

- THREE -

AN HOUR LATER, FORT STOOD OUTside his aunt's front door, his hand on the doorknob . . . but he just couldn't open it. There was no time to waste: They had to get to the Oppenheimer School as soon as they could. But going back meant telling his father and Aunt Cora everything, from the beginning—magic, Dracsi, Old Ones, all of it—and that made his blood run cold.

And just as they finished being freaked out about all of *that*, he'd have to tell them he was leaving to go fight a teenage dragon to save the world, not to mention he'd probably be staying at the school for a while, since they had no idea when Damian would actually be back.

Come on, just do it, he told himself, but how would he even start, once he was inside? Even if they believed everything he said, he couldn't imagine how angry and betrayed they'd feel once they found out how much Fort had been keeping from them.

At least he wasn't alone in this: Rachel had gone back to her house to do the same, no more thrilled by the idea than Fort was. Jia was lucky, in this if nothing else, since she was still under guard at the school, and her parents knew all about the books of magic. Not that being a prisoner was a good thing, but right now Fort would have traded places with her in a minute.

Fort took a deep breath, then grabbed the doorknob tightly, dreading what was to come. He turned it—

"Oh wow, you *didn't* die," said a voice behind him, and Fort screamed a bit in surprise, releasing the doorknob instantly to whirl around and face whatever danger had just snuck up on him, only to find Xenea staring at him with an oddly pleased expression. "I'm actually impressed," she continued. "I didn't think you humans stood a chance against the Timeless One." She looked around curiously. "Where's the dragon you've been hiding? Is she okay?"

"She's fine," Fort whispered, moving away from the door so no one inside could overhear. "And back to being hidden." He swallowed hard, dreading this next part almost as much as revealing everything to his dad. "But I do need to talk to you about her. I might have to do something, and . . ." He paused, feeling his throat constrict. "I mean, there's a chance that if things go badly, which they probably will, I mean, uh . . ."

Xenea raised an eyebrow as he flailed, so Fort decided to change the subject, hoping this conversation could wait, even if the one with his father and aunt couldn't. "What's happening to the Timeless One, anyway?" he said. "Is the queen going to . . . hurt him?"

Not that Cyrus was a better topic, but as much as Fort hated his ex-friend, part of him couldn't stop hoping he was okay, and the queen had just locked him away somewhere, instead of torturing him or something.

"Oh, I'm sure she froze him and is showing him off in the throne room," Xenea said, wrinkling her nose. "That's how she typically starts with her enemies, and once she's bored of gloating over him, she'll probably throw him in a dungeon for a few thousand years." She shrugged like that was a completely normal amount of time to be thrown in a dungeon. "But we need to talk about *your* bargain. The queen might have gotten the Timeless One, but that won't distract her for long, and she'll be checking on me about your dragon. Tell me that the older one is returning soon, so maybe I can finally go home."

Fort winced. "We don't know when he'll be back, and what's worse, he'll have probably mastered all six kinds of magic, so I wouldn't—"

"Ugh, you humans and your types of magic," Xenea said, rolling her eyes. "There's only *one* kind of magic."

Fort just stared in confusion. "What? There are six. Healing, Destruction, Time, Spirit, Mind, and Summoning."

She snorted. "First of all, you've got the names all wrong. Healing is Corporeal, Destruction is Elemental, and Summoning is—"

"Space magic, I know," Fort said, shaking his head. "Force of habit."

"And second of all, those are just *one* type," Xenea said with a long sigh. "You people have really messed magic up, honestly. If you don't die in all of this, maybe someday I'll teach you Tylwyth Teg magic, the way it was meant to be used."

Fort blinked, not sure what she was talking about, but realizing something. "Hey, since you know so much more about magic, maybe you can help us fight Damian? That way, if we beat him, you could bring him back to your queen. Your glamour is really powerful, and—"

"Doesn't work on dragons, actually," she sniffed. "What, you think Her Majesty would let those elder dragons live free on Avalon if she could magic them away?"

Fort sighed. Great. Of course it didn't work on dragons. Why *would* it? Why would anything make his life easier at this point? "If we can't stop Damian, he's going to bring the Old Ones back to try to defeat them once and for all. Which means—"

Xenea winced. "Which means this Damian dragon will be killed, and they'll take over your world again. *That* doesn't sound good. Does my queen know about this?"

"Probably, if she's interrogated Cy . . . the Timeless One," Fort said, the thought of the faerie queen torturing Cyrus for information making him nauseous. *He's an Old One. Stop thinking he's your friend. He* tricked *you from the moment you met him.*

"Hmm," Xenea said, beginning to pace around outside the front door. "Perhaps that's something I should discuss with her, then. I imagine losing this world to the Old Ones wouldn't be high on her list, considering if anyone conquers you human fools, she'd want it to be her."

"Oh, okay, good to know," Fort said, shaking his head as he turned back to his aunt's front door. "Well, if you aren't going to help against Damian, I've got to work on a backup plan. But first I have to tell my dad I'm going back to my old school."

"Oh, he's not there right now," Xenea said absently, then seemed to realize what she'd said and went quiet abruptly.

A cold shiver went down Fort's spine. "What do you mean, he's *not there*? Where *is* he?"

Xenea looked everywhere but at him. "How should I know? I could smell him if he were there, and he's not, that's all. Quit being so *paranoid*, Forsythe."

Fort just stared at her, his anger rising. What was she hiding about his father? This wasn't the first time something had come up between the faerie girl and his dad. They'd shared a look and some odd conversation each time he'd seen them around one another.

The last thing he had time for right now was Xenea's secrets. If there was something happening with his dad, he needed to know *now*. "What is going on between you and my father?" he demanded. "This isn't funny anymore, Xenea. You need to *tell* me what's happening here!"

Just as he finished, the front door opened, and Fort's father stood bathed in the light from the apartment's kitchen. "Fort?" his dad said. "It *is* you. I thought I heard your voice! What are you doing out there?" He looked past Fort and frowned. "Oh, hello, *Xenea*."

"I . . . didn't think you'd be here," Xenea said, looking nervous. "When did you get back?"

"Just now," his father said, giving her a strange look that made Fort even more curious, on top of being nauseous over what he and his dad needed to talk about in a moment. "I had a late interview, but I think it might have gone okay. How did you know I wasn't here?"

"By the smell," Xenea said, taking in a loud sniff, and Fort smacked his forehead, not having the energy to cover for her at the moment. Maybe that's what all the weirdness was about, his father sensing something was wrong with her, that she wasn't just a transfer student from the UK.

"Oh, you mean the smell of dinner?" Fort's father said to Xenea. "You can stay if you'd like."

Fort could tell he didn't sound too enthusiastic about the idea, and Xenea didn't seem thrilled about it either. "No, I really need to be going. Have to check in with my queen."

"The queen of England?" his father asked, raising an eyebrow.

"If the world worked the way it should, yes," Xenea said, then clapped a hand on Fort's shoulder hard enough to make him wince. "Good luck with things, Forsythe. I'll check back in with you soon about our . . . winged-lizard situation."

Fort groaned. "Only if I can figure out your *secret code*," he hissed at her, then pushed his father gently back into the apartment, hoping to cover for the fact that Xenea was about to just disappear into thin air. "Come on, time for dinner, like you said, Dad. I have to talk to you about something important."

As soon as they were both inside, Fort slammed the door shut, just as he saw the air start to shimmer. Hoping he'd closed it before his father saw anything, he turned to find his dad staring off into space anxiously.

"Are you okay?" Fort asked.

His father jolted abruptly, then smiled at him. "Totally fine!" he said. "Sorry, just remembering a promise I made to someone. What did you want to talk to me about?"

- FOUR -

FORT TOOK A DEEP BREATH, FEELING like he was trembling so hard from nervousness he might start an earthquake. "Um, it's about *school.*"

For the briefest of seconds, a worried look passed over his father's face, only to be quickly replaced by a grin. "Ah, so they finally figured out you're too smart for them and are sending you on to college instead? I *knew* it!"

Fort grinned back, even more anxious now. "Um, not exactly. Is Aunt Cora here too?"

"No, she's out for the night with some friends," his dad said. "How about we talk while we eat?"

He led Fort to the kitchen, where some pasta was boiling, one of the few things Fort knew his father could cook, at least without burning it. Fort helped get things ready, grabbing some plates and silverware as his father drained the pasta and served up two heaping piles for them.

"Don't tell me you got detention," his dad said, raising an eyebrow as they sat down. "What is it this time? Did the teacher get annoyed that you kept leading the class for her?"

Fort couldn't look at him, so instead locked his eyes on his plate. "No, it's . . . about the boarding school that Aunt Cora sent me to. They, um, want me to come back?"

A loud clank made Fort look up, and he found his father staring at him, a forgotten fork dropped on his plate. *"No,"* his dad whispered, shaking his head. "You're not going back there. I'm here now, and *I'll* be taking care of you."

Fort winced. This was already going worse than he'd feared. "It's not that simple, Dad," he said, his insides writhing around. The last thing he'd ever wanted to do was explain all the dangerous things he'd been up to while his father was in the Dracsi homeworld—and, well, for a long time after—but the time had come. "I have to tell you something that's going to sound, um, a bit . . . impossible, but . . ."

His father sighed, rubbing his eyes. "No, Forsythe, you don't have to tell me anything. You think I don't know what happened while I was gone, what happens at that school?"

Fort's eyes widened, and it felt like his heart might beat

through his chest. His father *knew*? But that wasn't possible. Dr. Opps had lied to his aunt from the beginning, and there was no way his dad could remember anything that had happened while he was unconscious.

Wait. He was just being paranoid! His father had to be talking about something else. "You mean like how the military is there?" Fort said quietly. "I know that's sort of strange for a school, but—"

"No, Fort, I mean that they've been teaching you *magic*," his father said, staring him straight in the eye.

This time, Fort dropped *his* fork with a loud clank.

"You . . . *know*?" he said, his voice cracking in surprise.

"Of course I know!" his father said, pushing away from the table and standing up to pace around the small kitchen. "I've known since I woke up. The military told me everything, Fort, but promised me that *you* wouldn't remember any of it, that they'd made sure that everything you'd gone through would be wiped out of your mind, that it wouldn't affect you any longer. I wouldn't have listened, but they showed me the other children casting spells, showed me video of *you* doing things I couldn't even believe!"

Fort just stared at his father, his mouth hanging open. How

was this possible? The military—Colonel Charles—had told his father about the school? It *couldn't* be. All this time, Fort had been hiding it from his father to not upset the man, only to find out now his dad had been doing the same for him? "But . . . *why* would they have told you?" he asked finally.

"Because they wanted me to keep an eye on you, to let them know if the memory wipe didn't take," his father said, his voice heavy with guilt. "They said that if it didn't work for whatever reason, I should let them know right away, so you wouldn't suffer from everything you'd been through. But as the days passed, I thought whatever they'd done had worked, since you didn't seem to remember any of it. I hoped it was all over, but then you started sneaking out, and now you're mentioning the school again. . . ."

Fort gasped. Sneaking out? He *knew* Fort had been leaving? "I, uh, was just visiting some friends from school. But how did you—"

"Know you were leaving?" his father finished, smiling sadly. "You're not as subtle as you think you are. And I don't even want to *know* what those claw marks are in your room."

Fort winced. "That would be Ember. She's not exactly a cat."

His father squeezed his eyes closed tightly, breathing in and out through his nose in long breaths. "Not a cat. Okay. Fantastic. I can deal with this." He opened his eyes back up and nodded. "So you *do* remember everything, and want to go back to the school. Fine. Permission *not* granted."

His words hit Fort like a slap to the face. "Wait, what? Dad!"

"There's no way I'm letting you anywhere near that place ever again!" his father said as he turned away from Fort to lean on the counter for support. "In fact, I think we need to get you out of here, go somewhere to hide for a little while, just in case the military comes looking for you."

"What?" Fort said again, standing up now as well. "I *have* to go back to the school, Dad. They need me! You don't understand what's coming—"

"Oh no?" his father said, turning around and looking both more scared and angry than Fort had ever seen him. "You think *I* don't get how dangerous that place can be? A giant monster took me away from you, Fort! I thought I was going to die! You're *not* going back into that world, no matter what. *End of discussion.*"

Fort gritted his teeth. "Dad, I get that you're worried about me. I would be too. But you don't know what I can do! I've learned so much and can actually *help* people with my magic.

If I don't go back . . . I've seen what's to come in the future, and I can't let it happen!"

"You don't get the *choice*!" his father shouted, something Fort hadn't heard him do in forever. "I'm your father, and *I* decide what we do. And I'm telling you that we're getting out of here, *tonight*. I've got a . . . friend who might help us, if we can make a deal with her. No one will be able to find us, and you'll be *safe*."

"I *know* how scared you are," Fort said, holding up his hands to try to calm his dad down. "But remember when you ran back into the Lincoln Memorial to save those people, even though it was collapsing? You did it in spite of how terrified you were! How can I do any less than you did? If I don't go back, other people are going to be hurt, or worse, and I *can't* let that happen, no matter what you say, Dad."

Now it was his father's turn to look shocked. "No matter what I say? I *told* you that you're not going back, Fort. That's all there is to it!" He pointed down the hall. "Go get your things. I'll pack what I have here. I want us out of here in a half hour at most."

Fort just stared at him. "I really can't change your mind?" he asked, almost pleading with his father. This had gone even worse than he'd expected, and he dreaded what he had to do next. "Please, Dad, just listen—"

"No," his father said softly, shaking his head. "We're done here."

Fort took a deep, shuddering breath. "Okay," he said quietly, and turned toward his bedroom. "I'll go get ready, then."

"Fort?" his father said as he moved to walk down the hall. "I'd do *anything* to keep you safe. I have no choice here. It's . . . it's just who I *am*."

Fort turned back to look at him one last time. "I know. And I'm so, *so* sorry."

His father gave him a sad smile, then left to go to his own room.

Fort watched him go, completely miserable inside. "And this is who *I* am," he whispered, then teleported away.

- FIVE -
TODAY

"I SHOULD HAVE LOCKED YOU ALL UP AND thrown away the key," Colonel Charles hissed, sitting at his desk next to Agent Cole, both of them tied with steel bars Rachel had pulled out of the wall. "I *knew* erasing your memories was too merciful! And I let your father go free, Fitzgerald. This is the thanks I get?"

Sitting at the desk in front of them, Fort went pale at the mention of his dad and turned away. It hadn't even been a full day since he'd teleported out of his aunt's house, and he hadn't spoken to his father since. Even thinking about him now gave Fort an empty feeling in the pit of his stomach.

More than anything, he just felt *lonely*, without Cyrus, without his dad. Thankfully, he still had Ember and his other friends at least.

"All right." Jia reached toward Colonel Charles with a glowing blue hand. "Maybe you should be *listening* more than talking right now."

Rachel gave her a proud look, then turned back to the colonel. "Gee's right. Besides, we're not here to hurt you."

A large, indignant growl came from Ember, who had turned into a cat again in order to fit into the office and now lay on Fort's lap. "Father, you promised me we *could* eat them if they disobeyed!" she said in English.

Both Agent Cole and Colonel Charles went pale at that, but Fort petted Ember fondly, appreciating the distraction. "Right, *if* they disobey. We haven't even told them what they're going to do yet."

"As if we'd listen to *you*, Fitzgerald," Agent Cole practically spat. "You've done nothing but undermine the security of the United States since arriving at this school. And I'll have you know I *did* say we should keep both you and Carter here, *behind bars*. If the colonel had listened, we wouldn't be in this situation right now."

"And humanity would be destroyed in a matter of months," Rachel said. "So before I turn my friend's dragon loose on the two of you, why don't you listen to Gee, and *be quiet*. It won't be long now until—"

"It can't be," said a new voice from the door. "Fort? Rachel? Jia? You're here—you're *all right*?"

They all turned to find Ellora standing in the doorway, frozen with shock. Fort's mood immediately brightened at the sight of her, even if most of the time they'd spent together had been trying to avoid being taken over by her former classmate and save what they could of London, and the world.

Rachel waved her in with a smile, but the British girl barely moved until Jia gently pulled her into the office and closed the door behind her. "It's really us," Jia said with a small smile.

"And no one's been Spirit magicked," Rachel confirmed. "We had the students release you as soon as we heard what they did to you. Sorry it took us this long!"

"But I thought they *captured* you all," Ellora said, still looking like she wasn't sure she could believe what she was seeing. "They were waiting for me when I arrived back here with Excalibur and took me by surprise. I couldn't even get a spell out before I was paralyzed by some Healer. They had to have a Time student on their side if they saw me coming, so I assumed you all were taken as well."

"They had *Cyrus*," Fort said quietly, his mood growing

darker again as he turned back to Colonel Charles, glaring at the man. "It's great you were listening to the enemy all along, by the way."

"*My* enemy is sitting right in front of me, you little monster," the colonel sneered.

"Cyrus provided good intelligence," Agent Cole said. "Just because you say he's working against us doesn't mean it's true. What did you do with him?"

"Did you not hear me earlier?" Rachel asked. "We beat him using Excalibur and took away all his magic. Because, you know, he was an *Old One*." She paused, letting that sink in, though both adults still looked doubtful. "Really? You're not going to listen to us on this?" She snorted and looked back at Fort and Jia. "This is what happens when people lie all the time. They think *everyone* must be."

"Wait, you aren't joking?" Ellora asked, moving to face Rachel. "Cyrus is an Old One? It can't be. He was one of us!"

"The girl's right, we have no reason to believe you," Colonel Charles said. "Not that it matters. Your little coup will be over before you know it."

"Oh, you mean the TDA guards you had as backup?" Rachel

asked, sitting down in one of the chairs and throwing her leg over an arm. "Yeah, we took care of them. Ellora, do you want to confirm that?"

The Time girl seemed to be lost in thought, and Rachel had to repeat her name again. "Oh, uh, yes, you got most of them, but there are still a few soldiers on their way," she said as her eyes turned black with Time magic. "Okay, I froze the rest, so we're safe. But can we get back to Cyrus?"

"He's the Old One of Time magic," Jia told her.

"And Merlin's younger self, of all things," Rachel said, shaking her head. "Which might make you wonder why Merlin wanted us to fight the Timeless One, then, but that's a longer story than we have time for. Cyrus has been manipulating us all, including Damian and Sierra, to get the other Old Ones back. Damian thinks he can defeat the Old Ones, once he's learned all the types of magic, but he's wrong. Instead, he's going to lose and unleash them on our world."

Ellora just blinked. "That's . . . quite a lot of information at once. Are you absolutely sure—"

Fort sighed, getting tired of no one believing them. "Let's just save some time and do this the easy way." In the language of magic, he said, *"Let everyone see what Cyrus did."*

"Except me," Ember said quickly as Fort's spell struck everyone else, jolting them with its power. As it did, his memories filled their heads, just as Fort had witnessed Dr. Opps's memories when they'd first met. Only this time, instead of seeing Discovery Day, the others all saw Cyrus removing his Timeless One outfit and confessing to his lies.

But as the others took in his memories, something odd began to happen to Fort: His mind began to . . . expand. Suddenly it was like he was looking down at the others from a distance, slowly rising into the air. He frowned and gritted his teeth, trying to pull himself back.

"It's really *true*," Ellora said, distracting Fort a bit and loosening his control. He felt his attention begin to wander as flashes began appearing in his mind of memories from various students around the school. Here was Sebastian, getting praised by Dr. Ambrose for his Healing spells, or Chad softly crying into his pillow, missing his parents.

What was going *on*?

"Enough of this," Colonel Charles said, bringing Fort's focus back to the office, if only for the moment. "Even if we believe what you just showed us—and we have no way of knowing if it was actually real or not—then what does it matter? We've been after Damian since *you* all woke him up, and we've trained for this. We'll stop him."

"No, you won't," Ellora said, shuddering a little. "The four of us had no chance against him, and that was *before* he learned Time and Spirit magic. If he has those two books, he'll basically be untouchable by anything human."

Ember patted Fort's hand with her paw, and suddenly the feeling of floating and the other students' memories all disappeared. "Thankfully, then, silver-haired human, it's good that you have *me*," she said to Ellora, who jumped in surprise at a talking cat.

"Oh, right," Fort said, barely able to concentrate. "This is Ember. She's the dragon you saw in my memories, just in cat form."

"Oh, right, of course," Ellora said, now looking even more confused.

"It's, uh, going to take us all working together to bring Damian down, Colonel," Fort continued, trying to think through the distraction. "He thinks he's the, um, chosen one. You know, from the books of magic? They all have that prophecy poem in the beginning, something about finding the six types of books."

The colonel just glared at him.

"Well, Damian believes the prophecy is about him," Rachel continued. "Because he's just *that* arrogant. If we don't stop him, he'll bring the Old Ones here and *lose* to them, because whatever that prophecy is, it has nothing on four eternal horrors from beyond. If that's what you want, then fine, we'll handle this on our own. But somewhere in there, I think you do actually care about protecting the world and will want to help." She leaned in to stare at Colonel Charles. "What do you say?"

The colonel sneered. "I say I'll see you all behind bars when this is over, Carter." Then he gritted his teeth, like what he was about to say was physically painful. "But for now the TDA and the Oppenheimer School . . . will stand by your side."

"Oh, for—" Agent Cole said, then went silent as Ember hissed at her.

"Good," Fort said, then gently put Ember on the floor and stood up. "Now that we're in agreement, you need to understand that the four of us here will be . . ."

He paused as his vision began swimming again.

"Fort, are you okay?" Rachel asked as if from miles away.

"Will be . . . ," he said again, his words sounding odd to him, like someone else was saying them. "Will be . . . in charge?"

And then he toppled forward as his mind expanded right out of his body.

- SIX -

Y*OU MUST SEE HOW IT BEGAN, WITH an explosion of Possibility,* said a voice, one Fort had never heard before. A woman's voice.

But there was nothing *to* see. Everything was utter black, a darkness beyond anything he'd seen before. This wasn't just an absence of light: It felt as if there was literally nothing around him, nothing anywhere, *ever*.

And then, abruptly, a glowing white pinprick of light appeared, and Fort found himself rushing toward it.

No, he wasn't moving. The pinprick of light was expanding, exploding outward, straight at him.

Where there had been nothing, now there was everything. Rocks and minerals larger than he could comprehend crashed against each other, sending pieces spinning off into space, or sticking together to form larger masses, even planets. Huge gaseous giants exploded again and again, creating stars, suns for new universes.

This is how it started, said the same voice, one Fort felt like he should know. It was comforting and familiar, even if he didn't recognize it. But still it made him feel safe, even as he hurtled through the newborn galaxies. *All of creation was filled with infinite potential.*

The space around him distorted, then snapped back into place as Fort found himself hovering above what felt like a very familiar planet, though it didn't look the same as the pictures he'd seen from space. *The Possibility force was drawn to this place, though by what, even it has no idea,* the voice said. *But whatever the reason, it was pulled to this new world.*

Down on the planet now, Fort's vision began to intensify, so that he could see even the tiniest of single-cell creatures, each one splitting in half in a spark of white light, then splitting again, over and over, each time giving off that same spark.

Even in the daze of the vision, Fort realized what was happening: This was *life*, living creatures appearing and reproducing for the very first time. The enormity of witnessing the birth of life on Earth made him start to cry, and tears rolled down his cheeks, leaving little white streams of light behind.

Everything was so . . . connected. All life emerging from the same light, the same spark. Even apart from it all, Fort still felt a part of it, surrounded by other living things.

He couldn't ever remember feeling so happy, so *safe*.

This creation of life was . . . new to Possibility, the voice said. *And it found itself endlessly curious about this new source of chaos and change.*

The single-cell creatures began splitting faster and faster until larger organisms emerged, first in the water, then gradually on land. The first dinosaur stomped right through the spot Fort was standing, and he watched it go in awe, not sure how he could be seeing this, or if he even wanted to go home: The vision was just too beautiful.

You hold the Possibility force now, Forsythe, the voice said. *You contain it within your mind. If you misuse it, if you turn away from the Possibility and seek to destroy it—*

"Fort!" he heard someone yell from a thousand miles away. A blue light lit up the world around him, and he looked down to find the same light glowing from his chest. Something began to pull him away, back through the years toward the present, but he fought it, not wanting to go, wanting to just stay where he was in the presence of the comforting voice, witnessing for himself what the possibilities were, what *magic* was.

The pull lessened, and he returned to the past, a feeling of elation flooding over him at the idea that he might stay here and take it all in.

"Fort!" he heard another voice yell, and this time he recognized it as Ellora's, the girl whom he'd once explored Spirit magic with, in a different future that had never come to pass. Weirdly, he could feel that same Spirit magic within him now, only it held no control over him as it had, and it struck Fort as discomfiting that it had ever held such a power, as if the Possibility was tainted somehow.

But feeling the magic as separate within himself seemed odd for some reason. Why *should* it be its own type, when all of magic came from the Possibility force? Why were there kinds of magic to begin with, all different colors instead of the one, living white glow he'd seen just now in Earth's history? Why—

"Father, now is *not* the time for this," said a new voice, Ember's voice. But strangely enough, this voice didn't come from a distance, but instead seemed to be everywhere, just as he was. He looked for her, and she coalesced beside him, a shining spirit in dragon shape that radiated affection toward him, along with worry and doubt.

"Why not?" he asked her, thrilled to have his dragon with him to witness the beginnings of their world. "Look at how things began, Ember. It's so beautiful. Everything just makes sense!"

"You are not ready, Father," Ember said, and now Fort could see that even she was struggling to keep herself together, to not disappear back into the glow of white light. "Neither of us is ready for this."

"We will learn!" he said, laughing in spite of himself. "Stay here with me, Ember, and together we'll figure it out."

She disappeared from view for a moment, and he frowned, not sure what had happened, even though he somehow knew she was okay. But just as quickly she returned, shaking her transparent head. "You will lose yourself in the chaos, Father, and I won't allow that," she said. "I will not give you up before you take me hunting!"

Fort laughed again, but Ember stayed silent, then reached out a paw toward him. "Come back with me, Father," she said. "This will always be here, when you're ready for it. But that time isn't now."

He raised an eyebrow in confusion but took her paw, trusting her completely. As he touched her, he once more felt pain, confusion, worry, all the things he'd left behind in the world, and he teared up even more now from the sorrow of it all.

His awareness of the beginning, his view of prehistory, and worst of all, the comforting voice all disappeared, and he began to split apart in every direction at once. The jolt was so shocking that he screamed in terror, loudly over and over, as his spirit re-formed, rocketing back toward the Oppenheimer School, toward his body. . . .

And then he was back in his own physical form once more. All the happiness, the safe, comfortable feelings of being surrounded by life were gone, and he never felt so *alone*.

He screamed even louder now, unable to understand how anyone could live like this.

"Fort!" Jia shouted, and again, cold Healing magic passed through him. "Are you back? Are you okay?"

But Fort couldn't stop shouting, not even with Jia's magic. Because it wasn't due to physical pain, though the sensation of having a body once more was almost too much to bear.

No, it was a loss, deep in his soul, of everything he'd just left behind. Even as he screamed, he could feel the memory of it fading, not even able to hold on to that much of it. He screamed and screamed. . . .

And then went silent as Ember smacked him with her cat's paw, right in the arm.

"Enough, Father," she said in the language of magic. *"Your wails are beginning to hurt my ears."*

"Fort, what happened?" Rachel asked, pulling him off Colonel Charles's desk to sit back in one of the colonel's chairs. "One second, you're fine, and the next, you passed out, then started screaming."

"How long . . . ?" Fort asked, his throat dry and raspy. "How long was I gone?"

Rachel, Jia, and Ellora all shared looks. "Maybe ten seconds?" Ellora said.

Fort's eyes widened. Ten seconds? But it'd felt like he'd been gone for a lifetime. How was that possible?

"Oh, *this* is wonderful," Colonel Charles said, still tied with Rachel's steel beams to his chair next to Agent Cole. "You little monsters can't even control your own magic. And *you* want to be in charge of the Oppenheimer School?"

"We don't *want* to be in charge," Fort said quietly, trying not to think about what had just happened. "We . . . we *need* to be. This is our one shot at taking Damian down. If we fail at that . . ."

He wanted to continue the sentence, to say that they'd have no choice but to destroy magic itself. But somehow, he couldn't get the words out, not after what he'd just experienced.

"Then we're all doomed," Rachel finished for him, flashing Fort a concerned look before turning back to the colonel. "Now, why don't you and Ms. Cole here go talk to the TDA soldiers and let them know they'll be taking orders from *us* now?"

Colonel Charles started to object, but Rachel quickly lifted the two adults up from their seats using the steel beams, then floated them to the door, where she released them into the hallway.

"This isn't *over*, Carter," Colonel Charles said, pointing a finger at her. "You think you're in control now, but when this Damian situation is taken care of, then—"

Rachel slammed the door in his face and whirled around to stare at Fort. "What was *that*?" she said. "Are you okay? It looked like the same thing that happened back when you learned every spell from the dragon dictionary. What is going on? Are you not able to handle that magic?"

He wanted to tell her he could, to promise he was fine, but he couldn't bear to lie. "I . . . don't know," he said quietly. "I don't know *what's* going on."

She sighed loudly, but when she spoke, her tone was actually pretty sympathetic. "Why don't you go rest for a bit and figure it out *before* we fight a dragon? The last thing we need is you falling asleep in the middle of it." She nodded at Ellora and Jia. "We three can handle things here for a while."

"Okay," Fort said, not having the will to argue. He stood up and grabbed Ember. "Maybe I just need a minute. A lot's been going on lately."

"That's not it, Father," Ember said to him in the language of magic. *"And you know it. The magic you learned is far beyond anything you've experienced before. You have to embrace it for what it is if you hope to master it."*

Fort swallowed hard, not even sure what she meant. It was all just magic, wasn't it? What could be beyond what he'd experienced?

Not that it might matter for much longer. If Rachel and Jia couldn't figure out a way to stop Damian, then all the magic in Fort's head would be going away with the rest of it, once he figured out how to end magic permanently.

Not knowing what to say, he put Ember on his shoulder and walked out in silence. Thankfully, Agent Cole and Colonel Charles had already disappeared, leaving Fort to wander away and into the halls without any clear destination, just wanting somewhere quiet to think.

Lost in thought, he brushed past several guards, some of whom tried to stop him, but seemed to think better of it when Ember murmured some words.

Fighting Damian already seemed impossible, since they had almost no chance of beating the dragon. But without the magic in his head, the magic he'd learned from the dragon dictionary, their odds got even smaller. All Fort had beyond those spells were Teleport and Heal Minor Wounds, and those wouldn't exactly cut it against Damian.

But if he *did* use the spells from the dragon dictionary and it knocked him out, sending him into another vision, then he could be putting both himself *and* his friends in even worse danger. That possibility was really the last thing he needed in the middle of a fight, or in any other part of life.

Of course, there was always plan B, destroying magic . . . once he figured out how to do that, at least. But if he knew that was the safer bet, why did the idea make him want to vomit? Was it part of the vision, or something more?

He clenched his fists, willing the sick feeling in his stomach to pass. What was he thinking? This was about the entire world, all of humanity! He couldn't let himself be thrown off by some weird vision. If they lost to Damian, there was no other choice, because they sure wouldn't have any chance against the Old Ones.

That meant Fort would have to figure out how to get rid of magic, once and for all. That was all there was to it. Rachel might try to stop him if she found out, so he couldn't tell her. And while Jia seemed to be at least open to it, he wasn't sure he could rely on her not telling Rachel, so Jia was out too.

Which meant this was all down to him. Fantastic.

As he realized this, Fort found himself in a familiar hallway, oddly walking toward a door he hadn't seen in a few weeks. Not entirely sure why he'd come this way, he paused outside the door as he reached it, then raised a hand to open it, but stopped and knocked instead.

No one answered, so he went ahead and opened the door.

His dorm room looked exactly the same as it had the last time he'd seen it, the night they'd gone to the Dracsi homeworld to rescue Fort's father. Oh, the room had been cleaned and emptied, but Fort could almost see himself sitting on one of the beds, with Sierra's mind-self next to him chatting away about their plan to steal the books of magic.

And on the other bed would have been—

Someone knocked on the door, making Fort jump. Ember hissed, so he placed her down on the nearest bed, then moved to open the door.

There, on the other side, was someone Fort had just been thinking about, his former roommate.

"Well, look who's back," Gabriel said to him with a humorless smile. "We need to talk, kid. *Now.*"

- SEVEN -

AT ANY OTHER TIME, THERE WOULD have been a million things Fort wanted to say to Gabriel, the son of Colonel Charles and brother of Michael, the only other person stolen by the Dracsi during the attack that took Fort's father.

Though it seemed like years had passed, it was a few weeks ago that Fort had felt almost like a little brother himself to Gabriel. But then his old roommate had betrayed them all in a failed plan to bring Michael back from the Old Ones, then threatened to drop Fort into a volcano when he'd refused a second attempt.

Even now, Fort found it hard to hate the other boy for what he'd done, not unlike his annoyingly conflicted feelings about Cyrus. Instead, looking at Gabriel, Fort could still see his friend, the boy who'd had his back and stood up for him.

It'd just felt so *good* to have a brother, if just for a few days.

But then he'd lost Gabriel just by doing what he still hoped was the right thing.

The worst part was, Fort honestly didn't know for sure if he *should* have pulled Gabriel out of the Dracsi dimension before he could rescue his brother. Michael hadn't seemed brainwashed at all, yet he'd still refused to leave, having been taught powerful magic by the Old Ones.

Could Michael have been saved? Fort still wondered, whenever he was feeling particularly guilty. Either way, he understood what it meant to lose a family member and be willing to do anything to get them back—though Gabriel sacrificing the people around him to do that did lose him some moral high ground.

Still, now wasn't the time to discuss any of this with Gabriel, as Ember leaped from the nearby bed straight at the other boy, hissing in a terrifying way, as soon as she laid eyes on him.

"YOU!" she roared, morphing from cat into dragon in midair. She slammed into Gabriel with her entire weight, sending him flying through the door of the room across the hall.

"Ember, no!" Fort shouted, but the dragon ignored him. Instead, she grabbed Gabriel by the shirt with her teeth, then tossed him against the far wall of the other—thankfully empty—dorm room, knocking the wind out of him.

"Evil human child!" she roared, the sound reverberating through the hall. "It is *your* fault that my creator was destroyed!"

Gabriel, struggling just to breathe, stared up at the dragon in amazement, clearly in shock.

Ember took in a deep breath, and Fort knew immediately what was coming next. He managed to open a teleportation circle right in front of her mouth just as a torrent of flames came billowing forth, melting some ice in the Arctic through Fort's portal instead of hitting Gabriel.

Fortunately, Ember's slight surprise over the portal made her pause for enough time for Fort to leap between the two of them.

"Ember, stop," Fort said, using magic this time as he closed his teleportation circle. A black glow of Time magic appeared around the dragon from his spell, but she just shrugged it off and pushed Fort gently yet firmly out of the way.

"I *won't*, Father," she said, her eyes fixated on Gabriel, who now was trying to scramble away from the enraged dragon. She clamped a paw down on his legs and dragged him to the floor below her, glaring at him with glowing eyes. "This one is the reason D'hea is gone. I've *seen* it!"

Fort's eyes widened. D'hea, the Old One of Corporeal magic? The creator of the dragons? But how could *she* know about that? "Gabriel didn't do anything to D'hea!" he shouted. "The other Old Ones were responsible for that, not *him*."

"And they were only involved because of *this* wretch," Ember said, sneering widely, which also had the effect—probably intended—of showing off her very impressive fangs. "My creator would still be here if not for this human. I saw it all using Time magic, after you told me about D'hea. And I promised myself I would hunt those who were responsible. Now—"

"Stop!" someone yelled from outside, and Fort turned with a sinking feeling to find several soldiers aiming lightning rods at his dragon from out in the hallway, somehow making the situation even worse than Fort could have believed.

Not that he was worried for Ember; she was far too powerful to worry about some lightning. But if his dragon ended up hurting a TDA soldier, whatever tentative hold they had over Colonel Charles could go straight out the window, not to mention that the soldiers didn't deserve to be attacked for trying to protect a student from a very angry dragon.

Fortunately, Ember didn't give the soldiers a second thought, not even when one zapped her with a lightning bolt. The electricity splayed off her scales as she gathered Gabriel up in her claws, pulling him closer to her teeth.

For a moment, Fort had no idea how to stop his rampaging dragon from eating Gabriel whole, if that's actually what she meant to do. It didn't seem possible that the little dragon he'd raised from an egg just a couple of weeks ago would be capable of such things, but he'd also never seen her so *angry*.

He wasn't even sure she was wrong, considering she had a valid point: Gabriel *had* caused D'hea's death in some ways, since without Gabriel's betrayal, D'hea would still be alive to raise Ember.

But as much as Fort hated to admit it, Gabriel also wasn't the only one at fault.

"If you blame him, Ember, you have to blame *me*, too!" Fort shouted, grabbing her head and pulling it around to look her in the eye. Her volcanic breath fell over him in waves, blowing his hair back with each blast as she glared at him, her razor-sharp teeth just inches from his face. "*I* was just as responsible. If not for me, D'hea would still be in that underground prison on the Dracsi world."

"You *freed* him," she said, narrowing her eyes. "Without that, I wouldn't be here, Father. I saw what you did as well!"

"And then D'hea helped me get my father back," Fort said,

nodding. He could hear the sizzle of the lightning rods from the hallway still, but the soldiers seemed to be holding back for now, which was good, considering their weapons were useless and would at worst annoy Ember further. "But I only came back home *because* I found my father. Gabriel didn't have that chance. His brother was taken by the Old Ones, and he couldn't leave his family behind."

"And he betrayed all of you in the process!" Ember roared, knocking Fort back a foot with the force of her yell.

"Yes, he betrayed us!" Fort shouted, getting angry himself. "But he did it because he loves his brother and couldn't stand him being alone or hurt. I can only hope I *wouldn't* have done anything like that if our situations had been reversed and my father was in the hands of the Old Ones."

Ember rolled her eyes, but Fort knew he was getting through to her. "You would never have done such a thing, Father," she hissed. "You *care* about other humans. This one has no such sympathy."

"Oh, come *on*," Gabriel started to say, but a look from both Fort and Ember quieted him down immediately.

"He was grieving," Fort told her. "And there's no worse feeling in the world than losing someone you love. Gabriel did some horrible things, yes, but you can't just roast him alive."

"I could eat him raw, if that is preferable?" Ember asked, raising an eyebrow, to which Gabriel responded with a small, high-pitched noise.

"That wasn't our deal," Fort said. "I told you before we came here that if you promised not to eat anyone at the Oppenheimer School, I'd take you hunting Old Ones. Now, are you trying to go back on your word? Because I can still ground you for a few centuries until you learn your lesson."

At least, he hoped he could. An angry Ember who didn't listen to him was a whole new ball game.

Fortunately, she seemed to be coming around. "*Fine*. I won't eat him, either raw or cooked. Happy, Father?" She sighed loudly enough to shake the room, then transformed back into a cat and scampered down the hallway to the horror of the TDA soldiers, meowing angrily to herself.

The soldiers, Fort, and Gabriel all watched her go for a moment, before the soldiers turned to the two boys. "So, um, is everything okay here, then?" one asked.

"Yeah, we're just having a little talk," Fort told him, and teleported the soldiers back to the cafeteria. Then he bent down and offered Gabriel his hand to pick him up. "So, roomie. What did you want to talk about?"

- EIGHT -

GABRIEL DIDN'T TAKE FORT'S HAND. Instead, he leaped to his feet and rubbed his bruised shoulders where Ember had thrown him against the wall. "You want to explain how you got a dragon?" he asked.

"Nope," Fort said, crossing his arms. "You want to explain why I had to save you, when last time I saw you, *you* tried to kill *me*?"

Gabriel snorted, then smiled slightly. "I'm not particularly big on apologies, so let's get to the important stuff: I was there in the cafeteria when you all showed up, so I know what's coming. And I'm here to make sure we're all on the same page." He gestured, his hands glowing green, and for a moment, Fort prepared for another fight, but Gabriel just opened a teleportation circle on the wall. "Come with me."

Fort snorted. He couldn't be serious. "Again, *last time* you tried to teleport me somewhere—"

Gabriel sighed. "Fort, if I wanted to throw you into another volcano, you'd be burning by now. Can you just forget about our history for a second?"

This time, Fort laughed. "No?"

Gabriel smiled widely and clapped Fort on the back hard enough to almost knock him over. "Good. I taught you well. Now quit complaining and follow me."

Without another word, he passed through the circle, leaving Fort alone in the now-destroyed dorm room.

For a moment, Fort considered not following. "Taught *me* well?" he murmured, glaring at the glowing green portal. "I rescued *you* from the Old Ones, even though you tried to stop me. But now that your whole betrayal thing is inconvenient, you want me to listen to whatever you have to say?"

"I can still hear you," Gabriel said from the other side of the circle, his voice crystal clear.

Oh, *whoops*. Fort blushed a bit, then ducked his head through the glowing portal, his embarrassment overriding his worry about what might be on the other side.

Instead of a volcano or any other horrible threat, Fort found himself in another bedroom, though this one was larger than the dorm room back at the Oppenheimer School. It also looked like a tornado had passed through, with dirty clothing thrown everywhere and various books and video game cases scattered around the floor. The walls were just as covered as the floor, with posters of bands that looked like they'd been around since Fort's father was young taking up every available inch.

Gabriel waved for him to come in farther, then closed the portal. Fort tensed up and almost reopened one back to the school on principle, but he stopped himself, knowing—or hoping, at least—he could jump away whenever he needed to. "So what's this about? Where are we?"

"Where do you think?" Gabriel said, moving carefully through the mess, not disturbing anything until he reached the bed, where he sat down. "Take a guess."

"Is this your bedroom at home?" Fort said, glancing around again. "Looks like you need to do some laundry."

Gabriel shook his head. "No, this is *Michael's* room. And it's staying this way until he comes back to us."

. . . *Oh.* That explained why the room hadn't been cleaned in months. Except as Fort looked closer, he realized that wasn't entirely true: If the bedroom hadn't been touched, there'd be dust everywhere, and there wasn't even a speck as far as he could tell, at least not on top of the clothing and other assorted items strewn about the place.

No, someone *had* cleaned, but left everything exactly where it was.

Again, Fort felt an emptiness inside, the loss of a brother like Gabriel in his life. Michael had an older brother who treated his abandoned room like a shrine. That was how much Michael was loved, and Fort couldn't help but wish he'd had someone like Gabriel too.

"Michael made his choice, Gabriel," Fort said softly, hating to throw that back at the other boy. But the last thing they needed right now was a *second* teleporter trying to open a portal to the Old Ones. "I don't think he wants to come back."

Gabriel clenched his fists, and Fort raised his own, prepared for an attack . . . but stopped when Gabriel gave him a strangely proud look, even through his anger. "You've gotten braver in the last few weeks," the older boy said with a nod. "Good for you."

"It helps that I know every single magical spell now," Fort said, fudging the truth by quite a bit, not that Gabriel needed to know that. "Makes it pretty easy to not be afraid of you."

Gabriel tilted his head curiously, then leaped off the bed straight at him.

Fort threw himself backward, slamming into the wall behind him even as he tried to open a portal between them . . . but paused as he realized Gabriel had stopped in the middle of the room, grinning from a few feet away.

"Not afraid, huh?" he said, and again Fort was reminded of the equal parts fun and annoying it'd been to have Gabriel for a roommate.

"What do you want, Gabriel?" Fort asked, trying to look as confident as he could. "I don't know how closely you were listening in the cafeteria, but we have to get ready to stop Damian, and this isn't helping."

"That's what we need to talk about," Gabriel said, moving back to take a seat again on the bed. "Damian's going to bring the Old Ones back, Fort. And who do you think they'll bring with them?"

That stopped Fort dead. Was he serious? All of this was because Gabriel assumed they'd bring his brother back home?

Except could he be right about that? If Michael was becoming some sort of apprentice to them, whatever *that* meant, they probably wouldn't leave him behind in the Dracsi dimension.

"They'll bring Michael—there's no doubt in my mind," Gabriel said, not waiting for Fort to respond. "He'll come home—I *know* he will. Damian will make sure of that, even if the Old Ones try to leave Michael behind. After all, it's Damian's fault Michael was taken in the first place, and he *owes* my brother."

The temperature in the room seemed to drop a few degrees as Fort realized what Gabriel was suggesting. "So you're on Damian's side?" he said quietly, his throat dry. "You want to *help* him bring the Old Ones back?"

Gabriel narrowed his eyes. "I'm on *my* side, my family's side. I don't care about the Old Ones, your dragons, or anything else. All I want is to have my brother back, and of all people, *you* should understand that."

Fort sighed. "Oh, I do. But my dad never got to choose, and your brother did. We can't know—"

Gabriel growled softly, his anger rising dangerously again. "*Choose?* You think that Spirit Old One gave Michael any choice? They *brainwashed* him, Fort!"

Fort winced and turned away. "It didn't seem like it, Gabriel. He sounded like he *wanted* to be there. I've seen some Spirit magic now—"

"And that's exactly how someone under Spirit magic would sound!" Gabriel shouted, rising from the bed, which again made Fort back away cautiously. "Don't get in my way again, Fort. I shouldn't have . . . reacted like I did, the last time—"

Fort rolled his eyes. "Oh, when you tried to kill me?"

"But I *am* going to get Michael back, no matter what it takes!" Gabriel shouted, then paused as he noticed Fort's hands glowing green as he prepared a spell. Gabriel took a deep breath and put his hands up in the air in surrender. "I'm getting this all wrong again. I don't want you and me to be enemies."

"You've got a funny way of showing it," Fort said, ready to teleport them to the school for backup the moment Gabriel attacked.

"But there has to be a way to get Michael home without letting the Old Ones take over," Gabriel said, and this time he sounded like he was begging, not demanding. "*Please*, Fort. *Work* with me and my father. He'll help you if he knows you're trying to rescue Michael. We can team up with Damian and *beat* the Old Ones. With all of us fighting together, we can make that happen! And then I can get my brother back and destroy those monsters in the process."

Fort just stared at Gabriel. Part of him wished he could

agree to it, to have Gabriel back on his side, to fight the Old Ones together. But Gabriel's teleporting wasn't exactly going to change much, and Fort still doubted they'd even have a chance against the Old Ones.

No, to stop them, he'd have to find a way to destroy magic on their world, so it would go away for good, unlike the last time . . . and Fort ached at the thought. Not just because he'd have to send Ember to Avalon, though that was a big part of it. But whatever that vision had been, back in Colonel Charles's office, some part of him felt so *comforted* by it that he wanted to go back into it and find out more, an idea that made him almost as nervous as Damian's arrival.

"Maybe we can find a way back to the Dracsi dimension to find your brother," Fort said finally. Gabriel gritted his teeth and turned away, so Fort pushed on quickly. "If we snuck in somehow, it might be possible to find Michael and persuade him to come back. But if Damian brings the Old Ones *here*—"

A flash of green light passed over him, and Fort found himself back in the Oppenheimer School dorm room, alone this time.

"Then we're *all* doomed," he finished to no one.

Well, *great*. Apparently they could add Gabriel to their list of problems now too. Fort groaned and dropped his head into his hands. Was the universe done with him yet, or could more go wrong, just for kicks—

"Hey," said a familiar voice, causing Fort to nearly jump out of his skin as Ellora appeared out of nowhere in a black glow. "We've got another problem."

Fort squeezed his eyes shut in frustration. "Oh, of *course* we do! What is it now?"

"I was using Time magic to see if I could figure out when Cyrus sent Damian and Sierra to," she said, "but almost all of the future is completely foggy to me now. I don't even want to *think* about what that means. But there was one time period where I could make things out, and, um, well?" She winced. "I think I found Sierra."

- NINE -

FORT IMMEDIATELY TELEPORTED HIMself and Ellora to the room with the dragon skeletons, one of the only places he could think of that might still be empty of students and soldiers. Fortunately, he was right, as the room was dark and silent when they emerged from his portal.

They were going to bring *Sierra* home. Apart from Cyrus—and he didn't count anymore—she was easily the one who knew Fort best, and he couldn't even describe how much he'd missed her since she'd left with Damian. Even when they weren't in the same place, having her in his mind had made him feel less alone, and he couldn't *wait* for her to be back.

"We still need Rachel and Jia," he said as he flipped on the lights. "Any idea where they are?" He could have located them both with a dragon dictionary spell, yes, but the last thing he needed was to have another vision—even if part of him still didn't think that sounded so bad.

"I'll grab them," Ellora said, and disappeared in a burst of black light, then reappeared a moment later with Rachel and Jia, the former looking excited, the latter much more surprised than anything.

"That was *amazing*," Rachel told Ellora, a huge grin on her face. "I really wish you could teach me that."

"I'm fine walking on my own next time," Jia said, then looked around. "Ellora told us what's happening. Where's Ember?"

Ember! Fort blushed, unable to believe he'd forgotten about his dragon after the talk with Gabriel. "She, ah, sort of got angry with me and stormed away, after, um, my old roommate came for a visit."

Rachel's mood immediately turned from excitement to anger. *"Gabriel?"* she shouted, her hands lighting up with a red glow. "Where is he? I could use a punching bag."

"He's *not* the priority at the moment, Ray," Jia said, pushing Rachel's hands back down to her side, where the red light faded away. "If we can get Sierra back from whenever she is, she'd be a huge help against Damian." She gave Fort a sidelong look. "But you probably *should* grab Ember before she roasts someone alive."

He nodded, then turned back to Ellora with an embarrassed look on his face. "I don't suppose you could find *her*, too? She had been in the hall outside the room where you found me."

The Time girl sighed. "You know I still have to run all over the place, right? Just because I do it in between seconds doesn't mean it's not tiring." Without waiting for him to respond, she took a deep breath, then disappeared again.

This time, she didn't reappear right away, and Fort wondered if it was a bad idea sending her after his dragon. Ember wasn't exactly in a good mood, not to mention the dragon skeleton room was pretty enclosed if she got angry, and—

Dragon skeleton room? Fort gasped, staring at the glass case on the other side of the room, filled with the bones of Ember's kind. Ellora was about to bring Ember into a room with dragon skeletons? What had he been thinking?

"Rachel, can you hide the displays here?" he shouted frantically, pointing at the museum case. "Ember can't see those—she's already upset enough!"

Rachel snorted and quickly fogged the air inside the display, effectively covering the dragon bones from view. "You could have picked somewhere else to meet, you know."

He nodded, just thankful they'd been able to avoid the issue.

"Sorry, I was just . . . There's so much going on, and—"

A cold, blue light filled his body, and suddenly he felt much more clearheaded. "That help?" Jia asked.

"Yes, thank you!" he said, straightening up just as Ember in dragon form appeared in a glow of green, a terrified-looking Ellora held tightly in one of her paws.

"Father," Ember said in the language of magic as she glared at him. *"Why did you send a human to fetch me? Do you realize how insulting that is?"*

"I wasn't sure where you were, Ember," he told her, gently unhooking her claws from around Ellora's arm. Once released, the Time girl quickly backed away from the dragon with a shudder.

"All you had to do was shout my name in your mind," the dragon said, shaking her head. *"We've been connected since I was born."*

That stopped Fort cold. They were connected? How had he never known that? And what did "connected" mean exactly? She couldn't hear his thoughts completely, or she'd have known he intended to send her away a few days ago, before realizing how awful that'd be for both of them. But apparently she could hear him yell her name? He might have to be careful what he thought around her now. *"I had no idea. I'm sorry about that,"* he said out loud.

"Are you okay?" Jia asked Ellora, who shuddered again.

"She shut down my magic like it was *nothing*," the Time girl said, staring at Ember, who hissed back at her. "I'm not sure you all realize how powerful she is."

"Of course they don't," Ember said with a shrug, then turned back into a cat and leaped up to Fort's shoulder, where she settled in, far too heavy to actually still be doing this.

"She's a dragon," Rachel said, frowning. "She's that powerful because she's literally made of magic. But she's on our side, so don't worry."

"I'm on Father's side," Ember corrected, purring in Fort's ear. Thankfully, none of the others spoke the language, so he didn't have to try to explain *that.*

Ellora just shook her head. "Forget it. Like I told you all on the way here, I found Sierra, a few months in the future. It looks like Cyrus sent her and Damian just far enough away for my government to ease up a bit on their security on the two books they were holding, thinking the danger had passed."

"Your government had *both*?" Jia said with a frown. "I knew they had the book of Time magic, but when did they find the book of Spirit magic?"

"During cleanup in London," Ellora told her. "They kept

the whole thing a secret, but Cyrus must have known if he sent them there. And if Damian had both, he could have used Time magic to speed up his learning like we did, to master both books in no time."

"It's good that we have you, then, to stop him," Rachel said, grinning at Ellora, who looked less convinced. Fort was with Ellora here: Damian had shut them all down already, even before he'd learned Time and Spirit magic. They wouldn't even have a chance now, barring some kind of miracle.

"If Sierra's alone there, then does that mean Damian traveled back in time already?" Jia asked, which made Fort even more worried. Why would he leave someone as powerful as Sierra behind? Had she tried to stop him, so he'd traveled back without her?

Weirdly, that thought actually cheered him up a bit. Not that it was good news that Damian had abandoned Sierra in the future or anything, but it *would* feel a thousand times better to know his friend was on the right side again. It still made Fort sick to think she was helping Damian with all of this, even if she was doing it for what she thought were the right reasons.

"Or maybe this is all a trap," Rachel said, looking at the floor, lost in thought. "For all we know, they're working together to set us up for something. Maybe Damian knows we can beat him, so he's trying to trick us somehow."

"Sierra wouldn't do that," Fort said, annoyed both at the suggestion that Sierra might betray them . . . and that Rachel might have a point. Fort hadn't even known she was going off to the future to retrieve the two books of magic until Cyrus had mentioned it, once it was already too late. And Sierra hadn't ever seen what Damian truly was, not like the others had.

But this was *Sierra*. Fort knew her better than he knew anyone else in the world, after practically living in her mind. There was no way she'd trick them—trick *him*—especially not to help Damian. Not sharing a secret was one thing, but betraying them? That was out of the question.

"I hope that's true, because we could really use her help," Rachel said, then shrugged. "So how do we get her back?"

"I can bring her here, right now," Ellora said. "But I didn't want to do it without talking to you all. She's alone there, as far as I can tell, but Damian could be hiding from me with his own Time magic. Like you were saying, Rachel, I don't know who we can trust here."

"Damian *must* have left her," Fort said, shaking his head. "And if he's here already, then that's even more reason to bring her back and find out what she knows. I say go get her, Ellora."

"I agree," Jia said. "The only reason Sierra helped Damian is because she was tricked by Cyrus. She's always been on our side."

Rachel sighed, squeezing her eyes shut. "I don't know her as well as you two do, so I hope you're both right. Okay, Ellora, let's do this." She opened her eyes again, giving Fort an annoyed look. "But you all need to be ready for a fight, just in case. Deal?"

"Deal," Fort told her, and Ember growled softly in what Fort hoped was agreement as well.

"Deal," Jia said.

"Okay, if everyone's sure," Ellora said, and began to glow with black Time magic.

And then she let out a gasp of surprise and disappeared completely.

"Well, hello, humans," said a voice from behind them, and the three whirled around to find Damian, looking years older than they'd last seen him. "It's been *far* too long, hasn't it?"

- TEN -

NO! THEY WEREN'T READY FOR HIM, not yet! And worst of all, Ellora had been right. Damian must have been using Time spells to master both that and Spirit magic, since his human form was now at least a foot taller, with hair down to his shoulders.

But the eeriest thing of all was the dead look in his eyes, coupled with the smile on his face.

"Damian!" Fort shouted, hoping to pull the newly older boy's attention away from Rachel and Jia, to give them a chance to attack. He had a spell readied as well, not even caring if it sent him into another vision, as long as it gave his friends an opening. "What did you do with Ellora?"

"Oh, she's fine," Damian said, and Fort noticed that the older boy was still glowing with a soft black light from Time magic. Was he really here, or was this just a Time projection? "I needed her gone, to make sure I had a clear view of what was happening back here. Those Carmarthen students have a nasty habit of fogging up Time magic, so I froze her a few weeks in the future. I'll release her when this is all over."

At Fort's side, Ember growled low and dangerously, and Damian glanced down at her. "Ah, the new blood," he said, narrowing his eyes. "You and I will have a lot to talk about, little one, but not now, not here. I should be done with these humans in a few minutes, though, so come back then."

He snapped his fingers, and Ember disappeared in a burst of black light.

The spell he prepared vanished along with Ember, and Fort leaped at Damian, growling wildly. "Don't you hurt her!" he shouted, only to collapse to the floor as his legs stopped working, his body now paralyzed below the chest.

"I wouldn't," Damian said simply, barely giving Fort a glance. "She's completely safe and will reappear fifteen minutes from now. In the meantime, we should talk."

Fort swallowed hard, not knowing what to do. For now he had to assume Ellora and Ember were both okay, since there wasn't much else he could do about it. At least Ember was probably fine, since if anyone was safe from Damian, it was a fellow dragon. Even if she wasn't, or if Ellora was in danger, he couldn't do anything about them now, not without taking Damian down first.

If that was even possible.

From the side of his eye, Fort noticed Rachel slowly inching forward, her hands glowing with shifting red and yellow lights, which meant she was using her newly learned Illusion magic, a combination of Elemental and Mind magic that Merlin had trained her in. "It's not too late to work this out, Dragon Boy," she said to Damian, whose smile didn't waver. "Cyrus was lying to you. You couldn't have known this, but he was—"

"An Old One?" Damian said, raising an eyebrow. "*Of course* I knew. Just because his mind was hard to read doesn't mean *I* couldn't do it. I let him think I was going along with his plan this whole time, so that he wouldn't get in my way." He tilted his head. "I wish you three hadn't taken him down, though. While one less Old One is a good thing, I really was looking forward to seeing his face when I destroyed him and his family."

Fort sucked in air through his teeth in a hiss. As much as he knew Cyrus was the enemy, Damian talking about hurting him still made Fort sick to his stomach. "So what, you know both Time and Spirit magic now?" he asked. "Because Spirit magic *changes* you, Damian. It happened to William, and it'll happen to you, too."

If anyone knew this, it was Fort, who both experienced it himself and watched a future-timeline Fort be utterly taken over by it.

Damian just laughed, then stopped, sniffing at the air. He abruptly reached behind himself and grabbed something that wasn't there, something invisible.

Instantly, the Rachel standing next to Fort disappeared, replaced by a new glowing orange Rachel now struggling to breathe in Damian's grasp. He lifted her off the floor as her Illusion spell faded, his strength in his human form far greater than it had been. "What's this, now?" he said, shaking his head. "I thought you wanted to work things out?"

"Let her *go*!" Jia shouted, and sent a bolt of blue Corporeal magic at Damian.

He reached out with his other hand to block it, his palm absorbing the magic without any effect. "Cause Major Pain, Jia?" he said, one eyebrow rising. "Wow, who knew you had it in you? Not that it would have hurt me, even if I *were* here. Fortunately for you, I'm still a few months in your future. But don't worry, I'm not showing up empty-handed: I'm here with a gift."

A gift? What was Damian talking about? And how could he be holding Rachel if he wasn't actually here? How powerful *was* his Time magic? Even if he'd spent years mastering it, how could he reach back into the past and touch things while still in the future?

But if this *was* just a Time projection, maybe a spell could cancel it. Fort opened his mouth to cast a counter spell in the language of magic, only for his tongue to freeze in place along with the rest of his body.

"What did I *just* say?" Damian asked, turning to Fort as Rachel fought and kicked out at him, her feet passing right through his body as if it really weren't there. "I thought we could have a real conversation here, children. But you all keep insisting on fighting me. Don't you even want to know why I'm not using Spirit magic on you?"

Fort groaned in frustration, unable to get any words out. He felt a cold sensation pass into him and saw a blue light coming from Jia, only for Damian to freeze her in place as well, her fingertips still glowing with Healing magic.

Damian sighed. "I guess this will have to be less of a conversation and more of me telling you what's going to happen, then," he said, and tossed Rachel across the room. She bounced against the wall hard enough to make Fort wince but still managed to push to her feet, glaring at Damian with a hatred that scared even Fort. "Like I said, I'm here to give you a gift."

"Is it the two books of magic you have?" Rachel asked, limping slightly as she moved back toward him. "Because *those* we'll take."

Damian laughed, though it sounded forced. "No, I had to destroy those, just like I'll do to the books you still have here at the Oppenheimer School. You humans can't be trusted with magic, not anymore. You're just too much of a pain to deal with, especially when I have to concentrate on my destiny."

Rachel and Fort shared a look. He'd destroyed the Time and Spirit books of magic? They'd done the same to the books of Mind and Space magic, which meant Healing and Destruction were the only ones left anywhere.

Without those, the Oppenheimer students would be stuck with whatever spells they currently knew. And at that level, they wouldn't be anywhere near powerful enough to stop Damian.

"What destiny is that?" Rachel asked, since neither Fort nor Jia could speak. "If this is about that stupid prophecy, you should know that Merlin said it's all just bad poetry. It doesn't really mean anything."

Damian sneered at her. "Don't bother lying. I've known the prophecy is real ever since I first laid eyes on it. I've always been meant for something greater than the rest of you, and the prophecy is what showed me the way. I am its *chosen one*, the magician who unearthed all six books and mastered them. And I *will* 'save all' by defeating the Old Ones. Once that's done, maybe I'll even turn your species into something worthwhile, if that's possible. A few centuries of me being in charge should be a good start."

Fort groaned again. *There* it was, the taint of Spirit magic—assuming this wasn't just who Damian was always going to be, once he got a taste of power. Neither option was particularly reassuring.

"Oh, no thanks," Rachel said, shaking her head. "We definitely don't deserve you ruling us. Besides, I think we're full up on power-hungry dictators already. Maybe go to the back of the line and wait your turn?"

Damian smiled again, his eyes still completely dead. "Funny. But that's enough from all of you. Like I said, I have a gift to pass on, and the longer we talk, the more I want to wipe you all out and start over from scratch, so let's get to the point, maybe?"

Rachel clenched her fists but somehow managed to keep her anger under control, which Fort admired her for. At this point, he wasn't sure he would have. "Okay, so what's this gift you keep talking about, then?" she asked. "If it's your sparkling personality, I hope it's returnable. Fort's right, the Spirit magic is definitely controlling you. You're even more arrogant now than you were before, which could never even be possible without magic."

Damian's smile faded, replaced by a sneer. "Nothing controls *me*, human! And you should be thanking me for destroying the Old Ones, not fighting me every step of the way. Why do you even bother? You know you have no chance."

"Oh, I wouldn't say *no* chance," Rachel said, and red light shot from her hands.

The floor of the room exploded up through where Damian stood, driving straight into the ceiling. Fort's eyes widened in surprise as he and Jia floated into the air. Rachel quickly tried to get them out of the room while Damian was taken off guard, since her physical attack wouldn't hurt his projection.

But before they even reached the door, they crashed back to the floor, sending pain shooting through Fort's body. Damian stepped out of the debris like a ghost, shaking his head.

"Rachel, this is getting embarrassing for you," the older boy said. "And I've had enough. One more outburst, and I'll remove you from time permanently. I can't let you keep getting away with attacking me. It'll send a bad message to any other humans that they can disobey me too."

She turned to face him again, but even Fort could see her hands shaking from fear, which made sense: If Damian could do all of this from the future, and they couldn't even *touch* him, what chance would they have when he was here in full power?

"Forsythe, maybe *you* will accept my gift, since Rachel doesn't seem to want it?" Damian said, turning to Fort, not even caring that Rachel could still move, apparently. "This is your last chance, so I'd say yes."

Fort closed his eyes for a moment, then nodded. Whatever this was about, Damian wasn't going to let it go until they played along. Even if the dragon intended to use Spirit magic on them eventually, then at least by agreeing, Fort wouldn't have to listen to him go on and on about it for an hour first.

Damian grinned. "Finally!" he said. "My gift to you is this: You have *one week* until I return. I'd use that time to prepare as much as you can, because it's all you'll have." He narrowed his eyes as he turned back to Rachel. "I want you to have all the time you'll need before you take me on, humans, so that when you fail, you'll know it's because you just aren't good enough."

Rachel screamed out in anger and shot an enormous fireball toward Damian, almost the size of one of the dragon skeletons behind him. But this time, instead of trying to stop it, the older boy just smiled slightly, then disappeared from its path.

In his place, a brown-haired teenage girl appeared, looking all around like she was confused about where she was. And then she saw the fireball.

"Sierra!" Fort shouted, his tongue unfrozen now that Damian had gone. Sierra screamed in surprise, but there was no time to dodge or get out of the way.

"No!" Rachel shouted, and tried to pull it back, but it was already too late. The fireball was moving with too much speed to be derailed.

Milliseconds before it would have hit Sierra, though, it passed through a portal and disappeared harmlessly into the Arctic as Fort managed to open a teleportation circle at the very last moment.

"Fort?" Sierra said, then dropped to her knees, looking exhausted.

He pushed to his feet and ran to her side, frantically checking her over to make sure she was all right, but from the looks of it, the fireball hadn't even singed her. "Are you okay?" he asked.

"Well, that was *not* the welcome I was hoping for," she said, then held up her hands to stop him before he could help her up. "Wait! Do you still have those evil necklaces that I made for Dr. Opps? If you do, get all that you can find and put them on me, because pretty soon you won't be able to trust a thing I do." Then she flashed a tired smile. "So what's new with *you* all, then?"

- ELEVEN -

AS CLOSE AS FORT HAD BEEN TO Cyrus, his friendship with Sierra was on a completely different level. They'd been inside each other's minds—even while Sierra was unconscious after the attack in D.C.—and she knew pretty much everything about him, even things his own father didn't know.

Which was why Fort was so confused right now. After everything with the Timeless One and finding out that Cyrus had tricked Sierra into going into the future, Fort just wanted to give his friend a hug and find out what had happened.

Instead, he stayed away from her as ordered, not having any idea why. "What are you talking about?" he asked, frowning. "What do you mean, we won't be able to trust you? Are you okay?"

She winced and turned away. "Damian mastered Spirit

magic and cast it on me. But it's not set to go off until the moment he arrives back here in a week's time." She glanced at him, looking absolutely devastated. "You won't be able to trust me, Fort. The necklaces would help, but it'd make the most sense to just send me away as soon as possible!"

Her words knocked Fort back, and he stared at her in confusion. "A delayed spell? But that's impossible!"

"He mastered Time magic as well," she said miserably. "Between the two, he's got me on a timer. It's best to just get me out of here before I do any damage, okay? Anything I learn between now and then, I'll have to tell him. You won't have any secrets if I'm around."

Fort just stared, having no idea what to say.

"I'm sorry about this, Mindflayer," Rachel said, coming up behind Fort. "But you're right. We're going to need to do something about this." She nodded at Jia, now unfrozen as well, who stepped forward, her hands glowing with Healing magic.

"It won't work," Sierra told Jia, shaking her head. "If I was already under his Spirit spell, maybe you could restore me to normal. But there's nothing to restore yet. The spell hasn't even happened, and won't for another week. I wish I could have warned you, but as soon as Ellora reached out to take me home, he grabbed her and disappeared himself a second later."

"I thought he couldn't see her," Rachel said, furrowing her brow. "How did he know she was coming?"

"He couldn't, and didn't, not exactly," Sierra said, rubbing her temples like she had a headache. "But it was a trap from the start. He hid his presence so it'd look like I was alone, figuring Ellora would come to get me, under orders. The moment he felt her magic on me, he could follow it back to the source and use his own spells on her."

Fort's head started pounding as well, and he grimaced, having had way more than enough Time magic with the Timeless One a few days ago.

"But if he's mastered Time magic, why would he care about Ellora?" Jia asked. "What would it really matter if he can see back here or not, if he's as powerful as he thinks he is? He can do anything she can already."

"Much, much more, actually," Sierra said, sighing. "But even if he's more powerful than she is, that wouldn't stop her from messing things up. If you were all really serious about stopping him, she could have gone back in time and kept him from learning he was a dragon, or kept Dr. Opps from ever finding him. But with her out of the picture, there's no way to stop him." She let out a huge breath. "If it helps, I wouldn't worry about her. He's trying to act like he's more mature now, after the time he spent mastering the last two books, so he won't hurt anyone who does what he says . . . or stays frozen in time, like Ellora."

That wasn't exactly comforting, but at least it meant they could probably wait to rescue Ellora until Damian was taken care of, since they had no idea how to find her at the moment.

Rachel and Jia shared a look. "You know, that's not a bad idea, keeping Damian from meeting Dr. Opps . . . ," Rachel said.

"Except it would cause a paradox," Jia said. "If Dr. Opps never brought Damian to the original school, there'd never have been an attack by the Old Ones, and so we wouldn't have sent Ellora back to keep them from meeting."

"I might take a paradox over the Old Ones taking over," Rachel said.

"We don't know what a paradox would even do," Jia said with a small smile. "It might destroy all of time and space."

"I'm just saying, could have been worth it," Rachel said, also smiling a bit.

Fort had no idea why they found this so amusing. Damian had just beaten them without even being present, and Sierra was on the clock. "Can we get back on topic please?" he said to them, and they both managed to look a bit guilty. "We haven't figured out what to do about Sierra yet!"

Jia bit her lip. "I mean, what is there to do? Like she said, we can put a bunch of her protective Mind necklaces on her, but we don't really—"

"Good enough for me," Fort said, and reached over to help Sierra to her feet.

Look who's such a gentleman, she said in his mind, though he could also feel how tired she was, a pure exhaustion down to her bones that she was trying to hide as best she could. *I missed you, you know.*

I missed you too, he told her, but held off on saying anything else.

He *wanted* to tell her that everything would be okay, that even though he'd been right this whole time about Damian, they'd still stop him, working together, and the Old Ones would never return.

He wanted to tell her all of that, but with their mind connection, he was too worried she'd know he was lying.

I'm just glad you're back, he told her, knowing that at least was honest.

She looked up at him with a terrible sadness, and in his mind, she said, *I heard all the rest of that, genius. I* know *how upset you are. But I really did think he was on our side, that he'd be the chosen one from the prophecy in the books that he thinks he is. You remember what it said?*

Before Fort could respond, Sierra's magic pulled up a memory, one from when Fort first opened a book of magic back when he was taking a test at the original Oppenheimer School, to see which discipline he was more suited for, Healing or Destruction.

The poem was in both books he saw that day, and with Sierra's help, he saw the words as clearly as if he were looking at them now:

One for the body, bones and skin,
One for the spirit, its spectral kin,
One for the mind, thoughts and dreams,
One for the world, from dirt to streams,
One for all space, wide and vast,
One for all time, future and past.
Seven from six, the rest unearthed.
One saves all, if proved their worth.

Something about going through the poem gave Fort a twinge in the back of his mind, like he was missing something. But that would have to wait. *That last part is what everyone's forgetting here,* Fort told her in her mind. *Damian could* never *be worthy of anything.*

And yet he was the only one with a chance against the Old Ones, Sierra said, looking away. *According to Cyrus, he could have beaten them.*

At the mention of his ex-friend's name, Fort tensed up. *There's something you should know—*

About Cyrus? Sierra said. *I already do—Damian told me.* He *knew from the start, he said. I don't know when he found out, but he let me believe everything Cyrus said, knowing it was all a trap, because Damian thought he could beat them anyway, that he'd be the one using Cyrus. He's gone* completely *off the deep end!*

"Okay, no private conversations, you two," Rachel said, putting her hands between them and pushing them physically apart. "Like you said, anything you find out now, you could give to Damian when he arrives, so stay out of *all* of our heads." She pointed at Fort. "That includes your boyfriend here."

In spite of the situation, both Sierra and Fort turned dark red at this. "We're not—" Fort said.

"He's just—" Sierra said.

"Nope to all of that. I couldn't care any less," Rachel told them. "And I'm serious. If you two go silent for even a minute, I'm going to assume she's stealing our plans from your head, Fort, and have Jia put her to sleep. You understand me?"

Sierra and Fort both nodded, though Fort looked at Rachel curiously. Plans? They didn't *have* a plan, at least not that he knew of. But maybe Rachel and Jia had come up with one? As far as Fort was concerned, it didn't matter anyway: If the fight just now proved anything, it was that Damian was way out of their league.

"Sierra, so you can confirm Damian is actually returning in a week?" Jia asked, sounding a lot more sympathetic to the girl than Rachel had.

Sierra nodded. "I get that you have no reason to believe me, but from everything he said, he wants you all to feel like you have time to prepare. He's got no reason to lie, anyway. . . . I'm not sure what you could do to stop him at this point."

That matched what Damian had told them, so either he was lying to all of them, or it was the truth.

But why give them the time to begin with? It couldn't really be about giving them time to prepare, could it?

"What's he thinking?" Fort asked Sierra out loud. "*Why* give us time to get ready? I get that he's so arrogant that he thinks it won't matter, but even a dragon has to have weaknesses."

Sierra looked down at the floor. "What weaknesses could he have now? You don't have a chance against him, not with the whole school on your side, or even the TDA. Trust me, I've seen what he can do now with all six types of magic he's mastered. He's on a whole new level from the rest of us."

"Sounds like someone's overconfident," Rachel said, though she looked just as rattled as Fort felt after their "fight" against the dragon minutes earlier. "Good. That'll help with our plan, and one week is more than enough time." She gave Sierra a side look. "Assuming you're not just setting us up for another trap?"

Sierra shook her head. "I swear to you, I'm telling the truth . . . as far as I know, at least. He intends to show up here one week from today, and when he does—bam!—I'm Spirit magicked. He could have been lying to *me*—"

"Except he really is just that arrogant," Jia said, wincing. "This is going to be *bad*."

"Not if we pull off our plan," Rachel said, then nodded at Sierra. "Gee, you want to put her to sleep for a few minutes so we can get her locked down?"

"Wait, what?" Fort said, surprised at his own shock. "You said you'd only do that if we were talking in our minds!"

"Yeah, well, now we need to discuss our options, and we can't have her overhearing anything," Rachel said, crossing her arms. "It's the smartest choice, Fort."

"But we could use her help!" Fort shouted. "She knows what Damian can do better than any of us. She could be a huge advantage—"

"Or a huge weakness, if Damian finds out about what you're planning from me," Sierra said, looking like she wanted to vomit. "Rachel's right: Put me to sleep, then get some of those Mind chains on me, like I said. It's the only way to be safe."

Fort shook his head. "No way. Those almost killed you, back in his office when you were controlling Dr. Opps's body."

"Only because I was using the magic at the time," she said, but even he could tell she wasn't sure. The fact that she was still willing to take the chance on feeling that awful pain again, though, told him everything he needed to know about whose side she was on.

Still, it looked like he was outvoted, including by Sierra. He sighed. "Okay, but can we at least make sure she's comfortable?" Fort asked Jia, who nodded.

"She'll have the most restful sleep of her life," Jia said, and cast her spell on Sierra. The Mind girl's eyes drooped, and Fort helped her lie down on the floor as she yawned widely.

"Oh, this is nice, Jia," she murmured, smiling gently. "I'm so sleepy, I . . ."

And then she began to snore.

They were all silent for a moment. Fort tried to wrap his head around everything that had just happened and how unfair it all was. And then Rachel turned to the other two.

"Okay, so, we're going to need a plan," she said, nodding thoughtfully.

"Great, so we *don't* have a plan?" Fort said, not even caring that Sierra was sleeping next to them. "I'd hoped you two had come up with this amazing plan that was going to beat Damian."

Rachel winced. "Yeah, that was just for her sake, in case she does eventually tell him everything. I wouldn't want them to think we've got nothing. But I've got faith in us! We can do this. All we have to do is analyze what just happened, what we know Damian can do, and then . . . find a way to, you know, make him *not* do those things."

"Oh, is *that* it?" Fort started to say, only to leap to the side as a burst of black light exploded next to him.

Ember appeared out of the light, fifteen minutes since Damian had sent her away, growling low in her throat. She glanced around in confusion, then settled her eyes on Sierra.

"Ugh, *another* human?" she said in English. "Where do you keep finding them all, Father?"

- TWELVE -

RACHEL AND JIA *DID* COME UP WITH A plan, though Fort had no idea how they could actually pull it off even if they had a year, let alone just a week—assuming Damian hadn't lied and planned on returning earlier.

Either way, it was going to take a *lot* of work on the part of the other students, half of whom didn't trust them, and even then, Fort still couldn't believe they had any kind of real chance against the dragon.

Fortunately, Dr. Ambrose agreed to help, and she ordered the Healing students to report to Jia for their part in the strategy, while Rachel had enough pull with the Destruction students that she basically strong-armed them into doing what she said.

Their plan didn't have much for Fort to do, so he told Rachel he'd work with Ember to prepare her to face Damian. But really, he knew in his heart that the only way to stop the Old Ones was to destroy magic, and that was going to require a lot of planning on its own.

The biggest problem was he had no clue how to end magic to begin with, or even where to start looking for answers. Then there was the fact that abolishing magic meant he'd have to send Ember away, which was hard enough without the horrible feeling he got every time he tried to think about destroying it . . . a feeling that seemed connected to his visions somehow.

All in all, Fort wasn't the most hopeful he'd ever been. And on top of all of that, he couldn't stop thinking about running out on his dad and how worried his dad must be. Fort had tried calling after Sierra's arrival, but he'd gotten his father's voicemail, which had sent a chill through him.

Was his dad not picking up on purpose? Or worse, had he left Aunt Cora's apartment and run, like he'd said they should, leaving his phone behind, so Fort had no way of finding him?

No, his father wouldn't do that. But it also seemed strange that he wouldn't pick up the phone when Fort called. Which he'd done only once, since hearing his father's recorded voice just sent him spinning into a combination of a guilt spiral and worst-case whirlpool. He'd try again once this was all over . . . assuming he was *able* to call at that point.

That wasn't a much better thought either, because what if this was the last week left for humanity? What if the Old Ones returned, just like they'd seen in the future a year from now, when fighting Cyrus, and Fort was giving up the only chance he had to speak to his father again?

There was no solving that problem, unfortunately, so while Fort tried to think of ways to fix the magic issue, he did as ordered and spent most of his time with Ember, making sure she was prepared for Damian's arrival this time. Even if fighting Damian wouldn't accomplish anything, he wasn't about to let his dragon get hurt in the battle.

"He surprised me, that's all," she growled at him, not happy about having to train. It didn't help that they were in an old gymnasium that probably had far too many unpleasant smells for her more sensitive nose. "I'll be ready for his Time magic next time."

"It won't *be* Time magic the next time," Fort told her, making her roll her eyes. "It'll be Spirit magic, or maybe something worse, if there *is* a worse. The moment Rachel and Jia order the attack, you have to go after him with everything you've got."

She nodded but turned away, and Fort didn't need a connection between them to tell him she was worried about something. "What's wrong?" he asked her.

She looked up at him with what could have been embarrassment. "You're going to laugh."

He couldn't help but break into a smile at this, though he covered it with his hand. "No, never, I promise. Tell me."

"I am . . . conflicted about destroying this Damian dragon," she said, watching Fort carefully for any laughter. When none appeared, she continued. "I am quite aware that he is our enemy and therefore should be hunted and eaten, but he is also the first of my kind that I've ever met." She looked down at the floor. "I feel humiliated to even share this, but, Father, I worry that if I feast on him, I'll have lost one of the few remaining dragons left."

Fort's heart immediately broke for her, and he quickly moved over to hug her around her long neck. "Oh, *Ember*," he said, squeezing his eyes shut as he hugged her. "First of all, please don't feast on him. That's . . . a lot. Second, there are other dragons. Avalon has a bunch of them. Maybe we can figure out a way to take you there?"

She pulled out of his arms and glared at him suspiciously.

"Those are the dragons you planned to have raise me. You don't still think they should, do you?"

He swallowed hard, wondering if he could just hide the truth from her . . . but no. He'd seen how that had worked out last time, with Xenea. He owed it to Ember to tell her everything. "If things go badly with Damian," he said slowly, "the Old Ones will take over our world. And if that happens, they might try to turn you into a Dracsi, which I'm *not* going to let happen."

She narrowed her eyes. "You *do* intend to send me to Avalon?" He could see her anger growing as steam began to rise out of her snout, but tears also formed in her eyes.

He knew what she was going through. Even talking about this made his heart hurt. "Only if we're going to lose to Damian!" he said quickly, hoping that would help. "Because I won't have any other choice, Ember. They'll take away your mind, and you won't even know who you are anymore. You won't recognize me, either! On Avalon, you'll be safe from them."

She looked away, though at least she wasn't attacking, or teleporting somewhere. "I understand your words," she said quietly, the tears in her eyes now turning to steam as well. "But I don't understand you sending me away alone. Wouldn't *you* also be safer on Avalon? If you come with me, then I would be content with going. Can you promise me that?"

He paused, having no idea what to say to that. "I don't know if the queen would let me," he said honestly. "But if I can get our whole family there . . . I promise I will try my best."

She gave him a suspicious look, then sighed, releasing a plume of fire to his side. "I do not like this, Father. But you speak the truth now, and that I can accept. And because of this, I have decided that destroying Damian will not only be advisable, but necessary."

Whoa. His little girl was getting more terrifying by the day. "We don't need to *destroy* him so much as stop him," Fort clarified quickly. "That's really it. Just keep him from bringing any Old Ones here."

"I could just wound him enough that he can still communicate, perhaps by blinking," Ember said, shrugging slightly. "Then I could still learn from him, but no one would have to go to Avalon?"

Fort winced, but before he could respond, a voice rang out from across the hall.

"Hey, New Kid." Fort turned to find Trey, the least evil of the three boys who'd bullied him when he'd first arrived at the

Oppenheimer School, standing in the gymnasium's doorway, waving. "Thanks for letting me train with Ember. I've been looking forward to it all day!"

"Ah, the Trey human," Ember said, nodding in his direction. "Perhaps we will play hide-and-hunt again?"

"Okay, but this time, I get to hunt first!" Trey said, and Fort rolled his eyes, though he was happy for the distraction.

Surprisingly, out of everyone at the school, Trey seemed the most comfortable—and friendly—with Ember, both in her cat form as well as when she showed off her dragon self to the students, trying to impress upon them how powerful Damian might be.

That had been under Fort's careful supervision, but even still, Ember had managed to intimidate almost the entire student body, with the exception of Trey, whom she somehow took a bit of a liking to . . . or at least didn't hate him like she did Trey's two best friends, Chad and Bryce.

Admittedly, that hate might have come a bit from Fort's connection with her, since Trey's friends Chad and Bryce had both fallen back into old habits now, calling him and Rachel the Ex-Spelled. And as much as Fort wanted to use one of his new spells on them, he knew it wasn't worth the possibility of falling into another vision, especially not in front of those two. He didn't even want to think about what nicknames might come from that.

"Of course," Fort told Trey, and gestured for him to come in. "I have to work on something else anyway, so I appreciate you training with her. Just . . . be careful."

"I'd never hurt her!" Trey said, looking shocked.

"Oh, he meant me," Ember said, and smiled widely, showing off all her teeth.

Instead of running in terror, Trey just laughed. "You're so adorable," he said, and scratched her chin. She raised her head for him to have better access, purring like a cat, even in her dragon form.

Trey's help couldn't have come at a better time, even if Fort still worried about Ember hurting the other boy. With his dragon entertained, that gave Fort a free moment to check on the school's "prisoner," whom he worried about almost as much as his father and Ellora.

He left Ember and Trey behind in the gymnasium, closing the doors behind him, only to flinch as a huge crash sounded from within. "We're okay!" Trey shouted after a pause, and Fort just shook his head and left, not wanting to know.

Sierra was locked away in a dorm room a few levels up, but

Fort had at least been able to make sure the room was comfortable. Jia had let her sleep for half the day until they'd figured out how to make her Mind necklaces work, so this was the first free moment Fort had to even check on her. He still hated the fact she was locked up at all.

Even with the necklaces, Rachel didn't want Sierra hearing anything she shouldn't, so she insisted the Mind girl be confined to her room under guard, just in case. Rachel didn't seem to appreciate when Fort pointed out this was exactly what Agent Cole and Colonel Charles had done to Jia, but that didn't change Rachel's mind either.

When he reached her room, he realized that the guards might be an issue, if they'd been ordered not to let anyone in, but they seemed to recognize him as he approached and knocked on the dorm room door. One problem down, at least.

"Come in," Sierra said, and one of the guards unlocked the door so Fort could enter.

As he walked in, he stopped just past the doorway, barely able to believe she was here after everything. Just seeing her there in person still gave him a little thrill, since so much of their friendship had been through their minds that it felt special for her to actually be here.

"Hello," he said as casually as he could, waiting for the guards to close the door as Sierra stood up from the bed, wearing an Oppenheimer School uniform now, just like Fort was. "I hope you are comfortable here, miss?"

"Oh, yes," she said, using the same mechanical voice as he had. "I am *quite* comfortable here, thank you for asking."

The door closed, finally, and Fort broke out into a grin, then hugged her tightly. She hugged him right back, and Fort felt the chains Rachel had made push into his collarbone. He pulled away to examine her work, only to step back in shock as he noticed a tiny, inch-tall Jia golem holding on to the chain. "Uh, what is *that*?"

"Oh, you like it?" Sierra said, showing it off. "Jia put it there so I wouldn't be able to take the charms off. If my hands come anywhere near the necklace, her little golem is programmed to use a Sleep spell on me." She grinned. "I think I'm going to use it to take a nap soon. I'm just that bored."

Fort leaned in for a closer look, and the little golem smiled at him. "Jia?" he whispered.

"Jia isn't here," the doll said in a weirdly deep voice. "I am completely autonomous so that Sierra will have her privacy."

"Jia's so thoughtful," Sierra said, only for her smile to fade. "I know I already said this, but I'm so, *so* sorry about everything."

"Don't," Fort said, stepping back to look at her. "It's okay. I get it. We all fell for Cyrus's lies. I just hate that Rachel's insisting on all of this." He gestured at the room, then the golem on the necklace.

Sierra waved off his concerns. "I'm fine! And Rachel's right. Until Damian's taken care of, I'm better off in here, so I don't see or hear anything I shouldn't. Just in case."

"Except if we figured out how to block his spell, you could be a huge help against him," Fort pointed out. "Since none of the rest of us know Mind magic." Okay, that wasn't exactly the whole truth, since Fort had the spell words in his head, but that magic wasn't something he could count on, and Rachel would fireball him if she found out he'd told Sierra about the dragon dictionary.

"*Damian* does," Sierra said. "*And* Spirit magic. There's nothing I could do that would help, really. And it's way too dangerous for the rest of you if I'm here when his spell kicks in. I could shut down the entire school before you could even move."

"So could he, unless you're there to stop him," Fort said, turning away. With as bad as things were, he really could have used Sierra's help in figuring out what to do about magic, but even more so as a friend. And to keep her locked up and not able to use her magic just seemed so cruel.

But she did have a point. Anything Sierra's Mind magic could do, Damian could counter.

"My guess? Your only hope is to surprise him," Sierra said, tapping her chin thoughtfully before frowning. "Though I probably shouldn't think about *how* you could do that, just in case."

Fort winced, turning away. Rachel and Jia's plan *did* revolve around surprising him, but not in the way Sierra probably meant. But even thinking about the plan made Fort feel guilty, though he knew she couldn't read his mind, not with the necklace in place. He could practically see Rachel warming up her fireball. "Whatever happens will have to be a surprise to you, too, I guess. *Ugh.*"

"Don't worry about it!" Sierra said, squeezing his arm as they both sat down on one of the dorm room beds. "Just teleport me away before the week is up, and bring me back when you've beaten him." He could hear how forced her optimism was, but he wasn't going to point it out. "Though I hate that we can't just talk like we normally do, in our heads."

She was right about that. Despite sitting right next to her,

Fort hadn't ever felt so far from Sierra, as used as he was to seeing her thoughts, and her seeing his. Even when she'd been off with Damian at other times, he'd still been able to "talk" to Sierra.

Now, especially with his dad not returning his call, everything with Ember, and Jia and Rachel busy, he would have given almost anything to have Sierra in his head again, just to feel like he had his friend back. As it was, he felt lonely even at her side.

"At least it will all be over soon," Fort said, then snorted. "Not that we can't use the time. There's a lot to do before Damian gets here."

Sierra nodded, then took a deep breath. "That brings up a question, Fort. What happens if . . . if Damian *wins*?" She put up her hands to stop him. "No specifics, of course! I just want to make sure you're thinking about it. For worst-case scenario."

Her worried look said more than her words did about what she thought their chances were against Damian. Not that Fort would argue the point. Even if they had more time, he still thought there was no way they could stand against Damian and his power, with or without Spirit magic, the most dangerous type of all.

After all, Fort had seen for himself how powerful Spirit magic was just weeks ago. William had taken Fort and his friends over without a second thought, and only Excalibur had saved them. Without it, they might still be under his spell, along with the rest of the world.

But Excalibur was gone now, and their only weapon against Damian's Spirit magic—not to mention the other types—was surprise. Didn't inspire much confidence, that.

But it wasn't like Fort's backup plan was going much better at this point.

"I'm thinking about it, yes," Fort told her quietly. "We'll try to keep the Old Ones from coming, but I shouldn't say anything."

"You're going to make magic go away again," Sierra said matter-of-factly.

He just stared at her in shock, then dropped his head into his hands. "Rachel's going to *kill* me. How did you know?"

She smiled slightly. "Don't worry, I didn't get it from you. That's just the only possible way to keep them out. I mean, that's how humanity got rid of them the last time, right? But how would you even go about it? Do you? . . . Actually, don't tell me. It's better I don't know."

"Yeah, don't worry, it's all under control," Fort lied, hoping she wouldn't see through him without her Mind magic.

"Good," Sierra said, her face showing exactly how not-good she found it. "Just in case you're still working out how to do that, though, maybe I could offer some suggestions?"

Fort faked a laugh. "You really think we don't know how to do it yet? We'd be in so much trouble if *that* were the case!"

She sighed. "Oh wow, I didn't know it was *that* bad. Okay. I don't know how to make magic go away either, but I do know the TDA has a *lot* of things they unearthed, from Discovery Day forward. They had to have found *some* clue about where magic went. There's no way Dr. Opps would have just let that go."

Fort blinked at her in surprise. "That's . . . a really good idea. You know, if we didn't already have a plan, which we do. But if we didn't—"

"Get out of here," she said, smiling wider now. "You're a terrible liar, and you need all the time you can get to research what they found. Come back if you need to talk through anything, you know, in general—no specifics."

Fort rolled his eyes. "You've already given me good ideas, so it'd be ridiculous not to come back." He blushed a bit. "So yeah, I'll probably be seeing you soon."

She turned red as well. "Do that. I've missed you."

A strange, warm feeling filled his chest, and he got up before he said something wrong. "Well, that's . . . I mean, me too. Missed you, I mean."

Perfect. Nailed it.

"You're better at speaking in your head," she said with a laugh, and pushed him toward the door. "Come back quick."

Without another horrible word, he knocked on the door to be let out, then left, not looking back just in case he somehow embarrassed himself further. Once in the hallway, though, he rounded a corner to move out of sight of Sierra's guards and paused.

Her suggestion had been smart, and he should have thought of it immediately. But any of the secrets the TDA had found would be locked up tightly, and even with their tentative truce, Fort couldn't believe Colonel Charles would give him access, or even let him know where it all was kept.

But there was *someone* who might know. Someone who Fort would have preferred to never see again, but it wasn't like he had much choice here.

He groaned, then set off, hoping this wouldn't be *too* painful.

It took Fort longer than he wanted, but finally he managed

to locate the right room, which happened to be in the renovated section of the school, where the officers stayed. Fort hesitated for a moment, then knocked.

The door cracked just a bit, and Gabriel peeked out, then sighed heavily before opening it the rest of the way. "*Great.* What do you want?"

Fort gritted his teeth but knew he didn't have any choice. "I have a deal for you," he said. "I need you to steal some stuff from your dad."

"I do that anyway," Gabriel told him with a shrug. "But what do I get for helping *you*?"

That was the real question, wasn't it?

"The only thing you want," Fort said, knowing he'd regret this. "I'll get you your brother back."

- THIRTEEN -

AFTER LEAVING GABRIEL'S DORM ROOM, Fort spent the rest of the day just waiting around, too nervous to concentrate on anything else. Only one of two things was going to happen as a result of the deal he'd just made: Either Gabriel would come find him with his end of their bargain, or the TDA would arrest him and lock him away. Because taking over the school was one thing, but the deal he'd just made with Gabriel was something else entirely. At least, that's the way Colonel Charles would see it, Fort knew.

Finally, when he was just about to explode with anxiety, there was a knock on the massive trophy room door, and Gabriel entered. He grimaced at the sight of Fort and shook his head, as if he couldn't believe he was doing this.

"Trust me, I'm not any happier about it than you are," Fort

told him, in spite of how relieved he was that Gabriel had finally shown up. "And just so you know, I didn't *want* to meet here, but I didn't know where else we wouldn't be seen."

The last time he and Gabriel had been together in the trophy room had been a happier time, when they'd still been roommates, almost like brothers. And now . . .

Gabriel walked slowly over to Fort, holding something small in his hand. "A deal's a deal," he said, pausing just out of reach. "Did you bring it?"

Fort nodded and pulled out a small grocery bag that had been tied shut. "But like I said, it's only going to work for you after everything with Damian."

Gabriel smirked. "And how exactly are you going to stop me from using it if I decide to ignore that?"

Fort raised an eyebrow. "You really want to be asking me that while I can still teleport this into the sun? Trust me, I'll explain how once I see what you brought." He paused. "I really didn't think this would be that big a deal for you, though. You told me you used to steal from your dad without needing a reason. Why would it bother you now?"

"Oh, it's not that," Gabriel said, narrowing his eyes. "It's helping *you* that 'bothers' me. I don't know why you want this, and I don't trust you any farther than I can throw you." He paused, looking around. "Which probably is about the length of this room."

"Fair enough," Fort said, and held out the grocery bag next to his empty left hand. "Trade you."

Gabriel grunted and gave him a tiny computer drive, then snatched the grocery bag out of his other hand. As the older boy untied the bag, Fort quickly inserted the flash drive into a tablet he'd teleported from a computer store—it wasn't stealing if he was going to bring it right back . . . he hoped—and began clicking on files.

"What is *this*?" Gabriel said, and started to reach into the bag.

"Stop!" Fort shouted, almost dropping the tablet in surprise. "Don't touch it!"

Gabriel paused, giving Fort a suspicious look. "It's a piece of paper and some kind of doll. Where's my *spell*?"

"The paper *is* the spell," Fort said, rolling his eyes. "I drew up a little ticket and put the dimensional portal spell into it. I was just going to use some silver, but you took so long, I decided to get creative."

Gabriel snorted. "So you're saying this paper—"

"Ticket."

"This ticket will open a portal to the Dracsi world?"

Fort nodded. "And that's no doll in there. It's a golem. I'm guessing you've already heard what Dr. Ambrose is having the Healing students do right now?"

"Something about . . ." Gabriel trailed off. "Wait, you're joking."

"No, that *doll*—actually an action figure if you want to get technical—is a golem. And Jia put a spell on it so that if anyone tries to touch anything in that bag before a week from now, it will put them to sleep for the next month." Fort grinned at him. "So be my guest, break our deal. You should have a pretty good nap, from what she tells me."

Gabriel scowled at him. "You could be lying about this."

"I could be," Fort said with a shrug. "But if you don't believe me, go watch what Jia's teaching the Healing students and see for yourself."

To be fair, Gabriel was more right than he knew, since Fort *was* lying, which he didn't exactly feel great about. But right now he couldn't think of any other way to get Gabriel to wait, and the last thing they needed was another portal opening to the Old Ones' world.

And because he knew Jia wouldn't approve either, he'd just teleported an old superhero action figure out of his childhood toys, now in boxes at his aunt's.

It was taking a big chance, yes. For all Fort knew, Gabriel would ignore him and try to use the ticket anyway. But it was the only idea Fort had had, and they didn't have the time to waste while he came up with a better one.

And if Gabriel did wait, then either it wouldn't matter, because the Old Ones would have returned, or Fort would be wiping out magic anyway, and the ticket would no longer work. But whether magic still existed or not was never part of the deal; the ticket *would* get Gabriel there, if he was able to use it.

That was a pretty lame loophole, but if it came down to that or humanity being ruled by the Old Ones, Fort would take the loophole . . . and just feel terrible about his lie to his once friend.

"Fine," Gabriel said, tying the bag closed again. "But if this ticket doesn't work in a week—"

"It will," Fort said, trying to fake some confidence as he purposefully turned back to his tablet. For all he knew, Gabriel hadn't even fulfilled *his* end of the bargain. He scrolled through the drive and clicked on a few files, just to check.

As far as he could tell, Gabriel *had* come through. These were exactly the files Fort had asked for, just like Sierra had suggested: everything the TDA had on magic, the school, Discovery Day, and all the items, skeletons, and books of magic they'd found.

In fact, if anything, there was too much. Fort paged through scanned reports, photos, scientific analyses of the carbon and radioactive dating of the dragon bones, lists of a thousand different boxes of historic magical items they'd discovered over the past thirteen years, and *way* more. Going through all of this would take hours, *days* even!

"That's what you wanted, right?" Gabriel said, moving over to look at the tablet.

"Was there anything you couldn't get?" Fort asked, quickly closing it down. Yes, Gabriel had seen all the files he'd copied to the drive, but Fort didn't need him finding out which ones he'd been looking over in particular. Not that he was too worried, considering how many there were. "Please tell me there wasn't anything else. I'd never have time for it all."

"That's it," Gabriel said, sounding annoyed. "*I* don't leave anything behind, unlike some."

Fort ignored that. "And no one saw you?" he said, putting the tablet into a backpack he'd brought.

Gabriel didn't answer, and Fort looked up nervously.

"Gabriel, no one *saw* you, right?"

"Well, um, my father did," Gabriel said, then shrugged as Fort's eyes widened in shock. "He was in his office when I got there. What was I supposed to do? I pretended like I came to see him."

"About *what*?" Fort shouted. "You hate your dad!"

Gabriel glared at him. "I don't . . . It's not like that! I *blame* him, but I don't . . . Just forget it. None of that matters. Anyway, I had the perfect thing to ask him about: how he planned on getting back at you, Jia, and Rachel when this was over, and whether I could help him with it." He grinned.

Fort rolled his eyes. "Perfect. But then how did you get the files?"

"Oh, I made him have lunch with me, then told him I forgot something in his office, which I did, on purpose," Gabriel said. "He lent me his keys, and I took everything I could find in his computer, then went running back to the cafeteria." He snorted. "This isn't my first job, kid. He and I have been through this before. Though that means he probably suspects something is up, and might figure it has to do with you."

Fort took a deep breath, then slowly let it out, trying to stay calm. The last thing he needed right now was more trouble with Colonel Charles.

"Oh, don't worry so much," Gabriel said. "I also threw two stink bombs that one of the Destruction kids made into the office just before I left. You know, to make him think I was just making his life miserable, as usual."

Fort laughed in surprise. "Wait, seriously? That's amazing!"

"No, it's strictly amateur hour," Gabriel said, actually blushing a bit. "I'm not proud of this performance, kid, but you didn't give me a lot of options, not when you needed it this fast." He crossed his arms. "Now, if you tell me what this is about, I can probably hide it better if he realizes what I took. Want to tell me what it is you're looking for in a bunch of catalog lists and photos of archaeological sites?" He pointed at the dragon bones in the museum case in front of them. "These fossils aren't enough for you?"

Fort bit his lip, not knowing what to say. Part of him wanted to tell the other boy everything, if just to stay on Gabriel's good side. But if Gabriel found out about the backup plan to destroy magic, he'd realize Fort had tricked him, and it'd all blow up.

Not that he wanted to leave Michael with the Old Ones. He'd wondered over and over since dragging Gabriel out of the

Dracsi world whether they should have left Michael there or not. But Michael hadn't been under Spirit magic, that much Fort was sure about. And if he didn't want to come home, how could they have forced him?

But now, if Fort succeeded, then Michael and his family wouldn't ever see each other again.

Just one more way saving the world meant leaving everyone with a *lot* of pain, and all of it apparently was on Fort's shoulders. Even having *one* friend on his side who he could talk to would have helped, but this was the only way to fix things, and he couldn't let his loneliness hold him back.

"I'm trying to figure out if there's anything we can use," Fort said after a long pause, hoping Gabriel wouldn't see right through him. "I was hoping we'd find some kind of powerful weapon somewhere in here, something that could take down a dragon."

Gabriel narrowed his eyes, and Fort looked away, figuring he looked guilty. Finally, Gabriel grunted. "Let me know if you find anything I could use. I owe that baby dragon of yours some payback."

"Good luck with *that*," Fort said with a nervous laugh, just happy Gabriel hadn't noticed his lie. "It's your funeral." He held up the tablet. "I'll erase this drive when I'm done."

"Don't care," Gabriel said, shrugging again. "It'll take him a while to figure out I took them, if he ever does. Those stink bombs were *powerful*."

With that, he turned and walked toward the door, then stopped right before leaving. "If this ticket doesn't work, Fort," Gabriel said, looking him right in the eye, "there's no magic or dragon on Earth that'll keep me from coming after you. You know that, right?"

"Yup," Fort said, digging his fingernails into his palms to keep his hands from shaking. "It does exactly what I promised."

"It better," Gabriel said, and closed the door behind him.

Fort waited a moment, then let out the huge breath he'd been holding and pulled the tablet back out. There was no time to waste, now that he had all the accumulated knowledge the TDA had put together over the last thirteen years.

At least he still had just over six days left, which had to be enough time to go through all the files and find whatever he needed.

After all, there couldn't be *that* many, could there?

- FOURTEEN -

SIX DAYS LATER, FORT HAD GOTTEN through only half the files and was ready to explode from worry and lack of sleep.

How could the government have dug up *this* much stuff?

The photos of cool-looking magical items were interesting at least, unlike almost everything else. Over half the files were just long lists of where things were stored, including states, military bases, warehouses, and even box numbers, all in an almost incomprehensible code.

Thankfully, he'd found that code in a different document, but then he still had to compare the two. And then there were all the expert analyses of the books of magic and other items, as well as analyses of analyses, memos on those, and memos on the memos.

How could anyone possibly get stuff done in the TDA with this much paperwork?

Three days into the week, Fort had actually considered just casting Learn on the flash drive and hoping for the best. But considering what had happened when he'd done that to the dragon dictionary, he thought it maybe wasn't a great idea, especially considering this flash drive contained more than enough files to fill a few thousand books the same size as the dictionary. The last thing he needed was to explode his brain from one stockroom list too many.

"Does everyone have their golem ready?" Jia said from the other room, and Fort looked up from his tablet, catching just a glimpse of her leading a class of Healing students. She had her usual golem held high in her hand, showing the little doll-like statue off, motionless for now.

But that would all change when she, and the other students, imbued their golems with magic.

He'd taken to studying the tablet in Dr. Ambrose's office, just off the Healing classroom, mostly because he wasn't too far from where Trey and Ember were training/playing—Trey had to stay close for healing his constant burns—but also because it was one of the few places he didn't have to answer questions about what he was doing.

"What *exactly* are you doing, Fitzgerald?" shouted a voice, and Fort jumped out of Dr. Ambrose's chair in surprise, readying a teleportation circle. But when he turned to find who'd just entered from the other door, he canceled the spell, blushing heavily.

"Hey, Dr. Ambrose," he said, wincing. "I was just using your office for some studying."

Dr. Ambrose strode over to him and grabbed the tablet from his hands before he could stop her, then sat down in the chair he'd just been using himself. She scanned through it a bit, her eyebrows rising along with his blood pressure. "These are top secret files, Fitzgerald," she said, not looking up. "*I* don't even have clearance to be seeing these. Where'd you get them?"

It was too late to make something up, so instead, he tried to fake it. "I think any need for top secret clearances is out the window now," he said, crossing his arms in what he hoped was a confident gesture. "You know, since Damian and the Old Ones are coming to destroy the world."

"So you stole them," she said, leaning back in her chair as his stomach sank into his shoes. Was she going to turn him in? Would she tell Colonel Charles? But before he could go through all the worst-case scenarios, she continued. "Good. Glad one of you took some initiative finally. The TDA barely know their brains from their behinds, and I for one would rather not be one of those Elder Ones' servants."

"Old Ones," Fort said automatically, just thankful she was on his side.

"Don't correct *me*, Fitzgerald," she said, tossing him the tablet, which he fumbled but managed to catch. "Frankly, the world is lucky that only kids can use magic so far. Imagine if adults had access to that kind of power? It took you all thirteen years to mess things up, mostly because of people like the colonel anyway. Adults would have done the same thing in under a month."

He smiled at that. "Let's hope we can fix everything we messed up."

"Speaking of, what are you looking for, anyway?" she asked, giving him a long look.

"Weren't you just meeting with Colonel Charles?" he asked, avoiding the question. Jia had assured him that Dr. Ambrose would be gone for at least an hour, or he'd have tried to find another place to study. "He told us he'd help with Rachel and Jia's plan, but I don't know that I believe him."

"Who knows with our dear colonel," she said with a shrug. "Even before you kids showed him up, he'd been perpetually about two seconds away from exploding. That tends to make it difficult to get things done, especially since I personally can't stand him and tell him so frequently." She glanced up at Fort again. "And stop avoiding my question. What are you trying to find in all those files?"

He held the tablet against his chest protectively. "Just some background on what the TDA has found over the years," he said carefully. "I thought there might be something in here that'd be useful."

"No you didn't," Dr. Ambrose said, her eyes narrowing. "Any weapons they had, Charles would have used against that thing in London, and you know that. No, you're after something else. Give it up, Fitzgerald, or I'll take back what I said and run off to tell him everything."

Fort sighed, hoping he could trust her. He moved to close the door to the classroom, where a dozen tiny golems were now scampering around the tables, then sat down across from Dr. Ambrose. "I don't even know what I was looking for, honestly," he said quietly. "I was hoping to find something about *how* magic disappeared, all those years ago. Or maybe why it came back. That might help too."

She stared at him thoughtfully for a moment. "Which means

you think you won't be able to stop Damian, and so you'll have to shut magic down again, to keep those monsters away."

His eyes widened. How did everyone seem to already know this? "Um, yes? How did you—"

"Because I have a *brain*, and I use it, Fitzgerald," she said with a sigh. "Don't lump me in with those TDA goons just because I work here too." She waved her hand as if to tell him to hurry. "So? What'd you find?"

"Nothing!" he said, leaning back in his chair dejectedly. "If there's anything in there, I either didn't see it, or I had no idea what I was looking at. Half of everything is in code, and the rest they don't even know what they found, so it's just 'bell,' or 'book,' or 'candle' or something. And the things I *do* recognize are basically useless garbage. A bag that holds an infinite amount of stuff isn't going to help against Damian, even if they seem to think it'll help with military deployments."

"You could trick him into it, I guess," Dr. Ambrose said. "How tightly do you think we'd have to tie it to keep him in there?"

"None of it told me how or why magic went away in the first place," Fort said, shaking his head. "Not even a clue as to when it happened."

She wrinkled her nose. "I was briefed on all of that Merlin/Artorigios garbage. Did you look up the files on him?"

"Him?" Fort said, then: "You mean Merlin? He's *in* here?" He tapped the tablet.

"How would *I* know?" she said, throwing her arms up. "Did you not hear me say I didn't have clearance?"

"Sorry, right," Fort said, and quickly typed Merlin's name into the tablet's search function, only to immediately deflate when it came up with nothing. "Nope, no mention."

"It was a good thought," Dr. Ambrose said. "Sounds like what you really need is one of those Time students. Did I hear correctly that you lost our only one to Damian?"

Fort winced. "Something like that."

"And that you permanently took away the magic of the rest of the Carmarthen Academy using that ridiculous sword that shouldn't exist?"

"Um, yes to that, too."

"Wow, Fitzgerald," she said, looking impressed. "When I brought you down for that briefing, I never thought you'd end up getting us into so much trouble. I should have just let you stay in the medical bay."

"Probably would have been for the best," Fort agreed,

wondering if it was too late to Time magic himself back to that point.

"Well, keep looking," she said, and stood up. "I'm going to go check in on this puppetry class." She frowned. "I still don't understand how Jia can teach them spells. I thought all magic was incomprehensible unless you read it from a book yourself."

"Merlin said that's just the basic books, the ones that showed up on Discovery Day," Fort told her. "He took Rachel and Jia back in time to when others were available, and those books didn't have the same restrictions. So Jia can teach them whatever she wants from what she learned."

"Huh," Dr. Ambrose said. "Too bad he didn't leave a forwarding number when he disappeared, or you could have just asked him all your questions. Though I guess if you took his younger self's magic away, he won't have any either." She opened the door, then threw Fort a dirty look. "No sitting in my chair, Fitzgerald. Believe me, I'll *know*."

With that, she left, and Fort stayed in his seat, not sure if he believed her or not, but not particularly wanting to find out.

It really *was* too bad he didn't have Merlin to talk to anymore. Yes, Merlin was Cyrus's older self, so Dr. Ambrose was right that he must have lost his magic too when they took it from Cyrus, which probably created all kinds of paradoxes. But he wouldn't need his magic to answer questions about how humanity had gotten rid of magic back then.

But that wasn't possible, not now. And the only others who might have been around at that time that Fort could think of were the skeletons in the trophy room.

If only *they* could talk . . .

Wait. *Wait.* Maybe they could?

Back when Fort had Jia's spells in his head, when he'd first arrived at the Oppenheimer School, he'd been reading ahead in the Healing book of magic. Farther in, he'd seen a spell, something that could help in just this situation. It was a long shot, but if Jia had mastered it, or even just learned it without casting it . . .

Fort leaped up from his seat so quickly he knocked the chair over and ran into the classroom where Jia was still teaching.

The assembled Healing students all went silent as he barged in, though their golems continued to climb all over them, several of them mumbling about interruptions. Dr. Ambrose had taken a seat at the back and looked at him with one eyebrow raised.

"Fort?" Jia said, looking concerned. "What's wrong?"

Fort blushed from all the eyes on him and quickly moved to Jia's side. The entire class leaned in to try to overhear, so Fort turned around and whispered something in Jia's ear.

"You want me to make a *zombie*?" she shouted in surprise, then realized the entire class had heard her and turned as red as Fort. "Um, keep practicing your golems, people. Looks like I'm going to be busy over our lunch break."

- FIFTEEN -

"I'VE GOT A BAD FEELING ABOUT THIS," Rachel said, shaking her head as she cut into the museum glass containing the dragon skeletons. "Zombies are *never* a good idea."

"They're not really zombies," Fort told her, trying to sound hopeful as Jia waited next to him, looking as nervous as he felt. "It's just animating the dead."

"In other words, *zombies*," Rachel said. "And so I repeat, *never a good idea*."

Fort sighed, not really disagreeing with her. But what other choice did they have? He could search through time to try to find the moment magic went away, but that risked another vision taking him down, not to mention that he had no idea *when* to look specifically, and there were a *lot* of days in the past.

Not that he'd told Jia and Rachel the real reason for this.

They knew he'd been looking through the TDA files, but considering Rachel's stance on the whole getting-rid-of-magic backup plan, he'd left that part out and told them that speaking to the magicians here might give them something to use against Damian. Which wasn't a lie, if not exactly the *entire* truth either.

"We *should* be okay," Jia said to Rachel, though she didn't look very confident about that. "I'm just going to animate them for a few minutes at most, and see what we can find out."

"What's the name of the spell, by the way?" Rachel asked.

Jia winced. "Um, Create Zombie?"

Rachel sighed deeply and moved the cut glass to one side using her magic, opening the way to the skeletons. "Perfect. That's exactly what we need on top of Damian and the Old Ones: a zombie invasion. With our luck, they'll infect everyone at the school, and we'll unleash an army of magician zombie kids on the country."

Jia smiled at her. "You're always saying half of the Destruction students have no minds of their own, so *they* should be safe from brain-eating zombies."

Rachel snorted. "That's true. I almost feel bad for Colonel Charles after teaching them for this long. *Almost*."

Rachel had been leading a class for Destruction students on Illusion magic, just like Jia had been teaching the Healing students her golem spells. Both seemed to be going okay, but there wasn't much time left, and a lot left for the Oppenheimer students to learn.

Things were coming down to the wire, and the closer they got, the more convinced Fort was that they'd need his backup plan no matter what.

He did wish he could have Ember with them for this, just in case the zomb—the reanimated dead—got out of hand. But he didn't want her seeing the skeletons of her own kind after everything else with Damian, so they'd just have to rely on their own magic to keep things in check.

"Ready?" Jia asked, her hands glowing blue. "I don't want to keep them around for long, so we're going to need to hurry."

Rachel nodded, creating a fireball and aiming at the nearest magician as Fort prepared a teleportation spell to the Arctic, hoping freezing cold would at least slow the zombies down. "Ready," he said.

Jia took in a deep breath, then cast her Create Zombie spell.

The human skeleton standing next to the largest dragon began to glow with Healing magic as muscles grew out of its bones, followed by a covering of skin, though neither looked healthy: The muscles had holes in them, and the skin looked diseased, which wasn't a great sign.

As the skeleton's body continued filling in, Jia gasped and dropped to one knee, sweat dripping off her forehead.

"Gee, you *okay*?" Rachel said, keeping her fireball aimed at the zombie but her attention now locked on the Healing girl.

"I'm . . . fine," Jia said, gritting her teeth. "He's just . . . fighting me!"

Fort stared at her in fear. The skeleton was *what* now? Fighting her?

"WHO ARE YOU *TO AWAKEN ME?"* said a voice like two rocks grating together. Fort slowly turned to find a pair of red, glowing eyes staring at him from the half-covered skull of the magician. *"SPEAK, OR I SHALL SILENCE YOU FOREVER!"*

"Um, this may not have been the best idea after all," Fort said to the other two.

"He's speaking magic, Fort," Rachel said, her fireball growing larger and hotter as Jia seemed to get more exhausted. "You're up. Hurry!"

Fort winced, then stepped forward, hoping the zombie magician wouldn't be offended by their weakest magic user speaking for the others. "Um, *hello, Your Majesty,*" he said, not sure how to address a zombie. *"We apologize for waking you up, but we have,* ah, *desperate need of information that only you can provide."*

The zombie stared at him for a moment, his eyes blazing, before he raised a hand and floated himself out of the display case and toward Fort, sneering at him through half-formed lips. *"YOU! SO YOU'VE COME TO TAUNT ME OVER EMRYS'S TRICKERY!"*

Fort's eyes widened. Emrys? That was Cyrus's—and Merlin's—Old One name. He quickly shook his head. *"No, not at all. I don't even know what trickery you're talking about. I just wanted to know how you made magic stop working."*

The zombie's eyes blazed with rage. *"YOU MOCK ME AT YOUR PERIL, CHOSEN OF THE SEVENTH BOOK. YOU ASK QUESTIONS YOU ALREADY KNOW THE ANSWER TO, AND HAVE AWOKEN ME FOR NOTHING!"*

Chosen of the Seventh Book? What did *that* mean?

"Fort, this doesn't seem to be going well," Rachel said, stepping over next to him. "Maybe we should quit while we're ahead?"

"YOU WOULD ATTACK ME WITH ELEMENTAL MAGIC?" the zombie roared, and raised a hand.

"Drop it!" Rachel shouted, and began to throw her fireball.

The zombie pointed a finger at her, and her fireball exploded back at her, knocking Rachel across the room.

"Ray!" Jia shouted, sending a Healing spell at the other girl before turning back to Fort. "That's it—we're done here!" She waved a hand, and the blue light around the zombie disappeared.

Only, nothing happened. The zombie turned to her and raised his hand again. *"YOU HAVE AWOKEN THE WRONG MAGICIAN, CHILD. BUT NOW I HAVE RETURNED, AND I WILL HAVE MY VENGEANCE ON THE TIMELESS ONE!"* He raised a hand again

Then he pointed a finger at Jia.

"No!" Fort shouted, and opened a portal between the zombie and Jia, but the creature's spell zigzagged right around his teleportation circle and struck Jia in the chest, knocking her to the floor as well.

"AND NOW YOU, CHOSEN ONE," the zombie said, turning back to Fort, his hand still raised. *"YOU WHOM EMRYS CONCEALED FROM US THROUGHOUT THE CEREMONY, HIDING LIKE A COWARD."*

"I don't know what you're talking about!" Fort shouted at the

zombie. "*But the Old Ones are returning, and we need to stop them. The only thing I can think of is to shut down magic, like you all did!*"

"*THAT WAS NEVER OUR INTENTION!*" the zombie shrieked, and the walls began to tremble around them. Rachel slowly picked herself up, readying another spell, but a blue glow appeared around the other magician skeletons, and they quickly zombified as well, then broke free of their museum cases and swarmed over her, while an elf and a dwarf skeleton did the same to Jia.

The giant cat that one of the magicians had been found with began to growl, then turned its red eyes at Fort.

"*MAGIC WAS OUR BIRTHRIGHT. WE WOULD NEVER HAVE FORSAKEN IT,*" the original zombie roared. "*THIS WAS ALL EMRYS'S FAULT!*"

The giant cat skeleton twitched, then leaped straight at Fort, who barely managed to teleport himself to the side and avoid it. But the cat was too quick and kicked off the floor from where he'd been standing and launched right at him again, too fast for Fort to react. It struck him in the chest, knocking him to the floor, its mouth full of fangs roaring just inches from his face.

"YOU HOLD THE KEY, CHOSEN ONE," the original zombie said, stepping over to Fort, who felt a cold chill go down his spine in addition to the terror he already felt. *"THE SEVENTH BOOK SEES SOMETHING WITHIN YOU. PERHAPS I SHALL TAKE THAT SOMETHING FOR MYSELF!"*

And then the undead magician leaned down and touched a finger to Fort's head.

A searing-hot pain exploded in his mind, and Fort screamed out . . . as did the zombie. Abruptly, an image appeared in Fort's head, four humans standing in the middle of a circle of rocks, with dragons and the large cat standing just beyond. And next to them was—

"No!" someone shouted. And just like that, the giant cat holding Fort collapsed into a pile of bones, each one clattering off him as it fell to the floor. The zombie magician's screams faded into a great, dying sigh, and he, too, collapsed, his undead flesh dissolving into nothingness. As Fort picked himself out of the cat's bones, he found that the other skeletons had also gone limp, now covering Jia and Rachel.

"Jia, thank you!" Fort said as he pushed himself to his feet.

"*I* didn't do this," she said, picking her way out of her own pile of bones. "Rachel?"

"It was me, *Father,"* said a voice behind them, and Fort sighed deeply, then turned to find Ember in her dragon form staring at him with disgust. *"I could feel your fear, so I came to save you. And* this *is what I find? You working magic on your own deceased? Hiding* dragon *skeletons from me? I thought we were done with secrets!"*

"*We* are, *Ember! I just didn't want you to* see them," he said, realizing how pathetic that sounded. Apparently she agreed, as she let loose a plume of flame that sent Fort diving to the floor. When the fires cleared, he looked up to find her gone.

"Oh, fantastic!" Rachel said, still trying to escape her pile of bones. "Now we've got *two* angry dragons to deal with." She glared at Fort and Jia. "See? *This* is why you don't mess around with zombies!"

- SIXTEEN -

SO RIGHT BEFORE EMBER RESCUED ME, the zombie magician . . . showed me something," Fort said, staring at the wall of Sierra's room. "A moment in the past. It looked like Stonehenge, maybe. I think that might be when they did away with magic a thousand years ago."

Basically, the whole idea had been bad from the start. He knew that now. And even thinking about the zombie made him want to crawl under some blankets and never face the world again. But if he was right about Stonehenge, and that *was* the time and place where they'd done away with magic, it might still have been worth it.

"Wow," Sierra said, interrupting his train of thought as she sat cross-legged on the bed, facing Fort. "Rachel's right. You *shouldn't* ever mess with zombies."

Fort rolled his eyes. "All right, not the time. But at least I know what to look into next. The only thing is . . ." He trailed off, embarrassed to even mention this next part. "He also called me something . . . odd."

"Odder than Forsythe?" Sierra asked, with a grin, then held up her hands in surrender as he glared at her. "Okay, don't get upset. I just mean it's not exactly a common name."

"Can you be serious for a minute?" Fort said, getting irritated. "We only have a few hours before Damian's going to show up!"

"Sorry, you're right," she said, nodding solemnly. "Did he call you 'mom'? I did that to a teacher once, and still want to throw up thinking about it."

Fort sighed loudly, and she laughed. "Oh, come on," she said. "I'm trying to lighten the mood. If these are the last few hours before Damian comes back and the Old Ones take over, then I'd rather have *some* fun, before it's outlawed or whatever."

"I'd rather they not *be* our last few hours," Fort admitted, but he smiled anyway.

"So what *did* he call you?"

"Um . . . the *chosen one*." Even as the words came out, Fort could feel his cheeks heating up.

Sierra's eyebrows shot up. "The chosen one? You mean like

what Damian is always calling himself?" She leaned in to look at him closely, making Fort blush even more. "Did you learn all six types of magic when I wasn't looking? Because that'd be pretty impressive."

He rolled his eyes, then stopped. Hadn't he done just that? If every type of magic was in Merlin's dragon dictionary, then he knew every bit as much magic as Damian did. Not that he could use it, considering the visions that came on out of nowhere.

But maybe that could mean that Damian *wasn't* the one the prophecy had been talking about? In fact, if it did refer to Fort, and this was his way of saving the world, it could even be confirming everything he was doing here.

But as much as that idea comforted him, he couldn't take the whole thing seriously. Him, a chosen one? The weakest kid at the Oppenheimer School? It didn't add up.

"I think I'd remember that," he said finally, knowing he couldn't mention the dragon dictionary. "He said something about me being the chosen of the seventh book—which, who knew there even *was* a seventh book—and how he wanted revenge on Emrys. That's Merlin's Old One name, by the way."

"Oh, that would make sense," Sierra said. "That's what the

Welsh called Merlin." At Fort's startled glance, she shrugged. "Listen, I was Mind magicking left and right while I was in the UK, trying to figure out where the Time book was. I picked up a lot of odd trivia."

Fair enough. "How would he even know me in the first place?" Fort asked, trying to get back on topic. "And what did Merlin have to do with any of this?"

"Well, to be fair, maybe he's not talking about Merlin," Sierra said. "Emrys is Cyrus, too, so maybe Cyrus did something?"

"Other than betray us all?" Fort muttered, then stopped to think about it. "Actually, you might be right. Maybe that's why the zombie guy was so upset, because Cyrus tried to mess things up with them, too? He's been trying to bring his family back for centuries, so it'd make sense that he could have been involved in whatever they did."

"I still don't get what this seventh-book stuff is about," Sierra said, tapping her chin. "They only found five on Discovery Day."

"And the Spirit book is six," Fort said. "Though it was stuck on Avalon."

They both went silent, and Fort's thoughts turned to something he hadn't told Sierra, how the magician had claimed

Emrys hid Fort during some ceremony. That had to be the moment at Stonehenge the zombie had shown him, which meant Fort had been there, somehow. Or was going to be . . .

"You know, you *could* always just ask Cyrus," Sierra said, giving Fort a sidelong glance.

That immediately derailed his own thoughts. "Um, what now? Actually I *can't*, because the faerie queen has him, and I'm pretty sure she doesn't want me showing up with a list of questions for her prisoner." And he was even less sure he'd want to see what the queen had done to Cyrus. The whole thing just made him sick.

Sierra shook her head. "You're not understanding. The zombie recognized you, so he's seen you before. And that means you're going to be taking a trip to the past somehow, probably for that Stonehenge thing he showed you."

Fort bit his lip, not saying anything. She was definitely thinking along the same lines he was, even without knowing all the information. But he couldn't tell her about holding the language of magic in his head, and how he could probably come up with the right words for a Time spell to actually go see the ceremony itself.

But it was definitely looking more and more likely that that was what he had to do. Or had *already* done. Ugh. Time travel was such a headache.

"Too bad there's no way to travel back to the past," Fort said, knowing Rachel would lightning bolt him if he mentioned even one word about the dragon dictionary. "I should probably go—"

"Except there *is* a way," Sierra said, shaking her head like Fort was hopelessly behind on all of this. "Or don't you have a dragon around here?"

Oh, right. That would make sense to Sierra, given that she didn't know about his power. "I don't actually know if she's still around," he said quietly, not particularly enjoying thinking about Ember any more than Cyrus at the moment. "When she got angry about everything after saving us from the zombies, she left, and blocked every finding spell I've tried. I'm guessing she's with Trey—"

"Wait, what finding spell?" Sierra said, frowning. "When did you learn a spell like that?"

Fort froze, his eyes widening. "Oh, it's . . . We found some magical . . . You know, someone created them for the TDA, and we found them, the silver . . . You know what I'm talking about."

"I'm not sure you could call that talking, actually," she said, looking at him strangely. "What are you *hiding*, Forsythe Fitzgerald?"

"Nothing!" he said quickly, wiping a drop of sweat from his forehead. "It's just . . . there are things you can't know, remember?"

This was all so bad. He hated, *hated* hiding things from Sierra and didn't feel a whole lot better about keeping Jia and Rachel in the dark. Every time he'd tried that in the past, it'd gone badly for everyone, especially his friends.

But he'd at least tried to come clean with Ember about Avalon, and Sierra herself admitted she didn't want to be told anything that Damian could later use against them. The dragon dictionary definitely fell into that category.

And he had reasons to keep things to himself. Good ones, even. Rachel had shot him down from the start, and both she and Jia needed to concentrate on their plan against Damian anyway. The last thing they needed was to worry about what he was up to.

He groaned quietly, wondering if this was all just a way to justify keeping everything from them. What if they *were* right, and he was going to make things worse? Or what if they were wrong, and not learning how to destroy magic left them ruled by the Old Ones?

Right now, he wished more than anything he had someone, *anyone* he could share this all with, like he'd had Sierra when they'd been stealing the Summoning book. But instead, he was alone and had to do what he hoped was right.

Even if he hated himself for it.

Sierra closed her eyes and rubbed her temples. "I'm sorry, I shouldn't push. And you're right—I shouldn't know anyway. Let's get back to the zombie. What did Jia and Rachel think of all of this?"

That wasn't exactly safer territory. "They, ah, don't know," he said, trying desperately to think of a lie that would cover it, only to come up empty. "Um, he was speaking a language they didn't understand."

Fantastic. This was just digging himself in deeper, and Sierra wasn't going to buy it any more than she had the finding-spell-magical-item ridiculousness.

Sierra raised an eyebrow. "I didn't know you spoke other languages."

"Oh, yeah, my dad was on a whole Latin kick for a while," he lied, turning to face the wall. "I got really good at it."

Fantastic. More outright lies.

He could feel her stare on his cheek and gritted his teeth to keep himself from just revealing everything. "It's true!" he said. "Want to hear some?"

"Do I want to hear you make up some words you think sound like Latin because you're lying to me? That doesn't sound like fun for either of us, no." She mumbled something he couldn't hear under her breath, then raised her voice again. "At least you have reasons to keep secrets from *me*. But why didn't you tell Jia and Rachel?"

"Because . . . they don't know what I'm trying to do," Fort said miserably. At least that much was the truth. "Rachel's against the, ah, backup plan we talked about last time—"

"Don't tell me don't tell me don't tell me!" Sierra said, putting her hands over her ears. When she saw he'd stopped talking, she dropped them. "Just because I guessed something doesn't mean you need to confirm it!" She went silent for a moment. "If that's how it is, then you need to use your 'finding spell' to locate your dragon, Fort. She's the only one who can take you to that zombie ceremony."

"I don't think they were zombies at the time," Fort pointed out, but he nodded. "You're right, I should go find Ember."

He stood up to say good-bye, then stopped as he realized something and crashed back to the bed. Finding Ember wasn't going to work, not if his dragon didn't want to be found. But that was all just an excuse to use his own Time magic anyway and visit the Stonehenge ceremony the zombie had shown him.

Only, how could he do that, if another vision knocked him out? Would he end up lost in time somewhere, or worse, just not ever wake up from it until after everything with Damian had gone down? He couldn't take the chance, not without someone to watch over him and wake him up like Jia and Ember had the last time.

Except Ember wasn't around, and while Jia semi-approved of the backup plan, she wouldn't help him without telling Rachel. And then it'd all be shut down.

That left only one person who might be able to help him, if a vision did happen. Someone with magic that could influence the mind itself, someone he trusted more than anyone, even if she'd soon be under Damian's spell.

Sierra.

Of course, without her magic, she wouldn't be able to watch out for him. But why were they really keeping her from using her spells before Damian's Spirit magic went off? Right now she was fully on their side and completely trustworthy. And if Fort used Time magic correctly, he'd be back before there was any danger of Damian's spell going off anyway. Besides, they'd have time after he returned for her to wipe her own mind of anything she shouldn't know. She had the magic to do it easily, and it was probably the smart thing to do even if he didn't tell her anything.

The more Fort thought about it, the more he decided this made sense. A small part of him wondered if he just really wanted to share everything with Sierra as usual, to have someone on his side here, so was taking too big a risk. But logically, he couldn't think of any downsides. Traveling by time meant he could return a few seconds after he left, and they wouldn't be running over the deadline.

He took a deep breath, hoping desperately he wasn't just justifying things to himself again.

"So, I've got something to admit," Fort said, and moved closer to Sierra, then reached over and grabbed the chain from her neck, the one with the little Jia golem still on it. Since the golem was only guarding against Sierra doing it, he was able to lift off the magical item keeping her spells in check without any problem. "I don't actually speak Latin."

"Um, what did you just *do*?" she asked, her hands immediately flying to her now empty neck in surprise. "Fort, you have to put that back!"

"I need your help," he said, and tossed the necklace to the floor. "And that means you need the full truth, at least for the next few hours."

- SEVENTEEN -

"YOU *ACCIDENTALLY* LEARNED THE entire language of magic?" Sierra said, her mouth hanging open. "From an—I'm sorry, what?—a *dragon dictionary*?"

"Maybe accidentally's the wrong word," Fort admitted. This all would have gone a lot easier if Sierra had been willing to just read his mind. He'd brought up the idea of her wiping her memories, and she'd agreed that it seemed smart. But even with that, she still worried about learning too much she shouldn't so refused to delve too deeply into Fort's memories with her magic. "I mean, I knew what I was getting into. . . . I just didn't realize what it could do."

"So you know every single spell there is?" Sierra asked, shaking her head in disbelief. "Why do you even need to destroy magic? You could probably take Damian down by yourself!"

"First of all, I don't just *know* the spells—I have to experiment until I get the words right," Fort said. "And second . . . well, I wasn't born on Discovery Day, and . . ."

And no matter what spells he knew, they'd never be as powerful as those of someone who'd been born on the day magic returned. Not to mention that dragons were something else entirely.

Sierra leaned back in. "Who cares about that? Magic isn't about sheer power. It's about how you use it, the imagination behind it. Even if Damian is stronger, between you, Jia, and Rachel—"

"There's a third reason too," Fort said. "And this is why I need your help. From the moment I memorized the dragon dictionary, I've been getting these . . . visions. They don't come on with every spell, but when they do, I've been knocked out, and needed help coming out of it."

This made her eyebrows shoot up. "Visions? Of what?"

Fort frowned. "It's sort of hazy, honestly, like a dream. There's a voice, a woman's voice." He paused, remembering how that voice sounded so familiar yet wasn't one he could ever remember having heard before. "I saw the beginning, I think."

"The beginning of what?" Sierra asked.

Of everything, Fort wanted to say, but for some reason, he hesitated to share it, not feeling like he could explain it correctly. "It doesn't matter. I've got the magic to go back in time and see what the magicians did to do away with magic, but if I have a vision in the middle of it—"

"You might never come back," Sierra finished, wrinkling her nose. "Okay, fair, you really *do* need help." Her face fell. "But what if I'm not strong enough to pull you out of it, Fort? I still think we need Jia here at *least.*"

It'd actually taken both Jia *and* Ember the last time, but Fort didn't mention that. "Her magic only affects it indirectly, by restoring me to a previous point. *You* can help push the vision away and bring my mind back here. Mind magic is *exactly* what I need. And no one's better at it than you!"

She smiled slightly. "Nice try with the compliments. But I don't know. I hate the idea of letting you down."

"Oh, don't worry about that," he said, waving his hand. "I let myself down a few times a day. I'm used to it."

She stuck out her tongue at him. "*Fine*, I'll do this. But if you get back late and I end up betraying everyone and doom the whole world, I'm blaming *you*, Fitzgerald."

"And I'll deserve it," he said, and stood up, reaching for his phone. "Okay! Let's do this, then. I just need a few minutes to make a call, and—"

"Are you kidding?" she said. "No, we're doing this *now*. The sooner you're back and I've wiped my memories of this whole week, the better. You can talk to whoever after you're back safe and sound, and you've told Jia and Rachel everything you've found out. That way it'll be too late for them to stop you, and they'll be able to help you with the whole destroying-magic thing, if they can't beat Damian."

She had a point . . . and a huge part of him was more worried about calling his father than traveling back through time, or even the visions. If his dad didn't pick up again . . . Fort wasn't sure he could handle it.

But he did feel much better after sharing everything with Sierra. Having her just made him feel so much less alone. And besides, was this really that dangerous? He was just going to send his consciousness back in time, not his physical body. He'd see what he had to see, then jump right back a few moments later at most. It'd be like almost no time had passed.

"Okay," he said, then laid himself down on the room's other bed. "So all you have to do is—"

"You don't need to Fort-splain Mind magic to me, buddy,"

she said, and put a hand on his head. Instantly he could feel her presence in his head, and just suddenly everything felt better. "I've got this. *No visions.*"

He nodded. "Thanks, Sierra."

Don't mention it, she said in his mind, and smiled. *Now go learn from the past, so we're not doomed to repeat it. Or we* are *doomed to repeat it, depending. I'm still a little unclear.*

Fair enough. Fort took a deep breath, then concentrated on the image the zombie had given him. "Be right back, hopefully," he said to Sierra, then before he could change his mind, whispered, *"Take me back to the moment in time,"* in the language of magic.

Immediately, the black glow of Time magic surrounded him, and the room around him disappeared.

As did Sierra's presence from his mind.

Fort immediately panicked, feeling like he'd just lost an arm or something equally important. *Sierra!* he shouted in his mind as his consciousness fell backward in time, to no response.

The black light around him began to brighten, to blur, and he could feel his mind expand again, just like before when he had a vision. Whatever Sierra had tried to do, it hadn't worked.

And now, she wasn't even there to help pull him back.

Not having much choice, Fort used all the willpower he had to hold on to the image of Stonehenge the zombie had given him, focusing on that in spite of the glow growing brighter all around him. The white light threatened to engulf him, even as his mind seemed to rise to meet it, and he screamed, pulling himself back as best he could, just hoping he could hold on—

Only for the glow to fade slightly, revealing a familiar-looking circle of rocks.

Except now, instead of being half in ruins, Stonehenge's multiple rings of stones were complete, with rock arches circling around a smaller circle of standing stones, each looking like they'd just been placed, unlike in the present. Fort stared at it in a daze, fighting to stay conscious as the vision played at the edge of his mind, slightly less powerful than it'd been a moment before, but still hard to resist.

Whatever was causing these visions was getting worse now, he knew. It could be that he was using these unmastered spells more, or that the spells were more powerful in general, but either way, he wasn't sure how long he could last here.

He'd just have to find out what he needed to know before the vision overtook him and jump back to the present, where, hopefully, Sierra could help.

Fort had arrived a few dozen yards from the rock formation, and from this distance, he could just make out five figures standing in the middle of the stone circles, humans from the looks of them.

Unfortunately, he was too far to hear what they were saying, so he willed himself closer. Even this small an act, though, caused the vision to grow stronger and his mind to expand back into it again. He growled in frustration, jerking his attention back as best he could, deciding that the edge of the stones would have to be close enough.

He leaned against one of the arches for support, not knowing how that was possible, if he was just here as a consciousness, but not especially caring at the moment. The magic was probably taking care of it, either way.

Fortunately, the voices were close enough to almost make out, so he slid around to the side of the arch and listened intently for what the gathered humans were saying.

"Good morning!" said a boy's voice to his left, making Fort almost jump out of his shoes. He whirled around in shock and found someone all too familiar glowing with black Time magic.

Still fighting the vision, Fort shakily raised his hands defensively, ready to open a teleportation circle. "Don't . . . even . . . try it," he said to the newcomer.

Cyrus frowned, staring at Fort in confusion. "I'm sorry. Was that not the proper greeting?" he asked. "Should I have just said 'hello'? I'm never quite sure with humans."

- EIGHTEEN -

WHAT ARE *YOU DOING* HERE?" FORT hissed, trying to keep his Teleport spell at the ready but finding it hard to concentrate with the vision still clouding his mind. Through the fog, he wondered how Cyrus could have escaped the faerie queen with no magic, but that didn't really matter now: He was here, and Fort couldn't let Cyrus stop him. "If you try anything, I'll teleport you to the bottom of the ocean!"

"Try anything?" Cyrus said, looking confused. "I mean you no harm. I just noticed a fellow visitor from another time, so I thought I might greet you. And I don't know that your Teleport spell will accomplish much, since neither of us is here physically." He tilted his head curiously. "I assume you're here for the same reason I am?"

A fellow visitor? How did he not recognize . . . ?

Oh. *Oh*.

Even with the vision trying to pull apart his mind, Fort realized what was happening: This wasn't the Cyrus he knew. It had to be a younger version, one who hadn't yet met Fort, or else the other boy would have recognized him. Cyrus had no reason to be lying now, especially if he'd broken free of Avalon.

But if this was a younger version of Cyrus, why was he here? Unless it was for the same reason Fort was, to figure out how magic had been nullified for so long. But why would he need that information?

Fort cursed. Because he wanted his family to return, and to do that, he'd need magic back. If this really was a younger Cyrus, he could be here to figure out how to reverse the loss of magic and start everything in the future that Fort was trying to stop.

And that meant Fort couldn't tell him *anything*, not if he didn't want this Cyrus to change things up and maybe make stopping the Old Ones in the future even harder.

"Did you hear me?" Cyrus asked, frowning. "You've been quiet an awfully long time."

Fort blinked. "Oh, I'm just, um, visiting," he said, leaning against the nearby stone again to steady himself as concentrating got steadily harder. "You know, random places . . . random *times* in the past." *Don't tell him this is your past!* "Or *future.* Whichever. Could be either, really."

Cyrus smiled. "Well, you picked a good time, then, considering how momentous an occasion this is." He raised an eyebrow. "May I ask your name?"

"Oh, it's Forsythe," Fort said before he could stop himself, then inwardly cursed for not making something up. Between the vision attacking him and the time travel, not to mention meeting someone he'd known for months for the first time, things were a bit hard to keep track of. "What's, ah, your name?" he added as casually as he could.

"Emrys," Cyrus told him, using the Timeless One's real name, before frowning. "You're human, aren't you? Maybe you shouldn't be here. There are plenty of other interesting times to visit, and this one is a bit of a private matter, actually."

Uh-oh. "Oh, don't worry about me," Fort said, waving Cyrus onward toward the stones. "You go ahead. I'll leave you all to it and just watch from a, you know, respectful distance. From back here, I mean."

All Fort could see now at the edges of his vision was pure white light, and he shook his head to try to clear it, with zero luck. The Cyrus in front of him frowned . . . then abruptly seemed to split in two as a second Cyrus and a second Fort appeared a few feet away, also talking to each other.

Fort blinked and rubbed his eyes. Okay, *that* couldn't be real. As he opened his eyes again, the duplicates were gone, with only one Cyrus remaining and no extra Forts. Phew.

"You're from my future, aren't you?" the silver-haired boy asked, and whatever satisfaction Fort felt from getting rid of the duplicates disappeared. Cyrus was seeing right through him, which admittedly probably wasn't that hard, considering the state of his mind at the moment.

"I am!" Fort said, his eyes darting around as he desperately tried to think of a reason he'd need to be there. "And that's why I'm here, to save your timeline. If I don't see what happens here, everything in the future might disappear! It's a whole paradox thing, and—"

Cyrus's eyes began to glow black as he squinted at Fort, then stepped back in shock. "Wait. You're . . . *him*? The one Merlin chose, the one who will be my . . . friend?"

"Um, yes?" Fort said quickly, barely able to follow what Cyrus was saying now, though part of him latched on to the word "chose." Was he confirming what the zombie had said? "You and I were . . . we *are* best friends!"

The surprise in Cyrus's eyes turned into excitement, which seemed like a good thing. "But how? I've never had a friend, and . . . oh, I see." His face fell as the black light disappeared from his eyes, and somehow, in spite of everything, Fort almost felt sorry for him. "We won't really be friends. I'm going to *lie* to you, pretend to be your friend so I can manipulate you into helping me get my family back." He sighed. "I can see why he picked you: You and I would get along really well. But it's for that same reason I'll have to use you too." He shook his head. "It's a horrible, never-ending cycle, and it has to *stop*. Somehow he and I need to figure out a way to end all of this."

"Oh, you didn't pretend!" Fort said, focusing on the only part of Cyrus's words he could follow. "I know you didn't. You couldn't hurt me when Rachel King Arthur was fighting you." He paused, feeling like the words were getting away from him a bit. "I mean Rachel, when she was an Artor . . . Agor . . . Merlin's apprentice."

Cyrus didn't seem to understand this, which was odd, because it made perfect sense to Fort. Either way, it didn't seem to be helping. But before Fort could fix it, he began to notice the grass and trees around him, even the stones of

Stonehenge swirling away into a mass of stars, which somehow at the moment felt like the most natural thing in the world.

From a great distance, he heard a woman's voice saying his name. "Forsythe!" she shouted, as if she were calling him home for dinner. Even the sound of the voice relaxed him, and he started wondering why he'd been so worried. He was here with his friend Cyrus, after all. He should be happy!

"So you're here now . . . to stop me in the future," Cyrus said, stepping closer. "I think I understand."

"Yes?" Fort said, feeling like he was supposed to lie about that, but not sure why anymore. "I was trying to figure out how to destroy magic permanently, so your family couldn't come back. Want to help? I could probably use it."

"No, I don't think I do," Cyrus said, looking at Fort oddly. "There's something happening to you, but I don't understand—" He stepped closer, his eyes glowing black again, and he gasped. "You've read the book! How is that possible? It wouldn't let anyone . . . *Where was it?*"

"The book?" Fort said, the word starting to lose all meaning the more he thought about it. "You mean the dragon dictionary? That's in his cottage, Cyrus. You know that—you were there too! At least before you destroyed the whole place. Where else would it be?"

Voices raised in the center of the stone circle distracted both Fort and Cyrus for a moment, though he still wasn't quite close enough to make out what they were saying. Fort stumbled forward, trying to hear more, only for the world to swing around him wildly, and he thought for a moment the vision had taken him.

But it was only Cyrus, yanking him away from the ceremony at the center of the stones. Somehow, the other boy could touch him, even though neither of them were present. Fort snorted. These Old Ones were sure good at magic!

"You shouldn't be seeing *any* of this," Cyrus said quietly. "Not that you'll remember it in your state."

"State? I'm from the *United* States," Fort said, the woman's voice calling his name now getting louder. He waved his hand in her direction. "One second, I'm just finishing up here!"

"See, this is exactly why we did what we did," Cyrus hissed, giving Fort an annoyed look while pulling him farther away from the stone circle. "It's complete chaos when left to your kind. It *needs* the order we provide to function. This?" He gestured at Fort. "This is what happens when humans are left to their own devices. *Chaos*. I can hardly bear it."

"No, those aren't bears," Fort told him, wondering why his friend was being so mean when everything was so connected, and the world was so filled with bright light. Cyrus and the magic were the same; they just couldn't see it. He just needed Fort to explain things, obviously. "No bears at all. They're people, just like you and me. Maybe not like you, because you're evil, but still—"

Cyrus gave Fort an appraising sort of look. "As annoying as this is, your babbling does come off as almost endearing. I wonder if that would work on other humans if I . . . eh, that can wait for now." He waved his hand absently. "First, I need to get you out of here."

"Babbling?" Fort said, completely lost now. "Can you hear it too? That's the woman. She's yelling my name. She says there are things I need to see still, and something about how everything is a possibility."

"Ugh," Cyrus said, sounding disgusted. He released Fort, who immediately dropped to the ground, the vision now crowding in from every side. "Go home, human," Cyrus said to him as the bright colors of the vision now fought against darkness, the glowing black of Time magic. "I'm sure I'll meet you again soon. I like the uniform, by the way."

"The what?" Fort said, looking down at himself. Oh, right, he'd had to borrow some school uniforms since he'd left home without any clothes. "Thanks! You did say the first time that you were used to me in green."

"I'll have to keep that in mind," Cyrus told him with a smile, just as everything disappeared in a mix of black and white light.

- NINETEEN -

YOU MUST SEE . . . COULD HAVE . . . , the woman's voice said, cutting off abruptly at times as Fort floated in a spiral of white and black light. The fogginess in his mind had lessened a bit, though it still felt as if he were in some sort of dream state, where logic and reality weren't so important anymore.

For example, he had no idea how he'd come to be floating here, or where he'd been before that. All of time seemed to flow out in either direction endlessly, past and future only depending on which way he faced.

Some tiny part of him shouted over and over about something he needed to do, someplace he needed to be, but it was easily ignored, especially as peaceful as the voice made Fort feel.

As the spiral of light began to fade, Fort stayed perfectly calm, even as he now found himself hovering over a world that looked like it could have been his own, yet looked nothing like the Earth he was used to. Instead of the skyscrapers and highways of his time, or the untouched forests and fields of days past, thousands of sweeping spires grew out of the lush green grass on the ground, extending off as far as he could see. Translucent walkways stretched between them, and on each one he could see human-looking figures walking—no, *floating*—just above them.

The spires themselves looked like they'd been formed from some kind of crystal, maybe diamond, but the shapes of the spires couldn't have been natural. Many defied gravity altogether, sweeping and soaring in ways that no foundation could have supported.

Not to mention that some of the spires floated above the ground, just as Fort did, twisting through the clouds. That also seemed a bit unusual, but not enough to cause any sort of anxiety or alarm.

In fact, if anything, the spires made Fort feel *more* serene, as if he was in touch with everyone and everything at once. How that was possible, he neither knew nor cared, just enjoying it for what it was as he moved along, something unknown pushing him toward an unknown destination.

That destination turned out to be the nearest spire. As Fort approached it, one of the crystal walls turned transparent, and a figure appeared behind it. Whoever it was bowed low, and the wall opened almost like a mouth, revealing a smiling girl around his own age.

A *human* girl.

She wore some kind of silken robe without any seams, like it'd been grown around her. Her hair was cut short and was the color of the sky on a sunny day, yet didn't look dyed.

"Welcome, Teacher," the girl said as Fort floated through the opening in the spire to land next to her. "We have been preparing for this moment for years."

In spite of all his questions, Fort found he wasn't confused or anxious. Things were too peaceful here. "You can see me?" he asked. "I thought this was just a vision."

The girl nodded. "From what we've been told, it was meant to be, but some stray Time magic disrupted that and sent you here, to us. As I said, we've been waiting for this for a long time."

"Waiting for what?" Fort asked. "And why did you call me Teacher?"

Her smile widened. "Please, come with me. We shouldn't keep the crowds waiting."

Crowds? Where *was* he, and how did they know he'd be coming? This was all so odd, and yet completely normal somehow.

The girl led him farther into the spiral, where water flowed like a whirlpool around the insides of the crystal wall, with plants of all types growing straight out of it. Some Fort recognized, while others looked completely alien to him.

"I wish I could show you around my library," the girl said as she led him to an opening in the floor, then stepped through it, gently floating down to the level below. Fort followed without knowing how and found himself in the middle of what looked like a shrine to books. "But you'd miss out on the important stuff if we stayed too long."

She moved toward another hole, while Fort glanced around as quickly as he could. The books looked just like paperbacks from his time, though he didn't recognize any titles. Still, there was nothing in any way abnormal about them, other than the fact they were behind translucent crystal, like they were being preserved.

"I have one of the largest collections of pre–Discovery Day books in the city," the girl said, beaming proudly as she descended through the floor once again. "I'd have loved if you could have told me more about them!"

The level below was open to one of the walkways, where dozens of people of varying ages, all wearing similar silken clothes to the girl's, waited in rows. As Fort appeared, the air began to shimmer around each one as they bowed, and a rush of warmth flooded his body, like he'd just been hugged by a hundred people at once.

"Welcome, Teacher."

"Thank you for everything you did, Teacher!"

"You look shorter in person, Teacher! . . . Ow, don't hit me—I'm just being honest!"

The girl sighed as she stared at the last person speaking, then turned back to Fort. "This all must be overwhelming to you, but we have very little time before you leave us, so we want to show you how beloved you are for what you've done."

The others all murmured their agreement, except for the one boy who muttered, "I wasn't trying to insult him. It's just interesting how we mythologize . . . Augh, stop smacking me!"

Even in his dreamlike state, Fort found himself feeling more nervous now. What was going on here? How was he being recognized by all of these people? And for doing what?

If this had to do with what the zombie magician had said, about him being a chosen one of something or other, Fort didn't like it one bit. Instead of being praised, he'd much rather have no one notice him so they could go wherever they needed to in private. All the attention just made him uncomfortable.

Uncomfortable, and a little proud. Only a small part of him, but still.

After all, if he really was the chosen one the books had spoken of and was going to save the world, maybe this was some kind of proof!

The girl led the way through the assembled crowd, which flowed in behind Fort as they passed, creating a sort of parade, making Fort feel even more awkward now. They floated down the pathway between spires toward what looked like a busier part of this town, or city, whatever it was.

As they passed, many of the spires overlooking the road opened to reveal onlookers, all of whom waved or clapped. "Thank you, Teacher!" one shouted.

"*Why* do they keep calling me Teacher?" Fort asked the girl, missing the peace he'd felt when he'd first arrived. "I've never taught anyone in my life."

"In your life *so far*," the girl corrected him with a grin, then turned back to the road.

That wasn't exactly an answer and didn't help Fort's mood.

It wasn't long before the spires on either side fell away to reveal a sort of park, filled with trees the likes of which Fort had never seen. Easily as tall as skyscrapers, they rose in a circle between the spires, almost blocking out the bright sun overhead.

The girl led Fort into the wooded area, where he could see another crowd waiting, this time standing in front of what looked like a large statue, a strange shimmering blocking him from making out what it was.

For a moment, Fort considered just running for it. Bringing him to a statue made him positive this was some chosen one craziness, and he wanted no part of it. But on the other hand, if it confirmed that he was making the right call by doing away with magic, then he needed to see it.

And if he got a little ego boost out of it, then that wasn't *his* fault, was it?

"It's so rare that we can personally thank someone who has done so much for us," the girl said as she moved to stop before a raised platform. She waved Fort forward, and without meaning to, he floated up onto the platform, staring at the shimmering before him. "But you deserve this, Teacher."

"This statue has stood for centuries," an older woman said from the top of the platform. "All in preparation for this day, when we can show you our gratitude in person. And please . . . when you can, pass it along to your comrades."

Comrades? Fort glanced up at the statue as the shimmering disappeared, and he gasped, both from shock and relief.

The statue rose a hundred feet tall, easily, with huge letters at its base.

THE MOTHERS OF OUR NEW WORLD, it said. And above that were two women, hand in hand, each one pointing off into the distance. THEY GAVE MAGIC TO THE WORLD.

And he *recognized* them. They were older, yes, but the resemblance was obvious.

"Rachel Carter and Jia Liang," the woman next to him said, sniffing loudly as a tear ran down her cheek. "It is thanks to them that we have everything we do today."

All the nervousness and tension of the last few minutes melted away, leaving Fort with a sense of peace again. "This will sound odd," he said, much happier now, "but someone just called me the chosen one. So I guess I thought with everyone thanking me . . ."

The woman's eyes widened. "Oh, my apologies, Teacher! Of course you are honored as well! You worked your whole life to bring magic to everyone, and we cannot thank you enough."

She pointed at the statue, where a series of small plaques filled the bottom.

"We'd heard something about a chosen one," the girl who'd met Fort said as he moved forward on the platform to get a closer look. "But considering how much nonsense that was, we just assumed it was made up for the story's sake. No one's chosen over anyone else, of course. You and your friends proved that: just people trying to do good."

IN THANKS the first plaque said. TEACHER SEBASTIAN.

The others were similar, thanking several other students from the Oppenheimer School, with the last plaque thanking TEACHER FORSYTHE.

So that was it. All the chosen one garbage had been some big mistake. His relief was overpowering, though that small part of him that had enjoyed it did feel a little sad now. It'd felt good to be important, if just for a moment.

And he wasn't exactly thrilled about what this meant for his plans. But maybe one didn't have anything to do with the other.

The girl had mentioned a story. What if there was more to that?

"I'm sorry, but what did you mean?" Fort asked, staring at his plaque. "What story's sake? What story?"

"The story of how you all brought back magic and spread it

to everyone, rich and poor," the girl said, beaming at him.

Just like that, any sense of peace or relief disappeared, and he stared at her in horror. Spread magic to everyone? That was the exact opposite of what he intended to do!

"Hold on," he said, raising his hands. "There's got to be some kind of mistake—"

"That you all didn't get statues?" the girl asked, blushing slightly. "Apologies for that, but from what we've heard of you, it didn't seem as if you'd have wanted one. Perhaps we can make one for a future visit?"

"No, that's not what I meant!" Fort said quickly, wishing he could think more clearly here.

"And now, unfortunately, we must send you back," the woman on the platform said, and raised a hand. The air began to shimmer all around him, almost like faerie magic, and the huge statue and trees and spires started to disappear.

"Wait!" Fort said, suddenly realizing he wouldn't get to ask all of his questions, dream or no. "But I have to *destroy* magic to save everyone, and I still don't know how—"

The woman stepped backward in shock. "*What* did you say?" she shouted, and the crowd began talking all at once. "But that's . . . monstrous!"

"You would destroy magic?" the girl who'd led him to the statue said, looking disgusted. "Why would you do something so awful? Look at what you'd be taking from your future! You *must* see—"

And then the girl, the statue, the crowds, everything disappeared, replaced by a dark, empty dorm room.

Sierra's room.

And she was gone. But the necklace was still there, lying on the floor where he'd left it.

Fort stared at it in horror. How long had he been gone? It should have been just a few minutes, but—

A blaring alarm cut through his confusion, ringing so loudly that it pounded in his skull. Fort's heart began to race as he looked around for Sierra, the vision or dream or future he'd just seen fading away in light of what was happening around him.

"Hello?" he shouted, getting more and more anxious with every second. *Sierra? Can you hear me?*

She didn't answer, which filled him with horrible dread.

What time was it? He pulled out his phone and felt his body go cold.

No. *No*. He'd been gone too long, lost in that vision. He had returned too late . . . *without* the knowledge he'd set out to find in the first place. And Sierra . . . He couldn't even think about it.

He still had no idea how to destroy magic, and now Damian's gift of a week had passed, and—

Something hit the school like a bomb, and Fort was thrown from the bed like he weighed nothing. Through the pain, he swore silently, knowing what that meant.

Damian was here. And they were going to *lose*.

- TWENTY -

SIERRA WASN'T ANSWERING HIS MENtal yells. That could mean two things: one, that Jia or Rachel had put a new necklace on her, since she couldn't touch it herself; or two . . .

Two, he couldn't even think about. But the fact that no Mind magic had attacked his brain yet at least gave him hope.

The plan Rachel and Jia had come up with hinged on tricking Damian when he first arrived. They knew he wanted the books of magic, so they planned on keeping the books in the cafeteria, where they could ambush him. Since the books made Damian's Time vision cloudy, that should have meant any trap they set would be a surprise.

So that's where Fort teleported first . . . only to find half of the room just *gone*.

The ceiling had collapsed, and debris had come crashing

down from the floors above to bury most of the tables and chairs. Fortunately, there at least weren't any students or soldiers around, so it didn't look like anyone had gotten hurt.

But if they weren't in the cafeteria, where *was* everyone?

Another loud boom shook the school, knocking Fort from his feet and into the pile of debris. He caught a steel beam to steady himself before landing, then pushed back to his feet and opened as many teleportation circles as he could in a line, hoping to find Rachel and Jia, Sierra, Ember, or at *least* some students.

The trophy room was still standing, but empty.

The briefing room in the basement was destroyed, just like the cafeteria.

The Healing classroom was also gone.

Colonel Charles's office had survived, but no one was there. Several phones were ringing at once, though, which, combined with the still-blaring alarm, made Fort immediately close that portal.

Why had he taken the chance on going back in time? His heartbeat raced so quickly that he could feel it in his head. He was supposed to be here, helping with the fight and protecting Ember and Sierra, if he could.

But now everyone was missing, and it was probably already too late. He had to find Damian and the others *immediately.* But how? Other than dorm rooms, Fort couldn't think of many places to check. Instead of teleporting, he made his way through the broken cafeteria doors out into the hallway and down toward the elevator, hoping to at least run into someone.

Unfortunately, not only were the halls empty, but the elevator wasn't in any better shape than the rest of the school. One of the doors was completely missing, revealing an empty shaft and no elevator. Not that it seemed safe to use in this shaking anyway.

Another explosion sent him stumbling toward the elevator shaft, but he teleported himself a short distance away before he fell and braced himself against a wall until the tremor stopped. Where could this be coming from? What kind of force would it take to shake the mountain? It had to be Damian, but where *was* he? And where were . . . ?

Oh, of course. Outside. They all had to be *outside.* That was the only possibility. Damian wasn't attacking the school directly; he was going after the mountain it was built beneath.

Except, Fort couldn't teleport outside. He'd never seen it.

They'd blindfolded him on the way in and out, along with all the other students, to keep the school's location a secret.

He growled loudly in frustration and worry, then teleported to the enormous round entrance door, which he *had* seen when he'd arrived. The door was closed, unfortunately, and probably locked, not to mention that it probably weighed a few tons. A lit keypad on the side of the door offered up a solution, if only Fort had the code to open it.

Another boom shook the school, this time louder. He could even make out the sound through the massive door, which was terrifying in and of itself, considering how thick it was.

But how could he get out there? He was *so close*, but without a code—

"Father!" someone shouted, and knocked Fort hard to the floor from behind. He panicked at first and rolled over to face his attacker, only to immediately feel a flood of relief as he found a pair of dragon eyes staring down at him in concern. *"You have returned!"*

"Ember!" Fort said, looking her over. *"You're not hurt?"*

She shook her head and backed up so he could stand. *"I was just outside with the others when I felt your presence. The two humans you warned me against eating are preparing their attack, while the elder, Damian, shows off."* She rolled her eyes. *"He's barely using any magic, just destroying this empty shell of a structure, I imagine to impress the humans. Why bother?"*

"Wait, so everyone's okay?" Fort said, relief flooding over him. *"Can you take me outside? I've never seen it, so I can't teleport out there."*

Ember snorted, little flames shooting out of her nostrils and singeing Fort's uniform. *"Oh, Father. Of* course *I can."*

Green light surrounded them, and abruptly they were on the side of a neighboring mountain, close enough to the school to see the entrance but far enough away to be safe. *"I don't even need a portal,"* Ember told him proudly, and he patted her head absently, not really having time to praise her properly as he surveyed the wreckage below them.

The other side of the massive round entrance door to the school was stuck in the middle of an enormous mountain, easily twice as big as the mountain Ember had teleported them to. The entrance, even as large as it was, was dwarfed by the mountainside itself and was dug back into the rock in a way that made it almost unnoticeable, other than the gated roadway leading to it. A couple of guard towers had stood over the roadway, but both were destroyed now, along with the gate that would have kept any hikers out.

The damage looked bad, but it was all just stuff. What Fort really cared about were his friends, and he didn't see them anywhere. For that matter, there were no students or TDA soldiers, either. Where *was* everyone?

The source of all the damage was apparent, at least: Damian hovered in midair in dragon form above the school's entrance, his massive paws glowing with red Elemental magic. He unleashed another spell straight at the mountain, and the shock wave almost knocked Fort from his feet again, even from this far away.

"Where are Jia and Rachel?" Fort asked Ember, his eyes searching over the entrance. "I can't see—"

"That's on purpose," Ember said, nodding down toward the road leading into the school. *"The leader human is using her Illusion magic."*

Right, that was part of the plan! In all of the confusion, Fort had almost forgotten. He followed Ember's gaze to the road and watched as both Rachel and Jia faded into view, followed by the assembled students of the Oppenheimer School directly behind them.

Jia held a Healing staff, while Rachel was covered in weapons, from lightning rods to what looked like unstrung bows, all strapped to her body, leaving her hands free. The other students held various items as well, reminding Fort that he should probably arm himself if he could, considering any magic he used beyond Teleport or a minor Healing spell could send him into another vision.

Feeling almost useless, he quickly opened a teleportation circle to the armory and, thankfully, found the room still standing, though almost entirely empty now: The rest of the students and TDA soldiers must have picked it over already. He grabbed a Healing staff through the portal and closed the magical gate behind him, deciding that if he could at least heal anyone who was injured, that would be something.

"Where are the TDA soldiers?" Fort asked Ember as Damian slowly lowered himself to the mountain in order to face the small army below him.

Ember sniffed in the air, then frowned. "I'm not entirely sure, Father. I don't sense them nearby."

What? What was Colonel Charles thinking? This wasn't the deal. Had the plan changed while he was in his vision? Because if not . . .

Before he could panic even further, Fort forced himself to take a deep breath. Jia and Rachel must have worked out something with the colonel ahead of time and were hiding him like they had the students. There's no way they'd have let him and the soldiers not even show.

Even if they were here, though, would it make a difference? As much as he had faith in his friends, Fort knew, just *knew* that they had no chance. All they had going for them was surprise, and that would only work because of Damian's arrogance, his belief that he was simply *better* than them.

If the dragon ever took them seriously enough that he resorted to using his Spirit magic, it would all be over.

"Damian!" Rachel shouted up at him. "Stop beating up the mountain and *face us*!"

Damian's massive dragon jaws split into what Fort assumed was a smile. "Ah, finally," he said, staring down at the assembled students. "I didn't think it'd take you *this* long to evacuate. I'm glad to see you all made it out okay."

He glowed red for a moment, and the ground began to shake so hard that Fort and Ember both collapsed to the dirt, as did all of the students below. A huge rumbling came from the mountain, and as Fort watched in horror, it collapsed in on itself, burying the school inside entirely.

"I'm done playing, humans," Damian said, hovering above

the cloud of dirt and dust that came billowing from the destroyed mountain. "You think you have power, but you have no *idea* what true magic is. If you don't want to find out, I'd surrender if I were you. *Now.*"

- TWENTY-ONE -

FORT JUST STARED IN SHOCK AS THE rock and dirt continued collapsing inward, filling in the underground space where the school had been. He almost couldn't believe that Damian had done it. At least there hadn't been anyone inside, something Fort had seen for himself when looking for everyone.

But if there had been, would that have stopped Damian?

Below, Jia and Rachel pushed to their feet, as did the rest of their student troops, if more slowly. Everyone was now covered in dust and dirt, but it didn't seem to bother them. In fact, none of the students had fled, which was surprising. Fort had figured at least some of the Destruction students would surrender, if not from fear, then from thinking they could learn from Damian.

But no, Rachel and Jia had the students locked down, and

Fort felt a swell of pride for his friends. Maybe they *could* pull this off.

"No one is giving up?" Damian said, sounding a bit shocked himself. "I didn't think you were *all* so misguided, but I should have known not to underestimate you."

"Why don't you come down here and underestimate us to our face?" Rachel shouted up at him, and the dragon growled.

"Last chance," he said, looking over the students. "If you want to survive—"

A bolt from either a Destruction spell or a lightning rod exploded up toward the dragon, only to deflect off his scales. He glanced down at the spot it hit in annoyance, then nodded his enormous head. "Okay then. You've made your choice!"

He took one last massive beat of his wings, throwing himself high in the air, then straightened his body and dove toward the students, straight at Jia and Rachel in particular.

It was all Fort could do to not open a teleportation circle then and there. Every muscle in his body tensed as Damian dove, and he could tell Ember was just as anxious, as she growled louder the closer Damian got.

But this was part of the plan, and the last thing Fort was going to do was get in their way.

"Get him!" Rachel shouted as Damian neared them. She and the other Destruction students sent more lightning sizzling out toward Damian, but the bolts again just hit his scales and deflected off harmlessly.

Damian glowed red with his own destructive magic as he prepared to unleash a belly full of dragon fire as well . . .

But he stopped abruptly, pulling out of his dive to hover above them angrily.

"You think I can't see through your Illusion spell?" he roared, his eyes now glowing with orange light. "Didn't we do this already, back in the skeleton room?"

The Illusion spell covering the students below him slowly melted away, revealing a small army of golems, each of which resembled the students who'd created them.

Next to Jia's usual golem, a Rachel golem made a rude gesture toward Damian, which just seemed to infuriate the dragon more. He let loose the fire he'd been holding into the air in frustration, then turned to survey the ground around him, searching for the actual students.

Fort held his breath, afraid to even watch. *This* was where everything could go wrong, if they weren't careful. If Damian found the students before they were ready . . .

"Now!" shouted a voice, and part of the mountain beneath Fort and Ember disappeared, revealing the assembled Oppenheimer students, each one glowing with their respective magical types.

Well, all but two.

Rachel and Jia, hands held tightly together, were now glowing with a purple light, a light that struck out to hit Damian's wings.

Instantly, the wings turned to solid gold.

With a roar of surprise, Damian dropped from the sky, his wings far too heavy to flap. He crashed into the ground hard, and the Healing students were on him immediately, each one casting what looked like a Sleep spell on him.

"Don't let up!" Jia shouted, adding her own magic to the fray, and the combined power of the entire group of students seemed to actually be overwhelming the dragon's natural defenses and power, as his eyes began to droop and his movements slowed. Fort's eyes widened, barely able to believe what was happening.

"Elemental and Corporeal magic, mixed?" Ember said, sounding almost impressed. "Not bad, though it couldn't have been easy, synching the magic up between them."

Fort nodded, not telling her that he'd had no idea *that* was coming. Apparently they'd been busy this past week!

While the Healing students put Damian to sleep, the Destruction students grabbed ahold of Damian's golden wings with their Elemental magic and wrapped them around the dragon, then melted the tips of the metal together, imprisoning him.

He roared again in response, but he seemed slow to react and wasn't casting any spells. If they could actually get him to sleep, they'd have a chance to take him down for *good.* After all Fort's doubt and worry about it, could their plan work? Could they really beat Damian?

Beside him, Ember sighed. "Oh *no*. Do you see it, Father?"

He felt his blood run cold at her words and turned to see her nod toward a spot in the air, right above where the illusionary army of students had first stood.

At first, he *didn't* see it. The orange glow faded into the setting sunlight too easily. But once he did, he knew it was already too late.

"No," Fort whispered, shaking his head. "No!"

A low, gravelly laugh sounded from the spot in the air, and the version of Damian on the ground disappeared. "You think you're the only ones who can use Illusion magic?" said a voice, and the dragon reappeared in the air, where he was hovering in place. "Did it feel good to win, humans, if just for a moment? Enjoy it, because it won't happen again."

And then he unleashed a torrent of fire on the students below.

"No!" Fort shouted again, and cast as large a teleportation circle as he could manage, sending the fire off into the Arctic somewhere. But even that wasn't enough, and most of the flames passed to either side of his circle, hitting their intended target.

The sight before him sent Fort to his knees, and he desperately wanted to look away but couldn't turn, couldn't stop facing his failure, as the fire exploded all around the students.

"No," he whispered, tears running down his face.

"Father, *look*," Ember said, nudging him with her head.

Somehow, a blue glow appeared in the midst of the dragon fire. Fort leaned forward, unable to believe it, but as the flames died down, he could barely make out a blue sphere, one of Jia's protection spells.

A sphere just large enough for two, no more.

Inside the sphere, Rachel huddled next to Jia, both looking devastated by what had just happened. The rest of the students . . . Fort couldn't bear to look.

He turned his gaze up at Damian, rage filling his mind. He expected to hear the dragon gloating, looking smug over his victory, but weirdly, Damian just looked surprised.

"What did you *do*?" he roared at Rachel and Jia. "I thought you'd have been able to block that! Why would you let them all be hurt like that?"

"*You* did it, you monster!" Jia shouted, releasing her protective sphere. "Look at what you've done, Damian. I thought you were doing this to *save* humanity from the Old Ones, not destroy it yourself!"

The dragon's mouth opened and closed for a moment. "I thought they'd be powerful enough to . . ." He trailed off, then shook his head. "This doesn't matter! You could have surrendered. I *offered* you the chance to surrender, but you refused! And the Old Ones *will* doom us all if they're not defeated for good. As the chosen one, I'm the only one who can beat them!"

"You think *you're* the chosen one?" Rachel said, sneering up at the dragon. "Why is that, Damian? Because you believe a children's poem? Or is it because Cyrus, one of the Old Ones himself, told you that you were?" He flinched at her words, but she didn't stop. "Which is it? Which lie are you using to justify taking out a bunch of innocent kids?"

Damian roared back at her, though it was hard to tell who he was more angry at, Rachel or himself. "Stop trying to confuse me!" he shouted. "I've seen the future, and only *I* can stop it—"

"Only you can *cause* it!" Jia yelled up at him. "Don't you get it? We destroyed the book of Summoning magic. No one else can bring the Old Ones back except for you. If you leave them where they are, we'll be *safe*, Damian!"

Again, it was like the words hit Damian physically. He shook his head, looking away from the destruction below. "That's not true! There are other ways. They'll find their way back if we let them. They're a threat to this entire world, and I *have* to face them!"

"You facing them is *why* they're a threat, Damian!" Jia shouted. "How can you not see that? You're playing right into their hands. We've seen the future where you *lose*. Cyrus took us there! But it doesn't have to be like that. It's not too late to stop all this!"

Damian growled again, but he seemed to be actually considering their words. Fort almost couldn't believe it: Were they really getting through to him? He wouldn't have thought that was even possible.

"You're not making sense!" the dragon shouted finally, cringing as if he was in pain. "I *have* to beat the Old Ones—they're the ones who made me summon the . . . who *started* all of this!"

Jia and Rachel looked at each other, then both put their hands in the air, surrendering. "Come down, Damian," Jia said quietly. "We're not going to fight you anymore. Too much misery has come from that already. Just come down and talk."

The dragon looked at them, his eyes flashing . . . only for his head to go limp as he slowly descended to the ground, his wings flapping heavily. He hit the dirt hard, and his body glowed blue for a moment, then transformed back to human once more.

Damian looked up sadly, past Jia and Rachel to the damage he'd done to the other students, and didn't say a word.

Rachel and Jia slowly moved closer to him, their hands held up. "It can still be okay," Jia said quietly.

"It can—she's right," Rachel said, then grinned. "Once we take your behind *down*."

"What?" Damian said, looking confused, but it was already too late. Behind him, the mass of golems created by the Oppenheimer School students attacked as one, swarming over Damian with a roar that couldn't have come from such small creatures.

"Get him!" one yelled, glowing with orange magic and morphing into a full-sized Moira.

"Oh, this is going to be fun," another shouted, turning into Sebastian.

One by one, all of the Oppenheimer students took their true form as they overwhelmed Damian, using a mix of Healing and Destructive magic to try to put him to sleep and entomb him in rock at the same time, respectively.

"What?" Damian shouted in confusion. "How can this—"

"*Double* illusion, Dragon Boy!" Rachel shouted, then slammed a fist made of rock right into his stomach. "I knew you'd detect my spell, but also that you'd be too full of yourself to look any further, so I just cast one illusion on top of the other. The golems were our friends the whole time!"

Jia stepped forward, warping Damian's limbs around him until he was tied up once again, this time for real. "Sorry, Damian," she said, not sounding the slightest bit apologetic. "But what you *thought* you did here? That's exactly why we're doing this."

"No!" he shouted, but his words were slurring now as more and more Sleep spells hit him, breaking through his natural defenses. "This can't . . . *You* can't do this. . . ."

The rock beneath Rachel launched upward, sending her flying in the air. A gust of wind from behind her propelled her forward, and she landed gently just in front of Damian, holding what looked like a chain made entirely out of silver balls.

"This comes courtesy of Sierra," she said, showing off the necklace. "We basically combined every remaining Mind magic chain together, and then Jia filled it up with Sleep spells besides."

Damian tried to shout again, but he seemed to be struggling not to nod off.

Fort couldn't believe any of this was happening. Their plan was actually *working*! All of this time, he'd thought for sure that Damian would destroy the Oppenheimer students, but together, Rachel and Jia had come up with a way to actually beat him!

"There's a part of Damian that doesn't understand the consequences of what he's doing," Jia had said a week earlier. "Trust me on that. If we can make him *think* he's beaten us, and badly, it might wake him up to what he's become."

"Which would then be the perfect time to take him *down*," Rachel had said, and the two high-fived.

Fort never thought it'd happen, never could have imagined

Damian would fall for it, but here they were. Could it be that he wouldn't have to destroy magic after all?

That would be good, considering he still had no idea how to do it.

Rachel placed the necklace over Damian's neck, then stepped back proudly. "Good night, Dragon B—" she started to say.

Then she froze in a glow of yellow magic.

So did Jia. So did *all* of the Oppenheimer students.

Fort's eyes widened, and he shook his head in horror.

No. Oh *no*. This couldn't be happening.

He looked all around the battlefield below, but he couldn't see her anywhere, couldn't find . . .

And then she appeared, with a small army of soldiers behind her. At her side were Colonel Charles, Agent Cole, and . . . and *Gabriel.*

Fort's whole body felt weak as he saw the entire plan unraveling before his eyes. They had lost, just like he'd thought they would . . . but not because Damian was too strong.

No, this was all *his* fault.

After all, he'd been the one to release Sierra from her Mind necklace, then hadn't returned in time to send her away or have her wipe her memories.

"Take that off my lord, would you, Rachel?" Sierra said, and a mind-controlled Rachel reached out and freed Damian from the silver chain. And then Sierra looked up directly at Fort. "Come on down, buddy! You're the one who made this all happen, after all."

- TWENTY-TWO -

THE OPPENHEIMER STUDENTS, ALL glowing yellow, backed away from Damian, canceling their spells. Without their Sleep magic, he was able to think again and immediately teleported out of the rock and over to where Sierra and the TDA forces awaited him.

"A bit late, weren't you?" he asked her as Fort just stared at them in shock.

She looked absolutely horrified by this, then bowed deeply. "I can't apologize enough, my lord!" she said, her voice quaking with guilt. "What punishment is appropriate? Should I wipe my own mind, or would you like to teleport me to the moon? I deserve it!"

Damian waved a hand, dismissing her request, and she stood back up, staring at him with a look of gratitude that made Fort completely sick to his stomach. There had to be a way to fix things! There must be a spell in his head, vision or no vision, that would cancel out Damian's Spirit magic on Sierra.

Fort brought the words to mind and opened his mouth, only to freeze as blue light surrounded him, paralyzing his body, including his tongue, stopping his spell before it even started.

Damian glanced up in his direction and smiled. "Wait your turn, Forsythe. I have to catch up with some old friends first."

Fort screamed in frustration, but it only came out as a sad moan. He could hear Ember growling next to him and knew she'd been paralyzed as well. His stomach turned over so much he would have thrown up if he hadn't been frozen.

"Colonel Charles," Damian said, moving to stand in front of the colonel and Agent Cole. "I notice Sierra's not using Mind magic on you. I assume she's made a deal with you?"

"Let's get one thing straight, *boy*," Colonel Charles sneered. "I'm here to get my son back and destroy the ones who took him. Once that happens, then all bets are off. We'll take you down *hard*."

Damian laughed in his face. "Sounds like fun." He glanced at Agent Cole, and a low growl came from his throat. "*You*. I remember you. You're the one who captured Sierra and me in London."

"Just doing my job," Agent Cole said, looking as disgusted as Fort felt. "In fact, if you two want to surrender now, I'd be happy to accept."

Damian stared at her for a moment, then raised a hand. She didn't even have time to react before disappearing in a burst of green light.

"That *wasn't* the deal!" Colonel Charles roared, stepping toward Damian, but stopped in place as his legs froze, paralyzed by Damian's magic.

"Oh, she's fine," Damian told him with a shrug. "I just dropped her in London and used some Illusion magic to make her look like a Dracsi. We'll see how merciful the UK army is feeling."

No! Fort moaned in frustration again. He hated Agent Cole almost as much as he hated Colonel Charles, but she didn't deserve *that*. Damian was even further gone than he'd feared, and it *had* to be the Spirit magic. But that still didn't explain how Sierra could be under his spell.

"Can we bring Fort down already?" Sierra asked, staring up at him. "He's thinking so loudly, and I can't block him out. We're too connected."

Without looking, Damian snapped his fingers, and a

familiar green light covered Fort. He immediately found himself standing opposite Sierra and Colonel Charles, neither of whom looked very happy.

"I'm sorry, Fort," Sierra said quietly, looking down at the ground. "I couldn't hold on to your mind, and when I went looking for it, it was just *gone.* I don't know where you went, but I couldn't find you anywhere. I looked for Jia, but by then too much time had passed, and my lord's spell kicked in." She looked back up, meeting his eye. "I would do *anything* for my lord Damian, of course. But I really wish I hadn't failed *you* in the process." She sighed.

Fort's heart broke at her words, but the feeling passed immediately as Colonel Charles groaned. "Do I have to stand here and listen to this nonsense?" He pointed a finger at Fort's face. "*You.* Gabriel told me you intended to destroy magic. You disgust me, Fitzgerald." The colonel sneered. "Not only would that have deprived our great nation of its most powerful weapon, but it would have also ensured I'd never see my son again. There was no way I was letting *that* happen. You forced me to ally myself with this . . . *creature.*" He pointed at Damian.

Gabriel moved to stand in front of Fort, who couldn't look away, not while he was still under a Paralyze spell. "You *lied* to me, Fort," Gabriel said softly, right in Fort's face. "You said that spell would take me back to the Dracsi world after all this was over, but it wouldn't have worked if you'd gotten rid of magic. Sierra told me everything, once Damian arrived." He gestured around at the mind-controlled students. "This, by the way? This feeling of losing, knowing there's nothing you can do to save the people you love? That's how *I* felt when you made me abandon my *brother*. So I hope you enjoy it."

Fort tried to respond, but all that came out was a low moaning noise. Gabriel just looked at him with disgust, then shoved him hard, sending Fort flying.

Fort landed painfully, his body still in the position he'd been standing in, his head hitting the dirt hard enough to almost knock him out. He groaned, but the pain quickly shut off as yellow light glowed around him, removing the pain from his conscious mind. "Hey!" Sierra yelled, moving to his side protectively. "Try that again, and I'll make sure *you* feel it all, not him."

"Whatever," Gabriel said, then stood behind his father.

Are you okay? Sierra asked in his mind as she felt around his head. *Does this hurt?*

Pain shot through his skull at her touch. *Yes!* he said in her mind. *All of it, but you being under his spell the most! Please, Sierra, you have to* fight *it!*

She looked down at him sadly, then slowly stood back up. *There's nothing to fight, Fort. This is how it's meant to be.*

It was as if he'd lost Cyrus again. Everything was falling apart, too quickly for Fort to even grasp how bad it was. He tried to respond to Sierra, but before he could, his body rose from the ground and floated over to where Damian was waiting. Even paralyzed, Fort could feel the magic radiating off Damian and cursed himself for failing everyone so badly.

Not only had he failed Sierra, but he hadn't even found a way to destroy magic. And worse, he might not have even needed to, because it looked as if Jia and Rachel's plan would have *worked.* Without Sierra's magic, they'd have actually stopped Damian.

And now there were no more options, no more backup plans. They'd lost. And the Old Ones would return.

"Forsythe," Damian said, staring at Fort like he was some kind of bug. "Sierra tells me you intended to destroy magic." He reached out a hand, and the invisible magic holding Fort in place tightened around his body, slowly crushing him. He tried to scream but still couldn't control his voice, so only groaned loudly. "I'm sure you didn't think this far ahead, but do you know what destroying magic would have done to *me*? I'm *made* of it, you pathetic little nothing!"

The pain was immense, and even if Fort could have spoken, he'd have had trouble coming up with any spells due to the extreme agony. He moaned again, just wishing there was some way out of this . . .

And then Ember plowed into Damian, knocking him to the ground.

"You do *not* hurt my father!" she roared, and lashed out with her teeth and claws, raking them across Damian's chest. Damian screamed in pain, then quickly morphed back into his own dragon form, now missing several scales where she'd attacked.

"You were paralyzed!" Damian roared at Ember, knocking her away with a powerful blow from his paw.

"I'm a *real* dragon," she said back with a sneer, showing all of her teeth. "Which means I'm as naturally resistant as you are, if not more so. I was *pretending*, Elder, until I had my chance to strike." She glared at him in a rage. "You have a lot to learn, don't you?"

Too quick for her to dodge, Damian grabbed her with

his teeth and threw her aside, then cast spells at once right at Ember, but the younger dragon just brushed them aside with her own magic. "He treats you like a *pet*," Damian said, sneering right back at her. "Has he let you out without a leash yet?"

Ember slowly smiled. "You sound scared, Elder. Good. You should be. From what Father tells me, you didn't know about your dragon heritage until recently. But *I* have been attuned with magic from the beginning."

Damian snorted. "That means nothing. We shouldn't be fighting, little one. We're the last two dragons and should stand against these humans. Join me, and I won't hurt you."

Ember laughed, then pointed at the missing scales on his chest. "It looks like *you're* the one who's hurt, Elder." With that, she launched herself back at him, even as several of Damian's spells exploded off her scales and into the TDA army, sending a group of soldiers reeling. One bolt of lightning almost hit Fort, but Ember managed to knock it aside with her tail, even as she raked her claws over Damian's haunches, making the older dragon scream out again.

"Do you not know what your 'father' plans?" Damian shouted at her, striking out with his own claws, only for Ember to teleport behind him and attack again. "Forsythe wants to destroy magic *altogether*! If he does so, *you* would *die*, too!"

Ember flinched at this but narrowed her eyes dangerously. "He told me that we might need to leave," she said quietly.

"We?" Damian said. "He never cared for you. He'd have given you up in a heartbeat."

No! That wasn't true, and Ember knew it! Fort struggled against his paralysis with all of his strength but still couldn't budge a muscle.

Ember, though, flashed him a glance, the slightest doubt entering her eyes, and it was enough. While she wasn't looking, Damian reached around and grabbed her by her neck. He pulled her forward, over his shoulder, and slammed her into the ground hard enough to almost knock the rest of the soldiers off their feet.

Don't touch her! Fort screamed in his mind, unable to do anything else. But even worse, he couldn't reassure Ember, let her know that he'd never have abandoned her, and he'd have done everything he could to still see her in Avalon.

But he'd hidden the truth in the past, and now she couldn't be sure. Just another failure on his part that would end up dooming them all.

"The humans can't be trusted!" Damian shouted at Ember as he held her head to the ground, avoiding her thrashing claws. "They'll promise you the world, but all they care about is themselves!"

"Lies!" Ember shouted, but she sounded less sure now, even as she struggled against the older dragon.

"No, *humans* lie," Damian told Ember, holding her down as he glared at Fort with pure hatred. "Because they lack our power, our connection to the chaos. They're jealous of us and must be controlled, ruled over, if we're to have peace. It's the only way."

"Father!" Ember shouted. "He's . . . I can't—"

And then she went silent as her eyes began to glow with a purple light.

Spirit magic.

NO! Fort couldn't let Damian take another of his loved ones away, not like this. He doubled his efforts to free himself, pushing against the magical hold on his muscles until he felt like his head might explode from the effort, but it was like the connection was completely blocked, and nothing moved.

Not knowing what else to do, he shouted *LET ME* GO*!* in the language of magic and put all of his willpower behind it, every last ounce of anger and guilt and sorrow he felt.

Just like that, he crashed to the ground, pain shooting through his body again. He groaned and pushed himself to his feet, not even realizing at first that he was free and could move.

"What?" Damian said, glaring at him in confusion. "How did you free yourself?"

Fort didn't say a word. He reached for the Healing staff on his back and held it in a defensive gesture. If he could hit Ember with it, the staff's magic might be able to restore her, since she'd only just been taken over.

"Let her *go*!" he shouted, and leaped straight at Damian. The dragon breathed a plume of fire at him, only for Fort to pass through a teleportation portal before the fire could hit and emerge just behind both dragons. He drove his staff down toward Ember's paw—

But Damian was faster. He swung out with his tail, sending the staff spinning off into the courtyard.

"So pathetic," the dragon sneered as he let go of Ember, who stood up, staring at Fort with the same rage that Damian had. "I don't know how you did that, but I'm glad you did. I've been waiting for *this* for far too long."

"Ember!" Fort shouted, holding his hands up in surrender, hoping she could somehow resist the Spirit magic like all the other spells. "Everything I told you was the truth. I'm sorry I ever hid anything from you. All I cared about was making sure you were okay. Please believe me!"

Ember growled low in her throat, and Fort could feel the heat from the building fire. This wasn't working; he had to get rid of that Spirit spell somehow!

"They all betray us eventually," Damian said to Ember as she let loose a dangerous-sounding growl and took a step toward Fort. "You would have learned that sooner or later. I just wanted to speed up the process."

Fort's one Healing spell wouldn't cut it, not against Damian's magic, which meant he'd need to use the language of magic again if he wanted to free Ember. He could already feel a vision coming on just from releasing himself, but if he could cancel Damian's Spirit magic, it wouldn't matter what happened to him: Ember could take care of the rest. He just had to give her a chance.

"I hope you can forgive me," he whispered to her in English, then changed to the language of magic. *"Free this dragon from— "*

Ember slammed against him, knocking him to the ground and disrupting his spell. "You lied to me, *Father*," Ember said, her teeth just inches from his face. "You told me you wanted me near, yet you would have sent me away or *killed* me when you destroyed magic. Damian is right—you *cannot* be trusted!"

"I'd *never* let you be hurt!" Fort shouted at her, barely able to argue—or even think—as the vision began to cloud his mind. He frantically tried to put together more spell words, anything that might be of use, but nothing was coming to him. "Ember, I *never* want you to leave me, but I need to protect you *and* the world—"

Before he could finish, she snarled, then launched an attack straight at his head, her jaws wide open.

"No!" Fort shouted, throwing his arms up to stop her, barely able to believe she'd actually hurt him . . .

But her teeth didn't close around him. Instead, he opened his eyes to find himself back on his feet, facing Damian.

"Wow, she wasn't pretending *that* time, was she?" Damian said with a wide smile. "That must have hurt, eh, Forsythe?" He turned to Ember, who obediently bowed before him. "I like the initiative, but this one is *mine*, young one. And I'm not done with him yet."

Fort stared at his dragon in shock. Even with everything, even with Ember being controlled by Spirit magic, he couldn't imagine she'd actually hurt him, not Ember. But maybe it wasn't just the Spirit magic. After all, he'd hidden so many things from her that she couldn't trust him anymore.

None of his friends could. All the things he'd done to try to help, or save someone, he'd ended up lying and betraying other people in the process.

And now here he was, alone against two dragons, and no one deserved that more. If he'd told Jia and Rachel what he was doing, they could have made sure Sierra was safe. And if he hadn't tricked Ember to begin with, trying to get her to Avalon, she'd probably still trust him.

No matter what Damian did to him, it couldn't be worse than how he already felt, staring at the hatred in Ember's eyes and knowing he'd just doomed the world.

You have much to learn, the woman's voice from the vision said, pulling Fort's mind away from Ember and Damian, the worst thing that could possibly happen at the moment.

He desperately fought against it, pushing back as hard as he could, but he knew he couldn't last long. The vision was just too powerful.

Damian grabbed the Healing staff in his jaws, then whipped it right at Fort, who managed to catch it in a daze as it slammed into his chest, almost fumbling it to the ground. "This has been a long time coming, Forsythe," Damian said to him, rearing up on his hind legs. "I've gone easy on you each time, knowing you weren't born on Discovery Day and therefore useless. But your constant interference must come to an end, and if I enjoy it too, well, who could blame me? Now *defend* yourself, with that staff or with whatever magic you think you possess."

Fort felt his legs go weak as the world around him shimmered, the vision crashing over him like a wave. He held up the Healing staff as best he could, remembering Sergeant Tower's instructions, but the staff shook in his hands as the woman's voice grew louder.

You must *see, Forsythe!* she said. *You have been chosen for this from the start!*

Damian reared his head back in surprise and anger. "Who is speaking to you? *You* were not chosen, you sad little human. *I* am the one destiny picked to fight the Old Ones! You were chosen for *nothing*!"

Fort had no idea how to even respond to that, or the woman's voice. The staff fell from his limp hands, and he stumbled forward, barely able to keep standing. "I'm not chosen," he said quietly. "I never wanted to be. I was just trying to help."

The world began to shimmer around him, something he

didn't remember from other visions, but for all he knew, he'd just forgotten. It wasn't like he was thinking the most clearly at the moment.

Damian began to laugh. "Then you failed, human. And now you pay the price."

Just like Ember had a moment earlier, Damian came straight at Fort, his jaws open wide enough to take Fort's head off.

But before Damian could reach him, something grabbed Fort from behind as his sight began to waver, and suddenly he was no longer outside the destroyed Oppenheimer School. Now it looked like he was standing in an almost familiar-looking castle, staring up at someone who could not possibly have been there.

"I'm breaking the rules, but I *couldn't* let you be hurt," Fort's father told him sadly.

Fort blinked, his mind completely fogged over now. "Wow, *this* is the strangest vision yet!" he said, just as everything went dark.

- TWENTY-THREE -

Y*OU MUST SEE IT,* THE WOMAN'S voice said.

But another voice, one from inside Fort, was louder: *You failed.*

And that inner voice kept Fort's mind in the present, even as he found himself standing on the edge of an island floating above the ocean, covered in fog. He looked around, every part of him wanting, *needing* to go back to the Oppenheimer School, to try to rescue Ember and his friends from Damian. He had no idea where the dream of the castle and his father had gone and didn't care. Right now he needed to wake up.

"Hello?" Fort shouted, looking all around him. But other than the sounds of the ocean below, he heard nothing in response. "Please, let me wake up! I don't know why I'm getting these visions, or what they're trying to show me, but I can't be here. I have to get back!"

All you have to do is see, the woman's voice said, this time from behind him. Fort turned, and in the distance, he could see a figure approaching through the fog.

"I've seen enough!" Fort yelled at whoever it was. "I don't have time for this. My entire world is about to be destroyed, and I have no idea how to stop it, but I can't stay here. Please, just send me back!"

You have been chosen for a reason, said the voice as the figure approached, still masked by the fog. *Your choice will—*

"Oh, *forget this*," Fort said, not willing to wait another second. He concentrated as hard as he could, then willed with all of his might for these awful visions to just stop, to go away already. *"Leave me alone!"* he yelled in the language of magic.

The woman seemed to cry out, almost in pain . . . and then she was gone.

So was the island, and the ocean below it.

Only Fort wasn't back at the Oppenheimer School. Instead, now he floated in a great darkness, almost like space without the light from stars.

Great. Of course he'd just make things worse by trying to end these visions.

"Please, let me wake up!" he shouted, but there was no response now. Maybe his spell had been *too* specific, and now the voice really was leaving him alone.

And that meant he could be trapped here for who knew how long.

Fort let out a primal scream, unable to take any more of this. His friends were trapped under Damian's magic, and somehow he was stuck in the middle of nothing, with no way to escape.

"Look, I'm sorry!" he said loudly, hoping whoever it was could still hear him. "I shouldn't have made you leave me alone. Please, send me back. I need to help my friends, my whole world!"

But there was no answer.

He screamed again in frustration, then forced himself to take a deep breath. Clearly yelling wasn't helping, so it could be that he was going about this the wrong way. Casting a spell had gotten him here, so maybe another spell would get him home?

"Send me back!" Fort said in the language of magic, then waited for something spectacular to happen.

And something spectacular *did* happen.

YOU DARE COMMAND ME IN MY OWN REALM? shouted the woman's voice, her words hitting Fort like knives, cutting into his body without a trace of blood, but causing just as much pain. *YOU HAVE LEARNED NOTHING FROM WHAT I'VE SHOWN YOU, AND I CANNOT UNDERSTAND WHY EMRYS WOULD CHOOSE YOU!*

The agony was intense, but somehow, Fort understood her words through the pain. *Emrys* chose him? That's what the zombie magician had said too.

Whatever it meant, he didn't have time for it now. He had to get back to the school before Damian summoned the Old Ones.

"Just let me *go*!" he shouted, looking all around for the woman and seeing nothing but darkness. "If I don't get back there and find a way to stop him, Damian will bring the Old Ones back to my world. They'll destroy everything, and I can't let that happen! I don't care if you're on *their* side or not—"

This time, the pain was easily a thousand times worse.

THEY DID THIS TO ME! the voice roared, echoing throughout the endless darkness. *I WILL NEVER FORGIVE THEM, AND I WILL HAVE MY REVENGE!*

The nothingness surrounding Fort broke like shattered glass

at the power of her words, falling away to reveal the same familiar-looking castle room he'd seen his father in at the start of the vision, and Fort found himself sitting on the cold floor, feeling very much awake now, and pain free.

He took in a huge breath, just happy for the moment not to be attacked by the vision lady, then slowly sat up, confused. The room in the castle didn't feel the same as the island in the vision had, and he wondered if it had really been a part of the vision the last time he'd seen it.

But if it wasn't . . . where *was* he?

"Thank goodness, you're awake!" said a familiar voice, and Fort's eyes widened as he turned to find his father sitting a few feet away, giving him a worried look. "What happened to you? You fainted, and none of my glamours would wake you up."

"None of your . . . what?" Fort said, not understanding any of this. So wait, the vision *was* still happening? Was this another message from the woman, trying to show him whatever she insisted he needed to see? But what did that have to do with his father?

And glamours were the magic the faeries used. Why would those matter to the woman?

His father, or the vision that looked like his father, rubbed his temples. "Look, Fort, I know this is going to be a lot to take in, especially with everything happening, but I couldn't let you . . . I was ordered not to interfere, but I just couldn't . . . I *had* to bring you to safety here on Avalon."

"You brought me . . . to Avalon?" Fort said, feeling even more lost than before. At least in the other visions, the confusion had felt natural, like how everything in dreams just made sense. But now it felt like his brain had combined a bunch of unrelated elements of his life, none of which belonged together.

"The queen forbade me, but I couldn't obey," his father said, coming closer. "I have all his memories, and I couldn't just . . . I'm too much like him, Fort!" The man grabbed his stomach, looking like he might throw up. "She did too good a job on me, and not only did I know everything he knew, but I *felt* everything he felt. I loved you like I was your father! Don't you see?"

Whatever this was, Fort didn't like it at *all*. He pinched himself, hoping it'd wake him up, but the scene didn't change. "No," he said quietly. "I really *don't* see."

His father sighed. "I suppose there's an easy way to explain it all."

The air around his dad shimmered, just like it had for Fort, back when he'd faced Damian outside the school. Only instead of falling into a vision or teleporting to a castle, his father was replaced by a faerie.

A faerie that Fort recognized. Specifically, the green faerie whom Fort had crashed into when first arriving at Avalon. Only now, instead of staring at him with hate like he had back then, the faerie gazed at Fort the same way his father had, with a sort of fatherly fondness.

"Now, let me tell you about something we call a changeling," the faerie began, only to gasp in surprise as Fort threw himself at him, snarling in wild anger.

- TWENTY-FOUR -

HE'D LOST EMBER. SIERRA. JIA AND Rachel. He'd failed to stop Damian and keep the Old Ones from coming back. The world was doomed.

And now he found out that through all of his failures, he'd never even had his father back.

The man he *thought* was his dad turned out to be fake, a faerie changeling.

His father hadn't woken up in the medical bay. Hadn't had long talks with him on the drive home from the Oppenheimer School. Didn't joke with him over pizza at his aunt's house. Didn't hug him good night.

Didn't try to take him away from everything when Fort had told him all the secrets he'd been hiding.

None of it had been real. He didn't even have his father.

And that meant he had *nothing*. Not anymore.

Almost from a distance, he saw himself slam the green faerie's shoulders down against the marble floor of the castle, screaming something in a rage. But the loss was just too much to even comprehend, and he couldn't do anything but watch as he attacked the faerie with all of his strength.

"What did you do with my father?" he heard himself scream.

"I *am* your father, Forsythe!" the faerie said, not even bothering to fight back, which just made Fort attack even harder. "Well, not in the way *you* are probably thinking, but in every other way. So all the ways that matter!"

The faerie's words cut through the fog in Fort's brain, and he forced himself to pull back, still in shock, but not sure what was happening now. "What . . . are you still him? Just turned into a faerie?"

The green boy winced. "Oh, no, not at all. I've always been a faerie. The queen turned me into your *father* so that I could report back on what human magic users were up to because—GAH!"

Fort pulled his fist back after punching the faerie in the stomach as the rage took over, any distance between it and his mind now completely gone as he embraced it. *"You've been lying to me this whole time!"* he growled. "I *never* had my father back! Where *is* he? Tell me, *now*!"

The boy shimmered and disappeared right out from under him, dropping Fort to the floor, only to reappear at his side, standing now and holding his stomach. "Really, son, we should talk about this," the boy said, sounding like he was in pain. "I have all your father's memories and feelings, so I really *do* see you as my son, just as much as he would. The queen forbade me from interfering in the battle against Damian, but I couldn't stand by and let you be hu—"

With a roar of anger, Fort launched himself at the faerie, knocking them both back to the floor, but again, the faerie used his glamour to escape. "Okay, young man, this is enough!" the faerie said when he reappeared a moment later, giving Fort a stern look. "I've been lenient on you so far, because I know how shocking this must seem, but this behavior *isn't* acceptable, and as your father—"

This time Fort kicked the other boy in the gut, doubling him over. "Enough?" he shouted as the faerie collapsed to the floor. "You took *everything* from me! He was all I had left, and *you stole him*!"

"Don't worry," the faerie gasped, looking up at Fort sadly. "I . . . forgive you . . . for this. And if it comes out . . . during your presidential election, I'll deny it to . . . the press, because I . . . I *love* you, son."

"Stop calling me that!" Fort screamed, and kicked out again, only for the faerie to roll away. Another shimmer, and this time Fort found himself unable to move, frozen in place. He shouted in anger and frustration, but no matter how much he struggled, he couldn't move.

"There, *now* maybe we can talk," the faerie said, standing up and brushing himself off in a way that reminded Fort *far* too much of how his father moved, all gangly and awkwardly. "As I was *saying*, I was forbidden from interfering, but I couldn't let that dragon hurt you. I begged the queen to send a contingent of warriors to your side, but she reminded me that our magic barely affects dragons, and it wouldn't have done any good. Not that she would have helped anyway, without getting something in return." He shook his head sadly. "What else *could* I do? I had to disobey her order, and—"

"Tell me where my father is," Fort said through clenched teeth, his mouth still working, thankfully. "*What did the queen do with him?* Tell me he's okay. If you've hurt him in *any way*—"

The faerie's face fell, and he looked away guiltily. "Ah, well, right, *that*. Well, your *other* father is still in his coma—"

The faerie's words sent a wave of rage crashing in Fort's head, and he could barely think as he doubled his struggle against the glamour holding him in place. "He's *not* my other father—he's my *only* father!"

"But the queen thought he might be useful," the faerie continued, "so she has him locked up here, in her castle. Something about wanting to learn humanity's weakness from him. Now, if she had asked me, I could have told her *my* major weakness is a good steak fry. Can't stop eating them!" He laughed, only to trail off at Fort's death glare. "So, uh, right. She fulfilled her promise to the letter, Fort, even if not the way you thought. He's perfectly safe and protected, as she agreed to. She never said you'd have him back."

"The bargain also never said anything about stealing him away and replacing him with a changeling!" Fort shouted, his whole body pushing to attack the boy again, then go after the queen. He couldn't remember ever being this angry in his life, not even at the Dracsi.

Those monsters had been mindless, almost like a force of nature. But the faerie queen and his fake father had done this *deliberately*.

Footsteps from farther inside the castle made the faerie flinch, and he raised a finger to his lips to shush Fort. "Let's keep it down, Fort," he said. "Remember when we used to play the quiet game on car trips—"

Fort gritted his teeth. "Yes I do, but you don't, *because you were never there*!"

The faerie sighed. "I know this is all a shock, Fort, but I thought I raised you to be more open-minded than this." Before Fort could even begin to respond to *that*, he felt his mouth freeze in mid-shout, and the air shimmered around both of them.

Two of the queen's guards entered the small room where the faerie had brought Fort and glanced around for a moment, even looking right through the spot Fort was standing in. But somehow they didn't seem to see him and shook their heads, closing the door behind them as they left.

"You aren't supposed to be here," the faerie whispered to Fort, reappearing next to the door. "If they find out I removed you from the battle, they'll throw me in the dungeons for a few thousand years." He looked back at Fort with a disgusting fatherly gaze. "Still, I'd do it again in a second to save you."

Fort tried to let the boy know exactly what he thought of *that*, but the faerie hadn't released his mouth yet, so he put all of his rage and hatred into his eyes instead.

That seemed to get the point across, as the faerie shuddered. "I *really* didn't think you'd take this so badly," he said, looking a bit hurt. "Wasn't I a good father? I kept up the act the entire time, since I of course knew everything you'd been through. And wasn't that a good story, about the TDA telling me about your memory and all? I thought that worked out rather well. Saved me trying to act surprised, at least, when you finally shared what'd been going on with me." He sighed. "I don't exactly have a plan as to what to do next, but we'll need to hide you from the queen. The only place I can think of on Avalon is with the dragons, if they'll take us. If not, maybe I can offer myself as a bargain for them to keep you safe."

The rage in his head kept Fort from following whatever the faerie was saying. All he could think about was how he'd tried to do good, tried to save his father from the Dracsi, save humanity and his dragon from the Old Ones, only to fail in every possible way.

And now he was alone in Avalon with *nothing*. No father, no dragon, no friends. If he hadn't been so angry, the utter loneliness and despair he felt would have taken up the slack.

The only reason he didn't just give up completely was the small hope that his father was out there somewhere in Avalon, still in his coma, but otherwise protected. He fought to push down the rage for now, just so he could concentrate on finding his dad and freeing him from the faerie queen.

When his father was safe, *then* he could unleash all of his fury on the faerie queen and this boy.

"I suppose we could look in a different dimension, too," the faerie continued, apparently having never stopped talking. "There's that dimension of gaseous beings that don't notice solid creatures, so that could work." He wrinkled his nose. "There's always the danger of smelling one of them by accident, though, which is basically their form of murder. Plus, they *stink*. So maybe we could try the dimension of giants instead. There must be mouse holes in their castles, something the right size for you."

Footsteps sounded again outside the door, and the faerie quickly cast his glamour once more. But this time when the door opened, it wasn't a guard, but instead someone Fort was actually happy to see for once.

"Oh, this has *got* to be a joke," Xenea said as she stepped inside the room and closed the door quietly behind her. "Seriously? You brought him *here*? I could smell his human stink from across the castle!"

- TWENTY-FIVE -

THE FAERIE BOY SHIMMERED BACK into view, looking even guiltier than he had about taking over Fort's father's life. "Ah, Xenea, you see—"

She snapped her fingers, and the faerie boy collapsed to the floor and immediately began snoring loudly. And just like that, Fort was free of his spell and could move again.

"Xenea?" Fort said, barely able to think straight now. Part of him wanted to thank her for freeing him, but the rest was just too furious to go there. "Did you know about my father?"

She held up her hands for him to stop. "No, I didn't know." She paused, like she was considering. "Well, okay, yes I did, but not the *whole* story. I mean, obviously I could tell he was one of the Tylwyth Teg, since he smelled like one. But he wouldn't tell me why he was there, or what was going on. But that doesn't matter right now."

"Doesn't *matter*?" Fort said quietly, holding himself back from attacking her now only because he knew she could easily take him down, like she had in the park. "The faerie queen stole my father and replaced him with this *boy*, and you're saying it doesn't *matter*?"

She winced. "Doesn't matter right *now*, I said. We have to get you out of here. If the queen knew you were back on Avalon or that *he* brought you here—"

"I didn't ask to come here!" Fort shouted, but quieted down as he heard footsteps in the distance again. "I was *trying* to stop Damian," he said after they'd passed. "Only I messed it up and failed everyone. And now I find out that I never even had my father!"

Xenea rubbed her temples like she had a headache. "Ugh. I don't want to get involved in *any* of this. The queen's mad enough at me already for not bringing her your dragon. The last thing I need to do is get lumped in with you and your dad here when she starts handing out lifetime sentences."

"He's not my father!" Fort hissed.

"Well, I need to find out what he was planning on doing with you, so I'm waking your not-father back up," she said, then snapped her fingers before he could stop her.

The changeling faerie immediately sat up, looking a bit groggy, as Fort restrained himself with all his might, just for Xenea's sake. "*That* was unnecessary," the faerie told Xenea. "If we weren't in the middle of hiding from the queen, I'd be tempted to turn you over to her for an unlawful glamour!"

"You just had a human acquaintance of mine under *your* glamour without his consent, *Helio*," she told him. "I'm happy to bring *that* up to the queen. Not to mention that you were supposed to leave him in the middle of the battle!"

"*You* were supposed to be delivering her the dragon!" said the changeling, whose name was apparently Helio—probably a completely fine name ordinarily, but one that now Fort hated with the white-hot intensity of a thousand suns. "If Ember hadn't been there, Damian wouldn't have been able to take her over, and maybe Fort would have had a chance. As it was, there was no way my boy could stand against them both—"

"I'm not your boy!" Fort hissed, forgetting about the restraint as he readied himself for another attack on Helio.

Xenea seemed to sense this, as she quickly stepped between them. "Listen to me, Forsythe," she said quietly. "No one would like to see you beat up Helio more than me. And if we have time later, I'll definitely make that happen. It'll be fun.

I'll even glamour up some of your pizza for snacks. But for now, the queen specifically ordered Helio *not* to bring you here, which means not only is *he* in a truly astounding amount of trouble—"

"Good!" Fort said, staring at Helio.

"I forgive you for this anger, my boy," Helio told him, making Fort growl in frustration. "I'm sure I'd be angry if someone who loved *me* saved *my* life, just because they hadn't told me a tiny little secret that was completely irrelevant."

"But!" Xenea said, holding Fort physically back now. "It's not just him. The queen is going to blame *you* for being here too. You can't just go talk to her, no matter what she's done with your dad." She cringed. "It doesn't particularly help that there are now *two* dragons out there, and she doesn't have either one."

"So why don't you glamour Damian over here, and we'll solve a few problems at once?" Fort said, torn in too many directions to even know where to focus his anger at the moment.

Xenea sighed. "You know our glamours won't do much against a dragon, especially now, when he's not exactly going to be taken by surprise. And as much as I hate to agree with Helio—"

"I forgive you too, Xenea," Helio said. "How could I stay angry at anyone who likes pizza that much?"

For a moment, Xenea looked like she might take a swing at him, which made Fort like her a lot more. "As much as I hate to agree with him," she repeated, "he's right: That battle wasn't exactly great for your general health. Damian was going to *destroy* you. But you knew that, right? That's why you had some secret plan?"

Fort gritted his teeth, not wanting to talk about how he'd failed completely at his "secret plan," or even worse, that she was right about going back. The way Damian was acting, Fort had no idea how far he'd go. "I let them all down," he whispered. "Ember, my friends, the whole world. And now it's too late. There's nothing more to be done. Damian's going to summon the Old Ones, and lose. And those monsters will take over the whole world."

Xenea and Helio looked at each other, then together held up one hand each. The air between their hands began to shimmer, and an image appeared, revealing Damian in dragon form holding the remaining two books of magic, Healing and Destruction, that had been in the possession of the TDA.

"Would you do the honors, little sister?" he asked, handing them to Ember, who stood at his side, looking proud.

Fort stared at the image in amazement. Ember was okay? And Damian hadn't opened a portal to the Old Ones yet! Could there really still be time?

"Of course, Revered Elder," Ember said, making Fort's stomach turn. She unleashed a plume of dragon fire straight into the books, and they burst into flame, disintegrating into ash within moments.

Damian wiped the remains from his paws, immune to the fire of his own kind. "And now magic once again belongs to dragons alone, as it was always meant to."

"*Now* will we destroy the Old Ones, my lord?" said another familiar voice, and Fort swallowed a lump in his throat as he saw Rachel move in to stand beside Damian, Jia at her side.

If he had just gone along with their plan, teleported Sierra away . . . they might be okay now, and Damian would be beaten. But instead, the Old Ones taking over felt inevitable, even if it hadn't occurred yet.

"We aren't ready," Damian told her. "I haven't finished arming all of the TDA soldiers." He paused. "And I'd imagine it'd be safer to put them under my control as well with Spirit magic."

"My soldiers are just fine under my command, Damian," said another voice, and Fort felt his anger rise again as Colonel

Charles appeared in the image. "They'll listen to me, and me alone."

"That better be good enough, Colonel," Damian said, his eyes narrowing as he showed his fangs. "Be thankful we have an agreement, or I'd use Spirit magic on you, as well."

Colonel Charles sneered at him and lifted the merged chain of Mind magic protective baubles from below his shirt. "Oh, I'm sure you could overpower all of these eventually, but in the meantime, my soldiers would take you down." He glared at the dragon. "Get me my son back from the Old Ones, and I'll make sure you have all the loyalty you need."

Damian tilted his head. "We are allies for the moment, Colonel, nothing more. And when this is over . . ."

"We'll see who's left standing," the colonel said.

"Get your soldiers prepared, then," Damian said. "We leave as soon as they're ready for Washington, D.C."

"Why there, my lord?" Jia asked.

"Because I want the world to see my victory," the dragon said, and grinned widely.

Xenea made a vomiting noise and dropped her hand, causing the shimmering image to disappear. "Ugh, how can you stand to even *listen* to their human ridiculousness?" she said to Fort. "Is that what you're all like inside, arrogant and convinced you're right?"

"Too many of us," Fort whispered, just trying to concentrate on the fact that his friends were all okay. As much as he hated the idea of them under Damian's Spirit magic, at least it gave the dragon no reason to hurt them.

Of course, that didn't mean he'd protect them against the Old Ones, either, especially considering Damian had no chance against them.

"Forsythe," Helio started to say, only for Xenea to glamour his mouth shut, which Fort was thankful for. The last thing he needed to do was hear his fake father speak one more word.

Not while Damian hadn't yet opened a portal. Because that meant there might still be time. And while even a glance at the green faerie made him want to punch through the wall, he knew that all would have to wait, at least for the moment, while there was still time to fix his failures.

But how? He literally had nothing left: no friends, no dragon, no magic, at least not without falling into visions. What could he do, even if he did have time?

The zombie's words came back to him through the anger and despair in his mind. The magician had called Fort the chosen one and said Emrys had concealed him during a ceremony.

But clearly Cyrus had done no such thing. All he'd done was send Fort back.

Did that mean he hadn't yet messed up? That maybe he had a second chance and could get back there somehow to find out what he needed to know to actually destroy magic?

But with Cyrus there, there was no way to do that. The Old One would just send him away again, maybe even quicker this time, after meeting him once. If only there was a way to get around him. . . .

And then Fort froze as he realized something. There *was* a way to get around the past-Cyrus. Even better, it was actually here on Avalon, too.

He couldn't deal with his fake father now, not if he wanted to save his friends and the world. There wasn't any time to waste, so his anger, his revenge would have to wait.

Assuming he could pull any of this off, which was very much in doubt.

"I have to speak to the queen," he told Xenea, deliberately ignoring the faerie boy next to her as best he could so as to keep control of his emotions.

Xenea laughed, then looked at him strangely. "Wait, you're

serious?" She gave him a warm look and put a hand on his shoulder. "It wasn't great knowing you, Forsythe. But thanks for introducing me to movies!"

"I have a plan to *fix* things," he told her through clenched teeth, "but I need something she has. I know you think it's dangerous—"

"Oh, it's beyond that," Xenea said. "You're definitely going to spend an eternity in her dungeons, and that's the best-case scenario."

So? What did *that* matter? He'd already lost everything he cared about. How much worse could a lifetime in the dungeons be? "Fine. I don't care. Sometimes you don't have a choice." He paused, remembering something that might help convince her. "Remember the alien movie? Where the woman went back for the others? You didn't think humans would actually do that, but that's exactly what I'm asking to do: Send me back in, and let me fight the aliens. If I don't, all of humanity will serve the Old Ones, Xenea!"

The faerie girl gasped and put a hand against her heart. "Do *not* try to manipulate me by mentioning my precious heroine, Forsythe," she said, then looked away. "Not that it didn't almost work . . ."

"I'm sorry, what is this about aliens?" Helio said, and Fort clenched his fists, not realizing that Xenea must have freed his mouth at some point. "Xenea, there's no way on Earth I'm letting *my* little boy battle an alien armada or something."

The anger flared in Fort's mind once more, but Xenea quickly moved to block Helio from his sight. "You have to be *sure* about this," she told him. "If I take you to the queen, we'll all be in trouble, and there'll be no way to protect you. You could live a good life here on Avalon, even in hiding, and we might find a way to free your father, too."

Free his father? The words sent a pang of sadness through Fort's chest, and he almost doubled over.

Maybe it was possible. And if so, he'd spend the rest of his life trying. But right now they only had a little time left before Damian opened a portal, and the entire world would suffer if Fort didn't at least try to fix things.

He had no choice. And that just made it an even worse betrayal of his father.

"I'm sure," he told her, his mouth almost too dry to speak.

Xenea shrugged. "It's your funeral, I suppose. Not literally, since the queen will make sure you live forever, but you know what I mean. Okay, let's get this over with, then."

With that, the whole room shimmered, and suddenly they were in the throne room that Fort had last seen just a few weeks earlier, when he, Jia, Rachel, and Ellora had first come to Avalon.

Except this time it was filled with faerie guards, all aiming weapons at him, Xenea, and Helio.

"The human child?" the queen of the faeries said from her throne, next to which a frozen Cyrus stood like some kind of statue on display. "You've returned? *Please* tell me this is about fulfilling our bargain?" She leaned forward, her eyes cold and deadly. "Because if it's not, then I imagine I shall be *extremely* cross."

- TWENTY-SIX -

THE SIGHT OF CYRUS, FROZEN IN TIME like a trophy for the queen, took Fort's already wild emotions for a ride. He knew he'd have to stay calm while speaking to the queen, but between his ex-friend displayed in the throne room and his father replaced by a changeling, calm might have been just out of reach.

At least losing Cyrus wasn't his fault, not like the rest of his friends. But that thought didn't make him feel any less lonely, standing here as the only human in the faerie royal court, with no one to help if anything went wrong.

Still, he had to try. Fort took a deep breath, making sure his anger was under control. But before he could speak, Helio leaped between him and the queen. "Actually, Your Majesty," the faerie boy said, "this was *my* doing. I've brought my son—this human child, I mean—here to make another bargain. Let him stay here on Avalon, safe and protected, and I will pledge my service to you for all of time."

"What?" Fort shouted, pushing past the boy as any attempt at staying calm evaporated. "No. That's *not* why I'm here." He knew he should get to the point, bring up what he needed, but his anger over his father and the changeling boiled over for a moment. "But if we're talking about bargains, then I'd like to know why you took my father from me and sent this . . . *spy* instead!"

"You *probably* shouldn't yell at her," Xenea whispered, backing away from Fort.

The queen slowly rose from her throne as the room began to shake, making the guards around Fort a bit twitchy with their weapons. "You imply I broke my bargain, child?" she roared. "I lived up to the very letter of the agreement! All you asked was that your father be kept safe, and I have done *exactly* that. You never specified *how* that should be accomplished. But if you would like to back out of the bargain, I can always retract my side of the deal as well."

The air shimmered in front of Fort, revealing his father asleep in a luxurious-looking bed . . . and then the bed burst into flames.

"NO!" Fort shouted, backing away in horror as he witnessed the worst thing he could imagine right before his eyes. He desperately tried to open a teleportation circle to wherever his father was, but the queen snuffed it out like a candle, leaving him no other option but to beg. "Please, Your Majesty, *don't hurt him*!"

The faerie queen slowly smiled, then snapped her fingers. The fire on his father's bed disappeared, as did the image itself. "Then why don't you share with me how you are living up to *your* end of the bargain?" she said, sitting back down in her throne. "Because I do not see a dragon here."

"Yes, he's broken the agreement!" Helio shouted, pushing his way forward again. "You should keep him here in your servitude, Your Majesty. There's no other way." Fort's mouth dropped open in shock, but Helio just gave him a loving smile. "I know that's not ideal, Fort," he whispered. "But you could *die* back on Earth. I can't let you get sent back!"

Before the queen could consider Helio's words, Fort pushed the changeling out of the way. "I haven't broken anything, Your Majesty," he told the queen, grinding his teeth together over the unfairness of it all. "My end of the deal was to owe you a favor, and you asked me to help Xenea find a dragon. Well, I told her exactly where he was. I even offered to help her capture him. But he was far too powerful for either one of us, so it's not her fault she couldn't fulfill the request."

The queen narrowed her eyes. "That is indeed the payment I asked for in return for keeping your father safe." Even the mention of his dad made Fort want to punch something, but he forced himself to stay calm, knowing that blowing up again would only make things worse. "But this Damian was *not* the dragon I had in mind. Xenea, where is the baby dragon?"

"She is, ah, under this Damian's Spirit magic, Your Majesty," Xenea said, giving Fort an apologetic look. "At this point, I'm not sure we could retrieve either one, even with the human boy's help. You know how resistant the dragons are to our magic."

The queen sneered. "I do indeed, but no one is more powerful than *I*."

All of the assembled faeries murmured their agreement, while Fort fought the urge to teleport them all onto the moon. If the faerie queen was going to listen to his next bargain, it'd help to not anger her, at least any more than he already had.

But he had to stay calm. Xenea was right: He couldn't yell, or even raise his voice at the queen, or she'd punish him for it.

Whatever else he was feeling, he had to push it down deep for now, if not for his sake, then for everyone who was counting on him.

"Your Majesty, I'm told you want a dragon to use to bargain with the older ones living here on Avalon," Fort said slowly, carefully choosing every word. "As you say, you're clearly more powerful than they are, but that doesn't mean they couldn't present some . . . annoyance. Well, I might be able to take care of them for you."

The queen raised an eyebrow. "You? A human with less magic than my children? How exactly could you rid me of the elder dragons?"

"By offering them something they want," Fort said, thinking of Ember, if he did have to destroy magic. He moved on quickly, though, before she asked too many questions. "But if I did this, it would take the place of our other bargain, so I'd need my father back safely, as well as—"

"There is no 'as well as,'" the queen said. "If you take care of my dragon problem, then I will deliver your father back to you in perfect health. But that is *all*, and I will withhold my end until you deliver."

No! He'd led with the wrong thing, too weak to do otherwise, but he needed *more* if he was ever going to stop Damian! "Then I'd offer you another bargain," he said, again trying to stay calm above all else. "Because you have something I need."

"Don't do this," Xenea whispered. "You're already pushing things, and you're just going to make things worse."

"Fort, *no*!" Helio said, much louder.

The queen waved a hand, and both went silent immediately. "And what is that?" she asked, sounding more curious than anything. At least she wasn't throwing him in the dungeon . . . yet.

"I need . . . *him*," Fort said, and pointed at the frozen Cyrus next to her.

A murmur went through the throne room, while Xenea slapped her forehead. The queen just stared at Fort in amazement.

"You want *the Timeless One*?" she said, as if she couldn't believe it. "You would take my trophy, the Eternal One who cursed my children to eternal youth? You think there's anything in this world that I would desire *more* than him?"

"Yes, Your Majesty," Fort said, hoping he wasn't making things a thousand times worse, like Xenea had warned. "Because I think I might have the magic to reverse what he did to your children. What if they could age again, normally, and grow into adults?"

Out of the corner of his eye, Fort noticed that the room was getting steadily darker, and the guards had begun to back away from him, like they were giving their queen room. That didn't bode well. Neither did the fact that Xenea had also put several feet between herself and him.

"I'm here, my boy," Helio told him from just inches away, making Fort roll his eyes.

"A lowly human could never know the secrets of the Timeless One's magic," the queen said, her voice low and dangerous. "Do not toy with me, child, for you stoke my anger!"

The room began to shake again, but Fort didn't back down, knowing he'd lose his chance the moment he did. "But that's not true, Your Majesty," he said as the shaking intensified, sending his heart racing out of fear, less for himself than what it would mean for the world if he failed here. The queen's eyes began to glow as she stared at him with a deathly cold look, and he shivered but continued on. "I have every spell that exists, all inside my head." He tapped his skull. "The Timeless One himself taught them to me, and I'm sure I could find the right one to fix everything."

Okay, Merlin hadn't taught him the spells himself directly, but it was close enough. And while Fort was pretty sure he could find the right magic, he had no idea if he'd be powerful enough to actually fix every faerie's curse. But at least he could *try*.

The queen leaned forward, and the air around Fort began to shimmer. A pressure began to build in his head, and he dropped to his knees from the pain, like a headache times a thousand.

"You speak the truth," the queen said, her words cutting through the pain of her presence inside his head. "You *do* have the words that command chaos!"

Fort tried to respond, but the pain was too intense, and he only managed to moan in agony.

"Please, Your Majesty!" Helio said, dropping to Fort's side. "You're hurting him!"

"It appears that you *do* have something I want," the queen said as the pressure seemed to grow with every passing second. "But not your performance of a spell. I want it *all*, every word inside your head, child. Give me the language, and I will give you the Timeless One."

The guards, Helio, even Xenea, all gasped at this, but Fort could barely think enough to care why. The pain was too intense, and besides, what good was the magic to him if he could never use it without having another vision anyway?

But he couldn't let it go just yet.

"You . . . can have it," he groaned. "But in . . . twenty-four hours."

If he hadn't figured out how to destroy magic within the next day, it would all be too late anyway.

Abruptly, the shimmering disappeared, and the pressure in Fort's head eased. The queen gestured, and Fort found himself back on his feet, standing right before the queen. She raised a hand and shook his.

"Then you have a *bargain*," she said. "The Timeless One shall be yours, in exchange for the language of magic inside your head, to be delivered within twenty-four hours from now." She smiled. "Don't think you can hide from me, child. I've marked you now with my power, and there's nowhere you can go that I can't find you."

Fort shuddered at that but was just happy to be out of pain and to have the deal made. If it was a mistake, then he'd handle that later. For now, it almost looked like he might actually have a chance to *fix* things!

"And now, for my disobedient children," the queen said, turning to Xenea and Helio. "What shall your punishments be for failing me?"

- TWENTY-SEVEN -

"WAIT, *WHAT*?" FORT SAID, STILL able to feel the chill from the faerie queen's hand where it'd touched his own. "But Xenea didn't do anything wrong!"

"That's my boy," Helio said, patting his shoulder again. "Sticking up for those who need help."

"Helio is *definitely* guilty," Fort growled.

The patting stopped.

"*Both* have failed me," the faerie queen declared, and the guards surged forward, now that it seemed like the faerie queen wasn't going to incinerate Fort on the spot. They surrounded Helio and Xenea, weapons aimed at the two faeries. "And they are well aware of the consequences of such actions."

"Xenea never disobeyed you," Fort said, throwing a look at the faerie girl, who shook her head as if to say this wasn't going to help. But as annoying as Xenea had been over the few days he'd known her, she'd also shown herself to be . . . well, not a friend, certainly, but an acquaintance, at least. And right now she was all Fort had left, and there was no way he could abandon her to her fate just for helping him. "I kept telling her to wait for Damian to come back and hid Ember from her. If you want someone to blame, then it's me who deserves it."

"Is that a fact?" the queen asked, gesturing toward Xenea with one finger. The faerie girl went flying forward with a surprised yelp, then came to a dead stop just inches from the queen. "Tell me, Xenea: Was this human able to deceive you as he said?"

"No, Your Majesty," Xenea said, looking away. "I had the dragon in my hands and could have brought her to you, but I . . . I felt sorry for the dragon. And pity for this human." She glanced back at Fort sadly. "He and the dragon had a bond, and I didn't wish it to be broken. It did not feel . . . *right* to me."

The faerie queen was silent for a moment, then broke into a laugh so abruptly that everyone in the room jumped. "And when did I ask you what you *felt*, child?"

"Never, Your Majesty," Xenea said quietly. "I merely offer

explanation, not an excuse. I am ready for whatever punishment you decide."

Fort growled softly. Why couldn't she have just let him take the blame? Xenea was in trouble only *because* of him. And he couldn't let her be punished for it.

"That's not the whole story, Your Majesty," Fort said, stepping closer to the queen, only to find several faerie weapons now pointed at his chest. He raised his hands in surrender to the guards but didn't stop talking. "I told her about Damian, a bigger, older dragon that would soon be available and tried to convince her that he would be worth immeasurably more to you in your bargaining with the Avalon dragons."

"Immeasurably, *nice* word!" Helio whispered, making Fort want to hit him again.

The queen seemed annoyed by Fort's words, but at least the throne room wasn't shaking again. "And when did I suggest Xenea could use her own judgment as to what I desired?" the queen asked.

"You didn't," Xenea told her, giving Fort a warning look. "And I'd suggest *everyone* be quiet now if they want to leave here without spending a few thousand years in the dungeon."

"We spoke about another deal, Your Majesty," Fort said,

ignoring her. "I told you I could take care of your elder-dragon problem, and you said you would release my father if I did. Well, if that's the case, then our original deal is no longer valid, which means Xenea didn't have the right to my dragon in the first place."

Xenea blinked at this, while the queen looked at Fort thoughtfully.

"It is true that our new deal would nullify the original and therefore would mean you would not have had to help Xenea," the queen said. "But *she* was ordered to bring me a dragon, and deliberately disobeyed."

Xenea's face fell, and Fort knew he'd lost his argument. But that didn't mean he was out of ideas.

"Then may I offer a suggestion, Your Majesty?" he said, and *now* the room began to shake again. Clearly he was irritating the queen and pushing his luck by continuing to talk, but he couldn't just let Xenea be sent off to the dungeons!

"You try my patience, human," the queen said.

"There's nothing Xenea hates more than the human world," Fort said before she could change her mind. "Ask her yourself if you don't believe me. She hated how we smelled, how we charged people for food and ate fungus, all of it."

"That *is* true, Your Majesty," Xenea said, looking confused.

"If you really wish to punish her, then what better way to do that than by sending her back?"

The queen raised one eyebrow, as did Xenea. "Now, wait a moment," Xenea said, but went silent immediately after a look from the queen.

"Intriguing," the faerie queen said. "But I have my own sort of punishment in mind. My dungeon—"

"Is what your children expect by now," Fort said, hoping she wouldn't send him there for interrupting. "All the faeries know that's the punishment if they disobey. Why not make them worry a bit more by changing things up? Xenea would be a thousand times more miserable in my world than in any dungeon, trust me."

"What exactly are you suggesting, human?" the queen asked, looking just intrigued enough for Fort to think he might have a shot at saving Xenea.

"Have *Xenea* help me take care of the dragons," Fort said. "You'll both be punishing her by sentencing her to a temporary exile on my world *and* you'll be helping ensure I succeed in solving your problem. It's a win/win for you!"

"A win/win?" the queen said. "Does saying the word twice make it doubly attractive to humans?"

"Pretty much," Fort said, then held his breath and crossed his fingers. If the queen didn't go for it, he couldn't just leave Xenea to her punishment, even if it blew up all his other deals. He had no idea what magic he might be able to use, since the queen was easily far more powerful than he was. But what other choice did he have?

"I approve of this idea," the queen said finally, and Fort sighed in relief.

But then the queen smiled. "And because Helio also deserves punishment, I will send him along with you as well."

As Fort's mouth dropped in horror, he felt the faerie boy's hand clap his shoulder. "You are as wise as you are beloved, my queen," Helio said to her, then lowered his voice. "This is great, Fort!" he whispered. "I'll be able to watch over you for *years* now!"

- TWENTY-EIGHT -

XENEA LED FORT—AND ANOTHER faerie whose existence Fort refused to even acknowledge—down a staircase that seemed designed to be spooky, with wet, slippery stairs when there was no water anywhere else and torches every few dozen feet making the eerie shadows dance.

The queen had unfrozen Cyrus but insisted on sending him to the darkest, most horrible dungeon cell first, just so he'd suffer a bit longer. Her cruelty reminded Fort of his own overwhelming need for revenge after the Dracsi attack in D.C., which now turned his stomach.

But at least she was giving Cyrus up. Now all Fort had to do was get the Timeless One's help.

Because if he didn't, humanity and his friends were all doomed. There was no one left to save them, rescue them. Just Fort.

He hoped with all his heart that he really *was* some kind of chosen one, if only because it meant he might have a chance.

"We're going to talk about your idea of 'helping me' later," Xenea said to him when they were out of earshot of the faerie guards. "I could do a few hundred years in the dungeons easily. I've done it before."

"Just stick with the plan, and you won't be in my world for long," Fort told her. He'd had a quick chance to tell her what he was thinking above, while the queen was wondering aloud where to put Cyrus. "As long as the dragons—WHOA!" He caught himself on the uneven wall as his feet slipped on the slick stone stairs. "*How* do these get so wet?"

"Oh, it's magic," Xenea said. "We like to create the proper mood. It's more for the prisoners than the visitors, but I'm not sure we've ever *had* a visitor."

"Anyway, I'm sorry about all this," he told her. "You were just trying to help me, and you don't deserve to suffer for it."

She sighed. "It's my fault for being selfless. I should have known better. But no bad deed goes unpunished, as the Tylwyth Teg say. I'll be okay."

"She really will be, Fort," said the faerie Fort was pretending didn't exist.

"Do you hear something?" Fort asked Xenea. "Like the worst person alive is trying to get our attention?"

Xenea looked over his shoulder. "Yeah, that's an apt description of Helio." She winked at the other faerie.

"Hey!" Helio shouted.

"Weird that whoever it is doesn't get the hint and *stop talking*," Fort said, and the voice behind him went silent.

"We're here," Xenea said as they reached the bottom of the stairs. "This is the lowest cell in the castle, where the worst of the worst get sent. Or, they would have, if we'd ever had a prisoner bad enough for it."

"There's always a first," said a voice from inside the cell, and Fort felt his stomach drop.

The queen had done as she promised: Cyrus was unfrozen, waiting for them.

They all went silent for a moment at his voice, until finally Xenea spoke. "You know what? I'm just going to leave you to all of *this*, then." She waved a hand at the cell and Helio both. "You better be right about the dragons!"

"I hope I am," Fort whispered, but she had already shimmered away on her own mission. Hopefully, she really would be fine, but that wouldn't stop Fort from worrying about her.

She would never have been in any of this danger if not for him.

Strange how just a few days ago, he'd been completely terrified about the faerie girl stealing Ember from him, and now he was sending her to negotiate with a bunch of Avalon dragons. If magic wasn't actually chaos and possibility, as Fort was constantly getting reminded in the visions, then it certainly led to both of those things.

"Well?" Cyrus said from inside the door. "Are you faeries here to torture me for information? If so, I should tell you, I already feel just about as horrible as I possibly can. I mean, I'll try to cooperate and all, but I wouldn't expect much."

Fort grimaced, then stepped closer to the door of the cell and peeked through the small barred window.

Cyrus was sitting against a wall with his knees held tightly against his chest. The cell was otherwise empty, all but for a bucket in the corner of the room that Fort could smell from there. He wrinkled his nose in disgust: The faerie queen wasn't messing around with her awful dungeon cells, apparently.

"Just get it over with already," Cyrus said, not looking up. "Maybe it'll be a good distraction."

"Sorry," Fort said quietly, then placed his hand on the door. "If I knew you were bored, I would have brought some mystery novels." As he'd been promised, the door's lock clicked open for him—supposedly *only* for him, according to how the queen had glamoured it a few moments ago—and he pushed it open as Cyrus glanced up in shock.

"Fort?" the Old One said, his eyes wide. "What are *you* doing here?"

Fort swallowed the lump in his throat as he stared at his former friend. He should forget about all of that—he *knew* he should. But seeing Cyrus now, after losing everyone else important in his life and feeling so alone through it all, it was just impossible to ignore that this was his former best friend trapped in a dungeon—even if Fort was here to free him.

"Shouldn't you *know* why I'm here?" he asked finally, trying to pretend he didn't care. The last thing he needed was for the Old One to think he could manipulate Fort still. "I thought you'd have foreseen all of this."

Cyrus smiled weakly. "For some reason, you managed to throw quite a few of my future visions out of whack. You never managed to behave the way I foresaw you behaving. So no, I had no idea I was going to be handed over to the faeries . . . or that you'd be here now." He lowered his head again, looking at the floor. "Honestly? I'd hoped somehow that my family might come for me, even though I know that's not possible, at least not until they take Damian over or something."

As much as Fort tried to resist, his heart broke over watching his friend suffer. Cyrus wasn't hurting from losing his magic—or at least not just that. He'd done this all for his family, and from what Fort had seen of the Old Ones, they would most likely just abandon him here in the hands of the faerie queen.

"Damian hasn't summoned them yet," Fort said. "It could still happen." And then he stopped, shocked at his own words. What was he *doing*, trying to make Cyrus feel better? The Old One had manipulated him from the start and didn't deserve his pity or compassion *at all.*

Cyrus snorted. "You're more optimistic than I am. I'm not going to hold my breath."

For the briefest of moments, Fort wondered if he could use this, turn Cyrus against the other Old Ones. It couldn't hurt to have the Timeless One on their side, even without his magic. He'd know all the Old Ones' secrets, maybe even share a way to defeat them. . . .

But no. Fort couldn't do that, not to his frie—*former* friend, no matter what Cyrus had done. It was just too cruel. "Well, maybe this will take your mind off things," Fort said to him. "I'm here to break you out."

Cyrus looked up again, this time in confusion. "You're *what*? Impossible. I don't believe it."

Now it was Fort's turn to snort. "You think I came all this way just to mess with you?"

"After everything I did to you, I wouldn't be surprised," Cyrus said, then turned away. "If you think I'm going to apologize, or, I don't know, help you against my family, you might as well leave now. I'm not doing either of those things. Even if they leave me here for the rest of eternity. They're still my family."

"I'm not asking you to turn against them," Fort said, choosing his words carefully. "But I do need your help. And in return, I can give you your freedom."

Cyrus gave Fort a side glance. "And what could you possibly need me for that badly? I'd imagine I'm the last person you'd want wandering around on their own."

This was the point where everything could fall apart, and Fort couldn't help shifting back and forth nervously. If he said too much or phrased it the wrong way, Cyrus would definitely refuse. But on the other hand, if Cyrus thought he was lying or holding something back, that would probably also sink the deal.

"Do you remember when we first met?" Fort asked carefully.

Cyrus gave him a confused look, then slowly nodded realization filling his eyes. "Ah, *I* see. That's what this is about. The timeline fits, and you've got a need. You want to find out how they made magic go away a thousand years ago." He rolled his eyes. "I told you, I'm not helping you against my family."

"I'm not asking you to," Fort said. "I want your help against *you*, that's all, the you from when we first met who sent me away before I could see what Merlin and the others were doing. I need to know—"

"I *know* what you need to know, Fort, and I'm not helping you." Cyrus stood up and reached for the door, pushing it closed. "If that's all, it's been nice seeing you again."

Fort grabbed the door before Cyrus could shut it. "*Are you kidding me?* I can get you out of here! Do you want to stay locked in here for the rest of your life?"

"Oh, I won't," Cyrus said with a shrug. "Merlin wasn't trapped in here, so I'm going to get out . . . *somehow.* Not sure when or why, but it's got to be a better deal than turning against my family." He tried to close the door again, but Fort pushed it open wider.

"Unless *this* is the only chance you ever get," Fort said, stepping into the cell now. "Cyrus, part of me hates that I'm here. You betrayed us and lied to me from the moment I met you!" He gritted his teeth, not knowing why he was saying these things, but not able to stop himself either. "And yet, even with all of that, another part of me still can't stand seeing you in here like this."

Cyrus blinked and released the door. "Sounds like a personal issue," he said, crossing his arms, though his eyes looked haunted. "What's that got to do with me?"

Fort started to respond, then stopped. He knew the other boy better than this. If Cyrus really thought he was going to get out of this dungeon and away from the faerie queen at some point, he had to know that Fort was his best option.

Which meant Cyrus needed something too.

"This isn't about your family, is it?" Fort asked. "What do you want?"

"What makes you think I want anything?" Cyrus asked, the hint of a smile on his face.

Right. Just another reminder that Cyrus was playing him, and any friendship they'd had wasn't real.

"You know what?" Fort said, turning to go. "Maybe you're right. You *should* wait for a better opportunity. I'll just leave you here, and—"

A hand caught his arm, stopping him.

"I want my *magic* back," Cyrus said, his voice low and dangerous. "And you're going to make that happen, Fort."

- TWENTY-NINE -

FORT BLINKED IN SURPRISE, NOT having expected that at all. "I'm going to do *what* now?"

"You're going to get me my magic back," Cyrus repeated, squeezing his arm even harder. "Don't play games with me. You must have known that's what I'd want."

"Uh, no, actually I didn't, because there's no way that's happening," Fort growled, pulling his arm out of Cyrus's grasp. "Even if I knew how, I would never do it."

"Oh, you'll find out how, if you want my help," Cyrus said. "I don't know if you really are my only chance to escape here, but I do know Merlin still had his magic after I lost mine, which means somehow, I must get mine back. And right now you're my best chance at that, considering all those magical words floating around in your head."

Fort stared at him. "Cyrus, there's no way I'd ever do it. I'm not giving an Old One access to magic!"

"Why not?" Cyrus asked. "You're planning on getting rid of magic altogether, aren't you? If you're so sure you can do that, who cares if I get my power back in the meantime? It won't matter once you're through."

"Because you could use your Time magic to stop me!" Fort said. "You already tricked me once. You think I'm just going to stand here and let it happen again? Even I'm not that much of a sucker."

"See, I'm not the one tricking you anymore. *You're* the one deceiving yourself, if you think you'd actually go through with destroying magic."

"You have no *idea* what I'm willing to do," Fort hissed, not able to believe any of this. Why had he thought Cyrus would be willing to help just to escape Avalon? The Timeless One was all about playing games with people's lives, all to help the Old Ones. Fort should have known this wouldn't work from the start. "This is ridiculous. If that's the only way you'll help, then we're done here. I'll find another way." He turned to leave.

"You're just as much a pawn of time as *I* am, Fort," Cyrus shouted as Fort passed through the doorway. "Neither of us can fight the future. Merlin *will* have his magic when I'm older, and the Old Ones will return to our world. You've seen it for yourself, when I fought Jia and Rachel. You can't change that anymore. Nothing can!"

Fort gritted his teeth as he stepped into the hallway, trying to keep his anger under control. Cyrus had to be wrong about that, or all of this was pointless. He couldn't let himself believe that the future was set, even if he had seen it, or there was no reason to go on.

Helio opened his mouth to say something, but a look from Fort silenced the faerie boy. Instead, Fort spun back around to face Cyrus.

"If that's true, then why bother helping you escape?" he shouted. "I'd much rather leave you here to rot!"

"That's not what you said a minute ago." Cyrus smiled slightly. "I don't get it either, but *you're* the one who misses his friend."

Fort just stared at him in amazement, then slowly shut the door. "*I* miss someone who never existed," he said quietly through the barred window as the magical lock clicked back into place. Then, without another word, he passed by Helio and began walking back up the stairs.

"Is that it, then?" Helio asked from the floor outside the cell.

"I don't want to hear one word from you," Fort told him, and continued climbing the stairs, but stopped as a voice yelled up from below.

"You're *not* going to leave me here!" Cyrus shouted. "You can't change the future, Fort, and I *will* get my magic back!"

"Good luck with that," Fort shouted back down, then started climbing again.

Below, he heard Cyrus growl in frustration. "How about I *promise* not to stop you with my magic?"

Fort rolled his eyes as he paused in mid-step. "Oh, really? You'd *promise*? That's all I'd need, then! You'd never break a promise!"

Cyrus swore softly. "You're not getting it! I won't *need* to stop you, because you'll be the one deciding not to destroy magic all on your own! Trust me!"

Fort shook his head in disgust and began walking up the stairs once more. Just as he was about to pass out of sight of the floor below, Cyrus's voice came floating up one last time.

"*Fine*. You can give me my magic back *after* you learn how to destroy magic. Is that good enough for you? Because I don't know any other way to make you believe me."

Fort went silent, considering this. As the seconds passed, he heard Cyrus start to tap the door nervously.

"Hey, you still out there? Did you hear me, Fort? That's the best I can offer! I'll show you how to get rid of magic, and you return my power. Do we have a deal?"

When there was still no response, Cyrus grabbed the bars on the door and began shaking it.

"Hey! You're not going to leave me here—I *know* you're not! You can't change what's already happened, Fort, and this has already happened. Someone had to break me out of here, and now we know it's you. So get back down here and *let me out*!"

Again, only silence.

Cyrus screamed in frustration and let go of the door. "Great, he probably teleported away," the Old One said quietly to himself. "Way to go, Emrys. You've got to be the first person in history to cause a time paradox entirely by being a jerk."

"Not just a jerk," Fort said softly. "A *huge* jerk."

Cyrus reappeared at the window, where Fort and a suspicious Helio were waiting on the other side of the door. "You came back?" And then he seemed to realize what had actually happened. "Wait, you let me think you left. You tricked me! Was that all just to punish me?"

Fort shrugged, not able to stop a smile. "Seems like that, doesn't it?"

"That was *low*," Cyrus said, narrowing his eyes. "Uncalled for, even for a human."

"Oh, I can still leave, if you'd prefer." Fort turned to go again, only for Cyrus to stick his hand out the barred window and wave for him to stop.

"I'm sorry, I'm sorry!" he shouted. "I definitely deserved it, and you're welcome to trick me all you want once we're gone. Now will you please open the door again?"

"The deal is, I find a way to get your power back *after* you help me learn to destroy magic," Fort said, crossing his arms.

"Yes, that's the deal, I agree. I'll sign on the line, whatever you want," Cyrus said.

"*And* you promise not to use your Time magic to stop him once you regain your power," Helio added.

"That too," Fort said to Cyrus.

Cyrus just blinked. "I'm sorry, who is this again?"

"Who am I?" Helio shouted. "Just the one making sure *you* don't pull any fast ones on the boy here." He clapped Fort's shoulder, which Fort immediately pulled out of his reach. "This kid's special in a way *you* clearly have never seen, considering how you've been treating him. But that doesn't mean we can't all get along and be friends from this point forward, since we're going to have to work together. Now, why don't we group-hug out these disagreements so there are no hard feelings?"

Cyrus just stared at him in horror. "I'm sorry, *what*?"

Fort sighed deeply and opened the dungeon door again. "It doesn't matter. Let's just go."

Cyrus quickly slipped out, as Helio smiled in an annoyingly friendly way at the Old One. But before Fort could move toward the stairs, the faerie boy grabbed his arm.

"Wait, Fort," he said. "There's no need to climb back up. I can glamour us back to your world, which will save us from attempting those wet stairs again. But first, do you have to use the restroom or anything?" He pointed at the small bucket in Cyrus's cell. "I mean, who knows when our next chance will be."

Cyrus just stared at Helio for a moment, then gasped. "Wait a second. Are you his *dad*?"

- THIRTY -

IN A SHIMMER OF LIGHT, FORT, CYRUS, AND Helio arrived back outside the second Oppenheimer School, thanks to Helio's glamour. There was no one around, but Fort was almost glad about that, since he imagined Damian would have left the injured behind when he took the others to D.C. That at least gave him some hope that all the students had made it through the battle okay, even if the entrance now looked like a tornado had touched down right on top of it—repeatedly.

"You know, this place has really fallen apart since I left," Cyrus said, looking around with his hands on his hips. "But I do kind of miss it. There were some good memories here." He gave Fort a small smile. "Remember when we tried to steal the book of Summoning magic, and it turned out *you* were lying to us about wanting to use it, instead of destroy it?" He patted Fort on the arm, mimicking the move Helio had done a moment ago. "We really are similar in so many ways."

Fort jerked his arm away, glaring at the other boy. "I lied, yes. But *I* actually felt bad about it. And more importantly, my lie wasn't going to wipe out humanity."

"Oh, come on," Cyrus said, rolling his eyes. "My family will turn humanity into their servants *at worst.* They won't actually wipe anyone out."

"Boys!" Helio shouted, stepping between them. "Arguing won't accomplish anything. We're going to have to work together if we want to get this done."

Both Cyrus and Fort stared at the faerie boy. "We're *not* working together," Cyrus told him. "We made a simple bargain, nothing more."

"And stop acting like my father!" Fort shouted, trying to hold back his rage over the changeling and failing miserably.

"There, now, isn't that better, agreeing on something?" Helio said, beaming. He leaned in closer to Fort. "Would you mind if I glamoured myself back into my human appearance? I wouldn't want folks to notice my green skin."

"Yes, I *do* mind," Fort told him. "You even *think* of making yourself look like my real father again, and I'll teleport you into a volcano." Before Helio could respond, Fort pushed around him to speak to Cyrus again. "So how long do we have? When will Damian be summoning the Old Ones?"

Cyrus shrugged. "How would I know? I don't have my magic, remember? But since the skies aren't red and the land isn't devastated, I imagine we have a bit more time left." He grinned.

Fort had to stop himself from punching the Old One right in his mouth. "Right," he said. "Then let's get to it: Show me how to destroy magic. Do I take us back to the point Merlin and the human magicians did it a thousand years ago right now? Will we have to fight that younger version of you to see what they did?"

"You know, I really didn't have any idea why a human was skulking around there at the time," Cyrus said. "But as soon as I sent you away, I looked into who you were—or who you would be. Turns out, my older self had so many plans for you—his little chosen one—that I decided to come up with my own ideas. Poor guy never saw that coming."

Fort gritted his teeth in frustration, not liking either Cyrus's attitude or being called the chosen one again. At least this time it seemed more like Cyrus mocking him than anything. "Is that where we should *go*, then?"

The other boy sighed. "Yes, but—"

"Good enough," Fort said, preparing the spell in his head. There was a good chance another vision might mess this all up, but—and he couldn't imagine ever thinking this at any other possible time—at least he'd have Helio there to help.

"Wait a moment," the faerie boy said, stepping between them again. "Fort, before you do this, I think there's something else you need to see."

Fort sighed heavily. "There's literally nothing you could want to show me that I care about." Instead of waiting, he started concentrating again on the image of Stonehenge he'd gotten from the zombie magician, preparing to cast his spell.

"What's this big thing, faerie child?" Cyrus asked, almost sounding curious.

Annoyance passed over Helio's face at that. "You know I'm only a child because your older self cursed . . . Forget it. It doesn't matter. What Fort needs to see is what happened the *first* time someone tried to hurt magic. He needs to know the consequences."

This actually made Fort pause. "What are you talking about, the first time? I thought the magicians at Stonehenge *was* the first time."

"According to my queen," Helio said, turning to Cyrus, "the first attack on the chaos force came from his family, millions of years ago."

Cyrus's eyebrows flew up. "My family? We didn't attack magic—we *mastered* it."

"Not according to my queen," Helio said simply, shrugging.

Fort groaned as he rubbed his temples, hating this. They needed to be figuring out a way to stop the Old Ones, not getting some history lesson. "Listen, Helio, I hate to say this, but I don't trust your queen any more than I do Cyrus."

Helio looked like he wanted to object, but simply nodded instead. "That's . . . understandable. But these stories have been around since the beginning: the tale of the Eternal Ones' home and how it came to be destroyed—"

"Right, *humans* did that!" Cyrus said. "That's what started all of this. Millions of years ago, your people showed up, Fort, and invaded our lands. That's why my family had to take them over!"

Fort's irritation turned to anger, and he clenched his fists. "You know what, Cyrus? If that's what happened, maybe we *should* see this thing Helio is talking about. I wouldn't mind watching some humans invade *your* home for once."

Cyrus sneered. "I thought you were in a hurry to burn magic to the ground."

Helio cleared his throat. "Actually, with Time magic, we can return a moment after we leave, so we won't actually be wasting any, well, time."

"See?" Fort said, nodding at the faerie boy. "Sounds like a plan, then." He paused. "But I don't know when I'm taking us to."

"The magic will guide you," Helio said, as Cyrus rolled his eyes. "Just ask it to take you to the creation of the Old Ones."

"Don't blame me if this all goes wrong," Cyrus said, sounding more irritated now. "Even *I've* never been back to see how my family became what they are. They set up some pretty heavy protective magical barriers, and I've never been able to break through, so if you think *you* can—"

"If anyone can manage, it's my . . . it's Fort, here," Helio said with a proud grin, and for once, Fort actually appreciated the compliment. "Besides, I'll be here to help."

The air around Fort began to shimmer as Helio started glamouring his own spell, so Fort closed his eyes and concentrated on something he never thought he'd want to see.

"Let us witness the moment the Old Ones were created," he whispered in the language of magic.

Black light began to glow all around them . . .

Only to start sizzling like an overloaded lightbulb.

"See?" Cyrus said, waving his hands in every direction. "I told you it wouldn't work!"

"You've got this," Helio said to Fort, and his shimmer increased. Somehow, Fort could feel the faerie's glamour pushing against whatever was holding them back, feeling out the barriers for weak spots, holes . . . and directing Fort's magic where it needed to go. As Fort and Helio worked together, the black light grew stronger once more.

"He's doing it!" Helio shouted, and even Cyrus looked surprised.

"This shouldn't be possible," the Old One whispered. "What did Merlin *teach* you from that book?"

Fort would have loved to brag a bit at that moment, but unfortunately, the world began spinning as the black glow grew brighter, and even with Helio's help, the effort was almost too much. Spots began to pop in Fort's eyesight, and he started to wonder if the black light was Time magic or another vision coming, when the light suddenly disappeared, leaving them surrounded by . . . well, he had no idea.

It was a city, at least as far as Fort could tell, but a city that looked like someone's imagination had come to life, without any natural laws getting in the way. Crystalline buildings much like the ones Fort vaguely recalled from a vision of the future rose from the ground in an oddly organic style, as if they'd grown there. Silky-smooth streets ran past—and even through—the buildings, while hovering flames made everything sparkle in a way Fort almost couldn't believe was real.

Even more impossible was the fact that the entire city seemed to be floating above what looked like the ocean, stretching off in every direction a few hundred yards below them. This was an island of wonder, and somehow, it felt almost offensive to think that the Old Ones had come from here.

"What . . . what is this place?" Fort asked, still weak from the effort of bringing them here.

Cyrus looked around in awe. "This is the golden age of magic, the home I've never seen. This is *Atlantis.*"

"And today's the day it's going to be destroyed," Helio added.

- THIRTY-ONE -

IF THIS WAS ACTUALLY THE LAST DAY OF Atlantis, Fort never would have known from the look of it. Everything seemed incredibly lively, with trees blooming with fruit he'd never seen before and people who looked basically human wandering the streets, or even floating above them.

He stepped over to where a male Atlantean was passing by, hoping for a closer look. Fortunately, they were all invisible to the residents of Atlantis, since this spell just brought their consciousness back in time, not their physical bodies.

For the most part, the Atlantean could have passed for a modern-day human. But the shape of his head was off just enough to be noticeable, more oval than round, with a protruding jaw, almost like the ones Fort had seen in museum exhibits of Neanderthals.

The Atlantean's clothes were something else entirely, flowing and floating like a toga in constant motion, each layer sliding around the Atlantean's body as the layer behind it replaced it.

All in all, it was hard to accept this place was real. It was like something out of a dream . . . or a vision. Was that what this was?

But no, Helio and Cyrus wouldn't have been here if a vision was all it was.

"Cyrus, what *is* this place?" Fort asked, not able to stop staring at the sights. "I mean, I know it's Atlantis, but . . ."

"I've never seen it either," Cyrus said, gawking just as badly. "Not like this. I found the ruins, of course. They're under what in your time is the Atlantic Ocean, close to Portugal and Morocco. But they were nothing like this." He sneered. "Not after humans tore it all down."

Fort's mouth dropped open. "You're saying *humans* destroyed all of this?" he said, not sure he could believe it. As airy and light as the crystalline buildings looked, whatever magic had created them must have been incredibly powerful.

"So I heard from my family over the millennia," Cyrus said, nodding as Helio sighed quietly. "I used Time magic to visit them when I could, and they shared our history with me."

"They lied to you is more accurate," Helio said with a snort.

"How long had humans even been around by this point, a few thousand years? There's no way they could have been any sort of threat against you *or* this city."

"Where do we go to see whatever it is that brought us here?" Fort said before Cyrus could start in on how bad ancient humans were again. "His family attacking magic, or whatever you wanted me to see, Helio. I don't like being here at all." Which was true, though not because of the city or its people. No, Fort was far more worried that he hadn't had a vision yet, which made him think it was more likely to happen on the return trip.

And what then? Would he trap the others somewhere in time, or would they return to their bodies while he got pulled into the vision? The last thing Fort needed was for Cyrus to escape because he was stuck with another lesson from whatever the visions were. Helio would be there, yes, but even with the faerie's glamours, Cyrus could probably still trick the other boy if it came down to it. That was the benefit of a billion years of experience at mind games, or however old he actually was.

Speaking of, hadn't Cyrus been born in the future? Merlin mentioned that he/they lived backward and were born at the end of time. So how could their family be from here, in the past? That didn't make any sense.

Fort opened his mouth to ask about it but went silent as Helio pointed toward an enormous tower in the distance, far taller than any skyscraper Fort had ever seen. "That's where we need to go," the faerie boy said, then glanced at Cyrus. "Our stories say that the Tower of Bal'ale is where your family set things in motion."

Cyrus nodded, staring at the tower like he was lost in thought. "That's where they put order to the chaos, yes," he said quietly, then shivered. "Something's off about this. I feel . . . a presence I shouldn't."

Fort raised an eyebrow. "You mean Merlin? Is he here too?" The thought that Cyrus's older self might be available to help—or at least ask for advice—gave Fort a bit of hope.

"No," Cyrus said, sinking Fort's optimistic ideas. "But weirdly, it feels similar to that, like there are too many of me in one place."

"Well, the sooner we get going, the sooner we'll arrive!" Helio said, waving the other two forward down one of the silken streets. "And the first person to ask 'are we there yet' doesn't get dessert for a month!"

It took them far longer than Fort would have thought to reach the tower, since it looked closer than it actually was, due to its immense size. Even without their physical bodies here, they still moved at the same pace they would have been able to walk, which led to some interesting questions about the magic involved, but none that Fort had time to find answers to at the moment.

Crowds of Atlanteans also filled the streets, and it felt odd to just pass right through them, so instead, they maneuvered as best they could around the city's inhabitants, which slowed them down even more. By the time they finally reached the tower, Fort was thrilled to find the crowds had thinned out a bit, if just so they could move more easily.

"Strange for a city so afraid of humanity attacking to not have any doors on the place," Helio said as they reached the tower, pointing at the open archways all around the bottom of the building. The tower was made of the same crystal as the rest of the city, a crystal that seemed familiar for some reason, though like nothing Fort had ever seen in nature or books. Where he'd come across it before, then, he had no idea.

The few people around the tower seemed to be entering and leaving freely, so at least they wouldn't have to walk through any guards or security. Besides, considering the level of magic Atlanteans clearly had available, for all Fort knew, they'd have some sort of magical gate that could actually detect visitors from other times.

Helio led the way, with Fort right behind. Cyrus trailed a bit, taking in everything with a look of wonder that actually made Fort feel a bit sorry for the Old One again, even against his better judgment. As awful as Cyrus was, Fort could still pity him for never having seen where he came from until now.

As they passed through the arches, Helio looked up, then froze in place, leading Fort to knock right into him, an unpleasant reminder that though they weren't actually here, the magic made it so they still felt solid to each other. "What's going on?" he asked the faerie, who didn't respond and instead pointed up.

Fort followed Helio's lead, and his eyes widened. As huge as the tower was, it turned out to be completely hollow inside, something Fort never would have expected. Apart from the Atlanteans floating up and down in a shimmer of light, it looked empty, just an enormous circular cylinder rising into the sky.

"Um, wasn't there supposed to be something here?" he asked both Helio and Cyrus. The faerie looked as confused as Fort felt, but Cyrus just smiled.

"Oh, it's just an optical illusion," Cyrus said. "I've seen parts of this underwater. There are floors every twenty feet or so. You can fly us up, right, Fort?"

Fort cringed, not liking that idea at all, though at least if he had a vision and dropped them all, they wouldn't be hurt, since they had no physical presence here . . . hopefully. "I can, but—"

"Oh, you've done enough," Helio said, clapping Fort on the back. "Let me take a turn."

Before Fort could object—or thank the faerie—the air around them began to shimmer, just like it did for the Atlanteans, and they floated off the ground. The similar effect made Fort curious. "Are the Atlanteans using glamours too, then?" he asked.

"Once upon a time, glamour magic was all there was," Helio said, giving Cyrus a dark look. "Of course, it was far more powerful in this time, because the Eternal Ones hadn't yet wounded chaos."

"You're going to see how wrong you are in a few minutes," Cyrus said, distracted by the tower as they rose, so his tone was less angry than usual.

As they flew higher, the other floating Atlanteans thinned

out even more, disappearing into the walls of the tower. At first Fort couldn't understand what was happening, but then he realized Cyrus was right: There *was* an optical illusion, as floors appeared on every side of them as they rose. Each floor was constructed to appear just like the inner wall of the tower, expertly designed so that the crystal floors were hidden in the side walls when looking up from below.

"Now, that doesn't seem smart," Helio said, pointing at one of the levels just above them. Fort glanced in the same direction and almost lost his concentration, given that several Atlanteans seemed to be magically creating a black hole in what looked like some kind of mystical laboratory.

Cyrus let out a huge gasp, but unlike the others, his seemed to be from excitement. "Think of what that must be like, having others just like you to experiment with!" he said, his gaze locked on the Atlanteans.

"If it doesn't blow up the whole planet," Fort said.

As they continued to rise, they soon found themselves alone in the air, far too high for Fort to chance looking down. They soon neared the top of the tower. He could make out the edges of a circular hole in what appeared to be the tower's roof, or at least a ceiling. But as they passed through that hole, he realized they'd just entered another room, this one much smaller, as more of the tower rose above them. How far up did this thing go?

"Guards," Helio said, pointing at two young Atlanteans, a male and a female, both wearing armor made of the same crystal as the tower. They each had what looked like a magical rod floating at their waist where a sword might be belted on and were standing at attention.

The armor. That's where Fort had seen the crystal before! The TDA had a set on display in their trophy room that looked *just* like the version the guards were wearing.

And that set had given Fort the same creepy vibes he'd gotten from the Old One Ketas in Sierra's memory at the time.

The thought had occurred to him then that the Old Ones might once have looked human, instead of like the terrifying monsters they now appeared to be. And Cyrus seemed to prove that point, considering his appearance.

But what could have turned them into such grotesque creatures?

If Helio was right, it sounded like they were about to find out.

- THIRTY-TWO -

HELIO GESTURED FOR THEM TO PASS by the guards. "Prepare yourselves, boys," he said, looking as nervous as he had with the faerie queen. "And be ready to send us back to the present at a moment's notice, Fort."

"But we're not really here," Fort said, frowning. "How are we in danger?"

"It's not just our physical bodies I'm worried about," Helio replied, which didn't help at *all*.

First Fort, then Cyrus, and finally Helio walked between the guards to find a spiraling hallway, one that sloped up toward what Fort figured had to be the top of the tower. As they walked, they passed by several more pairs of guards, which was disturbing in and of itself.

Whatever was happening here, the future Old Ones didn't want *anyone* to see it.

The rising hallway let out into a giant auditorium the diameter of the tower itself, with sloping bench seating surrounding an inner raised platform. The benches were empty, but on the platform were three men and three women, all Atlanteans of varying ages, talking quietly with each other like they were guests at a funeral.

As Fort had guessed, there were no screaming human faces or skull helmets on any of them, none of what he'd come to expect from the Old Ones. Instead, they had that same almost-human appearance as the other Atlanteans and were all wearing similar flowing togas to the ones he'd seen outside, even if these seemed to be a much higher quality, as if silk to the regular Atlanteans' cotton.

"My family," Cyrus said quietly, staring at them with a far-off look in his eye, then gasped. "Uh, what am *I* doing here?" He pointed at the youngest Atlantean man.

Fort squinted at the man Cyrus indicated. The Atlantean *did* resemble an older Cyrus, maybe in his twenties, only with black hair instead of silver. But how could that be possible? "I thought you were born in the future and live backward," Fort said, putting as much accusation in his voice as he could. "Or was that all a lie too?"

"No!" Cyrus said, looking honestly shocked at the sight of himself. "I swear, I've never even seen this ceremony—I told you that! I have no memory of any of it. That *can't* be me!"

His clear distress over this mollified Fort's anger a bit. "Well, if he's older, you *wouldn't* have the memory of it," he said, still having no idea what to think about any of it. Either Cyrus was lying—not exactly unheard of—or something weird was going on.

Beyond *everything* weird already going on.

"We should get closer," Helio said, then paused. "But not too close."

He led them down to the third row of benches and gestured for Fort and Cyrus to take a seat, then sat down on the aisle, his legs shaking up and down nervously, Fort noticed. Helio *really* didn't like whatever was about to happen, and he'd just heard it in stories. Hopefully, the reality wouldn't be that bad.

Cyrus, meanwhile, seemed to have moved on from his shock at his older self's presence and now was just gazing at his family with an odd look on his face. These were the siblings who'd left him in the faerie queen's hands, but he also clearly loved them and had spent hundreds of years fighting his older self just to bring them home. That was bound to give anyone some conflicted emotions.

Before Fort could ask about it, though, one of the Atlanteans raised his hands for silence and began to speak.

"My dear siblings," he said, and a chill passed down Fort's spine as he recognized the voice. It didn't have the same horrifying quality it had when it echoed through his mind back at the original Oppenheimer School, but he'd still have known Ketas—the Old One of Mind magic—anywhere. "The time has finally come."

They weren't speaking English, but somehow Fort could still understand their words. A slight shimmer in the air told him that Helio was translating, which he was thankful for, as he'd never have even thought of that.

The other members of the family all murmured their assent, including the older version of Cyrus—no, *Emrys*, Fort corrected himself: These were Old Ones. If this was a younger version of Merlin, he clearly hadn't had his change of heart yet.

"For thousands of years, Atlantis has stood as a beacon to the world, illuminating the majesty of magic for all to see," Ketas continued. "We have created the very pinnacle of civilization here, using the power that is our birthright. But you all know as well as I do that Atlantis is under attack from animals who have started *stealing* our magic away!"

Animals? Was he talking about *humanity* that way? It wasn't possible for Fort to hate the Old Ones more, but calling his people animals certainly didn't help.

But were human beings really stealing magic somehow? What was going on? Cyrus had said that humans destroyed Atlantis, but Helio seemed to think it was more complicated than that. Hopefully, they'd at least get the truth now.

"They'll overrun us if we give them an inch," one of the Atlantean women said, nodding angrily.

"The city sure *looked* overrun, didn't it?" Helio said quietly.

"You don't know what they've been through," Cyrus said, sounding both irritated and slightly confused himself. "My family told me that humans tried to take *everything* from us, because they were jealous of what we had and what we could do. They wanted our power and would do anything to take it!"

"These new creatures are *unworthy barbarians*," one of the other male family members said, looking disgusted. "How dare they try to use *our* magic?"

"We've waited too long as it is," the older Cyrus said, making the Cyrus next to Fort stiffen at the sound of his own voice. "Soon they might become an actual threat."

His older self's words hit Cyrus like a punch in the gut, and he went deathly pale. "What? They're not a threat now? But that's . . . that's not how they said it happened," he whispered.

"Yes, clearly these humans were doing such *horrible* things to your city, before they were even any threat," Helio whispered. "How *dare* they use your magic?"

"You don't know—" Cyrus whispered, but Ketas began speaking again, and Cyrus went quiet.

"We cannot allow these unworthy animals to sully our magic," Ketas said. "And because we are the foremost family in Atlantis, it falls to *us* to ensure only the properly civilized might use it from now on. What we do today will be remembered as the dawn of a new age of magic, one where only the worthy have access to its power."

"Cyrus, what are they *doing*?" Fort said, absolutely disgusted.

"They're . . . putting order to chaos," Cyrus said, sounding like he was repeating a phrase he'd been told himself, but his voice shook as he said it, and he looked even paler than before.

"For too long, magic has granted its chaotic power of change to just anyone," Ketas continued. "But we say *no longer* shall the lessers of this world have access to it! Whereas before, a feeling, a desire was enough for magic to grant you whatever you wished, as of today, only those with the knowledge of the words of power will be able to access it. And *we* will decide who can speak those words, no one else."

Wait, what? Magic hadn't needed spell words before? Was *that* what they were doing, forcing the language of magic onto the power itself?

And all so they would be the only ones who could use it? If anything, this was even worse than Fort had thought.

"They told me they were in danger," Cyrus whispered, almost too softly to hear. "They told me there were horrible invasions by the humans, leaving *half of the city* dead!"

"Do you see now?" Helio said quietly. "*This* is why we despise the Old Ones. The Tylwyth Teg haven't been able to learn the language, and what magic remains free now is just a fraction of what it once was. This is why the queen wants what's in your head, Fort . . . to regain the power she once had, before the Eternal Ones changed the rules."

"*Join me*, my family, and ensure that magic shall never be tainted by lesser creatures again!" Ketas shouted, and with that, the ceremony began.

THIRTY-THREE

"THEY *COULDN'T* HAVE LIED TO ME," Cyrus said, shaking his head as his family—and his older self—all formed a circle. "It's not true! If we looked at what humans are doing here, in the past, I'm sure we'd see what they were talking about!"

"Oh, I'm happy to show you," Helio said, and the air started shimmering in front of them. Within the shimmer, Fort could just make out what looked like human beings but for a few tiny differences, wearing primitive but well-crafted clothing, as if it'd been put together by magic. A few of the adults were spreading their arms over a table where several children sat, and shimmering fruit began to appear out of thin air. . . .

And then Cyrus slapped Helio's hand, and the image disappeared. "Don't mislead us with your fake images!" he hissed. "I'd *never* believe anything you showed me was real." He turned to Fort, who could barely look at his ex-friend now. "Think about it, Fort! Your people were basically *children* at this point. How do you think they'd handle magic? Of course they'd use it to attack!"

Fort clenched his fists, trying hard to hold himself back from punching the Old One. "You mean like what happened when *we* got access to magic, the children at the Oppenheimer School?" he asked. "Did *we* attack people we didn't know . . . or was that your family? Remind me how that went again."

Cyrus grimaced and looked away. "That's not what I meant. And this isn't personal, Fort. You're obviously one of the *good* ones, but so many of your kind just can't handle it. Think about what would happen if Colonel Charles had access to magic!"

Fort could feel his face burning now, and he rose to his feet to turn to face Cyrus, who flinched from his anger. "He would probably be awful," Fort said, gritting his teeth. "And yet he'd still be a thousand times better than *you* and your family."

"You're not letting me finish!" Cyrus said, putting his hands up in surrender. "*You* had the books that helped you learn. Your ancestors didn't have anything like that. They were just experimenting, and could have cast any number of world-ending spells—"

"You mean, just like how your kind experimented when *they* first learned magic?" Helio asked.

"Yes, which meant we knew what mistakes to avoid!" Cyrus said quickly. "We knew that when your people were ready, we could teach them—"

"You used humans as *servants*, Cyrus!" Fort shouted, not even caring if the Time magic kept him from being heard. As far as he was concerned, the soon-to-be-Old-Ones deserved to hear this too. "And they banned humans from learning magic until dragons taught them! Your family wasn't trying to prepare my people—they just hated them!"

Cyrus started to respond, only for his mouth to drop open as a white light lit up the auditorium. Fort glanced over his shoulder to find a glow almost too bright to see shining around Ketas and the others, six of them in total including the older version of Cyrus.

"Concentrate, my siblings," Ketas said. "Today we show the invaders that they are unworthy of the light, unworthy of the chaos, unworthy of the *power*!"

The light began to shimmer, and as it did, a tremor spread through the tower. Several of the family lowered their hands at the shaking and looked around in confusion.

"Focus!" Ketas shouted, and his siblings turned back to the center of the circle, raising their hands once more. "The power we seek is great and terrible, but *we* are its master! No more will chaos be free for all. *We* shall control it, and no other. *We* will bend the universe to our will, beholden no more to the fickle whims of magic and other creatures on this world. For *we* shall be the eternal masters of life and death, and none shall stand against us!"

The shaking increased now, and cracks began splitting in the crystal of the tower wall. From far away, Fort thought he could make out terrified screaming, and he realized it must have been coming from the streets below.

Was the destruction in the tower happening out in the rest of the city, as well?

"Say the words!" Ketas shouted, turning to his sibling to his right. "Say the words, and force chaos to obey only you! D'hea, *begin*!"

"Chaos that creates our corporeal body, you are mine to shape!" yelled the man that Fort now realized was the Old One of Corporeal magic, the dragon he'd freed from his prison on the Dracsi homeworld. A blue light appeared out of the white and engulfed him, and he screamed—this time in pain—as his body began warping and twisting.

"It's fighting me!" D'hea roared, his voice filled with agony. "I don't know that I can—"

"Keep going!" Ketas shouted, even as the tower's walls began to crumble away, and the floor cracked apart in an alarming number of spots. "We knew the chaos would fight back to keep from being controlled. We must defeat it! Q'baos, you are next!"

"Chaos that forms our ever-shifting spirits, you are mine to turn!" shouted the future Old One of Spirit magic. An orange light appeared this time and flooded over her. She screamed as well, as rivers of the same light began streaming into her from all sides. Fort cried out in horror, knowing what was happening behind those lights but not wanting to see it, not wanting to face it.

"Emrys!" Ketas shouted. Cyrus shuddered next to Fort, while his older self held his hands up to the center of the circle.

"Chaos of cause and effect, you are mine to reorder!" the young man shouted, almost proudly. Black light appeared around him, but unlike the others, the black light began to fade away.

And then, so did Emrys.

"Ketas?" he said, his body turning translucent, black light infusing every part of him as he disappeared. "I feel . . . *strange*."

"Emrys!" one of the others screamed, and even Ketas seemed surprised. But none could do anything as Cyrus's older self disappeared, leaving behind an empty spot in the circle.

"The magic is fighting harder than we thought!" Ketas shouted. "We cannot let it defeat us. Show your strength, my family! *Do not give in!*"

"You're hurting chaos itself," Helio said solemnly to Cyrus, who now had tears running down his face. "And it's fighting back the only way it knows how, by using itself against you."

"What do you mean?" Fort asked him. "What's happening to them?"

"It's turning their own power back upon them," Helio said. "If I had to guess, I'd imagine Cyrus's backward life started at this moment here. Time magic is cursing him, even as it's falling under his control."

Fort shuddered, barely able to even comprehend what was happening. "And . . . the others?" he said, nodding at D'hea and Q'baos, both of whom were still screaming in pain.

But they weren't the only ones. The shouts outside were getting closer, though their tone had shifted, now sounding more like echoes than anything. Fort looked over at the crumbling walls and yelled in surprise as he saw spectral, glowing

Atlanteans flowing into the tower, almost like they'd been pulled in by something.

In fact, they were being pulled . . . by the orange rivers of light surrounding Q'baos.

The spirits of the nearby Atlanteans funneled into the light, screaming as they disappeared into it, then into Q'baos's body itself. Faces appeared on her torso, yelling in agony, and Fort had to look away, not sure he could stand any more of this.

Helio had been right: This was a *truly* evil act, and he didn't need to witness it any longer to see that.

"We must complete the circle, or it will destroy us!" shouted another member of Cyrus's family, and Ketas and another woman nodded, though all three looked much more doubtful now.

"D'vale!" Ketas said, gesturing at the woman. "Take your power!"

"Chaos of earth and air, you are mine to form!" shouted the Atlantean, wincing in anticipation. Red light exploded up from the floor, covering her as flames exploded all over her body. She gritted her teeth but didn't shout out, attempting to control the fire instead.

"Ni'nev!" Ketas yelled. "It is down to the two of us. Take your magic, and we will finish this!"

Ni'nev, whose name Fort didn't recognize, nodded, still staring at the spot where Emrys had stood. *"Chaos of eternal space, you are mine to bend!"* the woman shouted, and green light erupted from the white, covering her fully. Her body seemed to shift out of view, appearing in multiple spots at once, as if she no longer occupied just one dimension.

Ni'nev was the Old One of Space magic? Fort vaguely remembered Merlin or Cyrus had mentioned something about her, but he couldn't bring it to mind, not with the chaos around him.

And then the floor of the tower fell away, crumbling into nothing. Fortunately, Helio's flight spell still seemed to be in effect, as they didn't fall. The central platform the Atlanteans had gathered on was gone as well, but a shimmering light told Fort they'd protected themselves before attempting the ceremony, as none of the future Old Ones dropped either.

"Chaos of the far reaches of thought!" shouted Ketas, the last Atlantean left, and he touched his hands to his head. *"You are* mine *to rewrite!"*

Yellow light surrounded him, cascading out of his eyes, mouth, and ears, morphing his head into what looked like some sort of skull shape. Fort stared in horror, then almost fell over as an earsplitting noise sent him reeling and the rest of the tower began to collapse out from under them.

"*Fort*, take us back!" Helio shouted, but Fort could barely comprehend his words over the noise of the destruction. The columns of light surrounding the Old Ones began to rise as one, then shot into the air, rocketing to places unknown, but their absence didn't seem to stop the chaos.

In fact, the screams out in the city only grew louder now, and as the tower fell away, Fort was able to see why.

Below them, the city of Atlantis was crumbling, falling into the sea below it. The shimmering, crystalline buildings toppled over, and the streets buckled as if the magic keeping them together no longer worked.

Cyrus just stared at it all in abject misery. "*We* did this?" he whispered.

"This is what you needed to see, Fort," Helio said softly as destruction reigned all around them. "Magic will not go quietly. It will fight against any attempt to harm it. I can't stand the idea of what happened to the Eternal Ones happening to you, as well."

Not having any words to respond with and unwilling to watch any longer, Fort nodded silently, then cast his Time spell, and everything disappeared in a black glow.

- THIRTY-FOUR -

FORT KNEW HE SHOULD BRING THEM back to the present, both to give Cyrus time to think about all the lies his family had told him, and also for his own sanity. He'd just seen something horrific, and there was a very good chance that if he tried something similar, he could end up like the Old Ones.

But it was for that reason that he knew he couldn't stop, couldn't let himself have a moment to think, or he might never go through with it. And then the monsters he'd just seen created would take over everything.

If there were any other choice, any other option, he'd take it. But he was all out of plans, and that just left the worst-case scenario. He had no one left to turn to, no one left to stand by his side other than an Old One who wanted something and a fake father whom he constantly had to remind himself not to punch.

And he was only this alone because he'd failed. He couldn't let his fear stop him again. Especially not if he really was some sort of chosen one.

So instead of returning to the Oppenheimer School, he brought them to a wet, grassy field a few dozen yards outside a circle of stones.

"Stonehenge?" Helio said, squinting at the stones. "So you're still going to go through with it." He flashed Fort a look but didn't say anything else.

"I don't have a choice," Fort said, shaking his head. That wasn't the truth, necessarily, but it was close enough. No matter the consequences, he couldn't live with letting his friends and the rest of the world down. And if it turned him into an Old One, or worse, then that was the price he'd have to pay.

"You could have given us a moment to breathe," Cyrus said quietly, not looking at him.

He looked at Cyrus and nodded, actually feeling a bit sorry about that. Maybe it was having his ex-friend around during a time he was desperate for a friend, or maybe it was just looking at another person suffering, but he did feel awful about what Cyrus was going through. He brought Cyrus's betrayal to mind, but even that didn't put a huge dent in his guilt.

But then he remembered Cyrus's twentysomething self thinking of humanity as animals, and suddenly he felt a lot less pity. "We had a deal, Cyrus. You get your magic back, and I find out how to destroy magic. Are you changing your mind now?"

Cyrus grimaced but shook his head. "A bargain is a bargain," he said, and slowly started walking toward the circle of stones. He glanced back over his shoulder at Fort. "Come on. We'll need to get closer. I'll deal with the other me when we find him."

Fort started to follow, but Helio stopped him. "He *believed* what his family told him," Helio said quietly, watching the Old One walk away. "And he's not the same boy as the one we just saw, the young man who had so much hatred for humanity in his heart."

Fort ground his teeth together, not wanting to hear any of this at the moment. The last thing he needed was another reason to sympathize with the ex-friend who'd caused all of this in the first place. "It doesn't matter. He can figure that all out later, *after* I stop his family from coming back."

"I wanted you to see what they did for a reason, Fort," Helio said, sounding so much like his father that Fort wanted to scream. "That ceremony was a desecration. The chaos force brought *life* to this planet, and—"

"I know—I've had visions lecturing me about it for a week now!" Fort shouted, making Cyrus stop and turn back to look at them. "You think I *want* to do this? *I don't have a choice.* I can't beat Damian, or stop the Old Ones by myself, and I'm not going to let them do to humanity what they did to Atlantis. If it hadn't been for the dragons, we might *still* be their servants, if humanity even lasted this long!"

"I know," Helio said, shaking his head sadly. "And I'll support whatever decision you make. I just needed you to know the full extent of what you'd be doing. It's not just humanity and the Eternal Ones that benefited from magic. This whole planet did, including my people. The years when it was gone from your world—"

"Were years when no horrible monsters were trying to enslave us," Fort said, glaring at him. "Sometimes you have to do bad things just to survive. *I* have to do them—me. No one else is going to suffer anymore for my mistakes. And if you can't accept that, then maybe you should wait here. I don't need you second-guessing everything I do up there."

And with that, he left to follow Cyrus, noticing that Helio

waited where they'd landed, staring at him sadly. A part of him almost wished the other boy had come, if just for the tiny, *minuscule* part of the faerie that reminded Fort of his father, but that just made him angrier, mostly at himself.

Fort caught up to Cyrus as they both reached the stones. He *thought* they had landed at the same spot he had last time, but the vision had messed with his mind then, so it was hard to tell. He looked around and nodded as he found the spot he'd leaned against the standing stone. "Over there," he said, pointing, just as a burst of black light appeared a few feet away from the spot. Was someone else traveling through time to this . . . oh.

Someone else *was*: himself from earlier that day.

As Fort watched, previous Fort arrived, looking a bit faint. He stumbled toward the stone Fort had just pointed at and leaned against it for support, trying to see what the magicians were doing.

"See?" Cyrus said. "It's not comfortable having multiple versions of yourself in one place, is it?"

Fort shook his head as he noticed another version of Cyrus, the one who was meeting Fort for the very first time, appearing next to his past self. It really was eerie watching something that'd just happened to him from the outside, though his memory of it was all so garbled anyway due to the vision.

"Right," Cyrus said, preparing to move. "I'll wait until he sends that you away, since I don't want to create a paradox by changing what happened. Not on top . . . of everything else."

Fort closed his eyes. He didn't want to get into what Cyrus was thinking, feeling, but he couldn't help himself. "Are you . . . okay?" he asked, hating himself for giving in.

"No," Cyrus said. "And I don't want to talk about it."

A few yards away, the other Fort looked in their direction for a moment but didn't seem to notice anything odd about another version of himself standing there. Except he *had* noticed! Fort recalled thinking it was just a duplicate of himself and Cyrus due to the vision, but he'd seen his future self at the time.

This was all giving him an enormous headache. But at least it meant that things were progressing as they should, and they hadn't messed up time on top of everything else.

And then the other Fort disappeared as Cyrus sent him away, and Fort's Cyrus started to walk over to his past self.

"You can handle . . . him?" Fort asked as he followed. The other Old One moved in their direction as well, a curious look on his face.

"Well, he has his magic, and I don't, which makes this a

thousand times harder," Cyrus whispered. "If we could have gone back to the present for a moment, I might have had time to point that out. But yeah, I think I've got this."

"What's the plan?" Fort asked.

Cyrus turned and gave him a small smile. "Let my older self handle things." And then he gestured, as if introducing someone on a stage.

"Your *what*?" Fort asked, only for a man in a long brown robe to step between them and the other Cyrus. Fort's eyes widened, and he almost shouted in surprise, holding himself back at the last moment.

"You shouldn't be here," Merlin said to the previous Cyrus, his back to Fort and present-day Cyrus. "You must know that, even now."

That Cyrus raised an eyebrow. "I just wanted to know how you did it. How you made magic go away." He tilted his head to look past Merlin at Fort and his older self. "Did you know there's another version of myself and that boy you chose standing behind you?"

"I'm hardly blind," Merlin said, his tone sounding like he was joking. But between these two, who knew what that meant? "Come now, it's time for you to go."

"You know it's just going to reawaken," the other Cyrus asked. "And I'll be ready when it does. You're going to put magic to sleep as deeply as you can, and humans will create a machine that stretches all the way down to the building blocks of chaos. They'll awaken it with their science, their *order*."

"Yes, their Giant Hadley Collision or some such," Merlin said, waving his hand. "They'll call it quantum this or that, but yes, they'll find the foundations of magic that even we can't fully hide, and it will return."

"So then you know all of this is useless," the other Cyrus said, looking to Merlin's side at the human magicians waiting in the middle of the stone circle. "All the manipulation, all the games you played just to get them here, and it'll last a little over a millennia at most."

"A bit more, but who's counting?" Merlin said. "You're asking why bother, when it's for so little time?"

"*Of course* I'm asking that," Cyrus said, sounding more irritated. "Why go to the trouble when it's all pointless anyway? A thousand years or more, they'll be back. I'll make sure of it!"

Merlin laughed, deep and low, then snapped his fingers, and the other Cyrus disappeared. The old man turned around to Fort and the present-day Cyrus and smiled at both of them.

"Imagine not doing something just because it's *pointless*," Merlin said with a wink. "Now, it's been far too many years, Forsythe. You must be here to learn how to destroy magic, then?" He grinned. "It's about time."

- THIRTY-FIVE -

BEFORE FORT COULD RESPOND, PRESENT-day Cyrus pushed past him. "You *knew* all along!" he shouted, poking his finger right through Merlin, since they still were just seeing this all through Time magic. "You knew they lied to us!"

"I did," Merlin said, his grin disappearing. "And I believe I warned you before not to trust them. But understandably, you wanted the family you thought you never had."

"Except it turns out I *did* have them, and I was just as bad as they were!" Cyrus shouted. "I thought I'd *always* been born in the future."

"Well, of course not always," Merlin said with a snort. "No one's born cursed by magic. Just by fate."

Cyrus growled in frustration. "Speak *clearly*," he shouted, and Fort had to cover a surprised snort. "No more riddles or vague prophecies. You knew Fort would be coming here to learn how to destroy magic, but you also must know it can't happen. You're *proof* of that!"

Merlin tilted his head quizzically. "Because I still have my spells in your future, so therefore it must exist? Are you suggesting that magic, the force of possibility itself, can't rewrite time? *You* do it every day." He shrugged. "Or at least you did until you lost to Rachel."

This time Fort didn't bother covering his laugh. Cyrus glared back at him. "Thanks a *lot*," the silver-haired boy said, then turned back to his older self. "That's different. He'd be taking away *all* possibility in the universe. Nothing would change; nothing new would ever come about. Why would you tell him how to do this if you thought he might go through with it?"

"So you actually didn't think I'd do it?" Fort asked, feeling less sorry for Cyrus again. "I thought you were just manipulating me again!"

"*Yes*, I didn't think you'd do it!" the other boy shouted. "You might have known that from the fact that I mentioned it over and over! It's not my fault you didn't believe me."

Merlin sighed and waved a hand. A glow of black light surrounded Cyrus, who froze in place. "Let's talk, just the two of us," Merlin said, and led Fort a short distance away from the circle, where the magicians were still preparing.

"You *know* why I need to do this," Fort said, not too upset about Cyrus being removed from the conversation, but still filled with the need to explain, to justify things to Merlin. If the older version of Cyrus would just agree with Fort's plan, he'd know he was right in going through with it.

And if Merlin didn't agree, well, Fort would still be alone. But the zombie magician had said Fort was the chosen one, and that had to mean *something*!

"It's the only way I have left to stop your family," he said to the old man. "Everyone keeps telling me I was *chosen* for something. If that's true—and if it is, I'd hate to be the one who chose *me*—then *help* me save the world, please!"

"Let me tell you a story, Forsythe," Merlin said, making Fort groan softly, though that didn't seem to slow Merlin down. "You *are* chosen for this, but not how you're thinking, not for any of that prophecy nonsense. Imagine taking *that* poem seriously." He nodded over at Cyrus. "My younger self isn't much of a poet. It barely even rhymes!"

Wait, *what*? His younger self? "Are you saying *Cyrus* wrote the prophecy in all the books of magic?" Fort said, his eyes widening. Did that mean that none of the chosen one stuff even mattered? If the situation weren't so dire, he'd almost have laughed at how upset that'd make Damian.

"Oh, I suppose it *is* a prophecy, if only because it's self-fulfilling," Merlin said. "Too many humans—too many sentients of *any* species—are convinced that they're better than others, more entitled to power. Cyrus added that poem to all the books the moment they were made to attract just those people, to use for his own purposes. People like Damian and, well, our friends here." He pointed at the magicians gathered inside the stone circles. "I have to admit, Cyrus did have some good ideas at times."

Fort blinked, not exactly sure what he meant by the magicians being like Damian. But that would have to wait. "So all of that about Damian bringing together the six types of magic to save the world is fake?" Fort asked, furrowing his brow, not mentioning that he'd wondered if it had applied to him, as Merlin didn't need to know *everything*.

"Oh, it's real," Merlin said, confusing Fort more. "Just as real as one and one add up to two. The six types of magic together merge into a seventh, and yes, theoretically you could use that power to do virtually anything, including save the world. But that's not the point here. Cyrus created his own prophecy to fulfill his plans, so don't let any of this chosen one garbage distract you."

"But the zombie . . . I mean, one of the magicians over there said that *you* hid me for some reason," Fort said. "I thought it had to do with being chosen. What was he talking about then?"

Merlin sighed. "I did choose you, yes, but only to make some hard decisions—and not because of destiny or that it was written in the stars. No, I chose you for your *heart*, Fort." He poked Fort in the chest. "I trust your compassion, your mind, and your wisdom. You tend to do what's right—even if you take some time to get there."

He blinked at that. "Ouch, first," Fort said, hoping he wasn't blushing too hard. "But second, how is that any different?"

"Maybe it's not," Merlin said quietly, looking away. "Maybe we set our fates when we choose our lives, our friends, those we can count on. And if that's the case, then I'm afraid to say you and I were destined to be friends from the start." He nodded at his angry, frozen past self. "Not that he'll admit it to you any time soon. He's got some growing up to do."

"I hope he does it quick," Fort said, before something horrible occurred to him. "Wait. So you're saying *all* of this happened to me because you set it up? My father being kidnapped by the Dracsi, William taking over London, all of it?"

"Oh, no, that was just random," Merlin said with a shrug. "Not everything the universe does has hidden meanings." He winced. "Well, that's not entirely true, but I don't want to scare you *that* much."

And yet he did anyway. "What is *that* supposed to mean?" Fort said, a chill going down his spine.

"Let me put your mind at ease," Merlin said. "We met originally due to random chance. You connected to Sierra, and that made you useful to my younger self. Yes, Cyrus then manipulated you with the rest, even as he became friends with you. But all of that was only due to who you are, and what you believe. Which brings us to the question that has led you here."

"How do I destroy magic, yes!" Fort shouted, as that at least was something he could understand.

"Always in such a hurry," Merlin said with a smile. "Forgive me if I wanted to drag out our final conversation a bit."

Fort's eyes widened. "*Final* conversation? What's about to happen? Am I going to . . . die?"

"You?" Merlin said, looking as surprised as Fort. "Yes, of course! But not at the moment. No, I was referring to me." He sighed. "If doing away with magic for a thousand years meant my family wasn't able to return here, where do you think that leaves me?"

Fort's entire body turned ice cold, and he stared at Merlin in horror. "I thought you'd just Time magic around it!" he said, not able to believe this. "You *have* to save yourself—you can't just let it all end here!"

"Unfortunately, that's exactly what I must do," Merlin said. "My time has come, as I always knew it would. I've lived a full life—several million of them, in fact—and I have no regrets."

"But *I* do!" Fort said, not willing to accept this. He felt something wet on his cheek and was surprised to find he was crying. "This isn't *right*. You don't deserve to die just to save us!"

"It's only fair, after the part I played in creating my family," Merlin said quietly. "You've seen the Atlantean ceremony by now, and know who I was. Actions have consequences—at least when you don't erase them with Time magic—and the time has come for me to pay."

Fort sniffed loudly, not sure what else to say. Somehow he had to convince Merlin that this was ridiculous, that he could just slip away into another time where magic still existed. The old man couldn't just give up; it wasn't *right*!

"Oh, come now," Merlin said, wincing at Fort's display of emotion. "Let's have none of that. I've lived for an eternity, and some of it was even quite pleasant!"

Fort laughed in spite of himself and reached out to hug the man, only for his arms to pass right through Merlin.

"Oh, now you had to go and do that," the old man said gruffly, then reached out and hugged Fort back, this time completely solid. Fort realized that he must have used his Time magic to make this happen, which made Fort cry even harder. "There, there, child," Merlin said softly. "It will all be okay."

"No, it *won't*," Fort said, burying his head in the man's robes. "You're dying, my friends are all under Damian's magic, and he's about to bring back the Old Ones, not to mention that the faerie queen has my father on Avalon. I'm alone in all of this, which at least would be worth it if I could save everyone. Only I still don't even know how to fix it! I don't know what to do!"

"You know plenty, Forsythe," Merlin said, not helping in the least. "You know all that matters, and I'll teach you the rest. But the final choice does belong to only you. I'm afraid neither I, my younger self, nor any of your family or friends can be of any help in that way." He nodded toward the center of the circle. "The time draws near, Forsythe. Come."

Fort looked back at Cyrus, who was still frozen. "What about him?" he asked.

Merlin smiled. "Oh, he'll be fine once you return to your present. The quiet will do him good. Now, let's go show you the last thing you'll need to make your decision: The *true* reason magic disappeared."

- THIRTY-SIX -

"MERLIN!" ONE OF THE ASSEMBLED magicians shouted, waving him over. "Have you finished talking to yourself yet, or is there more to come? They'll be here soon enough!"

Merlin sighed and glanced at Fort. "Insufferable, isn't he? I believe you met this one as a . . . What's the word you used, zombie?"

"Insufferable's a good word for him, then," Fort said, remembering how horrible the undead version of the magician had been. But that didn't mean the magician didn't have a point about Emrys, at any age. Even after all of Merlin's reassurances, Fort still didn't feel like he had a good grasp of what was happening, either with destroying magic to save everyone, or what all of the plans upon plans were behind the scenes.

Who was using whom here, and why did Fort keep getting

caught up in it? Was it just his own mistakes coming back to haunt him, or was there some larger purpose?

What *exactly* was he chosen to do?

As they approached, Fort noticed that the four magicians stood in the center of the rings of stones, but something was missing. "Where are the dragons and big cats?" he asked. "Aren't they the magicians' partners?"

Merlin glanced back and smiled. "Partners? Why, I suppose they are, in a way. But in a more *accurate* way, no, not at all. They'll be along by the end."

Okay. That didn't help in the least, but fine.

The magician who would attack Fort in a thousand years or so had long blond hair here and looked much healthier than when he'd been undead. He and the others all wore very similar clothing, hooded robes all around, though each held a different book in their hands.

"We have no more time to waste," the blond-haired man said. "Their pet human will be powerful enough to open a gateway here momentarily, and we don't yet have the power you promised."

"Cedric doesn't speak for the rest of us, of course, Eternal One," said a woman with dark skin and red hair. "This is a beautiful night, a full moon is in the sky, and I for one am glad to be here." She shrugged. "Though if you do break your promise, I can promise you'll regret it."

Merlin raised his hands, smiling slightly. "Patience, all of you. I will fulfill everything I have promised." He turned to the magician named Cedric. "We have time yet, a matter of days, in fact. Mordred is close, but not quite there."

Mordred? Why did that name sound familiar? Fort frowned, wondering if he'd get a chance to ask Merlin—or Cyrus—later. He moved in closer, hoping that none of the assembled magicians would be able to see him like Merlin could. That probably had to do with Merlin's Time magic more than anything, so he suspected he'd be safe, but he kept quiet just in case.

"You said we'd become more powerful than your kind," said another of the magicians, a woman with a shaved head and tanned skin. "How exactly will that occur?"

"You four represent the most powerful of all humanity, in each of the forms of magic," Merlin said, ignoring the question. "If you haven't yet met each other—"

"We have," Cedric said impatiently. "And we've all brought the books of magic you had us create. Though I don't know why you'd want us to make such dangerous items, for *beginners* of all people. I hate the idea that just *anyone* could learn what I know. How would we know they're worthy?"

A low murmur of agreement went up among the others.

"I know, I know," Merlin said, nodding sagely. "None of us want magic in the hands of those who haven't . . . earned it."

Fort swallowed some bile, not liking any of this. Hopefully, Merlin was just going along with their horrible words, but either way, this ceremony was starting to sound an awful lot like the one in Atlantis.

"I had to destroy a school myself!" the final magician said, this one with lighter skin and black hair cut close. "A colleague of mine planned on teaching peasants—*peasants*—how to use Mind magic. Can you imagine?"

"What did you do?" the red-haired woman asked.

"I erased all the students' memories, then wiped their teacher's mind completely, of course," the magician said, sounding disgusted. "I couldn't bear the shame if the world ever found out he was my nephew. Last I was told, he was still learning how to walk once more."

Another murmur went around as Fort's mouth dropped open at the people before him. They *were* human, right? Because if anything, they sounded more monstrous than the Old Ones had.

"My family had the same problem with some . . . locals," Merlin said, flashing Fort a subtle look that at least told him Merlin wasn't on board with any of this. "By creating the types of magic you have all now mastered, we ensured that no one could use them whom we didn't teach ourselves, and increased our own power a thousandfold over the old kinds of magic. And now—"

"Now your family is trying to return, so if we want to protect ourselves, *we* need something more powerful than what they have," Cedric said. "Which brings me to ask again, why are we wasting time? Let's begin the ceremony!"

"I just want to be very clear about what we're doing here," Merlin said, circling around to look at each of them in turn . . . including Fort. "My family imposed their own language upon magic, tying its power to their words. What you've done is take the next step, by making those words permanent in your books." He drew his own book from under his robes, and Fort gasped.

The Magic of Cause and Effect, it said. That was the book of *Time* magic!

"We're still missing one," the black-haired man said. "Where is the book of Spirit magic?"

"Ah," Merlin said, and turned a bit red, then plucked a

larger, familiar-looking book out of the air. "It's unfortunately been taken by the queen of the faeries in Avalon, but do not worry. I've already performed the ceremony on that book, so its power is awaiting the rest." He held up the larger book, and Fort's eyes widened as he recognized it.

It was the dragon dictionary Merlin had given him. What was *that* doing here?

The magicians, though, stared at it as if it were made of gold. "Is that . . . ?" one asked.

"It is," Merlin said. "Or, more accurately, it will be, yes. The seventh book of magic, one containing all the knowledge of the six others, the book that will bestow upon its owner the power of chaos in its *entirety*!"

The seventh book of magic? Fort almost choked. Merlin had handed over the seventh book of magic to him, just to help with some language lessons? But why? Cyrus had said Merlin knew Fort would use a Learn spell on it, so was this part of being chosen? He'd been meant to learn each type of magic?

If that was the case, then why? Merlin had said Cyrus's prophecy was true, in a way, and it mentioned a seventh book. But he hadn't made any sense when explaining it, and Fort was still lost even now.

All of the assembled magicians nodded, each looking almost hungry for what was to come.

"But what I didn't say," Merlin said with a smile, "is that this power can only belong to *one* of you: a chosen one."

"What?" the black-haired magician shouted.

"You tricked us!" said the bald-headed woman.

"He did no such thing," Cedric said, sneering. "How could you think that we all could share such power? Of course it was always meant for just one. If you didn't see that, your own intelligence is to blame, not Merlin."

"Agreed," said the red-haired woman. "I assume the one to receive this power will be chosen by magic itself?"

"Indeed," Merlin said, as Fort looked more closely at the book in his hand, wanting to be sure. It *was* the dragon dictionary, the same book Fort had used to learn the language of magic, down to the words on the cover that he couldn't read.

But how would the seventh book of magic make the power disappear?

"If you would all join me in a circle," Merlin said, gesturing for the others to move into place. Each one did, glaring at the others suspiciously, while Fort couldn't believe Merlin intended to go through with this. How could he give any of these monsters that kind of power? It would be just like giving it to one of the Old Ones!

That thought brought a strange memory to mind, his very first vision once he'd learned the dragon dictionary. He'd seen the universe from a distance, somehow, and everything had been so connected that he'd wanted to weep from its beauty. Even two species, the Old Ones and humanity, that had seemed so far apart once, looked like brothers and sisters to his eye during the vision.

And now Fort could see how that might be possible, only in the worst way. Merlin was right: Feeling entitled to power and wanting to keep it from others apparently transcended species.

"Cedric, you will be first," Merlin said, and nodded at the blond-haired man. "You must control the chaos and force that control into this tome through your own book. After each of you follow suit, the seventh book will contain the combined form of all magic and will be granted to whomever chaos deems the most worthy."

Fort wondered if he should try to stop this, to interfere if he could . . . but no, this had already happened, and it would save humanity from the Old Ones for a thousand years. As much as he hated to just let it go, it did seem to have a purpose.

"Is everyone ready?" Merlin said, giving Fort one last glance—and a wink—before black light began to shine all around the old man. "Then . . . let's begin!"

- THIRTY-SEVEN -

IN AN EERIE MIRROR OF THE ATLANTEAN ceremony by the Old Ones, the human magicians went around the circle, one by one, and did exactly as Merlin had ordered them to.

"Magic of earth and air, map your words of power to this tome!" Cedric shouted in the language of magic, and red light flowed from his book to the future dragon dictionary, making its pages glow with the same light.

Fort flinched, waiting for some kind of horrible curse to fall over the magician as it had in Atlantis, but this time, nothing happened. Instead, Merlin gestured for the next magician to continue, the black-haired man.

"Magic of our corporeal body, map your words of power to this tome!"

Blue light now mixed with the red, turning purple instead

of showing a spectrum, like Fort would have expected. Was Merlin's ceremony forming spells like the ones he'd taught Jia and Rachel, the magic that combined two different types? Or was this something different?

"Magic of cause and effect," Merlin said, a wide grin on his face as his own book glowed with the black light of Time magic. *"Map your words to this tome!"*

"Magic of eternal space, map your words to this tome!" shouted the red-haired woman.

"Magic of the far reaches of thought, map your words to this tome!" shouted the bald woman.

The colors in the pages of the dragon dictionary had already been muddied as soon as Merlin had gone, when a black light had joined the other two, but only grew worse with the next two. The book began to rise into the air, its pages flipping open and turning almost too fast to see as the light grew brighter from it.

"Magic of our ever-shifting spirits," Merlin said, and this time an orange light lit up from the book itself. *"Combine these powers as* one, *and choose the worthy master who might control you!"*

Somehow the addition of the orange light turned the overall glow from an odd sort of brown into a blazingly bright white, and Fort and the magicians all had to look away to avoid being blinded.

"Who is it choosing?" one of them shouted as Fort closed his eyes against the light. Even then, he could see it clearly, and he covered his face with his arm, hoping his vision wasn't going to be permanently damaged.

What that meant, though, was that he couldn't see what was happening.

"It has chosen me—I know it!" one of the women shouted.

"Do not touch the book until it has decided, or I'll burn off your hand!" said Cedric, or so Fort thought.

"Don't come near me, or—"

"*No*, do not touch it!"

And then he heard someone scream as they came flying straight at him—and then right through him. He turned to look and saw a robed body land hard outside the stones and not move.

"Myasa!" someone shouted from behind him, but it was too bright to look in that direction. Someone else screamed, and Fort realized that another of the magicians had been removed from the running.

But this didn't seem to be the book—the *magic*—choosing.

No, it was the magicians fighting among themselves, as far as he could tell, not even waiting to see who might be chosen.

Finally, the light dimmed enough for Fort to see. Where there had once been five magicians, including Merlin, now there were only two: Cyrus's older self and the one who'd been called Cedric. The others lay scattered inside the stone circle and out.

"It is *mine*!" Cedric said, a wild look in his eye. "None of the others were powerful enough to stand against me and therefore are not worthy to wield the all-magic!"

"So it would seem," Merlin said, and snapped his fingers. Instantly, several creatures appeared near the fallen magicians, including three dragons and a familiar-looking large cat. "Please take the fallen to their homes, that they might heal and witness the coming of a new world."

"It is as you said it would be," one of the dragons said, while the others each lifted an unconscious magician in his paws, then waited. The giant cat did the same, then backed out of the circle of stones, leaving just Merlin, Cedric, and the remaining dragon.

Cedric moved closer to the tome, limping a bit from some spell or another, and reached a hand out to touch it. His fingertips slid over the cover, and he jerked them back suddenly as if expecting a shock but quickly smiled, as the book didn't seem to have reacted at all.

"It *has* chosen me!" he shouted, and put both his hands on the floating tome. "The power of chaos, of all of creation, of life itself—"

A beam of white light shot out at him, striking him right in the chest, knocking him backward into the remaining dragon, who sighed, shaking her head. "This doesn't surprise me in the least, you little fool," the dragon said to Cedric as she gathered him in her massive paws, then turned to Merlin. "Is it time, Emrys?"

"Yes, Saila," Merlin said, and gestured to the other assembled creatures. "Please, take your partners and their books to the agreed-upon locations. We must be ready for the next step in this game."

"I can already feel it leaving," one of the dragons said, a green light fading in and out around him. "We don't have much time. I hope you're right about all of this, Emrys."

"As do I," Merlin told him, just as the dragons and the other creatures all disappeared in a glow of green. "As do I."

Now that they were alone, Fort found himself having no

idea what had just happened. "What was *that*? I thought this was how you all did away with magic!"

"And so we did," Merlin told him, nodding at the book, which again, didn't help Fort at all. Merlin seemed more tired than he had a moment before, though, and limped toward the nearest stone to lean on it. Fort quickly moved to his side, remembering their conversation from earlier, and suddenly dreaded what was to come.

He tried to help the old man to the ground, but his hands passed right through Merlin's body again. Merlin just grinned, then slowly sat himself down. "Thank you, my boy. But you should go now. You have much to decide and not much time to do so."

"I'm *not* leaving you like this!" Fort shouted as the sky seemed to lighten around him. Apparently they'd timed this to the sun coming up, as everything was getting brighter, but none of that helped Fort's mood at the moment. As conflicted as he was about Merlin's younger self, the old man had been . . . well, mostly kind to him, and as annoying as he was, he'd still helped.

But most of all, he couldn't stand knowing that this was the end for his ex-friend, and there was nothing he could do about it. "I still don't understand what I was supposed to learn," Fort said quietly, hoping Merlin wouldn't let himself pass away if he was still needed. "How did that make magic go away? What do I do to destroy it?"

"My family weakened the power of chaos in their quest for strength," Merlin said, his breathing slowing and his eyes drooping. "They did so by imposing order upon it, mapping it to their words alone. This weakened magic for anyone like your faerie friends who didn't know the words, while giving the remaining power to my family. But even so, they could never touch the most powerful type of magic. Not the way they were."

He slumped a bit, and Fort reached out in spite of himself, but again, his hand passed right through Merlin. "What type is that?" he asked quietly.

"It begins with Space and Time," Merlin said, wheezing slightly. "Those create the *where* and *when* of it all. Then the Elements take over, forming a world for a Corporeal being, complete with a Mind and a Spirit. Taken together, the six types of magic form the power of Creation, the final type of magic, able to change anything and everything, including magic itself. And that is what we've done here today."

Fort's eyes widened. "The magic in that book . . . can create things?"

"It can do *anything*," Merlin said. "And it has chosen its wielder, for good or ill." He pointed, and Fort looked down at himself, then gasped.

The sun wasn't coming up. Everything was getting brighter because Fort was surrounded by white light.

The book had chosen its user.

"Congratulations, Forsythe," Merlin said quietly. "You now hold total control over the entirety of magic in this dimension. Please try not to destroy us all?"

- THIRTY-EIGHT -

"NO," FORT WHISPERED, UNABLE TO believe it.

But there was no use denying it. The light was all around him, but it wasn't attacking him like it'd done to Cedric. No, it was almost infusing him with something, an energy he couldn't understand, could barely even comprehend.

Except he *knew* this feeling; he'd felt it in his visions. Was that what the visions were, the book trying to speak to him? Or . . . was it magic itself?

"The book chose *you*, Forsythe," Merlin said. "Because its magic *knows* you, as it knows all things. It has seen your thoughts, sensed your spirit, witnessed your actions through time and space. And in doing so, it has decided to trust you."

"I'm . . . the chosen one?" Fort asked quietly.

"Well, you're *a* chosen one," Merlin said, rolling his eyes.

"You think you're the only human with a good heart? Don't get arrogant on me at the end."

"Sorry!" Fort said quickly, but Merlin just chuckled, then began to cough. "I just . . . I still don't understand. It's choosing me, but does it know what I . . . what I have to do?" He couldn't even say the words, not with the light surrounding him, infusing him, filling him with its energy, its own sort of spirit.

"It knows," Merlin said, nodding slightly. "And it believes you will choose wisely, as it has. The rest is up to you."

And with that, he raised a hand weakly, and the tome disappeared, taking the white light with it in a glow of black Time magic. "Now it goes to wait in the future, when you will find it in your past. Or vice versa, I always forget." He laughed, then flinched from some kind of pain.

Fort winced, still filled with questions, still having no clue how to save everyone. He could barely bring himself to think about what needed to be done, not now that he knew that the book, that magic itself had *picked* him for some reason.

But didn't that mean it trusted him to save the world?

Merlin began to cough harder, and Fort quickly moved to his side. "Are you okay?" he asked, knowing the answer already.

"Magic is disappearing," Merlin said weakly. "We imposed

further order on it today, enough to weaken the chaos to the point it is almost gone. It will be forced to lie low, in what your kind will call a quantum something or other, until it's healed enough to return. At which point it will be up to *you* to decide what to do with it."

"But I still don't know how," Fort whispered. "Do I have to weaken it even more? Perform this same ceremony?"

"Why bother?" Merlin asked, then tapped Fort's head, his finger actually touching Fort. "You have the power of creation in there. You've had it since you took the book in, back in your future time. *You* hold magic within your hands now and can use it to do as you wish, including to destroy itself, if you choose to do so. It's up to you now."

Fort's mouth dropped open. He'd had the power to destroy magic all along, right within his head? Him? That didn't seem right! Books choosing people and Merlin trusting his heart were all well and good, but this was too big, too much for just himself!

But who else was there? He was alone now, and the choice was his. And he knew what he had to do . . . didn't he?

"I can't believe you knew this was all going to happen from the start," he said to Merlin finally.

"Or I'm just making it up as I go," Merlin told him with a smile, which somehow was even worse. He waved a hand again, and now a black glow surrounded Fort. "Go home, boy," he said. "You've got work to do."

"No, wait, *Mer—*" Fort shouted, then disappeared.

- THIRTY-NINE -

"—LIN!" FORT FINISHED, THEN WENT SILENT as he found himself back at the destroyed Oppenheimer School entrance along with Helio and a now-unfrozen Cyrus. A wave of nausea hit him, and he had to lean against some of the rubble just to stay standing.

"Did he freeze you, too?" Cyrus said, looking disgusted. "I can't tell you how much I *hate*—"

"No," Fort whispered, barely able to comprehend what had just happened. "He sent me home because . . . because he's dying. And he didn't want me to see it."

A look of shock and maybe even pain passed over Cyrus's face, before he covered it with a quick laugh. "Oh, I'm sure he's fine. He and I are meant to live until the end of time."

Helio put a hand on Fort's shoulder, and for the first time, Fort didn't try to remove it as quickly as possible and instead gave the faerie boy a quick smile of thanks. "If it makes you happy," he said to Cyrus, "I did find out that the humans who did away with magic were no better than your family. Maybe even worse. They all turned on each other for power and barely even cared that they were trying to stop the Old Ones from returning."

But Cyrus didn't seem to hear him, lost in his own thoughts. "It must be a trick somehow," he whispered. "It's just not possible. I can't just . . . *No*."

"Hey," Fort said, pushing on his shoulder to get his attention and hopefully distract him. "Our deal was for you to help me find out how to destroy magic, if you remember. But you didn't do *anything*. Merlin did all the hard work with your younger self."

Cyrus looked over at him, the anxiety in his face fading a bit. "Well, you should have specified that in the agreement. I thought you'd have learned better from the faeries about all of that by now."

Fort rolled his eyes, hoping this would keep the other boy's mind off whatever had happened to his older self. "And what's this about the Old Ones having had a human learning magic a thousand years ago? His name was something like Morgan, or—"

"Mordred," Cyrus said, nodding. "One of the Artorigios' sons, if I recall. Not a big fan of his father, so he learned enough magic to go looking for my family in another dimension, and asked them for power."

"But why would they give it to him?" Fort asked, thinking about Michael, Colonel Charles's son, and how the Old Ones had done something similar with him. "I thought they hated humans."

"They do," Cyrus said. "But if you've noticed, my sister, Ni'nev, the master of Space magic, went missing when my older self turned her and D'hea against the rest of my family, meaning they had no way to open a portal between the dimension they were exiled to and here."

"So they needed a human to do it?" Fort asked. "Why not just learn Space magic themselves? They could use what spell words they know and put together a few Space spells eventually. At least enough to get them back."

"Not by themselves," Cyrus said quietly. "Too many words were missing for one of my siblings to figure Space magic out by themselves. And from what you've seen, can you imagine any of them sharing their powers with the rest of my family? No, they could only use a stranger, a human in this case. Teach them what they needed to know, let the human put together some Space magic, and—bam!—there's your way home. Then they can do away with the human and have no threats to their own power." He sighed. "I'm sure they're doing the same with Michael."

A chill ran down Fort's spine. "So even if Damian doesn't bring them back . . ."

"They'll return eventually," Cyrus said. "Assuming their little apprentice can handle it. Mordred could up to a point, but he lost his mind in the process. And before you ask, I have no idea if Michael will ever get there, since it's never gotten that far, not with Damian's help."

Fort turned away, anger boiling inside him. "Then it's time I end this altogether. Apparently no one can be trusted to do the right thing and actually *help* other people, no matter who they are."

"There are always those who seek power," Helio said. "It doesn't matter if they're Tylwyth Teg, human, or Atlantean. But that doesn't mean there aren't good people as well, those who fight against injustice." He shrugged. "Even if it takes a bargain or two."

He might have a point, but where were those people now?

Seeing the human magicians turn on each other just made Fort wonder why Merlin even asked him to decide. Obviously humanity couldn't be allowed to have magic any more than the Old Ones could. There was just one thing left to do.

And if he really did have the magic of a seventh book inside his head, he was the only one who could do it. Merlin must have known it'd come to this, after setting it all up. But why not just explain things from the start?

"The seventh book," Cyrus said quietly. "That's what you're wondering about, isn't it? How Merlin could give you the seventh book of magic and tell you it was just some dictionary."

Fort looked over at him in surprise. "You don't have your magic. How did you know what I was thinking?"

"It's what *I'd* be thinking," Cyrus said. "And something I still wonder. I can't believe he hid it from me for so long, only to hand it over to you at the earliest possible moment."

"I think it was only ever going to work for me," Fort said. "It *chose* me somehow, back in the past."

"So where is this book now?" Helio asked. "If Fort needs it to end all of this, we'll have to find it. . . ."

"Oh, it's gone," Cyrus said, looking a bit ambivalent about it even as his cheeks turned red from embarrassment. "I destroyed

Merlin's little out-of-sync cottage a few weeks ago, so the book's lost in non-time somewhere."

Non-time sounded like something Fort didn't even want to think about. "It's okay. I learned everything in the book already," he said to Helio. "It's all in my mind, which means . . ." He paused, the enormity of everything hitting him again.

"Which means only you were going to be able to destroy magic," Helio said quietly.

"And that Merlin had this planned even throughout your whole game," Fort said, looking at Cyrus in awe.

"Oh, don't pin this on *me*," Cyrus said, holding up his hands to stop them. "He's on a completely different level. I thought I could win our game, and he beat me with *children*. After making me make friends with them! It was cheating at the highest level, and I can't help but admire him for it."

"But that doesn't tell me what I *do* with the book," Fort said, tapping his forehead. "Merlin said I'd have power over magic itself, but am I just supposed to cast a spell that destroys it? Won't it fight back?"

Cyrus looked at Fort almost fondly. "Oh, Fort. Weren't you paying attention? You have the power of Creation magic in your head, the sum total of the other six types of magic. There's nothing *to* fight back with. It's *all there*. You can do literally anything you want."

"Like wishing for more wishes!" Helio shouted.

Cyrus sighed deeply at him, then turned back to Fort. "It's *nothing* like that. But before you go off destroying anything, we had a deal, and I need you to fulfill your part of it."

Fort's mind was racing, and he almost didn't hear Cyrus. Even with all that power, he still could barely cast a spell without falling into some vision or another. Were those really magic trying to speak to him, or maybe fight back somehow? Whatever it was seemed pretty intent on showing him all the uses it had.

And magic had been pretty useful throughout time. Yes, if he destroyed magic, he'd save humanity from the Old Ones forever. But he also had no idea what that might do to the world itself. Even when magic was weakened over the last thousand years or so, it was still around, just buried deep in a place so small they didn't have the knowledge or technology to see it.

And if Fort destroyed it, it'd be *gone*. No more quantum physics, and that was just the beginning.

But if he didn't, the Old Ones would rule everything. He didn't have a choice; there *was* no choice. This was why he'd been chosen, to make this choice to begin with. His choice, and his *alone*.

A wave of loneliness hit him, fighting with his uncertainty to see which would win.

"My magic, Fort?" Cyrus said, pulling Fort's attention back to the present. "I made sure you found out how to destroy magic. Now it's your turn. Give me back my power. You've got everything you need in that head of yours."

Fort opened his mouth to respond but realized he had no idea what to say. Could he really just give an Old One back their magic, especially the Timeless One? There were so many ways Cyrus could still stop him from ending magic if he wanted to.

"You don't have to do this, Fort," Helio said quietly. "I know I always told you to keep your word . . . sorry, your *father* always told you that. But in this one case, both he and I would agree it's okay to break your promise."

Cyrus sneered. "I guess I'm lucky Fort is a better person than that, then."

Fort sighed, staring at his ex-friend as he wondered if Helio was right. Cyrus had promised not to interfere with things if he had his Time magic back. And his magic would let the silver-haired boy escape to another time period where the power still existed, so he wouldn't be hurt if Fort did away with it all.

But could he trust Cyrus, after everything? Yes, the Old One had learned some horrible truths about his family, but they were *still* his family. And giving him back his Time magic would mean Cyrus could keep Fort from ever being born, and stop the plan altogether without technically interfering with it directly. He and Merlin had certainly found loopholes to promises before.

But the more Fort thought about it, the more he came back to the fact that the Old Ones weren't any worse than the human magicians he'd seen, not at their core. And if he broke his promise here, how was he any better than they were?

He was already doing the worst thing he could think of to save the world. At least this let him balance that a bit with saving Cyrus, too.

"Okay," Fort said, and Cyrus grinned widely in victory. "But I really don't know where to start with it."

"I told you, the power in your head can do *anything*," Cyrus told him. "Just say the words, and command the magic to return to me."

Well, it was worth a shot. Fort closed his eyes and concentrated on Cyrus glowing black with Time magic once more.

Somehow, though, everything felt more possible than when he'd tried spells at random before. Maybe it was everyone telling him he could do anything, or maybe he was just gaining confidence, but making the image in his head real only seemed like a matter of when, not if.

"Let Cyrus have access to his power again," he said in the language of magic.

White light began to glow around Cyrus, and he let out a wild shout in excitement. "It's coming—I can feel it!" he yelled as Fort began to waver, all of the energy in his body suddenly gone. His muscles started shaking, and he took a step forward, only to drop to one knee.

"Fort?" Helio said, but he wasn't quick enough to stop Fort from collapsing as the white light grew brighter, surrounding Fort, the ground around him, and everything he could see.

"My magic!" he could hear Cyrus shout. "It's returning! Fort, you did it! You really—"

And then his voice disappeared, along with Helio and even the ground. The white light faded, leaving Fort somewhere else entirely: a cozy-looking living room, one he'd seen before. It wasn't too big or too small, but just right for a small family, maybe of around three.

Was this another vision? Had he fallen unconscious again?

But it didn't feel the same as the other visions. The other times, he'd passed out and heard a voice in his mind.

This time, there was no voice. Instead, he looked up to find a woman waiting for him, sitting on what looked like a comfy couch.

"Hello, Fort," said the same voice he'd been hearing throughout the visions. His mother looked down at him with a loving smile. "It's time we spoke in person, I think."

- FORTY -

. . . MOM?" FORT SAID, THE WORD FEELING both completely alien and 100 percent right at the same time. "Am I . . . dreaming? Is this another vision?"

His mother put a hand on his shoulder. "I *am* your mom," she said. "Or at least a possibility of her. The power in your head chose me to speak to you, pulled me out of your memories so that we could talk."

A possibility of her, taken from an image in his mind? What did that even mean?

And then Fort stiffened, remembering something he'd tried not to think about since. This version of his mother came from the vision that Cyrus had shown him when he'd promised Fort his parents back, if he'd just join Cyrus's side.

"You're *not* her," Fort whispered, a feeling of revulsion filling him as he looked at the form of his mother now. "And you thought that talking to me in the form of my dead mother would be a *good idea*?"

He turned to go, not able to even *consider* speaking to whatever this was in front of him, but there were no doors out of the living room, no exits anywhere. "Let me go," he whispered, not looking at her. "I *won't* talk to you, not like this."

"I'm afraid I can't, Fort," said whoever it was behind him. "We need to speak. The time for your decision has come, and I still have a lot to show you."

The disgust in his stomach morphed into rage, and he whirled around to confront his "mother." "You don't get to decide what I need to see!" he shouted. "I know what I have to do, so *let me out of here*!"

Even looking at his fake mother made him sick. She was sitting so calmly on the couch that could have been his family's in some sort of alternate future, if only he'd sided with Cyrus.

"You haven't seen what is possible yet," the woman said, looking sad now. She gestured, and suddenly Fort was sitting next to her on the couch, and the television was on. "All you can think about is saving the world, and that's obviously pretty important! But what you're missing is that you have the power to also make it *better*."

The television flickered, catching his attention, and he turned to find another memory he'd have preferred to forget: the Dracsi attack on Washington, D.C.

As he watched, the image seemed to push out from the television, surrounding him on all sides until the living room and his fake mother were both gone, replaced by the destroyed National Mall in D.C.

At the moment, a Dracsi's hand was pushing up through the Reflecting Pool, so it wouldn't be long before it took his father from the Lincoln Memorial again.

Fort's heart beat so hard it could have broken through his chest, but he forced himself to stay calm. This was all just a vision, none of it was really happening. He closed his eyes, unwilling to be a part of whatever this was.

"You don't have to be afraid," his mother's voice said, echoing through the sky from a great distance. "You have the all-magic now, Fort. You can do *anything*, just like Cyrus told you."

As she said the words, an incredibly intense light pierced through Fort's eyelids, and he opened them to find himself glowing as bright as a star.

"You hold the power to change anything you want," his mother's voice said. "The force of possibility that brought me here *chose* you, Fort. It wants *you* to control its chaos over anyone else."

Incredible power filled his body, instantly dispelling any fear he'd felt at the sight of the Dracsi. His eyes widened in surprise, and he even smiled, feeling more confident in himself and his power than he'd ever felt in his life.

This wasn't the same magic as a beginner Healing or Teleport spell. This wasn't the natural talent of a student born on Discovery Day—or even a dragon. This was something . . . different, *new*.

"Try it," his mother's voice said, still from a long way away. "See how it feels."

Fort took a deep breath, then raised his hand, letting the power flow through him. The words for any spell he could think of appeared in his head as needed, and he smiled.

Then he pulled the Dracsi straight out of the ground.

All around him, the silent, fleeing people—probably under Sierra's control—stopped and turned to stare at the now-flailing creature hanging in the middle of the air, dwarfing the monuments around it. It roared, but Fort snapped his fingers, and it immediately went silent.

"That's it," his mother said, and Fort could hear the notes of pride in her voice. But he wasn't done yet. He waved his other hand, the words to the spells he needed passing through his mind with but a thought, and instantly the damage to the Mall mended itself, repairing the Reflecting Pool and the Washington Monument to a condition better than new, practically sparkling in the glow of his light.

A distant memory of revenge flitted through his mind, but he rejected it, feeling disgusted by his past obsession with it. This wasn't like when an alternate version of himself had used Spirit magic to take over the country: No, he still felt pity for the Dracsi, knowing it was just a dragon that had been transformed against its will.

But he could help with that, too.

Another spell, and the Dracsi shrank down to a more reasonable size, morphing into dragon form as it went. Only this time, instead of dissolving back into magic as had happened when D'hea had tried the same thing in the Dracsi dimension, Fort reversed the damage done and gently laid the now fully restored dragon down upon the ground.

"I'm sorry for your pain," he said to the dragon in the language of magic. *"How do you feel?"*

The dragon looked at him in confusion as a still-silent crowd stared at it in wonder. Fort traced the magic holding them together back to Sierra and saw that it was actually she who was curious about what was happening, which made sense. She'd never seen anything like this before, after all.

"I have no memory of how I came to be here," the dragon said. *"Who are you? Where is this place?"*

Fort started to respond, but before he could, the image pulled away from him, depositing him back on the couch next to his mother. The confidence and power he'd felt a moment ago disappeared, but he knew they hadn't gone far: All he had to do was embrace the magic inside his head, and he'd have all the spells he could possibly need.

"Do you see now?" she asked, giving him a fond look. "There are more possibilities than you can imagine, Fort. You can do whatever you want with all of this power, my little chosen one. You could even *destroy* the Old Ones, if that's what you wanted."

- FORTY-ONE -

"WHAT—" FORT SAID, BUT THE television changed scenes, pulling him back in once more.

Now he stood on the grounds of the old Oppenheimer School, the one destroyed by the second Dracsi attack. Damian hovered in the air, his mind controlled now by Ketas, the Old One of Mind magic. And as Fort watched, Damian/Ketas was using that magic to take over the assembled students below.

Again, Fort felt a power like none he could have imagined previously filling his body, and he snapped his fingers, the words to the spells he needed passing through his mind with the speed of thought. Instantly, Ketas's spell was disrupted, and Damian fell to the ground, landing hard but unhurt.

The four monsters coming through Damian's portal turned toward their new enemy, and Fort could feel their fear even from a distance. He smiled and teleported over to them, just a few feet away. "Well, hello," he said to the surprised Old Ones. "I'm sorry, but today's not going to be your day."

Then he shut the portal behind them, trapping the Old Ones in the Dracsi dimension once again, and cracked his knuckles.

This was going to be *fun*.

Only before he could move, he found himself back on the couch with his mother once more, the feeling of power gone just as before.

"There's nothing you couldn't do with the all-magic," his mother told him, beaming with pride. "Without the threat of the Old Ones, you could turn the world into a paradise!"

The television showed another scene, this time of food appearing magically for hungry children and hospitals releasing their patients, cured of their many diseases. Fort watched in wonder at what he would have thought of as miracles becoming everyday occurrences and realized she was right: He *could* do all of these things.

But he wouldn't.

"No," he told his mother, shaking his head. "I'm sorry. But I can't do this."

Her proud expression melted away, and she tilted her head

in confusion. "What do you mean? You *can*—I just showed you how. You can change the world, not just save it. We could have a heaven on Earth!"

He looked away, but she just put a hand on his face and turned him back toward her. "We could be a family again," she said, her voice now cracking with sadness. "Me, you, and your father, all together, like we should have been from the start."

Fort's heart broke as he gently pulled her hand from his cheek. "You don't understand. *No one* can have this kind of power. I've seen what it does, whether it's Atlanteans or humans or even a faerie queen: It's never *enough*."

"But this is *all* of the magic!" his mother said. "There literally isn't anything beyond it. You could do whatever you want!"

"And that scares me more than anything," Fort said, shivering at the thought of it. He shook his head. "I'm so sorry, but I can't be trusted with it. Even just the Spirit magic alone turned me into someone I despised—"

"That's because the Old Ones corrupted it!" his mother said, standing up now and staring at him. "The magic within you can be purged of that curse. You have that power. Take it, Fort, and burn the old ways to the ground. Change this world into something new, a world of plenty for all!"

She had a point, and for a moment, Fort wondered if he should consider it. There *were* so many changes he could make, fixes to the world that would save so many lives. . . .

But the fact that he was tempted meant he already wanted it too much.

"I'm afraid I can't," he said, and stood up as well to face his mother. "I know we won't be better off without magic, but no one will rule over us either, so at least things won't get worse. I just can't risk it."

She stared at him for a moment, then slowly smiled. "Oh, my darling little Forsythe," she said, and reached out to pull him into a hug. In spite of knowing this wasn't actually his mother, Fort let it happen and hugged her back as tightly as he could. "You turned into the person I always hoped you would."

"So you're not mad?" he asked, pulling back to look at her, not sure why that mattered so much to him. "You and, um, magic?"

"Mad?" she said. "Why do you think it chose you? Merlin gave the chaos to someone who would learn not to be tempted by fame or power, who would choose what was best for others over themselves. And that's why you're its chosen one, *truly*."

Fort winced. "I just told you, I don't want that—"

"Which is exactly why you're perfect," his mother said with a laugh. She put a finger on his forehead. "Now all you have to do is see *all* the possibilities!"

And with that, his mind exploded in a burst of white light.

- FORTY-TWO -

EVERYTHING WAS POSSIBLE. THE LIGHT showed Fort that.

Every single choice he could ever make could be made. And somewhere, it played out, whether in this dimension or another.

And it was all because of magic.

Magic was what connected everything, because nothing was separated to begin with: It all began as one, and would someday be one again.

He wasn't alone. No one was.

And magic was there to remind him of that, always.

It was the potential in all things to change, to become something new, become something better.

And it was beautiful.

Nothing awful was permanent, not with magic. Nothing good couldn't be improved.

Everything could be changed, fixed, returned to one.

Tears streamed down Fort's face.

"I think I see it," he whispered. And he did.

He saw why some people wanted power for themselves and feared those they didn't know. Because they were scared, fearful of the unknown.

He saw why others wanted to be important, to be special, instead of just being who they were. Because they feared they weren't good enough to begin with.

And he saw why he'd been chosen: because he was willing to see these things and understand them . . . eventually, at least.

But more importantly, he also knew that magic belonged to *everyone*, and couldn't, shouldn't be controlled by any group. Which meant there was only one thing to do.

And as Fort considered it, filled with the power that made change possible, he realized that everything actually could fit together, if he just made the right choices at the right moments.

Xenea and the elder dragons. Ember. The faerie queen,

and his bargain with her. Cyrus. Damian. The Old Ones. His friends. All of it.

And then he smiled at how it all fell into place, even as the light began to fade.

"You now have the knowledge of the all-magic and can use it as you wish," he heard his mother say. "You know what comes next, then?"

Part of him felt sadness that the connectedness was going away, but he knew it wasn't really; it was always there. He just wasn't seeing it as clearly. He'd have to remind himself of this moment, often, so he'd never forget it.

"Yes, I do know," he said to his mother.

"And what is that?" his mother asked, beaming at him.

"I have to destroy magic," he said, smiling at her. "But thank you for letting me see my mother one more time."

Then he snapped his fingers and ended the vision.

- FORTY-THREE -

FORT OPENED HIS EYES TO FIND HELIO staring down at him with concern. "You're awake!" the faerie said, almost shouting in excitement. "Are you okay, son—I mean, Fort?"

Fort nodded, feeling strangely better than he had in months. "I'm just fine," he said, and gave Helio a smile. "Thanks for the concern, though."

Helio raised an eyebrow at this. "You're not going to yell at me to get away from you?"

Fort grinned wider. "It's not your fault you're struggling with memories and emotions that the queen gave you in order to trick me. I just appreciate you sticking around to help."

Helio winced and put his hand against Fort's forehead. "You must be sicker than I thought. We need to get you to an emergency room."

Fort laughed and gently pushed the faerie's hand away. "I really am feeling good. Like I've slept for the first time in a year." He slowly stood up, marveling at how everything just seemed to work together, from his mind to his muscles. It really *was* magical, in a lot of ways.

"Cyrus left while you were unconscious," Helio said, watching Fort carefully, like he thought Fort might collapse back into anger or despair at any second. "I'm worried he's going to find Damian and help bring his family back, now that he has his magic."

Fort nodded. "He might. But that's okay. We should probably get going too."

Helio nodded. "So you're going to do it? Destroy magic? That's really the only way?"

"Is it the only way? Probably not," Fort said, feeling like he wanted to laugh again. "But sometimes you have to burn everything to the ground just to start fresh, you know?" He clapped Helio on the shoulder and gave him a long look. "You really have been a good friend, even if it's due to fake memories. I just wanted you to know I appreciate it."

Helio sighed. "I see. The vision took your mind somehow. Don't worry, Fort, we'll get you fixed up." He cast a glamour, and the air around Fort shimmered, but nothing happened. Helio frowned. "Why didn't that work?"

"Eh, you did your best," Fort said.

Helio just stared at him for a moment, then took out what looked like Fort's father's phone from a pocket. "There's got to be a hospital around here somewhere." He held it up in all directions. "Why is there no signal out here? Doesn't the TDA need cell towers?"

Fort rolled his eyes, but his smile stayed put. "I'm fine, really. Are you ready to go? We should really be getting to Damian now." His eyes glowed yellow. "If I'm seeing things correctly, he's about to open a portal to the Dracsi world."

"What *happened* to you?" Helio asked, looking confused. "You sound so . . . confident now. Not that you shouldn't! I've always had all the faith in you, son . . . I mean, *Fort*. But are you sure you should be fighting Damian in your condition?"

"Oh, we're not going to fight Damian," Fort said. "We're going to help him. Come on."

Before Helio could respond, Fort's hands glowed green, and he and the faerie boy disappeared in a burst of light.

They reappeared in Washington, D.C., on a set of marble steps familiar to both of them, though Helio would have known them only from Fort's father's memories. Scaffolding ran up and down most of the Lincoln Memorial from the attacks less than a year ago, while a dome covered the space where the Reflecting Pool had been between the memorial and the Washington Monument.

The memory of the place still sent a chill down Fort's spine, but somehow, that was okay. His father was safe, even if he *was* in Avalon, and it wasn't like the Dracsi could hurt either of them anymore.

"Um, Fort?" Helio asked from his side. "We didn't use a teleportation circle."

"Nah," Fort said, scanning the land around them. "I don't need those anymore."

"Since when?" Helio asked, but Fort just shrugged.

Surrounding the National Mall were TDA troops, and it looked like they'd had the time to evacuate any tourists. There were even some standard military soldiers helping with crowd control, making sure the few surrounding blocks were also closed off.

"Would you mind helping me look for Damian?" Fort asked. "Try your glamour—I think he might be using magic to hide the Oppenheimer School students."

Helio nodded, and the air shimmered briefly. Then he gasped. "Not just them," he said softly. "There are more TDA soldiers too. *Lots* of them, and they all have weapons."

"Oh, good!" Fort said. "It's about time we wrapped this all up." He looked in the direction Helio pointed and squinted his eyes, which were now glowing blue. "Okay, I see them. It looks like the TDA aren't under his Spirit magic, which is good. But they'll still be taking orders from Colonel Charles, so we'll have to deal with that. Not exactly a surprise, though."

"You're not going to . . . hurt them, are you?" Helio asked, sounding nervous. "I know they betrayed you all back at the school when Damian attacked, but they're just doing what they think is best. And I wouldn't want the boy I raised . . . I mean, I wouldn't want *you* doing something you'd regret."

"Nope, they'll be fine," Fort said, continuing his scanning. "Ah, *there* we go. I found Damian and the others." He squinted again at the hill where the Washington Monument had stood and now Damian gathered his inner circle. "Looks like he's got Ember, Jia, Rachel, and Sierra all close by. Makes sense. He probably thinks I'm going to come after them first."

Helio didn't look too happy about the assembled forces. "So what's the plan? I'm happy to fight at your side, but from the looks of it, they have an army, *two* dragons, and a ton of human magic users, while we have, um, *us*."

"Look on the bright side!" Fort told him. "It looks like Cyrus didn't come to help Damian after all. Maybe he's rethinking everything!"

"That's the bright side?" Helio asked. "Yes, to be fair, I'd rather not be facing an Old One as well—"

"See?" Fort said. "That's the optimistic spirit we need. Don't worry, we'll be okay. Now why don't I go and say hello to them?"

"Go and say . . . Fort, the only advantage we *have* is surprise! You can't just throw that away!"

Fort turned to Helio, giving him a fond look. "This isn't fair to you, what the queen did. I should take the memories away and send you back."

Helio immediately shook his head. "I'm not going *anywhere* until you're safe. I don't care if these emotions are fake, I'm still feeling them, and worried sick about you. If you're staying, *I'm* staying. And I'll do anything in my power to protect you."

Fort bit his lip, almost overcome with gratitude. "Thank you for that," he said softly. "You didn't choose any of this, but you're sticking by me anyway." He tilted his head. "Maybe someday you and my father can actually meet."

"He's probably the only one in the world who understands how anxious I am right now," Helio said with a shiver.

Fort smiled. "Don't worry. Whatever happens, we'll figure it out. Now c'mon, it's time to go say hi to Damian."

And again, before Helio could object, they both disappeared.

- FORTY-FOUR -

ELDER, BE CAREFUL!" EMBER SHOUTED, a moment before Damian noticed that Fort and Helio had arrived. "My father has returned!"

Fort knew she had no choice, that Damian's Spirit magic had forced her to turn them in, but it still hurt. And with every passing moment, he missed the certainty that it would all work out he'd felt while filled with possibilities in the vision. But he had to stay optimistic and stick to the plan.

"Hello, Damian!" he said, waving as the dragon and Fort's friends all turned toward him, each of them glowing with their own magic specialty. "Sorry to go missing like that back at the school, but I had some things I needed to see."

Damian tilted his head curiously. "Ah, the coward has returned." He started to speak again, only to sniff loudly. "You smell different, Fitzgerald. What are you trying to pull?"

Fort quietly smelled his armpit. “Sorry about that,” he said, wincing, reveling in knowing this would annoy Damian, even if it was petty. “It’s been a long day. But don’t worry about me. I’m not here to make any trouble.”

“Since when could you make trouble?” Damian growled. He nodded at Fort, and Jia, Rachel, and Sierra stepped forward. “Take care of him, will you? It’s time for the portal to open.”

“I *just* said I wasn’t here to fight,” Fort said, shaking his head as yellow Mind magic shone around it, courtesy of Sierra. Just like Ember, this one hurt, but he blinked the spell away while pretending to freeze in place, not wanting to interfere with things.

Jia followed Sierra’s magic with a Paralyze spell of her own, which Fort also canceled, but he let Rachel’s swirling ribbons of fire continue to surround Helio, threatening to burn him if he moved. That one would be way too obvious if he ended it now.

Not that Helio knew what was happening. “Fort!” the faerie yelled, and started to cast a glamour to free himself.

I’m fine, Fort said in Helio’s mind, his pupils turning just the barest hint of yellow as he did. He hoped none of his Spirit-magicked friends would notice. *We need Damian to do what he came here to do. Don’t break free just yet, okay?*

All right, but I hope you know what you're doing, Helio said, ending his glamour. Fort sent him back some warm, fuzzy feelings, then turned his attention to the older dragon.

"I don't remember ordering you to go easy on them," Damian said, and the three girls all looked down at the ground, ashamed. "Still, we can take care of this later. It's time."

With that, he leaped into the air, his dragon wings spreading out wide as he rose far above the National Mall. He had to still be invisible to any lingering tourists who'd escaped the TDA and military evacuation, given that no one started screaming in horror.

As he reached the height of a few hundred feet in the air, Damian paused majestically, hovering in place as he glowed green with Space magic.

This was it: the moment Fort had been fighting against ever since they'd defeated the Timeless One. And here he was, just letting Damian get away with it. Yes, it was all part of his plan, but that plan had made so much more sense just a few minutes earlier, when he'd been able to see all the possible outcomes.

Now he had to fight to stop from shaking anxiously. As it was, his hands began to sweat, and he risked wiping them on his pants, since the others were all distracted by the dragon.

It wasn't too late. He could still end this all, keep Damian from casting the spell, and put things off for another thousand years. . . .

But no. He'd been chosen for a reason, and he had to see this through. It was time.

Even so, as Damian roared his spell and an enormous portal opened to another dimension, Fort had to keep from throwing up at what he'd just allowed to happen. The view of the other side of the portal made him want to scream in terror, and he knew right away that this was the home of the Old Ones in the Dracsi world.

A small part of him, the part that still held on to what he'd seen in the vision, decided that the Old Ones were trying too hard. Why embrace magic's curse this much, unless to try to intimidate people?

Somehow, the thought that the Old Ones were that insecure made him feel better about the whole thing.

But the remaining tourists around the National Mall didn't have that luxury.

Screams sounded from the streets around them, and Fort fought to keep from turning his head to see what was happening, even if Sierra and Jia were too distracted to notice he wasn't under their spells. From the corner of his eye, he could see a few remaining civilians and a mass of regular military personnel pointing and shouting in absolute fear, which meant Damian hadn't made the portal invisible along with everything else.

Knowing the dragon, he would want everyone to see this. After all, he thought he was about to defeat the Old Ones, then rule the world. Why shouldn't the people see his victory?

The TDA soldiers were more prepared for what was coming and continued their evacuation of the remaining civilians, as well as any military now who couldn't handle what they'd just seen. That was good. The fewer people Fort had to worry about, the easier this would be.

"OLD ONES!" Damian roared through the portal. "You have threatened my world for too long. I have come to destroy you, once and for all! Face me if you dare!"

Fort wrinkled his nose. It wasn't just the Old Ones who were trying too hard. Damian was laying it on a bit thick.

But the dramatic call-out seemed to have done the trick, as four humanoid shapes appeared within the portal, and a freezing chill swept through everyone within sight of the National Mall.

They had come.

Ketas, the Old One of Mind magic, wore his customary skull

helmet and crystal armor, which Fort now recognized from the guards in Atlantis.

D'vale, the Old One of Elemental magic, lit up the now-darkened Mall as her body burned with fire.

Perhaps the most dangerous of them all, Q'baos, the Old One of Spirit magic, was also the most horrific, with her body covered in the screaming faces of her people, the Atlanteans who'd been pulled into the Spirit magic curse.

And the fourth . . .

"Michael!" shouted someone from the ground, and Fort glanced over to find Colonel Charles and Gabriel standing not far from the hill, both staring up at the human boy the Old Ones had kidnapped in their first attack so many months ago.

When Fort had last seen Michael, the boy's body had been in a state of constant change, shifting between fire like D'vale and a weird sort of diamond, even turning transparent. His eyes, though, had been the worst, resembling the horror of the Old Ones' home more than anything.

Now, though, his body had returned to human, at least as far as Fort could tell from a distance. He looked larger than he had before, stronger, too, but otherwise he could have been any other student from the Oppenheimer School.

But in spite of his family's shouts, Michael didn't look at them. Instead, his eyes were locked on Damian, and he had an unreadable expression on his face. Did he know that the Old Ones were just using him to return to their home, in case Damian had never opened a portal? Or had he decided to fully join the Old Ones, taken in by whatever madness they'd put him through?

Fort held his breath. They'd be finding out soon enough.

YOU ARE A *FOOL*, YOUNG DRAGON, came Ketas's voice in their minds, sending everyone but Fort and Helio to their knees in pain. Even Damian seemed to flinch as he hovered in midair, though he tried to act like he was unbothered. YOU'VE GIVEN US EXACTLY WHAT WE WANTED.

"You underestimate me," Damian said, and grinned, showing off his enormous fangs. "I have more power than the dragons you've faced in the past. Each type of magic is *mine* to control."

A horrible laugh echoed in Fort's head, and around him, everyone writhed in pain, even Helio this time, which brought the faerie far too close to his burning ribbons of fire for Fort's comfort. He blinked quickly, and the flames disappeared, replaced by illusionary ones. He probably should have done that from the start, honestly.

NO ONE CONTROLS MAGIC BUT MY FAMILY, YOUNG DRAGON, Ketas responded.

"Until now," Damian shouted, breathing fire into the air. "Your reign of terror ends here, *today*. And after I have destroyed you, I will lead this world to a new—"

And then he stopped abruptly as his wings began to dissolve.

"What?" he shouted, even as he plummeted from the air, the minerals in his wings melting away into the air around him as he fell.

"YOU SPEAK TOO MUCH, DRAGON," D'vale said, and Fort's eyes widened. Without D'hea and his Corporeal magic, Fort figured Damian's body at least would have been safe. But D'vale's Elemental magic could be equally dangerous when used in this manner.

Just before he hit the ground, though, Damian teleported himself back into the air, his wings glowing blue as they grew back instantly. "Then I'll let my actions speak *for* me!" he roared, and Fort rolled his eyes. "Let us *end this*!"

And with that, the three Old Ones and Michael passed through the portal, the real battle began, and Fort desperately hoped he hadn't made a huge mistake.

- FORTY-FIVE -

DAMIAN ROARED AND DOVE TOWARD the Old Ones, his various claws lighting up with multiple types of magic. A black light rocketed toward Ketas, a Time spell to freeze the Old One of Mind magic, while blue Corporeal light surrounded D'vale, wrapping her fiery body in on itself. And for Q'baos, yellow Mind magic struck hard, and the Old One shouted out in pain.

"*Whoa,*" Helio said, looking impressed by the display. "He's not bad. Could he actually have a chance?"

Fort didn't respond, not wanting to sink the faerie boy's hopes. Because this fight hadn't even begun, unfortunately.

The black Time spell struck Ketas, but the Old One disappeared, reappearing elsewhere in multiple spots as his Mind magic created dozens of illusions of himself at once. Each Ketas struck out cruelly at Damian, sending Mind bolts searing into the dragon's skull, and Damian roared out in pain, whether all were real or even just one.

D'vale, meanwhile, sizzled out of her Corporeal tangle by transforming into lightning, then rocketed straight at Damian, morphing into a solid block of iron at the last moment to knock Damian from the sky with the force of the blow.

As the dragon sped toward the ground, Q'baos was upon him, covering Damian in an eerie, orange light. "YOU *DESPISE* YOURSELF," she commanded the dragon. "YOU CANNOT SUFFER ANOTHER MOMENT OF YOUR EXISTENCE. ATTACK, AND WIPE YOUR STAIN FROM THIS LAND FOREVERMORE!"

Damian nodded obediently, then dug his claws into his own chest. The pain set him off roaring again, apparently disrupting the Spirit magic, as he turned on Q'baos, eyes burning with hatred.

"You *can't* beat me!" he shouted, his words much less formal now that he was losing. "I am a *dragon*, and we were made out of magic itself!"

The other two Old Ones floated down to join their sister, surrounding Damian on three sides.

AND WE ARE THE *MASTERS* OF MAGIC, Ketas thought in all of their heads.

All at once, the three Old Ones attacked. Yellow and orange light combined, while an enormous spout of magma exploded from the ground toward Damian, obstructing Fort's view. Smoke rose from where the lava struck the remaining grass on the ground, making it even harder to see what had happened to Damian, but the fact that the Old Ones had paused in their attack, confident in their victory, wasn't a great sign for him.

But when the smoke and magma did finally clear, Damian was gone.

"NOT QUITE SO WEAK AFTER ALL," D'vale said, sounding almost excited as her fire grew brighter. "FINALLY, A REAL OPPONENT. WHERE IS HE, KETAS?"

HE IS BLOCKING MY MAGIC, Ketas said in their minds. I CANNOT FEEL HIM. BUT IT WILL ONLY BE A MATTER OF TIME.

The ground beneath them began to rumble, and Fort wondered if D'vale had set off some fault line with her magma attack. But as the shaking intensified, he realized he was wrong and slowly smiled as the ground burst open, and an enormous dragon claw as big as a Dracsi's emerged, grabbing all three of the Old Ones in its grasp.

"NOW YOU'VE MADE ME ANGRY!" came a roar from

below, making the ground shake even harder, to the point that most of the soldiers and Fort's friends were knocked from their feet. Damian, now easily as large as the Washington Monument, pulled his way up from the ground, then unleashed a cargo-ship-sized breath of fire on the Old Ones clutched in his claw, a flame so hot Fort could feel it from a few hundred yards away.

But before it could hit, D'vale sent the dragon fire spinning off into the sky, while Q'baos and Ketas resumed their attacks, attacking the dragon with both Mind and Spirit magic. But Damian snapped out with his gigantic jaws, and his fangs closed around the three with a loud, bone-rattling thud, prematurely ending both colors of magic.

He grinned, then opened his mouth again . . . but the Old Ones were gone.

"WHERE DID YOU RUN TO, LITTLE MONSTERS?" Damian roared, looking around the National Mall, though he moved much slower now, due to his massive size. "ARE YOU AFRAID? ARE YOU GOING TO RUN BACK TO—"

A human shape came flying out of nowhere to strike Damian right in the lower jaw, sending the dragon flying backward with the force of the blow. His gigantic body crashed down hard on the remains of the TDA dome, crushing it beneath his massive weight, while above him, Michael floated in the air, glowing with a dull white color as he surveyed his victim.

"Michael!" Colonel Charles shouted again, and left his soldiers behind, sprinting toward the spot below his son. But he didn't make it even a few feet before Gabriel opened a portal in front of his father, and the two teleported over to where Michael waited for Damian's next move.

"Mike, what are you doing?" Gabriel yelled up at his brother. "You're on the wrong side. You need to fight back against the Old Ones!"

Michael glanced down at his family, without any recognition in his eyes, then flicked a finger. Gabriel and Colonel Charles both went flying toward the hole beneath the National Mall. Fort clenched a fist, and the two stopped just before falling into that hole, and he quickly teleported them back to the TDA, hoping they'd stay out of it for the moment.

This battle was *not* the place for family reunions.

Back on the ground beneath Michael, Damian groaned, then shrank back to his normal size, unable to hold his Corporeal enlargement in place anymore. As he did, Michael surrounded him with blue light and yanked him into the air, then held Damian in place just in front of himself.

"DID YOU REALLY THINK YOU COULD BEAT MY MASTERS?" he asked, his voice far closer to the Old Ones' than human now. "THEY TOLD ME I COULD PLAY, AS LONG AS I LEFT YOU ALIVE FOR THEM."

"Michael, let him go!" Colonel Charles shouted again, though at least he stayed where Fort had put him. "I don't know what they did to you, but I'm here for you, son! Come down here, and I'll fix all of this!"

Michael slowly turned to where his father and brother waited. "IT SEEMS AS IF I SHOULD KNOW YOU," he said, raising an eyebrow. "YOU LOOK FAMILIAR, BUT LIKE SOMEONE I HAVEN'T SEEN IN DECADES."

Gabriel and his father looked at each other. "No, Mike, it's been a few months, that's it," Gabriel shouted. "Do you remember when you and I last talked?"

"GAB—riel?" Michael said, shaking his head as if to clear it from a daze, his voice dropping in power. "Is that you?" He flinched in pain, and his Old One voice returned. "YOU SHOULD LEAVE. THIS WORLD IS NO LONGER SAFE FOR YOUR KIND."

"We're not going anywhere without you, son!" Colonel Charles yelled up, though he looked shaken.

Michael glanced down at him in annoyance now, which didn't seem like a great sign. "I'm not the boy you remember," he said quietly. "*Please*. Gabriel, take him away. I don't want you two seeing this."

Before they could respond, a rainbow of colors struck Michael, only for him to brush them away absently before turning back to Damian. "CAN'T YOU SEE I'M SPEAKING TO MY FAMILY?" he asked, looking more irritated than hurt.

"Your *masters* were going to destroy you, once you brought them back here," Damian told him, looking a lot less sure of himself now. "You were always their backup plan, if they couldn't find me. But it's not too late to save yourself and fight back against them!"

Michael slowly smiled. "OH, I THINK YOU ARE MISTAKEN." He blinked, and blue light surrounded Damian, shifting him back into his human form. Only Damian's shocked expression told Fort that something more had happened, and he swallowed hard, not liking this at all.

The light faded, and Damian let out a choked cry. "What did you do to me?" he shouted.

"I GREW TIRED OF YOUR DRAGON RESISTANCE

TO MAGIC," Michael told him. "SO I MADE YOU FULLY HUMAN."

Fort's mouth dropped open, and he cursed, not having expected this. Should he fight back now? It might not be too late. . . .

But it *would* destroy the rest of his plan, that he knew for sure. He just had no way of seeing what possibilities led where anymore, and that made him more nervous than anything.

"You took my magic!" Damian shrieked, flailing around in Michael's magical grasp. "What did you do to it? Give it *back*!"

"OH, THAT WOULD BE YOUR FAULT," Michael told him. "YOU WERE THE ONE WHO AGED YOURSELF, STUDYING THE VARIOUS KINDS OF MAGIC OUTSIDE OF TIME. I JUST ADJUSTED YOUR SYSTEM SO THAT YOU'D BE TOO OLD TO ACCESS IT."

Damian screamed again, this time in pure agony, and Fort clenched his fists, doubting everything now. *Fort,* Helio thought in his mind. *You have to do something about this!*

Fort winced but shook his head, not even bothering to pretend to be paralyzed anymore. *Not just yet! I'm still waiting for something.*

And hopefully he wouldn't be dooming the entire world by doing so.

The three Old Ones floated down near Michael, who seemed to be enjoying every one of Damian's screams. "WELL DONE, APPRENTICE," Q'baos said.

"YOU HAVE MADE US PROUD, HUMAN," D'vale said. "YOU'VE GROWN IN POWER EVEN MORE QUICKLY THAN WE COULD HAVE HOPED."

"THANK YOU, MASTERS," Michael said, and turned to bow low before them.

The three Old Ones glanced at each other, then struck out at Michael at once with their magic.

UNFORTUNATELY, THOUGH, WE CANNOT ALLOW ONE OF YOUR DISGUSTING KIND TO WIELD SUCH MAGIC, Ketas said.

Michael cast his own counter spells, defending himself in surprise, but with his attention stolen, Damian plummeted from the sky, no longer able to hold himself up without any magic. Fort flicked a finger, and the former dragon disappeared in a small green burst, only to land on the ground just to his side.

"What?" Damian said, looking up at Fort in surprise. "How did—"

"Shh," Fort said, and knocked him out with a Sleep spell

before turning back to Michael and the Old Ones. Damian would have a lot to answer for later, but right now Fort had more urgent concerns.

"MA-sters!" Michael shouted, trying to resist their attacks but slowly being pushed back. "Why are you doing this? I thought I was serving you well!"

"YOU WERE," Q'baos said.

BUT YOU ARE STILL HUMAN, Ketas added.

"AND THEREFORE ARE UNWORTHY OF THE MAGIC," D'vale said. She reached out, and Michael began to scream, his body separating into its various minerals, starting with his fingers, and running up his hand.

FORT! Helio shouted.

Fort felt a bead of sweat slide down his face. This was it. If he was right, then this was the moment that it all hinged on. But if he was *wrong*—

But just before Michael's hand disappeared entirely, his whole body froze in a burst of black light, canceling D'vale's attack.

The three Old Ones glanced down to find a lone silver-haired boy on the ground below them, looking up at them in disgust.

"I *really* hoped I was wrong about you all," Cyrus said to his siblings, shaking his head. "But it was never about humans invading and taking our magic, was it? No, you're all just a bunch of cowards, and honestly, I'm ashamed I ever called you family."

"Yes!" Fort shouted, and couldn't help grinning at the sight of his friend's return. Finally, everything he'd seen in his vision had started falling into place. This was going to take some careful maneuvering, but he knew it could work, if he just made sure the timing was correct.

Helio! he shouted in the faerie boy's mind. *I need you to go find someone for me and tell him what's going on here. Tell him to bring as many friends as he can!*

Find . . . who? Helio asked, sounding confused even in his thoughts.

Fort sent the faerie a mental image, both of the boy he was going to find and where to find him, and Helio's eyes widened. *Are you serious? They've never been my kind's biggest fans.*

I need your help with this and wouldn't ask otherwise, Fort told him, pushing his honest sincerity over that thought along with it, and Helio sighed.

Okay, I'll be back momentarily, he thought, and started to shimmer, then paused. *But don't do anything dangerous while I'm gone!*

Fort smiled and waved as the faerie disappeared, then turned to Jia, Rachel, Sierra, and Ember, canceling out Damian's Spirit magic with a snap.

"Hey, everyone," he said quickly, before they could react. "I'm going to need your help. While Cyrus distracts the Old Ones, we're going to destroy magic—*together*. Sound good?"

- FORTY-SIX -

D*AMIAN!"* RACHEL ROARED, AND LEAPED straight at the slumbering former dragon, her hands on fire.

Fort quickly cast a spell, and she froze in midair, a look of surprise coming over her as she tried to turn to see who'd stopped her but ended up flailing around instead. "Sorry about that," he said. "But we don't really have time for that just now."

"Don't have *time* for it?" Jia said softly, the look in her eyes even more dangerous than Rachel's, if that was possible. "I think I'm going to *make* some time. And some pain, too."

"These two speak truthfully, human," Ember said in English. Fort noticed immediately she hadn't called him Father, which meant that even without Damian's Spirit magic, she was still angry with him, and he swallowed a large lump in his throat, hating that. "He deserves to be punished in eternal fire for what he's done to us. And I'm happy to provide it."

"They're right, Fort," Sierra said quietly, not looking at him. He could almost feel the guilt radiating off her, in spite of the fact she'd had no choice in fooling them. Not to mention that she wasn't speaking in his mind, which told him more than her words that she didn't want him seeing what she was thinking. "He needs to *pay*. This is all his fault."

A burst of magical light caught Fort's eye, and he looked over to find that Cyrus had disappeared, while D'vale now looked at least a few millennia older, her body just glowing embers instead of a full, raging fire. Q'baos, meanwhile, was frozen in black light, though Ketas seemed unhurt, glowing brightly with his own Mind magic as he searched around for his brother.

Unfortunately, that meant the most dangerous Old One was still free. No matter how good Cyrus was, Ketas would be able to beat him. As Merlin had said once, Time magic was naturally weak against Mind spells, given that even a Time magician couldn't move faster than thought.

They'd have to hurry.

"You can all get your revenge later," Fort told his friends, trying to ignore their angry—and hurt—looks. "Right now we've got one chance to stop the Old Ones, and we're going to need help. Some of it, you might not like." He paused, sending out a call in his mind. "And some of it's just going to be a bit odd."

Forsythe? came the answer. *Has the time come to hand the dragon over?*

Sort of! Fort responded in his mind, hurrying on before the other could respond. *How about you bring your new friends here, and we'll work out the details?*

Wait, what? But—

"I do not follow your orders, *human*!" Ember roared, pulling Fort back out of his mind just in time to watch her launch a burst of dragon fire at Damian. Fort barely knocked the fire off course as it was about to strike the former dragon.

"Michael turned him human!" Fort shouted at her, more scared at what she'd almost done than mad. "He can't even use his magic. He's basically helpless now, so could we concentrate on the bigger problem?"

Who's Michael? asked the voice in his mind, and he sighed.

Just get here when you can! Fort shouted back, then quickly moved back to his friends. "I get that this is all coming pretty fast, so maybe there's time for some magical catch-up. Sierra, could you do me a favor?"

She still wouldn't look at him. "Whatever you need," she said quietly, and again, he noticed she hadn't responded with Mind magic. That hurt as much as Ember's new title for him, but again, it'd have to wait.

"Show them all what I've seen in the last few hours, and what we have to do about it," he said, tapping his head. And while she did that, he'd bring in the last two people they'd need.

Sierra nodded, and before Ember or the others could object, yellow Mind magic covered each of their heads, and they all went quiet now, giving Fort a moment to think. They'd have his plan down in a few moments, and things were in motion with his first set of allies—assuming they *would* be allies. But it all still hinged on how long Cyrus could last against his family members.

And however long that was, it wouldn't be enough if he didn't hurry.

YOU WERE ALWAYS THE WEAKEST OF US, EMRYS! Ketas shouted in everyone's mind, and the others around him all shook in pain from the force of his mental voice, even under Sierra's spell. AT LEAST YOUR MAGIC CAN STILL BE

USEFUL TO US, IF NOTHING ELSE. OUR EXILE WILL HAVE NEVER BEEN IF WE ERASE HUMANITY FROM HISTORY ALTOGETHER!

Yikes. *That* didn't seem good and had never been a possibility Fort had seen. He'd have to finish this before Ketas found Cyrus, or it might all be for nothing.

He immediately used his own Time magic, as well as a quick Teleport spell, and brought the final two people he needed to his little group, then cast a Mind spell to link them into Sierra's. Again, everyone went quiet, though now he was going to have to do more explaining when Sierra was finished.

"Fort, you've got to be *kidding* me with this," Rachel said, shaking off Sierra's spell first as she moved toward him. "You honestly think this will work?"

"Of course!" he said, mostly confident and faking the rest.

"But how do you know . . . ?" She turned and caught sight of the two new arrivals. One, Ellora, who Fort had just pulled from the future Damian had sent her to, was probably a comfort to Rachel, since they all trusted the Time girl.

Gabriel, though, was another story.

"*What* is he doing here?" Rachel said, pointing at the colonel's son, who was still under Sierra's memory spell.

"We need him, Rachel," Fort said quietly, knowing how she felt. "You know the plan, and we're going to need someone with experience in each type of magic."

"*You* have that now," Rachel growled as her hands began crackling with lightning. "*He*, on the other hand, handed us over to the Old Ones last time they were here! What makes you think he won't do it again?"

"Because they just tried to kill my brother," a low, angry voice said, and Fort looked over Rachel's shoulder to see Gabriel shaking off the Mind spell as well. "I don't want to be here any more than you do, but if this plan actually has a chance, then I'm in."

Rachel gritted her teeth and threw Fort another look. "You didn't answer my question. You have every kind of magic in your head right now. So why can't we use you?"

Fort winced. "That's going to change in a second. Sierra?"

She sighed and glanced up at him, and the guilt in her eyes almost broke his heart.

"You once gave me a few of Jia's spells while you were in a coma," Fort said quickly, before Rachel could see where this was going. "Think you can do that same thing awake?"

Sierra slowly nodded. "I can, and I know what you want me

to do. But remember what happened to Jia? She lost the spells completely. If I do this, you'll be left with *nothing*. No magic whatsoever. Are you sure about this?"

"Very sure," he said, completely lying this time. "Now please, give everyone here all the power I have, so we can fix this for good."

- FORTY-SEVEN -

"FORT, WHAT ARE YOU DOING?" RACHEL said, and Jia started to object as well, but before she could say anything, he felt Sierra's presence in his head, her voice speaking over theirs.

Real talk, she said. *I know you don't know for sure this will work. But I* do *know you've got the power to do . . . well, whatever you want! You could try to take down the Old Ones by yourself, and maybe even succeed. Why are you doing it this way, instead?*

He bit his lip, not sure how to respond with anything but complete honesty. *I'm no chosen one, Sierra. None of us are. The only way we're going to make this work is* together. *And right now that means you six need a little push.*

She sighed deeply. *Okay. But just in case it doesn't work, I want you to know—*

He stopped her there. *There's nothing you have to say to me,* he told her, pushing all of his warm feelings for her into her mind. *You said it earlier: This was all Damian.*

Relief flooded back, along with some warm feelings of her own that made him blush. But before he could say anything else, she nodded at him and started her magic.

Yellow light lit up his world, and he could feel the presence of all-magic in his head, the power that had given him so much confidence and awareness of possibilities . . . and then he felt it melt away, sinking into the minds of his friends. And Gabriel's, too.

"Whoa," Rachel said, stopping in mid-objection to look around with glowing red eyes. "What did you do, Sierra? I can see what everything's made of. I can see the *atoms* in things!"

"We're all so *beautiful*," Jia said, glancing at the others with her newfound Corporeal spells as tears slowly slid down her cheeks. "I almost can't believe this. Is this what magic actually is?"

"It's what it could have been," Fort told her. "But we weren't selfless enough to let it be."

The rest of them seemed just as impressed by their new powers, all but Ember, who rolled her eyes, probably having lived this every day of her life, and Ellora, who was presently shaking, covered in black light. Fort quickly stepped over to her, not sure what to do if she was caught in some sort of time loop. "Are you okay?" he whispered.

The black light faded, and she turned around to look at him. "I am now," she said, letting out a huge breath. "Honestly, I needed a moment to myself just to *deal* with all of this. I'm tired of coming in at the tail end of things here and being expected to just join in without even having a chance to think!"

He raised an eyebrow, hardly able to deny any of that. After all, to her, they'd just been fighting William the day before. "But you're feeling better now, then?"

She nodded. "I just needed a little time. Fortunately, I had all I could want."

He smiled, then moved to address the others. "You should all now have what you need to go through with things. But none of this is going to matter if the Old Ones get ahold of Cyrus before we finish. For that reason, I think we need to go in order." He looked at Ember. "If you wouldn't mind covering Spirit magic, I think that has to go first. Otherwise, we could all be back under their spell in seconds."

The dragon nodded. "It's the most foul of all magic anyway."

No one disagreed with that. "Then, I think we have to do away with Time magic," Fort said, looking at Ellora. "If

Ketas takes over Cyrus, then he could erase all of humanity."

Ellora nodded. "Works for me. Can't say I'll miss being stuck elsewhen in time again."

Fort turned to Sierra. "After that—"

"No," she said, shaking her head. "If we lose Mind magic next, there's a chance that the spell I just cast could go with it. And that'd mean all the power you just passed along to everyone would revert back. Mind magic has to go last."

Fort cringed but nodded. That would mean Ketas would be the last to lose *his* magic, after they destroyed the rest. That wasn't great. But Sierra had a point and left them with no other option.

"Then we need people protecting you," Fort said. "Jia, can you—"

"No," Rachel said, stepping into the middle of the group. "I'm the one with Illusion magic. I can keep us hidden *and* defend us the most easily if we're attacked. Elemental magic goes just before Mind magic."

Fort sighed, but he didn't have any better ideas. "Okay, then it's Spirit, Time, Space . . ." He pointed at Gabriel, who nodded, glaring back at him. "Corporeal, Elemental, and Mind."

"That's all fine," Jia said. "But why are you going over this now? Where are *you* going?"

AH, they heard Ketas's voice in their heads, and now Fort felt the pain worse than any of the others, given that all of his magic was gone. He fell to his knees as Ketas continued. THERE YOU ARE, LITTLE TIME WORM.

Fort glanced up, his head still pounding, and found Cyrus a few dozen yards away from Ketas, but slowly walking toward his brother with quavering steps, as if controlled by Ketas's magic.

This was it. They had to start *now* and still would need more of a distraction.

"I'm going to save my friend," Fort said, and turned to leave, readying a teleportation spell in his head . . .

Except there were no spell words there. All of his magic was *gone.*

"Um, Gabriel," he said, looking back over his shoulder. "Would you mind sending me over there?" He pointed at Cyrus.

"Are you joking?" Rachel shouted, throwing an illusion up over them to hide the group. "You have *nothing* to defend yourself with, Fort! One of us should go!"

Fort looked over at Jia and nodded at the staff on her back. "Can I borrow that for a second?"

"No!" Jia said. "Rachel's right. You won't last a minute!"

"I can, and I *have* to," Fort said. "I've seen how this all goes, and this is the only way. The rest of you are necessary for the ceremony, and I'm the only disposable one."

"Human, *no*," Ember said, and she looked up at him with wet eyes. "I won't allow this. You need protection now, more than ever. Even if you are horrible and make poor choices."

"I'll be okay," Fort told her, and cupped her scaly cheek fondly. "I won't be alone, after all. Seriously, it'll—"

"Oh, just go already!" Gabriel growled, and before anyone could say anything else, he pulled a teleportation circle down over Fort, sending him across the remains of the National Mall to land just a few feet from Cyrus.

In spite of everything, Fort couldn't help but smile at that, both for Gabriel being Gabriel, and how much Ember was going to take him down later.

But for now, he had a job to do, and that was to save Cyrus, and hopefully distract the Old Ones in the process.

Unfortunately, he had no idea how to do either.

Ketas glanced down at him, and his skull mask split into a grin. *YOU,* he said in Fort's head, and Fort once more fell to the ground at the force of his power. YOU DARE TO FACE US WITH NO MAGIC TO SAVE YOU?

Feeling completely naked without his spells, Fort looked up hopefully at Cyrus. "It's okay. I'm not alone," he said again.

Ketas's divided attention gave Cyrus just enough control for the silver-haired boy to turn and look at him. "Fort, I'm so sorry," he said quickly, but went silent as the yellow light around his head intensified.

DO NOT LOWER YOURSELF IN A HUMAN'S PRESENCE! Ketas roared, and Fort thought his head might explode now. He yelled out in pain but knew he had to push through this. His friends just needed a few more seconds to start. . . .

"I understand . . . why you did it, Cyrus," Fort said with a groan, pushing back to his feet in spite of the agony still radiating through his head. He knew the silver-haired boy couldn't hear him, not with Ketas in his mind, but that didn't matter: It still needed to be said. "We'll work it . . . out later, okay? I have a feeling . . . we're going to be good friends again, if the future . . . is any indication."

Q'baos and D'vale, now freed from Cyrus's spells, floated over to Ketas's side. Michael had also been freed, but he still lay on the ground, not moving, probably from D'vale's attack.

"A HUMAN, FRIENDS WITH ONE OF OUR KIND?" Q'baos said, sounding disgusted.

"THIS CANNOT STAND," D'vale said, and lifted a hand.

Her magic surrounded Fort and pulled him into the air. He looked over at Cyrus, who had his eyes on Ketas, and he wished the other boy had been able to hear his words, because he wasn't sure he was going to get any more.

"THIS WILL BE PAINFUL," D'vale said, and she sounded excited about that.

And then the worst pain in Fort's life began as his body began to disintegrate, just as Michael's had done. It started in his fingertips and felt like red-hot knives cutting through each one, separating out the various minerals that made up his muscles, skin, and bone.

"HOW WE EVER LET THIS HAPPEN—" he heard Q'baos say, as if from miles away, but then her voice went silent abruptly.

And then the pain stopped too.

Fort gasped in relief and looked up, not sure what was happening. Q'baos shuddered like she was going through the same thing he had just been.

"Chaos that forms our ever-shifting spirits," Fort heard Ember shout, her voice sounding as if it were coming from all around them, instead of over in the now magically invisible group. *"I RELEASE you from our control!"*

This was it. The plan had begun, and if it somehow managed to work, then they might actually have a chance at not only stopping the Old Ones, but maybe even fixing the world, too.

And if it didn't, then humanity would be serving the Old Ones for all eternity, if not wiped out of history altogether first.

Q'baos's mouth opened, but no noise emerged. Instead, the screaming heads all over her body began shouting in joy as they dissolved away into nothingness, until all that was left was a small, scared-looking Atlantean woman.

In spite of the agony he'd just felt, Fort grinned.

WHAT IS THIS? Ketas shouted, but the pain wasn't as bad this time, like the Old One's shock had interfered with his power. Q'BAOS, WHAT IS HAPPENING?

"I don't *know*!" she shouted, looking around in terror. "The power . . . it no longer obeys my commands! My spell words aren't working!"

"Don't . . . you . . . know?" Cyrus said, smiling as well as he fought back against Ketas's Mind control. "Fort's . . . destroying . . . *magic*!"

The three Old Ones—or now, two Old Ones and one Atlantean—all turned to look at him.

"Well, I'm destroying *your* kind of magic," Fort said as a

shimmering portal opened behind him, and six elder dragons appeared inside it, an annoyed-looking Xenea leading them. At the sight of them, he just grinned wider. As he'd told his friends, he knew he wasn't alone out here.

"WHAT HAVE YOU DONE, HUMAN?" D'vale said, her fire turning white with anger.

"We're taking your spells," Fort told her. "No more special power for those who think they're better than everyone. We're reversing what you did to it, returning the chaos back to how it was before *you* all took control of it." He shrugged. "I think it's time that magic returned to the *people*, don't you?"

- FORTY-EIGHT -

DESTROY THE ETERNAL ONES!" ROARED A dragon, and the six massive creatures came flying straight toward them. Fort's eyes widened as he realized he was standing directly in their path, but fortunately for him, Xenea shimmered him to her side, out of the way of the deadly dragon attack.

"What were you *thinking*?" she shouted as D'vale and Ketas defended themselves, with one dragon immediately taken over by Mind magic and another enveloped by the ground below, their battle already threatening to destroy the entire National Mall. "I thought they were just a backup plan for Ember!"

"Well, they can have Damian, if they still want him," Fort said, nodding over at what looked like empty ground, thanks to Rachel's Illusion magic. "Though I think he's fully human now, so they might not."

"What is *happening* here?" Xenea said, just as Ellora took her turn.

"Chaos of cause and effect, I RELEASE you from our control!" she shouted, and again, her voice came from all directions due to Rachel's spell.

And suddenly too much was happening for Fort to keep up with.

Cyrus screaming in agony grabbed his attention first. The silver-haired boy began to convulse as he aged, grew younger, then reversed again over and over, while a dragon swooped down to devour him.

"Xenea!" Fort shouted, pointing at Cyrus. "Grab him!"

"Oh, for the love of my queen," she said, sounding weirdly different, but Fort barely noticed as the dragon descended, plowing through the spot Cyrus had been just as the Old One shimmered out of sight.

He appeared at Fort's feet, now unconscious from whatever he'd just gone through, though at least his age seemed to have stabilized. "Do you think you can heal him if he needs it?" Fort asked, turning to Xenea, then gasped.

The faerie girl next to him was no longer anywhere close to his age. Instead, she'd grown a few feet taller and now resembled the faerie queen in size as well as age, as the curse of childhood from the Timeless One had apparently worn off.

"Huh!" Xenea said, looking down at herself. "*That* was unexpected!"

She wasn't wrong about that. "Do you think that happened to every faerie, then?" Fort asked.

"It must have," Xenea said. "The queen's going to be thrilled." She frowned. "But Helio's going to be even more insufferable now."

Fort's thoughts turned to his fake father, and he hoped the faerie boy—no, faerie man—was okay on his mission.

"I don't know," he said. "He might be growing on me."

Xenea made a disgusted face and rolled her eyes, then turned back to the battle before them. "The Eternal Ones won't let this go on for long, Forsythe. They're surprised now, but they've beaten dragons before. Whatever you're doing, you're going to need to hurry."

She wasn't wrong about that, as Ketas had already taken out four of the dragons with his spells. As resistant as they were to magic, the dragons still stood almost no chance against the Old Ones, who were just too powerful.

But all they needed was time. And there were still a few friends on their way—at least, he hoped they were.

"Chaos of eternal space," Gabriel shouted, his voice echoing around the National Mall. *"I RELEASE you from our control!"*

And that was it for Space magic. Unfortunately, the Old One of Space magic was long gone, so it wasn't going to help them now. Though part of Fort regretted never being able to teleport again.

For a moment, he almost panicked at the thought that Helio might not be able to return either, but no, the faeries used the older form of magic, weakened by the Old Ones, but still workable. So he should be able to make it back okay, assuming he'd had luck.

As if he'd summoned the faerie just by thinking of him, a shimmering portal appeared, and what looked like the entire population of dwarfs—sorry, Dracsi-kin—emerged, with Helio next to a familiar-looking younger dwarf.

"My friends!" the young dwarf, Sikurgurd, shouted. "The elf speaks the truth! Q'baos's power is gone, and we are now *free*! Now is our chance to take back our lives for good!"

A roar went over the Mall, and the dwarfs began rushing the Old Ones en masse, shaking the ground with their trampling boots.

"Um, what are *they* doing here?" Xenea asked him, wincing.

"Those little monsters *hate* us. We've never gotten along."

"Helio seems to have done okay," Fort said. "Do you think you could go grab him and bring him over to where Rachel and the others are? They could use all the protection they can get."

She snorted at him. "This is a *lot* of freebies I'm giving you here, human. You're going to owe me." On that ominous note, she disappeared in a shimmer, leaving Fort with the still-unconscious Cyrus.

With the dwarfs' attack in full-swing, the two remaining dragons managed to regroup and now were working together against both D'vale and Ketas. But Fort knew even with an army, the dwarfs wouldn't last much longer against the Old Ones. At least the Dracsi-kin were fairly resistant to magic, especially Ketas's Mind magic, if he remembered correctly, so could hopefully buy Fort's friends more time.

"Chaos that creates our corporeal body, I RELEASE you from our control!" he heard Jia shout and felt a thrill go through him, as they were now down to just the last two types. Again, it would have been nice to take out another Old One, but D'hea had already lost whatever power he'd had with his life to D'vale. Not to mention he'd actually been at least a tentative ally.

But even if there were only two left, they were the two Old Ones still present, and some of the most powerful of the family. And in spite of their resistance to magic, the dwarfs were getting trounced, with D'vale throwing dozens of them across the Mall at a time and sending yard-long bouts of flame at the rest. She had to be avoiding lightning in particular, given how good the dwarfs were at utilizing it.

"What have you *done*?" shouted a voice, and Fort sighed, wondering why Xenea hadn't figured that out yet. He whirled around to find an adult faerie facing him, but it wasn't Xenea.

"Your Majesty!" Fort said, bowing low to the faerie queen. This was *not* the time to annoy her, at least not any more than he already had. He frantically searched for something to say, then realized he had a bargain fulfilled. "As promised, we took care of your dragon situation, so our bargain is complete!"

"I don't care about our bargain!" she shouted, then paused as she seemed to realize what she'd said. She looked over Fort's shoulder to where the last dragon had just fallen to D'vale and raised her eyebrows. "Oh. Well then. That's actually quite nice, thank you." Then she turned back to Fort. "But more importantly, my children's curse has been lifted! What miracle made this happen?"

"Right, isn't that great?" Fort asked, dreading what was coming next. Because their other bargain had been for all the magic in his head, which at the moment amounted to right about none. "Maybe keep in mind that we gave you that for free when it comes to our other deal."

She narrowed her eyes and touched a hand to his temple, then pulled it away in horror. "You are *empty* of their magic, child! You have broken our agreement!"

She held out a hand, and Fort rose into the air, held tightly in an invisible grasp. But hopefully unlike D'vale, the queen would give him a chance to speak before trying to dissolve him. "I didn't break anything!" he said quickly. "I promised you could have whatever magic was in my head, and you *can*! I never said how much would be there!"

The queen sneered, then dropped him hard to the ground. "A technicality," she spat.

Fort groaned, then slowly pushed himself to his feet. "Maybe," he said, wincing in pain. "But it's still true. I'm fulfilling our deal, which means our bargain is over."

The queen gritted her teeth, and tiny lightning bolts sliced through the air all around her, a smaller display of anger than he was used to seeing from her. But granted, they didn't typically meet in the middle of a battle against the Old Ones. "I . . . concede that you have met the terms," she growled. "Therefore I shall deliver to you your father, right here and now."

"Wait!" Fort said, throwing up a hand. "Can you hold off until this is over, so he won't be in danger? You just got your children freed from their curse. Doesn't that earn me a little mercy?"

"Mercy?" the queen asked, raising an eyebrow as thunder rolled in around the lightning. "I am *overjoyed* by the return of my children. But you made no deal for breaking the curse, and so I give you nothing in return."

Fort swore silently, then looked out over the field, remembering something Xenea had hinted at several times. "You know, everything's going to change here, if we can stop the Old Ones," he said quickly. "It wouldn't surprise me that if you were willing to help, maybe there'd be some room for you and your children here. Maybe even on your former island?"

The UK government might not love the faeries moving back in, but right now, all Fort cared about was making sure his friends finished the ceremony. If it'd help, he'd offer the faerie queen the moon.

The queen's eyes flashed in surprise, and then she slowly smiled. "Perhaps there is room for a new bargain after all."

- FORTY-NINE -

ENOUGH OF THIS! KETAS SHOUTED AS the two remaining Old Ones rid themselves of the last dwarven attacker and turned their attention to an empty spot in the field, right where Rachel and Sierra were waiting. D'VALE, THERE ARE THE HUMANS TRYING TO TAKE OUR POWER FROM US. WE MUST DESTROY THEM!

D'vale gestured, and the illusion Rachel had put up was swept away in an instant, revealing just her and Sierra still standing; the others all lay on the ground, exhausted from their part.

Helio and Xenea quickly put up a shimmering shield, but a bolt of red light struck it, and the shimmering disappeared as Helio fell with a shout of pain.

"Chaos of earth and air," Rachel shouted out, only for a Mind spell to slam into her head, silencing her.

"No!" Sierra shouted, and cast her own spell to cancel Ketas's attack, but the earth beneath her feet opened, and she fell in. Rachel grabbed her at the last second on a cushion of air.

"DIE, FOUL HUMANS!" D'vale shouted.

"You first, Eternal One!" shouted the faerie queen, appearing at D'vale's side. And in her hand she held the remains of a broken sword, its flames rising high into the air without burning her at all.

D'vale sneered as the remains of Excalibur sliced down toward her. Not even trying to block it, she just waved a hand and shattered the weapon into its component atoms. But as it disappeared, the queen attacked with her own magic, having used the sword as a distraction, and D'vale's flaming form began to distort, causing her to scream in pain as her body was caught up in a shimmering grasp.

RELEASE HER! Ketas roared, and a Mind bolt struck the queen, collapsing her, but now it was too late.

"I RELEASE you from our control!" Rachel finished, with Sierra standing protectively over her, and this time, D'vale screamed in such agony that even Ketas seemed surprised, as the Old One of Elemental magic's body began to *burn* beneath her own magical flames.

"SAVE ME, BROTHER!" she shouted, but he just stared at her in confusion, his Mind magic offering no solution to the fire consuming her.

Ketas's spell now gone, the faerie queen stood back up and grinned. "Magic finally has its revenge," she said, then went flying backward as another blow from Ketas struck her. She landed hard and didn't move, though Fort could see she was at least still breathing.

THIS CANNOT BE HAPPENING! Ketas roared, and again, his words pounded in Fort's head like a sledgehammer. YOU ARE NOT *WORTHY* OF TAKING OUR POWER AWAY!

"Yeah, well, it looks like you're wrong about that," Rachel said, rising to her feet unsteadily and helping Jia do the same. With Ellora at their side, they moved to stand in front of Sierra, who surrounded them with a dome of yellow Mind magic. "Looks like you're the only one left, Skull Face. You ready to join your family in Loser Town?"

I WOULD RATHER *DIE* THAN BE BEATEN BY YOUR KIND! Ketas roared, and Sierra's dome shattered under his power.

Helio! Fort shouted in his fake father's mind, hoping the

faerie could still hear him through his own magic. *Can you bring me there? I need to help!*

A shimmer surrounded him, and before Fort could even take a step, he appeared next to Xenea and his human friends, standing all together as a group, even if most of them were now completely out of magic.

Helio smiled at him but looked incredibly exhausted, like the last spell had been all he had the energy for. Hopefully it'd be enough, though Fort wasn't sure how.

"Oh hey, New Kid," Rachel said, her eyes on the Old One. "Glad you could join us. You probably shouldn't have, though."

THIS IS YOUR PROTECTION? Ketas roared. TWO FAERIES AND SOME POWERLESS HUMAN CHILDREN? He struck out again, but his spell hit a new, shimmering wall, which barely held.

"The moment I start to say the words, he's going to take us all out," Sierra said quietly from behind them. "Xenea's spell isn't going to cut it, and I can't even slow his spells down. He's way too powerful."

"Maybe," Fort said. "But we have to try." He looked at Xenea. "Can we help somehow?"

"*Of course*, you ridiculous humans!" she shouted in annoyance. "All of you, add your magic to mine!"

"Um, how do we do that?" Rachel asked.

Fort's eyes widened as he realized what Xenea was saying. They didn't have the Old Ones' spells anymore . . . but there was no reason they didn't have access to the older, original kind of magic now. After all, humanity had been using it without being taught since Atlantis was around.

"Just ask magic for its help instead of commanding it!" Fort yelled. "It's there for us, it always has been, but it doesn't want to be controlled!"

The others looked at him doubtfully, but he just shook his head. "Trust me," he told them, hoping he was right. "If it doesn't work, all of this has been for nothing. But it's there—I know it is!"

Without waiting for a response, and seeing Ketas readying another spell that would destroy Xenea's wall, Fort closed his eyes.

Mom? he whispered in his head, picturing a shimmering wall so powerful no spell from Ketas could get through. *I don't know if this is how it works, but we really could use some protection.*

Please?

He opened his eyes just as the Mind bolt hit Xenea's wall . . . only it barely had any impact.

"Don't just sit there, humans!" Xenea shouted at the others. "Do what Forsythe said!"

"She's got a point, Ray," Jia said, taking Rachel's hand as the two moved to stand in front of the others.

"I mean, if Fort can do it," Rachel said, and grinned at him. Then both closed their eyes and began concentrating.

Immediately the shimmering wall solidified, and the next bolt didn't even come close to breaking it.

THE OLD MAGIC CANNOT BE SO POWERFUL! Ketas shouted, his voice not even painful anymore. THIS IS *IMPOSSIBLE*! WE WEAKENED IT WHEN WE TOOK CONTROL!

"And we strengthened it by releasing that control!" Jia shouted back.

"Nice one, Gee," Rachel murmured.

Ready, Sierra? Fort asked her in his mind.

Nope, she said, and he could feel her sadness, that she'd miss being inside his mind with him, closer than close. *But let's do this.*

"Chaos of the far reaches of thought!" she shouted.

NO! Ketas roared, and this time, his magic came at them from all sides, hitting Xenea's wall with such force that it crumbled, even with the help of Fort and his friends.

Fort called out to his mother once more, but his magic wasn't strong enough, and one Mind bolt managed to break through to strike Sierra in spite of it. She screamed out and fell to one knee.

"I . . . ," she said, then shuddered, and a new voice came from her mouth. "I WILL NOT LET YOU DO THIS."

Anger hit Fort so hard that he could barely think, and he wanted to fight, to punch, to hit something, anything that would make the Old One release her. "Get *out* of her!" Fort shouted, too upset to even think about trying magic again.

"Sierra!" Jia shouted, and the air started to shimmer around Sierra's head. Rachel joined in, and the shimmering intensified. Sierra's face started to contort, like she was fighting just as hard as they were.

"Release . . . ," she said, but trailed off, going silent once more.

At the sound of her voice, Fort's anger disappeared, and he rushed to her side, practically begging his mother to protect her.

"YOU HUMANS ARE NOTHING MORE THAN

ANIMALS!" Ketas shouted from Sierra's mouth, staring directly at Fort. "YOU ARE NOT WORTHY OF THE POWER!"

He looked up at the Old One through Sierra's eyes, then felt something deep within himself, a power he thought he'd given up. It rose through his body, up to his head, and he smiled.

"THE POWER SAYS OTHERWISE," magic said through Fort's mouth, and pushed Ketas straight out of Sierra.

"From . . . our . . . *control*!" Sierra finished, taking with it the final power of the Old Ones.

Ketas began to scream, but for once, it wasn't in their heads. Fort pushed to his knees, just high enough so he could watch as the former Old One's crystal armor cracked in two, the skull helmet falling off in pieces, revealing a familiar-looking Atlantean.

Only this Ketas was missing his skull, leaving his mind visible to the world.

Fort winced in disgust, then closed his eyes and asked the magic for another favor. When he opened his eyes again, a shimmer had covered Ketas, and beneath it, his head was healing, solid once more.

"Why did you do that?" Xenea shouted at Fort, picking him

up from the ground by the shirt and holding him in the air. "After everything they put your kind through, you would help him?"

"They're no different from us," he said, shaking his head. "Just . . . afraid." Then he grinned. "Plus, I'm not letting him off the hook that easily. I thought your queen might have ideas on how to punish them for a few millennia?"

Xenea slowly smiled as well. "You know what? We're even again if you let me tell her."

She dropped him to his feet, which almost sent him back to the ground, given how weak he felt. As his friends all stood up as well, Sierra hugged him tightly. Everyone else seemed okay, even Ember, who started making her way over to where the elder dragons from Avalon were waking up, moving slowly but steadily.

The end of the Old Ones' magic was probably going to be hard on her, given that the Old Ones had created her kind. But Fort had a feeling the newly strengthened all-magic that was left would be kind to the dragons.

He sighed, looking around at what remained of the National Mall, and couldn't believe it was over.

They'd destroyed the Old Ones' magic and brought back the original version in its place.

That meant magic would be usable by anyone, trained or not.

Including adults.

Which meant that things were about to get *extremely* interesting.

- FIFTY -

IS EVERYONE OKAY?" JIA ASKED, LOOKING around at the rest of them before blushing. "Oh. I was going to offer to heal you, but I'd forgotten I can't do that anymore."

"Yes, you can," Xenea told her, rolling her eyes. "It just doesn't require spells. Imagine what you'd like, and ask magic to do it, just like when you were helping with my wall. Much easier this way, and doesn't force one of the ultimate powers of the universe to do your bidding, which seems smarter all around."

"So now everyone can use magic?" Rachel said, looking a bit intimidated. "Don't get me wrong. I think that's great, and will solve a *lot* of world problems. But it's also going to make for some new ones." She glanced over at where Colonel Charles huddled by his unconscious son Michael, with Gabriel moving to join him. A group of medics was approaching, so Fort figured they'd all be okay . . . assuming Michael would be able to get over whatever it was he'd seen in the Old Ones' home. "I mean, think what our friend the colonel will try to use it for."

"But he won't be the only one with the power," Fort pointed out. "Every government, every military, every single *human being* in the world will have the exact same magic he does, so no one will be any more powerful than anyone else."

"And if we can cure diseases and make food out of nothing, there'll be even less reason for wars anyway," Jia added, brightening a bit. "You know, Fort, this whole plan of yours worked out pretty well!"

"Yeah, New Kid, I have to admit, you didn't mess up *too* badly here," Rachel said, clapping him on the back so hard it sent him reeling. "Still, we're going to need help, getting everyone up to speed on how to use it and all. And probably pretty quickly. The longer we leave it, the more magical accidents are going to pop up. The last thing we need is for some kid to wish he didn't have any homework, so his whole school disappears."

"Good luck with that," Xenea said, and turned to walk back to where her queen was waking up. Before she could go, though, Fort stopped her.

"You know, she did exile you here," he said. "And while I know this world isn't your favorite, we could really use your help."

"With what?" Xenea said. "All the Old Ones are defeated. Even if they try something now, they won't have any more power than you do. And it looks like your dragon is making friends anyway." She pointed to where Ember stood in the middle of the elder dragons, who seemed to be doting over her. Fort's heart broke at the sight, even if he knew it was for the best.

"That's not what I meant," he said, tearing his eyes away from Ember. "Like Rachel said, we're going to have a lot of people suddenly able to use magic with no idea how. We could use someone who knows what they're doing. You know, a teacher."

As he said the word, a memory came to him of the utopia he'd seen in the half vision, half Time spell of the future, where plaques had labeled him and a bunch of the other Oppenheimer students as teachers. He almost laughed at the thought but held it back so as to not offend Xenea.

The faerie woman, though, was under no such pressure and laughed in his face. She paused when he didn't join her, then laughed again, even harder.

"She's in," Fort told Rachel and Jia, letting Xenea tire herself out. "But we're going to need more than just her, if we want to really get the knowledge out there."

"Well, I'm up for helping," Jia said, shrugging. "Assuming my parents are still okay with it. We've had a lot of practice with learning magic, and it'd be kind of nice to teach it some more. I liked when I was helping the Healing students learn to create golems."

"Ugh, we're going to be teachers now?" Rachel said, sticking out her tongue. "I'd assumed we'd be like joint presidents or something, leading the world into a new utopian society."

Fort went pale as he remembered the statue the teacher plaques had been on, one of Jia and Rachel that called them the Mothers of Our New World.

Maybe Rachel wasn't far off.

"Let's do it," Sierra said, putting her arm over Fort's shoulder, both out of fondness and for support, as she didn't seem much more stable than he felt. "It'll be nice to get back to learning without government agents trying to throw me in jail or something."

"We'll have to talk to Sebastian's mother about everything the TDA and Colonel Charles got up to," Jia said. "That could clear everything up, assuming she'll listen."

"Eh, we know more magic than she does now," Rachel said. "She'll hear us."

"I'm in too," Fort told the others. "You know, until my dad makes me go back to school or . . ." He trailed off, realizing he was forgetting something important. In spite of the queen agreeing that his bargain had been met, his father hadn't returned from Avalon yet.

He whirled around, looking for the faerie queen, but she'd shimmered away, probably to make arrangements to invade the UK, something else Fort would have to explain. Considering she'd helped save the whole world, though, hopefully they'd be open-minded about it.

But that didn't help him get his father back, and he wasn't that confident with this new kind of magic that he was sure he could open a portal to Avalon. Still, it wouldn't hurt to try—

"Fort?" someone shouted out, and Fort whirled around to find Helio waiting a few feet behind him in a shimmering portal, a smile on his face. "There's someone here to see you."

The now-adult faerie stepped aside, revealing . . .

"Fort!" his father shouted, and limped toward him, grinning widely.

Fort's mouth dropped open, and he moved so quickly that

he closed the distance between them in seconds, throwing himself into his father so hard he almost knocked them both over.

"Tell me it's really you," he whispered, hugging his father as tightly as he could while tears streamed down his face.

"Is that in doubt?" his father asked, hugging him back.

"It's him," Helio said, then held up a hand. "I swear it's him. Trust me!"

Fort laughed and buried his face in his father's chest, not wanting to let go even for a minute. But some hot breath on his arm made him turn to find Ember waiting patiently for them both.

"Um, I notice we're back in D.C., and there are big, scaly black monsters still," his father said, looking at the dragon next to him. "Care to fill me in on this?"

"Ember, this is *my* father," Fort said, introducing them. "Dad, this is Ember. She's basically my adopted dragon." At least, she had been. The way he'd been planning on sending her to Avalon if he'd done away with magic completely still might be something she hadn't forgiven him for.

"Grandfather," Ember said, bowing her head low. "It is a pleasure to meet the real you." She looked back at Fort and sighed. "I have to admit, Father, these new elder dragons aren't quite as bad as I thought they'd be. I am not often wrong, but in this case, I think you were correct that I would enjoy their company."

Again, Fort felt a pain in his chest, but he was determined not to make this hard for her. "So, you're going to go live with them?" he asked, his voice cracking as the words barely made it out.

Ember's eyes widened. "Why would you even ask that? Of course not, Father! I belong here with you. *They* have decided to move *here*, since there are two young dragons for them to watch over on this world and none where they come from." She sneered, baring her fangs. "Yes, Damian is now human, but they think that won't be much of a problem to fix. They're far more worried about his attitude. Very undragonlike." She narrowed her eyes. "Believe me, I've made them extremely aware of his failings."

"Good," Fort said with a smile, and hugged her close too.

"Fort, seriously, *what is going on*?" his father whispered in his ear. "I'm seeing what look like elves, dwarfs, dragons, and a *lot* of military people around here. Are we okay?"

Fort glanced around, taking it all in, as helicopters flew in overhead, and more TDA soldiers returned to the field. Ellora was helping some Healing students make sure others were okay, while Sebastian glared in his direction, shaking his head dismissively as if to say he could have done this better.

At least not *everything* was going to change.

A few dozen yards away, he saw a silver-haired boy walking away, only to stop and turn back. He and Fort locked eyes, and the silver-haired boy waved once, then continued on without looking back again.

"Yeah," Fort said to his father. "I think things are going to be great."

- FIFTY-ONE -

"THIS IS THE *WORST*!" RACHEL SHOUTED, pacing around the small room backstage, filled with various magically created fruits and snacks. "Have you *seen* how many people are out there?"

"We knew it was going to be a lot," Jia said, grinning at her. "And you *love* ordering people around!"

"Not like *that*!" Rachel said, pointing at the door. "The place is packed. How many does it seat again?"

Fort opened his mouth to say but quickly shut it again at a look from Jia. He smiled widely at her in response, and she stuck out her tongue at him.

"Rachel," he said. "This can't be *that* bad. You've snuck around military bases, fought Old Ones, and saved the world."

"Not with twenty thousand people *watching* me do it!" she shouted.

"Oh, it's a lot more than that, with all the TV stations taking it live," Fort pointed out, only for Jia to smack his arm.

Rachel growled loudly, then dropped her head into her hands. "I thought this whole new world was going to be *less* terrifying. Can't I just go shoot some fireballs at Damian or something?"

"Considering we're asking him to help us teach, you probably shouldn't," Jia pointed out. She reached out and hugged Rachel close, while Rachel made a high-pitched whining noise. "You're going to be *great*!"

"Ugh, fine, let's get this over with," she said. "At least you didn't let my parents sit in the front row, right?"

Fort and Jia looked at each other. "Of course we didn't," Jia lied.

"They're in a skybox somewhere," Fort added, also lying.

Rachel glared at them both. "I hate you both. Except for you, Gee." She squeezed Jia's hand, took a deep breath, then flung the door open and marched out toward the stage.

Fort and Jia watched her go for a moment. "She really is going to do great," Jia said quietly. "Can you believe what we're doing here? The whole world is going to be watching."

"They needed to know," Fort said, though he wasn't sure he

even comprehended how big this was about to be. "It's going to change everything."

On the monitors overhead, they saw Rachel approach a podium set up for this moment, and Fort welled up a bit inside, incredibly proud of how confident, how calm she managed to look in spite of being terrified.

"Good morning, students," she said to an absolutely silent crowd. "That might not be how you think of yourselves, but from this morning forward, *all* of you are now students. As you know, the world has changed dramatically since the attacks in Washington, D.C., and Maryland over a year ago. But most of you don't know the full extent. Well, I'm here to show you."

She stepped to the side of the podium, and the air around her began to shimmer.

The crowd audibly gasped as overflowing piles of fruits, vegetables, and other foodstuffs appeared out of nowhere.

"Welcome to the Utopia School for Magic," Rachel said, stepping back to the podium. "As of now, you're all enrolled. And lessons start immediately."

EPILOGUE
STONEHENGE, 1500 YEARS AGO

"GO HOME, BOY," MERLIN SAID. "YOU'VE got work to do."

And before Fort could respond, Merlin sent him away.

The old man took in a deep breath, then looked around the circle of stones. "It's been . . . a *good* eternity, I think," he said, closing his eyes.

A hooded figure stepped out from behind the stone Merlin was leaning against and sat down next to him. "It has," the figure said. "At least from what I've seen of it."

Merlin opened one eye and half smiled at the man. "I knew you wouldn't leave me to face this alone." He groaned. "Remember after you fixed magic, and I went on a tour of the world to find myself?"

"And I had to rescue you from the faeries, twice?" the hooded man said. "I believe that's when I forced you to come to our new school."

"Blech, teaching children has never been my strong suit," Merlin said, then coughed weakly. "Thank you for coming, my friend."

"Of course," the man said. He pulled off his hood to reveal an older human, with short white hair, far too old to be time traveling. He took Merlin's hand in his. "What kind of best friend would I be if I hadn't?"

"I'm glad you changed my mind about you humans," Merlin said to the man, patting his hand. "You've made these years so much more . . . fun."

"I'm glad you like them, because they didn't want you leaving without saying good-bye either," the human said as various people began shimmering into view all around the circle of stones.

Two women, middle-aged and regal, waved from one side, their arms around each other.

"My victorious Artorigios and her apprentice," Merlin said, smiling sadly. "I always told Rachel she'd save the world."

"Jia's the one doing most of the work," the human said, nodding in greeting to his two old friends. "Rachel's just the one in the spotlight."

An enormous black dragon wrapped her neck around both the human and the Old One, then looked up at Merlin with steam coming from her eyes. "I'm sorry to see you go, Emrys," she said. "In honor of our friendship, I won't consume you as I otherwise would."

"I'm enormously honored," Merlin told Ember, and petted her on the head, making her purr like a cat.

More friends showed up, each saying a silent good-bye to their friend, until two last ones appeared, mirroring Merlin and the older human on the ground.

"Ah, look at us," the human said, nodding at his younger self and the silver-haired boy next to him. "We were just starting the school at that point, if I remember right."

The younger Fort waved, and his older self waved back. Cyrus started to do the same, then looked away, overcome with tears.

"Such a softie," Merlin said, wiping tears from his own eyes. "No wonder he couldn't go through with taking over the world."

"We did change it, though, didn't we?" the older Fort asked his best friend. "And there's still so much to do."

"You'll have to accomplish it without me," Merlin said sadly.

"I'm afraid my time has come, and where I go now, I'll have to go alone."

The older Fort shook his head and reached a hand out to his friend. A shimmer covered Merlin's body, and the old man disappeared into the night.

"See, that's where you're wrong, my friend," Fort said quietly, and smiled at all his old friends and his younger self. "We're *never* alone."

ACKNOWLEDGMENTS

There's not much else to say, is there, other than good-bye to Fort, Rachel, Jia, Cyrus, and everyone else who made this series so magical for me. And hopefully you!

And just like Fort, I could never do any of this alone, either, so I need to give all my thanks to the following people: Corinne, my teacher in magic; Michael Bourret, my agent; and my two editors at Aladdin, Liesa Mignogna and Anna Parsons, who more than earned their own dedication in this book. Next time, you two!

I also want to thank (again) Mara Anastas, my publisher at Aladdin; Chriscyntheia Floyd, deputy publisher; the marketing team of Alissa Nigro and Caitlin Sweeny; Cassie Malmo and Nicole Russo in publicity; Sara Berko in production; Elizabeth Mims in managing editorial; and Laura DiSiena and Mike Rosamilia, the designers of the book; Michelle Leo and the education/library team; Stephanie Voros and the subrights group, too; Christina Pecorale and the whole sales team; and finally Vivienne To, because she's the reason anyone even picks my books up.

While Revenge of Magic might be ending, there'll be more stories from me, including a spin-off from my first series, the fractured fairy tales of Half Upon a Time, coming soon. So hope to see you again, and thank *you*, readers, for sticking through the whole series with me!